Advance Praise for
CAM GIRL

"Raeder's best book yet. It has the grit, language, and heat you'd expect, but there's more. Raeder has clearly dug down and bled and studied the mirror to reveal the ugliest and most beautiful parts of herself, and human nature. *Cam Girl* is a rich and unflinching narrative."

—Emery Lord, author of *Open Road Summer*

"*Cam Girl* is a beautiful exploration of gender and sexuality that begs readers to question how well we know those closest to us, including ourselves. Raeder's trademark sensual lyricism is in full effect here, but it's the fraught yet tender relationship between Vada and Ellis that will have you glued to the pages until the oh-so-perfect ending."

—Dahlia Adler, author of *Under the Lights*

Praise for
BLACK IRIS

"Intense and visceral, *Black Iris* is as sharp as a knife and beats with a heart that is double-edged and dangerous."

—Lauren Blakely, *New York Times* bestselling author

"Provocative, seductive, and skillfully written, *Black Iris* stands out from the crowd."

—K.A. Tucker, *USA Today* bestselling author

"Like an afternoon special on bullying gone impossibly dark, Raeder's dizzyingly intense, drug-addicted queer teenage revenge fantasy takes its reader on a sexy, bloody journey of pure emotion that's by turns expressed, denied, and turned back in on itself . . . A twisting timeline dancing over a year's events makes every moment seem both immediate and angrily steeped in memory. Major themes include depression, mania, and the ways that the use and abuse of drugs affect access to the reality of self and the world's essential nature; but the soul-searching always comes in the context of action, everyone around hit by the shrapnel of exploding feelings. This is an exhilarating ride for our inner underdog, craving a taste of what it would feel like to just get back at everyone if we were reckless enough not to care about the consequences."

—*Publishers Weekly*, starred review

"Risky, brave, bold. A suspenseful powerhouse of a novel and one of the best books I've read this year."

—Karina Halle, *New York Times* bestselling author

"Fearless, inspiring, and a story that does more than just keep you enthralled. It holds you by the damn throat."

—Penelope Douglas, *New York Times* bestselling author

"Erotic, poetic, heartbreaking, captivating, and full of mind-blowing twists and turns."

—Mia Asher, author of *Easy Virtue*

Praise for

UNTEACHABLE

"With an electrifying fusion of forbidden love and vivid writing, the characters glow in Technicolor. Brace yourselves to be catapulted to dizzying levels with evocative language, panty-blazing sex scenes, and emotions so intense they will linger long after the last page steals your heart."

—Pam Godwin, *New York Times* bestselling author

"*Unteachable* is a lyrical masterpiece with a vivid story line that grabbed me from the very first page. The flawless writing and raw characters are pure perfection."

—Brooke Cumberland, *USA Today* bestselling author

"Raeder's writing is skillful and stunning. One of the most beautifully powerful stories of forbidden love that I have ever read."

—Mia Sheridan, *New York Times* bestselling author

"Edgy and passionate, *Unteachable* shimmers with raw desire. Raeder is a captivating new voice."

—Melody Grace, *New York Times* bestselling author

"A simply stunning portrayal of lies, courage, and unrequited love. Raeder has a gift for taking taboo subjects and seducing us with them in the rawest, most beautiful way."

—S.L. Jennings, *New York Times* bestselling author

ALSO BY LEAH RAEDER

Black Iris

Unteachable

CAM GIRL

LEAH RAEDER

ATRIA PAPERBACK

NEW YORK   LONDON   TORONTO   SYDNEY   NEW DELHI

ATRIA PAPERBACK
An Imprint of Simon & Schuster, Inc.
1230 Avenue of the Americas
New York, NY 10020

First Atria Paperback edition November 2015

ATRIA PAPERBACK and colophon are trademarks of Simon & Schuster, Inc.

For information about special discounts for bulk purchases, please contact Simon & Schuster Special Sales at 1-866-506-1949 or business@simonandschuster.com.

The Simon & Schuster Speakers Bureau can bring authors to your live event. For more information or to book an event, contact the Simon & Schuster Speakers Bureau at 1-866-248-3049 or visit our website at www.simonspeakers.com.

Manufactured in the United States of America

10 9 8 7 6 5 4 3 2 1

Library of Congress Cataloging-in-Publication Data

Raeder, Leah.
  Cam girl / Leah Raeder. — First Atria Paperback edition.
  pages ; cm
I. Title.
PS3618.A35955C36 2015
 813'.6—dc23
                    2015028559

ISBN 978-1-5011-1499-1
ISBN 978-1-5011-1500-4 (ebook)

For all the girls I've lost

—WINTER—

–|–

A car crash is a work of art.

At first it's Cubism: the hood folding, doors crumpling, windshield splitting into a mosaic of shattered light, the whole world breaking into shards of color and noise and tumbling around you like a kaleidoscope. Screeching tires and cold air and gasoline and your own scream are all just bits of debris flying around, gorgeous chaos. When the tires stop spinning and the engines die, you're left sitting in a smashed puzzle of metal and glass, trying to figure out which way the pieces go now, why some are stuck together and won't come apart. Why there is an eye next to a foot, steel where there should be skin.

I listened to a soft dripping and the sigh of steam. By then it had become Surrealism. My hands were puppet hands, one arm bent at a bizarre angle. A deflated airbag lay in my lap like a bloody surgery sheet. The seat belt (I buckled up, I didn't really want to die) was some kind of medieval bondage device and I clawed at it senselessly before clicking the release button. Then I saw her.

Ellis slumped in her seat, limp against the seat belt. Red-gold hair hung in her eyes. She was utterly still.

I kicked my door open. Staggered through the electric prongs of the headlights to her side of the car. My right arm was heavy, pulling toward the ground, so I used the left to haul her out. Impressionism now: the dashboard glow dappling her pale skin cyan, black ice reflecting swirls of white starlight. My breath spiraling wildly into the sky. I cried her name as I pulled her onto the road, her legs dragging.

"Wake up, Elle. Please, please, wake up."

You idiot, I thought. You know CPR.

I brushed her hair off her forehead, leaned close. No warmth on my ear. My right arm had begun to tingle and buzz and it was going to make this difficult. I took a deep breath, but before my mouth met hers she coughed and her eyelids fluttered open. Details became acutely clear, almost Pointillist: stars glittering in her eyes, ruby droplets freckling her skin. I touched her face, smearing the blood.

"Vada?" she said weakly.

"Can you move?" I couldn't take my hand off her cheek. "Move your arms. Ellis, move your arms. Okay. Now your legs."

She obeyed.

I grabbed her in an awkward one-armed hug but hugging wasn't enough so I kissed her cheek, her mouth, cupped her face and stared down into it. "Are you okay? There's so much blood." I wiped her face again but it only got worse. "Where's it coming from? Are you hurt?"

We both noticed my right arm at the same time. The sleeve of my hoodie ripped to tatters. The sliver of white showing through red near the elbow.

"Oh my god," Elle whispered, her breath musky and sweet. Tequila.

I let go of her.

The other car.

His headlights made an X through ours, a crucifix of light across the blank black night. We were on a highway bridge between nowhere and eternity, the ocean glinting beyond the treetops. The other driver lay sprawled facedown on the ground. My eyes traced the path he'd taken through his windshield, the bloody stripe running over the hood of his Jeep.

"Vada," Ellis said.

I dropped to my knees at the man's side, feeling for breath, pulse. My right arm was completely numb now. When I lifted his head, a warm red gush flooded my palm.

"Call 911." My voice was calm.

Elle fumbled in her coat pocket and then at the screen and almost dropped her phone. As I watched I thought, She's drunk. God, she is so drunk.

I took her phone and painted by numbers with the stranger's blood.

"I need an ambulance." I described the river nearby, the bridge.

Elle sank to the ground beside me, those lucid green eyes locked on the body. Her glasses were gone. She couldn't see how bad it really was.

On the asphalt, pieces of skull lay scattered like pottery fragments.

Can you tell me what happened?

"Car accident. This guy wasn't wearing a seat belt and he's . . . on the road."

How many people are hurt?

"Three. We're okay but this guy is—we need an ambulance."

It's on the way, miss. Is the man breathing?

"I don't think it really matters anymore because *I can see his brain.*"

My voice remained calm but Ellis clapped a hand over her mouth.

The dispatcher asked another question. Elle stared at me, horrified, over splayed fingers.

In a few hours, she wouldn't remember any of this. The concussion and the alcohol would blot it out.

But not me. I'd never forget.

"Vada," I said. "My name is Vada. I'm the driver."

−2−

Dots. Pretty dots of color, chrome blue and oxide red, strewn with firefly blurs of peach and gold, all smudging together. I stared at them for a while before my vision focused like a camera lens, the circles shrinking, becoming shapes. Room with white walls. Plaid shirt, sleeves rolled up. Black-rimmed glasses. A face I knew better than any other, her mouth moving slowly.

"Vada? Can you hear me?"

I opened mine to respond, then immediately closed it. My right shoulder twinged. I tried to cover my mouth to hold in the vomit, but my arm was stuck at my side, weirdly wooden. I looked at her helplessly.

Ellis hit the call button for the nurse.

A man came in and added something to my IV. Elle stood beside the bed, smoothing my hair back from my forehead. I closed my eyes and made sure only breath left my mouth.

Last night was fuzzy and soft, silvery, a half-erased sketch. But as the drugs kicked in it came back in sharp dark strokes. An oxygen mask over my face, cutting off my questions with frozen air. Losing track of Elle in the other ambulance. Hospital lights streaking overhead like glowing road stripes. A doctor explaining to me, in my shock-addled daze, that they had to operate and I had two choices: save the arm, or—

My eyes shot open. I clawed at the sheet with my left hand. Ellis laid hers over mine. "Don't touch."

"Did they take it? Oh my fucking god, did they take my—"

"No." She squeezed. "Look at me, Vada. You're okay. It's still there."

I breathed hard, staring at the sheet wild-eyed. Still wanted to rip it back to confirm visually that I was whole, that they hadn't amputated. How would I know? I couldn't feel a thing. I remembered a desperate incantation as the anesthetic washed over me in a black wave: *Please don't take it. Dear God, please.*

Elle touched my face and turned it up toward her.

"Baby," she said in that lilting voice, "I promise, you're okay."

My claw grip transferred to her hand, twisting it in mine. She winced but didn't let go.

I glanced around the room. Pale sun poured through a window, kindling the few spots of color: lilies spilling from a vase in a froth of pink starbursts, cards arrayed on the sill—Dalí and Kahlo prints from my classmates. My gaze refocused on Ellis. Her face was drawn, eyes dashed with violet shadow.

"Were you hurt?" I said.

"Mild concussion."

"Anything else?"

"No." She smiled briefly, faltered. "They said you pulled me from the wreckage like some superhero. You were bleeding so badly."

My mind skittered over fragmented images. Her closed eyelids, spattered with freckles and blood. A screaming wildness rising in me as I thought, for an awful moment, *She's gone.*

" 'They said'? You mean you don't remember?"

Elle shook her head, the movement slight.

"Do you remember anything?"

"They said not to focus too hard. Concentration is bad for a concussion. No books, games, or memories."

"Shit. I'm sorry."

"Don't be." She stroked my hand. "Just wanted you to see a friendly face when you woke up."

"There's nobody I'd rather see."

I meant it with my whole heart. Ellis lowered her eyes, a lock of ginger hair sweeping over them.

We both looked at my arm beneath the sheet.

"What did they do to me?"

"They saved it."

"But I can't feel—" I made a fist around Elle's hand and she bared her teeth, but I couldn't release. I had to hold on to something. "Elle, I can't move my arm." I pulled at my right shoulder with every surrounding muscle. It wasn't heaviness. It was . . . nothing. There was nothing there. Shreds of pain, fraying off into oblivion. "*I can't move my arm.*"

Carefully, she extricated her hand. "That's normal. It'll take a while for the nerves to heal."

"Am I paralyzed?"

No answer.

"Ellis, am I fucking paralyzed?"

Her eyes filled up, sea green shivering with sun. She brushed my face with her fingertips. "They don't know yet." Her voice dropped to a whisper. "I'm sorry. I'm so sorry."

They don't know.

I slammed the emergency call button over and over till the nurse reappeared.

"I don't want to be conscious right now," I said.

"Are you in pain?"

Was he for real? I couldn't move my drawing hand. My everything hand.

"Eleven out of ten."

He slid a needle into the bag and the colors blurred again, dissolving into darkness. The last thing I saw was Elle's face, two glass threads running down it.

———

The car hit the river in a burst of black petals, water flowering all around us in inky dark bouquets. Cold jets shot through the crumpled door and webbed windows and I yelped when they touched my skin, and realized I was still conscious. I turned with horror.

Ellis hung from her seat belt, unmoving.

Automatically I clicked my belt button. At least I thought I did. But my hips were stuck and when I looked down, my hand was all red, the fingers splayed at strange angles, as if gripping mush. In my mind I sensed myself moving that hand to the button and clicking again, but my eyes showed only a mangled ball of meat stubbing itself dumbly on the buckle, failing.

I'd done this. This was my fault.

Water rose over my ankles.

"Ellis," I said.

Not a sound. Not even breath.

We sank slowly at first, then faster as the river surged into the car. I twisted and fumbled. Couldn't get free.

Water at my calves.

"Ellis."

Something sharp. I needed something sharp. I tried to reach the glove box but the seat belt cut into my chest, made it hard to breathe.

"Elle, wake up. Please."

Water at our waists.

A ghastly chill climbed my legs, crept up my bones, deadening me with cold. In one last muster of strength I mashed my belt buckle and miraculously, it released.

My whole lower body was numb. Deadweight.

The waterline reached my breasts. An infinite heaviness pushed the air out of me.

Ellis sat motionless as we sank.

I love you, I didn't say. Instead I took a deep, deep breath, struggling to hold it as the chill tried to spook it free. When we went under, I'd give it to her. A last kiss of life.

Uncontrollable shivering. No feeling in my fingers or toes. I closed my eyes, reopened them underwater. Elle's hair floated around her face in lurid red ribbons, like skeins of blood.

At least we stayed together.

Till the very end.

———

I sat bolt upright. Hospital bed. Something trilled frantically, a machine about to explode—the heart monitor, matching my pulse.

Ellis lurched from a nearby chair. "It's okay," she said, rushing to my side. "It's okay. Don't scream."

Was I screaming?

"We were in the river." I grasped her forearm. "The car was sinking. I couldn't wake you up. I never meant to hurt you, I just—"

Didn't want to lose you.

My mouth fell as I heard the words in my head.

"Vada?"

I settled back into the bed. "Nightmare. I was having a nightmare."

We were never in the river.

Just a dream.

Oddly, I could still feel imaginary frostbite searing through my arms. Wait. *One* arm. The immobilized one.

I wrenched Elle's wrist, and her face scrunched up.

"I can feel it," I said through gritted teeth. "It hurts. Like a motherfucker. But I feel it."

"I feel it, too."

I looked at my hand on her, and let go. "Sorry."

"It's okay." She smiled. "Pain is good, Vada. It means the nerves are working."

"They're really, really working."

Her smile turned tremulous, that watery quality it took on just before she cried. She so rarely did. And only in front of me. I could never watch without joining her.

"Don't cry, you big nerd," I said gently.

"You either, dork."

My right arm was on fire and it felt fucking glorious. I could *feel*.

Elle leaned in and half hugged me, resting her forehead against mine. Her tears and touch made me drop the tough-girl act. Pain flared through me, striped every nerve from fingertips to brain stem with living fire. My arm sizzled like a sparkler firework but it wasn't dead, it was bright and sweet with agony, and I began to laugh in delirious relief.

"Are you okay?" Ellis said.

"You're here." I brushed her cheek with my knuckles. A tear laced between them. "And I'm whole. Yeah, I'm okay."

She cupped my chin in her hands, let a thumb stray over my bottom lip, then the top one, as if to ensure I was real. My heart played a skittery staccato on the monitor. Elle's breath smelled like mint grown in shade, a forest coolness—the scent of her vaping liquid. Her face was so close. Freckles dusted her cheeks like cinnamon, sandy against milk-white skin. I skimmed a finger over them.

"Excuse me," a voice said from the door.

We jerked apart.

New nurse, female. She bustled in and checked my IV and vitals. Ellis skulked near the window, looking silly, a redheaded scarecrow, too tall to be inconspicuous.

"How do you feel?" the nurse said.

"Terrible." I beamed. "It's fucking amazing. I can actually feel stuff."

Her eyebrow twitched. I caught the slip of a smile. Then she said, "Only immediate family is permitted after visiting hours."

Ellis and I blinked at each other. What an absurd thing to say. No one in my life was more *immediate family* than her.

"She's my best friend," I said. "She's—"

The nurse—Halsey, according to her ID—interrupted. "I'm sorry. Legal family only. Is she your partner?"

Strange that such an innocuous word could freeze me up so fast.

Partner.

Your best friend is your partner, right? The person you've lived with going on five years. Shared your life with. Shared everything with. Matching tattoos, an encyclopedia full of inside jokes, a scrapbook stuffed with memories. The person whose heart you know better than your own. Because you've listened to it so many nights, that small, fierce tapping against your ear, your jaw. A little bird hurling itself at the bars of its cage.

Elle stared at me, waiting for my answer.

"No," I said.

Her mouth fell.

I wanted to disappear.

"Miss," Halsey began, and Ellis said, in a raw voice, "It's fine, I'm leaving," and something rose up in my chest like a tidal wave.

"Don't go," I called as she reached the door. "Elle, please don't go."

She turned back partway, wearing that wounded expression that wrecked me every time, and words formed in my throat—*Fine, she's my partner, whatever you want to call it, just let her stay*—and then heel clicks sounded from the hall, and a voice that filled me with warmth and dread.

"Here you are."

My mother stepped into the room, flawless, as if she'd walked straight off a photo shoot and not half a day sitting in coach on some shoestring airline. Camila Pérez Bergen: nearly six feet tall, skin the tone of aged brass, bone structure that could facet diamonds. Her withering eyes sized us up in one sweep. She kissed Ellis's cheek and hauled her by the elbow back to my bedside. I got two kisses and a series of *tsk*s and a sigh.

"Let me see," she said perfunctorily, plucking at the sheet.

"Mamá," Elle said—my mother called Ellis her third daughter—"careful. She's healing."

"Explain this to me, *chiquita*. Apparently I'm the only one in this fucking hospital who speaks English. Can she work? Do art?"

My mom spoke rapid, flawless English with a Puerto Rican accent, dipping deep into vowels, rolling and hissing consonants agilely, musically. Her voice always reminded me of a song picked up in the middle, her words one long lyric.

"She has nerve damage," Elle said, eyeing me askance. "Think of a puppet. You know how the strings move the arms? Hers were cut. Not all the way through, but bad enough."

"Is she in pain?"

I rolled my eyes. "I'm right here. You could just *ask* me."

Neither looked my way.

"Yes," Ellis said. "A lot of pain. But that's sort of good. It means the nerves work. The doctors sewed them back together, but that's only a partial fix. Her body has to heal them fully."

"*Gracias a Dios*. I thought she was paralyzed. I was sobbing on the plane. People thought I was going to a funeral." Yet her makeup was immaculate now, of course. Mamá rubbed Elle's shoulders. "You should be a doctor. So much smarter than the ones here."

Ellis blushed furiously. The nurse cleared her throat.

"Ma'am, are you the patient's mother?"

My mother narrowed her eyes, not dignifying that with a response.

"I'm sorry, I need anyone who's not immediate family to leave the—"

"We are all immediate family. Thank you." Mamá gestured to the door.

Despite myself, I caught Elle's eye and traded a small smile with her.

No one got between my mom and her family. Ever.

But the smile faded swiftly. They hadn't told me I had nerve damage. What the extent was. The prognosis. My right arm was crawling with fire ants, but I didn't want more painkillers. I wanted to know, for sure, that I was still whole. More specifically, to what degree.

When the door clicked shut my mother rounded on us. "What have you told the police?"

Elle blinked, owlish. I shifted in the bed.

"Did they question you?" Mamá pressed.

"Yeah. That night." I scratched crosses into the sheet with a nail. "I told them what happened. I was driving, it was icy on the bridge. The other guy hit us."

My eyes flicked to Ellis. She swallowed.

"And you, *chiquita*?"

"They didn't question me yet. Because of my head injury." Elle spun a lock of hair around one finger. "I'm supposed to give a statement later this week, but . . . I still don't remember anything."

"Do you remember getting in the car?" I said. "In the passenger's seat?"

She squinted at me.

"I buckled you in. You drank too much and felt sick. I made sure your seat belt was secure. You were on your phone right before he hit us. Remember?"

Remember how you were breaking my heart?

Elle's breath quickened. Very softly, she said, "Are you coaching me?"

I didn't answer.

My mother frowned, then clapped her hands, startling us both.

"Enough for now. We can revisit it later." Her gaze settled on me, dark and weighted with expectation. "Why don't you tell me how you've been, since you don't answer my calls anymore, *mija*?"

"I'm really tired."

"Always tired, tired. Too tired to talk to your mother."

"Too tired to hear how disappointed you are," I snapped.

Mamá's eyes flashed.

"Come, *flaca*." She put an arm around Ellis. "I'm starving and you're too skinny. Let's find something to eat."

At the door Elle glanced back at me, a specter of hurt in her face. I turned toward the window and watched dusk fall in shades of blood and old bruises. When I was alone I recited the story to myself, the car crash story, until the details were sharp and straight in my mind, honed to a razor's edge.

———

My mother stayed for two days. We'd had enough of each other after two hours.

Every time doctors came by she acted like I was a baby, not twenty-two. She made them tell her everything, then had Ellis re-explain in layman's terms while I sat there mentally headdesking.

Compound fracture of the radial head. (Broken elbow.)

Distal radius fracture. (Broken wrist.)

Multiple phalangeal fractures. (Broken fingers.)

Soft tissue injury. (Bruises on the inside.)

Injury to radial, ulnar, and carpal nerves. (Puppet strings cut.)

The doctor said, "It appears you braced against the steering column at the time of impact." (Elle said, "Imagine trying to stop a truck with your palm.")

The insurance investigator said, "There were two impacts. The other car rear-ended you, then you hit the bridge rail." (Elle looked away, her eyes shadowed.)

The cop said, "We will not be pursuing criminal charges, Ms. Bergen. We wish you a speedy recovery." (Elle was not in the room.)

When they finally let me out of bed—my arm strapped tight to my chest, throbbing through the meds—I snuck into a supply room, stole a white coat, and put it on Ellis. We made rounds and talked to the other patients. She loved this kind of stuff. Her and her big soft heart. She'd listen to any sob story, no matter how obviously fake or drug-induced. It was better than her staring at me with that hangdog expression, her eyes glimmering with questions.

We'd both taken a Breathalyzer that first night. Standard procedure for any serious crash. I was stone-cold sober. Elle's BAC was 0.11.

I tried not to think about white shards on black asphalt.

"He can barely see," I said, pulling Ellis away from an old man who mistook her for his son. "He thinks you're a boy."

She shrugged.

"Doesn't it bother you?"

"Why would it?"

"Because you're not his *son*?"

"He's alone, Vada. If it makes him happy, it doesn't hurt to let him believe that."

"Don't lead people on. It's cruel."

She recoiled as if I'd hit her.

"Sorry," I muttered. "My arm hurts. It's making me bitchy."

It was making me more than bitchy.

THINGS I COULD NO LONGER DO WITH A FUCKED-UP ARM:

1. Shower alone.
2. Dress myself.
3. Handle my fucking period.

Mamá was right to baby me, because never in my life had I felt more powerless than when I went to piss and saw blood on the paper. It hit me then, harder than anything else had: this was my life now. I couldn't wash my own hair. I couldn't put a bra on. I couldn't put the fucking menstrual cup in.

Once upon a time I had a bit of a Cinderella complex. I resented the mundane chores that consume your life when you're poor: hauling clothes to a coin laundry, lugging groceries home on city buses. I wished for freedom, fantasized about a life where my days weren't measured in cups of rice, where I didn't have to decide between eating protein that week or having a beer to unwind after working a double shift *and* studying my ass off for finals. Well, I got what I wished for. Just like in fairy tales, the wish wasn't worth the price.

Please, I prayed. Take it back. Let me scrub my clothes in the tub again. Let me work. Let me suffer and ache.

This isn't freedom. This is the cage. I was so wrong.

Elle knocked at the door and I wiped my tears away. "Yeah?" She passed me my phone. On it, a text from her:

Write down anything you need. I'll go get it. She won't know.

I texted back, **my savior.**

While Ellis was gone, all Mamá talked about was my younger sister, Ariana. Ari was dating some hotshot lawyer, Ari was in love, Ari was getting engaged. My twenty-year-old sister had already been engaged twice. Instead of going to college, she majored in heartbreak.

"You could have been married by now," my mother said, sighing. "Living in a nice house, with a baby to keep you busy. Then this never would have happened."

Just like you, I thought. "That's not why this happened."

"Then why?"

Subject change. "You seriously think I'm old enough to have kids?"

"Seventeen was old enough for me."

"I haven't even finished college."

"You already have a degree. Why do you need another?"

"Because I—" I cut off. Still no good answer beyond *because I want it.* But when I thought hard, sometimes the answer was *Because I'm stalling. Because I'm not ready to be an adult yet.* "I don't know."

"What do you know? Besides that my life isn't good enough for you."

"Stop projecting. No one's judging you, Mamá."

"Every choice you've made is a judgment on me." She picked at her nails. "Ari wants children."

"Good for her. I'm not my sister."

"Yes. That is clear."

Then she started talking about wedding dresses.

When Elle returned, I whispered, "Please get me out of here before I hurt myself and others."

The doctors insisted I use a wheelchair. Ellis pushed me down eerily quiet halls in the dead of night, the harsh light tinting our faces ashen, ghoulish. When we passed the nurses she pushed me fast, sprinting down the corridors as I shrieked in surprise and glee. She grinned down at me, that rake of red hair all mussed, cheeks pink. So pretty.

"Speed demon," she said.

I smiled, but part of me was in the car, watching the odometer tick up. Fifty-seven. Fifty-eight. Fifty-nine.

"Demon," I agreed. "*El diablo.*"

The cafeteria was deserted this late, so Elle bought me gummy worms out of a vending machine. Gummy anything: my go-to comfort food.

"Do you know what tonight is?" she said.

I bit a worm and stretched it transparent. "Nope."

"New Year's Eve."

The worm snapped against my teeth. I'd lost all track of time. Some friends from school were throwing a big New Year's bash, and I'd planned to take Ellis. I'd planned to show her the latest painting I was working on. I'd planned so many things.

My mother loved to say, *If you want to make God laugh, tell him your plans.*

A sinking feeling opened up in my chest, widening, plunging, and heavy things inside me slid toward that precipice.

"What are you thinking?" Ellis said.

"How much I can lose in one fucking night."

She touched my shoulder, lightly. "I'm still here. You haven't lost me."

It didn't mean much. Not when she couldn't remember the crash. If she did, she'd take that promise back.

"What do you want to do tonight?" she said.

"Wallow."

"Aside from that."

"Maybe some navel-gazing. An hour or two of angst."

"Vada."

I sulked at the cafeteria counter. A display of kid's meal toys caught my eye: lacy tiaras, magic wands. I pictured Ariana in a Disney princess dress.

When we were little, Mamá was our queen, looking like a million bucks in Gucci heels while scrubbing grilled cheese off the floor. Never mind that the Gucci was thrift store and the grilled cheese bought with food stamps. She wanted a do-over. Wanted us to marry rich and rewrite her life story. I was more interested in watercolor paints than wedding gowns. By the time we were teens, Mamá had shifted her hopes to Ari.

Ellis followed my gaze.

Suddenly I knew what would cheer me up.

I didn't even have to tell her. I just smiled.

Elle was comically bad at stealing. First she looked straight up at the security cameras. Then she positioned the wheelchair to block the view, and kept repositioning to get it perfect. Then she knocked the toy display off the counter, which made all her prep pointless.

"If I go to jail for stealing a tiara," she said, "I will never forgive you."

"But you'll be a legend. The prince who stole a crown for the exiled princess."

This pleased her. She set the tiara on my head, blushing.

"We need something for you," I said.

"No. No way am I wearing—"

I jumped up and dashed around the counter before she could stop me. I was light-headed, dizzy from poor circulation, but I grabbed a plastic apron from a bin and tossed it to Elle with a flourish.

"What am I, the royal cook?"

"No, goofus. You're the prince. Put it on."

Only your best fucking friend will tie an apron cape around her shoulders and pretend to be your Disney prince.

"Let us survey my lands," I said, strolling back to the chair. "Please roll the throne to my viewing tower."

From the roof of the parking garage you could see clear to the Atlantic. It was freezing, a hard, metallic cold that seemed to make the air ring. My breath flew away in scraps of pale tulle. Midwinter in Maine is hell. Dante's Hell, Ninth Circle style. Ocean infused the air, salt and grit studding the breeze with a million tiny barbs. Might as well have left the blanket indoors. I used to think of myself as tough, born in a blizzard and raised on the West Side of Chicago, but I wasn't prepared for this sheer brutality, the way each day hit you like a kick in the teeth.

Ellis took out her vaping pen and I savored the warm steam she exhaled, the scent of sage and mint.

"What happened to the car?" I said.

"Insurance covered it."

"Did you pick out a new one?"

"No."

I pulled the hospital blanket tighter around my shoulders. "What are you waiting for?"

"I don't want a new one. I don't want anything."

"Why not?"

Her fingers combed through my hair, grazed the nape of my neck. I shivered harder than I had at the cold. "Let's not talk about that. Let's just be happy tonight."

It was right there. This thing we were skating around, the thin, fragile ice at the center of a dark pond. I could ask her. I could push us both into the black.

Instead I said, "This is our fifth New Year's together."

Elle sat on the stone coping of the roof. Her smile was distant, sad. "Which was your favorite?"

"The first."

The smile wilted. "Are you sure *you* don't have a brain injury?"

"What's wrong with year one?"

"The furnace broke down. We covered the windows with garbage bags to trap the heat."

"Then we made the best fucking pillow fort anyone's ever made."

"Okay, the fort was kind of awesome."

"You kept trying to calculate the load-bearing capacity of our couch pillows." I laughed. "Such a nerd. You got shitfaced on lemon drops."

Elle gave a prim toss of her head, the fake cape crackling. "I didn't know vodka could taste like candy."

"Remember getting all handsy with me?"

"I did not!"

"You so did. God, you were so pure before we met. And now look at you." I smirked up at her, a bit meanly. "Prince Ellis, the fallen. Getting drunk at parties. Hooking up in bathrooms."

My toes brushed the rim of that dark heart in the proverbial pond. Elle felt us teetering near the edge, too.

"Remember?" I said. "At the party, before the accident?"

"No," she whispered.

"But you remember wanting to go back to Chicago. I know you do, Elle. Because you still want to go. You don't really want to be here."

We stared at each other through a haze of breath and steam. From far away came a soft roar, like the ocean rising. As I looked up at her, the wind tousling her short hair and that silly cape till she seemed almost regal, I didn't see my best friend but some gamine tomboy prince. Someone I could run away with.

Someone I already had.

My right shoulder jerked suddenly, playing a muscle memory: gripping a drawing pencil, pushing it against paper. Capturing this moment. But it was only memory. My arm remained straitjacketed, a wire of pain twisting around the bone.

"You were right," I said. "I'm an asshole. You're better off leaving."

Ellis sighed, a wall of white cloud cutting us off for a moment. "I'm not leaving when you're hurt."

"Don't stay out of pity."

"It's not pity. It's because you're the most important person in my life. Even if it's not mutual."

"What, the nurse? You're mad I wouldn't say some arbitrary word in front of some random woman?"

"There you go again. Making me sound petty and unreasonable because I—"

She fell silent as the faraway roar rose higher, and a haunting scream pierced it. I stood and a streamer of light rolled across the sky. At its apex it burst into a red chrysanthemum, a hundred fiery petals falling into the ocean. Fireworks.

"It's midnight," I said. Elle's eyes lowered, watching my mouth and then drifting back up. I went warm all over, little threads of heat shooting out to my fingertips, my lips. "If you start this new year with me, we'll be stuck together."

"I never wanted to go. But you won't give me a reason to stay."

"I'm your reason. Like you're mine." I brushed her cheek. "Everything's new tonight. Let's be new, too."

Our breath hung silkily in the space between us, a ghostly tissue spanning mouth to mouth. Something made from the two of us, knitting us together. Overhead another firework burst and then another, electric blue, shocking purple, as I leaned in to close this space, to share one breath.

And then my fucking phone rang.

I stepped back, dizzy. Sat in the wheelchair and glared at the screen. "Shit. Guess who?"

Ellis laughed nervously. "*Tu mamá.*"

"Let's go before she melts down Maine."

We avoided each other's eyes on the elevator. But she traced my jawline with one finger, and I took that hand and pressed it to my mouth, brushed a kiss across her knuckles.

"Happy New Year, my prince."

Her hand stayed on my shoulder the whole way back.

My mom met us in the room in full *español* mode. "Letting your beloved mother leave without a good-bye? What if the plane crashes?"

I responded in Spanish, too. "Planes are safer than cars. And that's really tasteless when we were just in an accident. Please speak English in front of Ellis."

"She understands more than you think." Mamá gave me a strange look. "As do I."

I got out of the chair, shaking the tiara from my head. "So you're going home?"

"I booked an early flight from Boston. I have to be at work tomorrow."

"Well, thanks for dropping by."

"Vada." My mother touched my arm as I headed for the bed. "Come with me."

"Where?"

"Chicago."

Elle watched us with big unblinking eyes, probably not parsing more than every fifth word. But the name of that city alarmed her.

"I can't, Mamá."

"This is serious. You're not playing house anymore. You'll need months of further care."

My jaw tightened. "'Playing house'?"

"Transfer to a college back home. Ari's fiancé will help us pay."

"Do you even understand how grad school works? I can't transfer. I'd have to start over." I snatched the tiara again and crushed it with my good hand. "And I'm not taking money from some stranger."

"Your future brother-in-law."

"I've heard that before." To Elle I said, in English, "She wants me to come home."

"Maybe you should, Vada."

I gaped. "You're taking her side?"

"Do you know what kind of physical therapy you'll need?"

My meds were wearing off, pain rumbling in the marrow. Soon there would be lightning jags lancing along my nerves. I pretended the tension in my body was all anger.

"No, I don't. I've been trying not to focus on the nightmare ahead of me. I've been trying to stay fucking *positive*."

Ellis raised an eyebrow, and I heard how ridiculous I sounded and almost laughed. She always brought me back to earth.

"I'm staying," I told my mother, still in English. "My life is here now. My school, my friends." I swallowed. "And Elle is here. I won't leave her."

"I made a reservation for her, too."

Now we both gaped.

"Thank you, Mrs. Bergen, but I can't—"

"Unbelievable," I interrupted. "Still controlling my life. Thinking you know better. My choices are never good enough for you, Mamá. I'm never good enough."

"I won't hold this against you," she said icily. "You're in pain, and upset. Let's go home."

"I *am* home."

I half shouted it. Because I couldn't explain, not in words. Only with lines on paper, tides of color. This place, this new life we'd started, away from my mother's meddling and Elle's awful parents, where we could finally be our real selves—this was home. This was *ours*.

In the last painting I started before the crash, two silhouettes ran into the night ocean. The water was so thick with stars it looked like liquid glitter. Spray kicked up from their heels, shimmering trails of galaxies. Rising on the horizon, instead of the moon, was Earth: a deep-blue pearl wrapped in tatters of white mist. One silhouette's hair was long and the other's short, but nothing else indicated what they were—young or old, girls or boys. One pulled the other onward by the hand, but a trick of perspective made it different each time you looked: Sometimes the long-haired one was leading, sometimes the other. Sometimes, as you looked, it switched right before your eyes. The only certainty was that they were going in together.

(—Bergen, Vada. *Follow Me into Forever.*
Unfinished; oil on canvas.)

My mother's gaze flicked between me and Elle.

"What is really going on here?" she said in a hushed voice. "Is there something I should know?"

"No. I told you. I'm still in school. I have a life here."

"I should go," Ellis said. "I'll give you two some priv—"

I gripped her shoulder, firmly. "Stay."

My mother watched us, her eyes glinting with sharp thoughts.

"*Chiquita*, tell her to come home."

Ellis bit her lip.

"Don't drag her into it," I said. "Just let me live my life, Mamá."

"What kind of life?"

"My own."

"Your own. I see." She breathed deeply through her nose. "A life you have to hide from your mother. From everybody. What kind of life is that?"

"Don't you dare judge me." Ellis put a hand on my spine, stroked softly, soothingly, and my fury fell but my voice remained bitter. "You know why I keep things from you? Because everything I do is wrong in your eyes. I'm not perfect like Ariana. I'm the black sheep. The fuckup. The disappointment."

My mother stood to her full height. Her voice struck like a slap. "I've never been disappointed in you. If I have high expectations, it's because I would expect no less from myself. The world looks down on you, expects nothing from you because of the color of your skin and your mother's family name. They don't want you to fail. They want you to not even try. If you try, you will never disappoint me."

At that moment I wanted nothing more than to grab Elle's hand. "There are things about me that *would* disappoint you. Things I can't change."

"Like what?"

"I'm not having this discussion now."

Mamá snorted. "You've made mistakes? Who hasn't? I never liked the boys you chose, but I never stopped you from seeing them. I still run into Raoul. He asks about—"

"I'm not talking about fucking Raoul."

Her gaze refocused, cold sun burning suddenly through fog. "You think I don't know what you're talking about? Do you really think I'm that blind?"

Elle's hand left the small of my back, but I sensed her heart smashing hard, inches behind mine.

"Why do you hide this from me? Both of you, why? *Chiquita*, I have known you as long as *mija* has. I love you like my own blood."

"Leave her out of it," I snapped.

"You think I don't understand? You spend all your time together, alone. It is one thing to be best friends, but the lines are becoming blurred. Come home. Be around other people. You'll grow out of it. It's not healthy, what you're doing. Either of you."

"Stop, Mamá. Just stop." I moved away from Ellis. If I was taking arrows to the chest, I didn't want one piercing me and hitting her. "You don't know what you're talking about."

"Whose fault is that? This is the first time you've spoken to me in months."

"And why do you think that is?"

"You are ashamed."

"Because of *you*. You taught me shame. You always said making art was pointless. You spent all that money on my stupid Confirmation dress instead of buying me some cheap paint like I begged for. You're pushing me to get married before I finish school. That's not me. I don't want to relive your fucking life for you and fix your mistakes. I want to live my own."

Mamá's mouth opened, but no sound came out. I'd gone too far.

"Vada," Ellis said. "I'll just go, okay? You should talk. Without me here."

"I have nothing else to say to her."

My mother's eyes ricocheted between us. I expected wrath, but instead she said, quietly, "There is a seat waiting for each of you, *mijas queridas*."

My beloved daughters.

"Thank you, Mrs. Bergen," Elle said.

"Take care of her, *chiquita*."

Then she kissed our cheeks and was gone.

I reeled backward into a chair, as if some great weight had just vanished and I'd lost my balance.

"Vada." Ellis tugged my arm, startlingly rough. "Go after her."

"Why?"

"Tell her you love her."

My jaw clenched. "She knows."

"What if you never see her again? What if those were the last words she hears?"

I have nothing else to say to her.

I caught my mother at the elevator doors. She heard my footsteps, or sensed me. When she whirled around I crashed into her chest and she seized me in strong arms. My injured one was crushed between us, but I didn't care.

"*Te quiero,*" I mumbled into her shoulder. "*Te quiero, Mamá. Y yo también la amo.*"

She held me for a long, long time. The elevator dinged and shuttled past over and over. She didn't speak. I wasn't sure how to take that. But when she finally left, I knew my last words had come straight from my heart.

I love you, I'd said. *I love you, Mom. And I love her, too.*

Querer. Amar.

Two different words. Two different loves.

———

Her hands.

I obsessed over them. Drew them in all their moods. Deft and nervous, fluttering quick as the flick of birds' wings, her fingers a blur of white feathers—or slow and tantalizing as they lifted my shirt, unhooked my bra, brushed the skin over my hammering heart. With one nail she'd trace the knot of fire in my chest to the place it came undone just below my navel. I sketched her hands a thousand times in my notebooks, and in my dreams her hands sketched my skin a thousand more.

New Year's morning I woke in a wash of watery blue light.

Ellis sprawled awkwardly in an armchair, one coltish leg flung across the floor. My shoulder shifted in small, abortive orbits, drawing her in my head. Miming the movements hurt but I didn't stop. Here's the truth: every line you agonize over is etched into your memory. Onlookers see the finished result, polished and prettified, but all the artist remembers is the labor. The grueling, gloriously bloody becoming.

"What are you looking at?" Elle said, catching me staring.

"Nothing."

The sky turned shades of cold metal, tin and zinc, and when she wheeled me outside into the thick stillness we both glanced up, searching for the first snowflakes. A pinprick of ice touched my tongue. When I lowered my head, Ellis was watching me with a wistful expression.

"What are *you* looking at?" I said.

"You." She shrugged shyly. "It's just nice to see you happy."

Something warm ran down my spine, a droplet of sun.

The hospital garden looked spray-painted with winter, a silver powdercoat of frost laying atop everything. Other patients passed with their attendants, smiling benignly. We meandered down stone paths lined with witch hazel. I plucked a frond, idly broke off the ice whiskers. Ellis knelt suddenly before a bank of snowdrops.

"Oh my god," she said.

"What?"

"This. Doesn't it belong to you?"

She turned on her heel and held it up in both hands: a crown of woven witch hazel, spidery threads of red and gold, with snowdrops tucked into the braids like gems.

My mouth hung open. "Ellis."

She rose to set it on my head. I grabbed the dangling end of her scarf.

"When did you do this?" I breathed.

"It was stolen long ago, Your Highness. We've been searching for many years. What a great irony, to find it here in our own kingdom."

I laughed, a little wildly. "You are so ridiculous. I love you."

She was trying not to laugh, too, and she blushed and lowered her eyes. My bashful prince.

Something hot stung my cheek.

"Oh, no. Vada. Don't."

Great. I was totally crying.

"I'm just—this is really nice," I said. "Being happy again." With you.

I scrubbed my tears on her scarf, which earned a laugh. We got up to walk. Ellis hovered at my side and after a while I took her hand, walking close and slow, arm in arm. We circled a pond where thin glass leaves of ice floated atop dark water. On a bench across from us, a man in a beanie watched. Instinctively I turned around.

"What's wrong?" Ellis said.

"Let's go this way."

We walked into a copse of spruce, the air spiced with balsam and menthol. The path bent and the civilized world disappeared and for a moment, we could've been in some forest deep in the heart of Maine, utterly lost. I started to relax, wrapped my arm around Elle's waist. Then I heard footsteps crunching up the path.

I stepped away from her. "Want to head back? I'm kinda tired."

"Okay."

When she reached for my hand again I drifted a step farther off.

"Vada, what's wrong?"

"Nothing."

"Are you avoiding people?"

"Just look at me." I gestured at my ragged ponytail, the goofy crown, the wrinkled pajamas. "I'm not fit to be seen in public."

"You're not fit to be seen?" She moved closer, grasped my hand. "Or this isn't?"

Again, instinct: I recoiled, shook her off.

Then immediately did a double take and said, "Ellis, I'm sorry, I didn't—"

But she was already stalking down the path, leaving.

"Fuck," I growled.

She must have taken off running, because by the time I got out of the trees she was nowhere in sight. Fucking track star. No way could I catch up.

I trudged back to the wheelchair and tried to push it one-handed, but it kept veering off into the snow. So I started kicking it instead, which was a lot more satisfying.

Goddammit, Ellis. What did you expect?

Seeing my mom always put me in a bad headspace. Seeing the way other people saw us. When it was just us in our little fantasy world it was fine, but Mamá had to remind me how childish and *unhealthy* it was.

The lines are becoming blurred.

Come home. Be around other people.

You'll grow out of it.

Like we were kids playing make-believe.

I ripped the crown from my head, but I couldn't shred it with one hand. So I pressed it to my mouth to hold in a sob, because fuck emotional stability, apparently.

"Excuse me," a man said.

I jumped. Beanie Guy stood beside me. Blond scruff, broad-shouldered. Ruggedly handsome. Fortyish.

"Need some help?"

For a bizarre moment I thought he was talking about the crown. I looked pitifully at the chair.

"Oh. No. Thanks."

"Please," he said, cracking a smile. "I won't make you sit. But let me help."

I really just wanted him to go away, but if I tried to tell him off I might burst into tears. Then he'd definitely go all Good Samaritan.

"Whatever," I said.

He kept pace with me on the path back. I clutched the crown in a fist, and he glanced at it.

"Is she your girlfriend?" he said. "The redhead?"

I almost tripped. "What?"

"I saw you together. You looked happy."

My fist furled tighter. Then I tossed the mangled vines into the snow. "She's a friend. Not that it's any of your business. Are you a patient?"

"No. My son was."

"Oh."

We walked in silence another half minute. I felt his eyes on me. Too avid, too interested.

"Was?" I said.

"He passed away."

"I'm sorry."

"It's all right." The man's eyes defocused. "It's comforting, to see other people his age. Reminds me that life goes on."

Beanie Guy was making me feel like a sublime shitheel. "What happened to your son?"

"He was in a car accident."

I stumbled.

The man caught me, carefully avoiding my injured arm. The large hand on my hip made my skin crawl.

"I'm okay," I said, not looking at his face.

"You're Vada, aren't you?"

I didn't answer. I stopped moving, stared at the ground. My vision swam, too bright, weirdly pixelated.

"Do you know who I am?" the man said.

I made myself look at him. "Your son was the other driver."

He nodded. No emotion in his face, just that avid intensity. "My name is Max."

"I'm really, really sorry—"

Max clapped a hand on my shoulder. The good one, but it jolted my whole body and pain jittered up my spine. "It's okay, Vada. It was an accident. Not your fault." The hand on my shoulder tightened like a pincer. "I've been wanting to meet you."

"Why?"

He let go with a rueful smile. "Didn't mean to scare you. I just wanted to talk without Ellis around."

Max said our names fluently, familiarly. As if he'd been saying them to himself, night after night, like a litany.

"Maybe we shouldn't be talking without—"

"You were driving, right?"

My mind raced. This wasn't a cop. Just the father of a dead kid. He seemed . . . sad. Merely sad, lonely, desperate to connect to some part of his son's final moments.

Jesus, some kid was dead, some kid my age.

"Yes," I said. "I was."

"The police said you were sober. It was nice of you to be the designated driver for your . . . friend."

A chill cascaded down my back.

"I'm so sorry," I mumbled, edging away. "For your loss. But I really need to go. I'm sorry."

Max didn't stop me. He stood still in the winter garden, watching me backpedal and turn and run.

———

VADA: where the fuck are you?

VADA: all your shit's gone from my room

ELLIS: In a cab.

VADA: bailing on me again

ELLIS: I just need some space. To think.

ELLIS: I'm not leaving.

VADA: I met Max

ELLIS: . . .

ELLIS: What did he say?

VADA: he said it's okay we killed his kid

VADA: which maybe you should've fucking told me

VADA: before I learned it from the dead kid's dad

ELLIS: I thought you knew. You were lucid that night.

VADA: I've been blocking out a traumatic event, Elle

VADA: did you not recognize the signs?

ELLIS: I thought you just didn't want to talk about it. I was trying
to distract you.

VADA: telling me I killed a human being is a bit higher up the
priority chain than playing make-believe

VADA: god

VADA: you're so

VADA: fuck

ELLIS: I'm so what?

VADA: what did you tell him?

VADA: he asked all sorts of questions

ELLIS: Like what?

VADA: like what the nature of our relationship is and shit

ELLIS: What did you tell him?

VADA: nothing

VADA: I don't tell strangers our personal business

ELLIS: Of course. God forbid you tell anybody the truth.

VADA: oh fucking stop

VADA: this is so not the time

ELLIS: I didn't tell him anything, either. He scared me.

VADA: he scared me, too

ELLIS: Where is he now?

VADA: lurking around the hospital like some fucking ghoul

VADA: probably stalking me

ELLIS: You'll be out soon.

ELLIS: You're almost ready for outpatient.

VADA: and then where?

ELLIS: Home.

VADA: where the hell is that anymore?

ELLIS: With me.

VADA: god

VADA: I fucking killed somebody, Ellis

VADA: I killed a human being

VADA: oh my fucking god

ELLIS: It was an accident.

VADA: no it wasn't

ELLIS: What?

VADA: don't talk to Max

VADA: don't talk to anyone

VADA: if the police question you, tell them what I told you

VADA: you got in the passenger seat

VADA: do you understand me, Elle?

ELLIS: It was me, wasn't it?

ELLIS: You're covering for me.

VADA: jesus

VADA: no

ELLIS: You are.

VADA: stop it

VADA: delete these messages when we're done

VADA: don't be stupid

VADA: you did nothing wrong

ELLIS: Why are you talking like this?

VADA: like what?

ELLIS: Like I'm guilty. Like you're protecting me.

VADA: I am protecting you, Elle

VADA: from your own fucking naivete

VADA: you always say things without realizing how other people hear them

VADA: you don't understand how the world works

ELLIS: Fuck you, Vada.

VADA: I'm not judging you

VADA: I'm just saying

ELLIS: You're saying I'm a liability. I get it.

ELLIS: You think I'm some dumb, naive child.

VADA: will you stop with the martyrdom

ELLIS: I know you're hiding something.

ELLIS: About the accident. Something I can't remember.

VADA: what does it fucking matter?

ELLIS: Because I know it was me. I know it's my fault.

VADA: jesus christ

VADA: you're the prince of self-pity

VADA: you'd be happier if I HAD let you get behind the wheel drunk, wouldn't you?

ELLIS: Didn't you?

VADA: I'm not fighting about this

VADA: just keep your story straight

VADA: make sure it matches mine

VADA: and don't fucking tell anybody our personal business

ELLIS: It's the same fight. Over and over.

VADA: don't even start

ELLIS: You don't really want me here.

ELLIS: I embarrass you. Shame you.

VADA: will you stop?

VADA: this is about a fatal car accident

VADA: not some episode of our never-ending soap opera

ELLIS: No, it is about us. Everything comes back to that.

ELLIS: This wouldn't have happened if things weren't so messed-up between us.

ELLIS: If you'd just be honest with yourself. With me.

VADA: I'm as honest as I know how to be

ELLIS: You never stand up for us.

ELLIS: You let your mom walk all over you. That was your chance to tell her.

VADA: THAT'S when you wanted me to tell her?

ELLIS: You let her define it. You let her call it unhealthy.

ELLIS: You always let other people define what we are.

VADA: I don't even fucking know what we are

VADA: how could I define it?

VADA: maybe it is kind of unhealthy

VADA: I don't know

ELLIS: I'm so tired of this, Vada.

VADA: you're tired?

VADA: what are you fucking tired of?

ELLIS: Being the cross you have to bear.

ELLIS: Sometimes I'm even tired of you.

VADA: you know what?

VADA: fine

VADA: fuck you

VADA: you want to be the martyr? be my guest

VADA: you're better off without me

ELLIS: What are you saying?

VADA: what do you think I'm saying?

VADA: go home

VADA: stay the hell away from me

VADA: I killed somebody

VADA: I dragged our stupid drama into the real world and now someone's dead because of it

VADA: I'm toxic

VADA: this has gone way too far

VADA: just stay away from me

VADA: go back to Chicago, or whatever

VADA: just leave me alone

ELLIS: You don't mean this.

VADA: I mean it with all my fucking heart

VADA: I'm blocking your number

ELLIS: Vada, please.

ELLIS: Let's talk this through.

VADA: there's nothing to talk about

VADA: it's the same fight over and over, just like you said

ELLIS: That doesn't mean I want it to end.

VADA: that's where we're different, Elle

VADA: you're the idealist and I'm the realist

VADA: this doesn't work

VADA: you and me

VADA: we're a fucking mess

ELLIS: Please don't go.

VADA: I love you but I can't do this anymore

VADA: it's better this way

VADA: I'm sorry Ellis

VADA: I love you

VADA: bye

—SPRING—

My drinking buddy banged on the kitchen door again.
I grabbed my phone off the nightstand. One hour till work and I'd been up half the night, curled into a ball in the bay window, teeth clenched, riding out the pain. Three months since the accident and I still didn't have fine motor control in my right hand.

At twenty-two I was relearning life as a lefty.

When he hit the door this time, the glass squealed alarmingly.

Bastard was going to break something.

I staggered past the bed, pulling the blanket around my shoulders. If he broke shit, Mrs. Mulhavey would add it to my weekly rent. Which I was already late on. Which he knew, and offered to cover.

I said no, of course. Taking money from a man I'd wronged was below me.

I padded through the freezing kitchen, cold linoleum kissing my soles, and flung open the door. He stood with one hand poised in midair.

"Max," I said, shivering. "What are you doing?"

"Did I wake you?"

"You probably woke half the city. What's up?"

"Can't sleep."

"Me either."

He took a flask from his jeans and swigged, then offered it to me. I shook my head.

I smelled the whiskey on him, strong. He'd missed the last ferry to the island. Next one came near dawn. So I'd keep him company till he could get himself across the bay and home.

Because this was our thing now. Holding each other back from the edge.

I stepped outside and sat on the sea-worn wooden rocker. Salt hung heavily in the wind, the rawness of the ocean like an exposed wound, dark and tender. Once upon a time you said we'd live beside the ocean, Ellis. Mermaids returning to our true realm. Well, I'm here, alone. It wasn't supposed to be like this.

"You'll get hypothermia if you sit outside drinking all night," I said.

"Wouldn't be a bad way to go."

He went for another swig and I grabbed the flask, tucking it into my blanket. "You're cut off, buddy."

Max sank onto the rocker bench, defeated.

He was a Jekyll-and-Hyde drunk: one side charming and gregarious, one morose and maudlin. Tonight was the latter. Red-rimmed eyes, lit with a crazed grief. Moisture beading on his skin. I pictured a tipsy Poseidon, kelp strung in his beard, armored in conch and coral, a whalebone trident dangling from one fist. My fingers twitched. I could see the sketch in my head.

He was going to get confessional. That's what he was here for. Catharsis. Day to day he was like me, walled up, but when we drank together we let ourselves say the things we couldn't normally say.

I miss her.

I miss him.

It's our fault.

The cold made my bad hand cramp. I hunched over, and Max said, "How's it feel?"

"Awful."

"I envy you."

"If you felt like this, you wouldn't."

"You could get rid of it, if you wanted. Be free." He gave what might have been a smile. "My wound's on the inside. There's only one way to stop that kind of hurt."

I shivered again, not from the cold.

Max wore a flannel shirt, no coat. Without asking, I slid toward him and tossed the blanket around his shoulders. We didn't touch, staring straight ahead into the mist, but after a while our heat merged beneath the cover.

"What kept you up tonight?" I said.

"Baseball." Breath left his mouth like smoke. "Training started today. I watched the kids do warmups."

His son, Ryan, had been a ball player. All-star, scouted by colleges. Apple of his dad's eye.

It was good to remind myself of that. Of the person who'd been killed instead of me.

"I used to coach," Max said. "Today I sat in the stands and watched. And I started thinking, I don't belong here. I'm not a parent anymore. Just some fucked-up middle-aged man, watching young boys play."

I shifted uneasily, the rocker swinging. "You'll always be a dad. Like you'll always be somebody's son."

"I'm nobody's anything. My parents are dead, my son is dead. I have no ties to this world."

You have me, I thought, but didn't dare say it.

"What kept you awake?" he said.

Ryan. Ellis. You.

"The pain."

"Your arm?"

"My life."

He laughed hoarsely, understanding.

We rocked in silence awhile. Eventually he slumped and dozed off. I watched him as the sun came up and bruised his skin in reverse: plum, then lilac, then salmon. Now my hand ached to draw, to capture the bronze grit on his jaw, the damp hair curling over his forehead. *Neptune, Sleeping*, I titled him.

The urge to make art is a hurting. An ache, like desire. Like loneliness.

Except I couldn't draw anymore. The hand that once spoke for me was dead, mute. It couldn't even make a fist without pain stropping my spine like a razor, straight to the brain stem.

I slipped out of the blanket. As I stood, Max clasped my bad hand.

"Careful. That hurts."

"I want to feel it. I want to feel the way you feel, Vada."

"No, you don't. Physical pain isn't better than emotional. It all sucks." I tugged. "Let go."

I could have gotten free. No other man touched me like this without getting my fist in his face. But Max was different.

I'd taken his son away. So it was only fair to let him take little pieces of me in return.

I let him clutch harder, and harder, refusing to cry out, until I sat back down and he hugged me, desperate. We held each other in an awkward embrace.

He didn't speak, but I understood. Perfectly.

———

I waited for her every morning. Walked down to the wharf at dawn and sat shrouded in fog, watching runners pound past on the cobblestones, silhouettes against the white sun. Their breath trailed behind, the air from a hundred lungs twisting into knots, clinging, dissolving. I waited for the fireball streaking across the gray harbor.

Ellis Morgan Carraway, my former best friend.

Max wasn't the only ghost haunting the living.

When I caught the flash of red I ducked behind a car, camera raised. I was broke as shit but my one indulgence was a pricey point-and-shoot and I snapped photos as she flew past. I could never quite capture her face. Just her hands rising and hovering with each stride, as if reaching for someone else.

I let the camera swing from the wrist strap, my hand rising in response.

Gone.

Ex–best friend. Ex-soulmate. Ex-everything.

If I were still seeing my psychiatrist he'd say the same thing Mamá did:

You're codependent, Vada. Build a life without her.

Anyone who calls you "codependent" has never had a best friend. Best friendship is a healthy codependence.

I followed her at a distance and she slowed, planted her hands on her knees. She wasn't really winded. I knew her too well. She glanced around, bangs hanging in her eyes. Nobody near. Only my breath gave me away, but morning mist rolled in over the docks, cloaking everything in pale smoke.

She took off again, determined.

Straight for the water.

I chased, passing the chain-link fence where friends and lovers had hung hundreds of locks to symbolize their devotion. We had a lock there. A brass lion's head. We'd latched it tight and tossed the key into the Atlantic. *"Love you forever,"* she said, and I said, *"Forever isn't long enough."*

Let me correct myself:

Friendship is a healthy codependence if you're still actually friends.

Elle jogged past the piers, toward the old train yard, where rust-eaten boxcars lay on broken tracks. Rime coated everything like cellophane, crinkling beneath my shoes. I weaved behind beached boats, her shadow.

Where was she going? There was nothing out here but an abandoned bridge that led nowhere.

Ellis veered off the footpath onto the seawall.

It was a shambles of piled rock, a ten-foot drop onto knife-edged limestone and deep ocean. This early, no one would hear her cry if she fell.

My heart heaved. It was like she knew I was there. Like I had to follow, or I might lose her forever.

Stalkers are excellent at rationalizing their behavior.

I'd been athletic once, Elle's running partner, but since the accident I'd let myself go. Drank myself to sleep, filled my waking breaths with weed. I struggled to keep up while her shoes skimmed slick rock without slipping. Elle ran right on the edge of oblivion, never glancing down. If she fell, the best I could do was call 911. I couldn't even swim.

What kind of idiot moves to coastal Maine when she can't swim?

Vada Bergen, who never thinks ahead. Who lives by impulse.

Elle's foot skidded on ice.

I almost yelled, but some wiser instinct clamped my mouth shut. I paused in the lee of a schooner, watching.

She tossed her arms wide for balance, caught herself on nothing but air. Stood there staring at the ocean, her breath frothing into the cold. I was maybe fifty feet away. I could have called her name. I could have stepped out and said, "Stop punishing yourself. Let's forget it all and start over. Again."

Instead I watched her shake it off and lope toward the city, passing me without a glance.

This is what they don't tell you about losing someone: It doesn't happen once. It happens every day, every moment they're missing from. You lose them a hundred times between waking and sleep, and even sleep is no respite, because you lose them in your dreams, too.

When she was gone I went down to the water and sat on the seawall, my legs dangling. I felt the pull of it, that promised erasure, the annihilating blot of the abyss. It's strange living near the ocean. Living near this edge of eternity, this falloff into nothingness.

The truth was, if she fell in I'd jump after her, but not to save her. To drown myself at her side.

I was already drowning in dry air. Just dying to finish it.

Sometimes I'd sit on the dock and let the magnetic tug of the ocean draw at me till I lay flat on the planks, my body pressed as thin and small as it could go. Longing to be pulled under. To disappear.

You're depressed, Vada, the psychiatrist would say. *Take this pill and pretend it will fill the hollow where you used to be whole.*

You fall in love with it a little. Depression. It's an abusive romance. It hurts like hell but you don't want it to stop, because at least hurt is a feeling. At least it reminds you you're still alive.

It was a two-mile walk back, my lips chapped and the chill lodging bone-deep in my marrow, just like loneliness.

———

At work I slapped on a fake smile and poured espresso and steamed milk into cups. I didn't see a single face, only the play of light on my own hands. The right looked normal unless you knew where to check for grafting scars. Ghost hands. The world they'd once shaped now passed straight through, nothing but a cold rush in my veins. My left was still clumsy.

I hefted a coffee kettle with it, poured a whole mug before my wrist twisted, mug and kettle and a pastry platter crashing to the floor, all over my pants, my shoes, my life.

Which was how I ended up in my boss's office, wishing I were invisible.

"It was my fault," I said to the floor. I was very good at saying that when it didn't matter.

Curtis rolled a joint and offered me the first hit.

"I'm on the clock."

"Our little secret?" He exhaled. Sweet smoke clotted the air, the earthy perfume of forest animals and wild girls.

"I'm good."

"We need to talk, Vada." He was my age, college dropout. Around here, college didn't mean much. Most jobs required a pair of sturdy hands. Unlike mine. "This is your third incident. I don't ride your ass about it, but it's starting to cost me."

Funny thing was, I'd planned to ask for a paycheck advance. Month behind on rent. I'd promised Mrs. Mulhavey I'd have it today.

"I can work a double this weekend."

"Weekend's already scheduled."

"Curt, look. My insurance doesn't cover everything. I have to pay half this shit out of pocket." No more pain meds. Couldn't afford them. "I'm not asking for charity. I want to work. Is there anything you can do?"

Please don't fucking make me beg.

He toked, held a lungful of smoke as he rolled his blood-shot blue eyes all over me. "I can give you some extra shifts."

"Thank you," I said dully, knowing what came next.

"We'll keep you on register. No heavy lifting. Good work ethic's worth more than a few broken dishes." He shrugged. "You know, I'm off this weekend, too. We should hang out."

There was no "should." I'd do it, or find a new job.

We met at a bar a few months back. I'd asked the owner if she could train a new bartender and she said, *You're pretty, hon, but pretty don't cut it. I need experience.* Pretty got me a referral, though. Out in the alley I found Curtis sitting on a pier piling with a blunt. He was rawboned-skinny but wearing only a T-shirt and vest in winter. Typical Mainer. He whisked a joint through the night while he talked, a tiny meteor streak. Maybe he could use some extra coverage at his coffee shop. We could chat later. Meanwhile there was a party at Someplace in Somewheretown and we should go. I went, and my half-healed hand ached and I hadn't fucked anyone since the night of the accident and I felt borderline subhuman, so I smoked Curt's weed and gave him a handjob in his truck, mostly to see if I still could. I lasted two minutes before the pain turned my bones to ripsaws and shredded my skin from the inside. I finished him with my mouth.

I really needed that job.

It was a mistake. I know that. He still doesn't.

"I'll text you when I know my plans," I said, and made for the door.

"Friday. After nine."

"Wait for my text."

"I'll pick you up."

I almost spun around and slugged him. You don't whittle down a yes. A yes is something that's built up, not conceded out of desperation, a hunk of raw meat tossed to a starving dog just so you can flee the moment.

But instead of saying no like I meant to, I carved a piece from my body and threw it to him. "I'll go, but I can't stay late. Finals are coming up."

"It's only April."

"It's grad school, Curt."

"Art school."

I turned. "What is that supposed to mean?"

If Elle were here, she would've flashed me the warning look. *Temper, Vada. This is your boss.*

"I mean, it's not, like, med school."

"It's master's-level work."

"Didn't they give you medical leave?"

I swallowed. My throat felt like a fuse, fire eating its way down. "I didn't take it. I don't need it."

Straight lies. I was behind on everything, no hope of catching up. Yesterday I downloaded the forms for medical withdrawal.

"But you're handicapped. Why not, you know, take advantage?"

My right hand shot out before I could stop myself. I grabbed the collar of his T-shirt and wrapped it in a fist, drawing his face close to mine. "Does this seem like a fucking handicap?"

Curtis gaped, expelling weed fumes. He was stunned enough not to notice how my hand shook. How weak my grip actually was. How tears collected in my eyes and threatened to paint my pain all over my face.

He pried me away. "Sorry. Poor choice of words."

I muttered something pseudo-apologetic.

"It's fine," he said, looking elsewhere. "Go ahead. Take the rest of the day off."

"I didn't—"

"You'll miss the bus."

Dismissal.

The walk to the stop didn't cool the hot spike drilling through the center of my chest. I missed the bus anyway. Of course. I sat on the hood of someone's car and made a fist and smashed it on my thighs, but that wasn't satisfying, so I hit the hood, too, which set off the car alarm, which was a little better. Tourists on the sidewalk stared.

I wanted to scream. Let everyone know how not okay I was. But all I did was side-eye the car as if it had thrown a tantrum on its own. Sometimes people actually feel relief when a machine breaks down—it's not okay to show your not-okayness publicly anymore, everyone thinks you'll shoot up a movie theater or a classroom, but when a machine malfunctions we can pretend to disapprove while secretly we're cheering, living through it vicariously, willing it to spin and vibrate and explode, take out someone's eye or hand, do something real. We want someone, something else to revolt, because we can't.

What the fuck is wrong with me, Ellis? How am I supposed to make sense of anything without you?

The alarm finally died and the quiet pulsed as rawly as screamed-out air.

———

My landlady was waiting for me in the kitchen.

I stood on the porch, peering through the window. Sometimes you see disaster coming, the edge of the bridge rushing up, dark water waiting, and you're so fucking empty and hopeless you don't bother to avoid it. You don't swing the wheel, slam the brake. You speed up. Meet your doom head-on.

I went in and sat at the table.

Mrs. Mulhavey smiled, not unkindly. Pushed a mug of hot cocoa over. I didn't drink, but wrapped my hands around it. Heat merged with pain, muscle fibers pulling apart by millimeters, not pleasant but at least different from the ache I was used to. If I could choose my pain, I'd prefer unraveling to exploding.

We faced each other. Regret tightened her smile.

"I don't have the money," I said in the same monotone I'd used with Curtis. "When do you need me out by?"

"Next week, dear."

No argument. We'd already had that discussion. I was a good kid, Mrs. Mulhavey said, a good kid dealt a bad hand, no pun intended, but she had bills to pay and meds to buy, too. It didn't move her that I was out of options. I didn't have cash for the security deposit everyone else wanted. This was my end of the line, and fate took it away from me. Like I deserved.

I thought about getting up from the table and walking out the door and simply not stopping. Leaving all of this. My few run-down possessions, old sketchpads, canvases, paint cans unused for so long the lids were glued shut. A strand of Christmas lights bordering my bed and the photos taped above it. Me and Ellis, when we were happy. When we were us.

Mementos from someone else's life.

"I'm sorry," I said.

"I know, dear. I'm sorry, too."

I looked at her lined face, wrinkles filling with afternoon shadow. The older we get, the more shadows we let in.

There was nothing left in me that shone. If I could still do a self-portrait, all I'd draw would be a silhouette.

Mrs. Mulhavey fetched something and set it before me. Tissue box. One firm pat on my shoulder, then she left me to sit in dignified silence, crying.

Friday night I got dolled up and let Curtis take me to a house on the ocean. We split a joint on the drive down the coast. Spruce towered to either side of the road, black bristles merging with black night, our headlights and a handful of silver dust scattered across the sky the only illumination. He drove past the bridge where Ryan's Jeep had collided with Elle's car, where the three of us crashed into each other's lives and only two walked away and then those two walked away from each other. I felt nothing. Do you know how much blood is soaked into every mile of asphalt, how many graves you drive over each morning on the way to work?

This world is so thick with ghosts it's a wonder anyone can breathe.

The house stood on a bluff over the water. Mixed crowd, some early twenties and rowdy and drunk, others older and chill, smoking weed or eating shrooms. Curtis walked around with me on his arm and introduced me as his girlfriend. I didn't correct him. When people looked at us, they didn't see anything out of the ordinary. Just a girl and a boy. Pink and blue. Skirt and slacks. Normal. They asked about my major, where I worked. They didn't blink and say things like, *Wait, are you two together? Are you a couple? Are you dot dot dot?*

It felt so good, being seen for who I was, instead of what.

A girl kept catching my eye. Pixie-slim, dark brown skin contrasting sharply against an ivory dress. Her curly hair bounced with each step. No matter where we went she appeared after a few moments. A guy hovered at her side, lean and blond, wearing an open-throat Oxford.

"Know them?" Curt said.

"Nope."

"I think they want to know you."

He tried to introduce us but I ducked away, pretending I had to pee. And then I just . . . didn't come back. I wandered through the house, through conversations, stopping to listen to someone discourse on a film or a book, laughing at their jokes, moving on before anyone asked me personal questions. For some reason I didn't want that elegant couple seeing me with Curt. There was something about them, something honed, hard. Something too much like me.

Weed made me restless, hyperaware of the shift of light and shadow. I sketched scenes in my head: a woman and a man arguing, glimpsed through a window, their voices mute but their breath clouding in the chill, steam serpents circling, lashing. A girl in runny mascara sitting on the dock, her hair a dark tempest whirling around her face. A couple kissing in a doorway, her hands twisting his shirt as if crumpling a drawing. Human beings connecting in anger and longing and lust.

I felt queasy and I hadn't even drunk anything. If loneliness has a physical manifestation, it's nausea.

Where are you? Curtis texted.

I thought about meeting him at his car. Getting in and running a hand up his leg. Blowing him, but not letting him come. Going home with him and fucking him in his dank apartment that smelled of marijuana and coffee and then, in the afterglow, telling him how Mulhavey was tossing me on the street and how *grateful* I'd be if he spotted me some cash for a new place.

Never in my life had I traded sex for money. But was this really a life anymore?

meet me, I started typing, and the black girl in the white dress swept through the room. The blond guy strolled after her, pausing at my side. I'm tall like my mother. I had a couple of inches on him.

He smiled at me, a twinkle of mischief in it, a dare, then trailed in her wake.

I pocketed my phone and followed without hesitation.

This was what I'd been missing for so long:

Mystery.

The two of them waited in a sitting room. Instinctively, I closed the door after I entered. It was empty save for us. Low light, tinged sepia from a nicotine-stained lampshade. Sagging sofas and nicked wooden chairs, salt- and sun-bleached, that typical Maine look, as if everything was a found object washed ashore in a storm. The guy leaned against a wall, arms folded. The girl stood at the center of a hemp rug and gazed at me.

"Come here."

Her voice was deep and commanding.

I'd been in bad situations plenty of times. These two didn't set off my threat meter. She was clearly in control, and whatever she wanted, it was up to me to consent.

I went to her.

Sometimes people sing out to be drawn. She had the kind of face I could draw again and again without growing bored. Gazelle-like, large doe eyes, fine bones tapering to a neat mouth. Something haughty and proud in it. Queenly.

"How did you find me?" she said.

"Who are you?"

"Who are *you*?"

Alice in Wonderland, apparently.

"I'm just here with a friend. I don't know who you are."

The girl studied me, skeptical. "You're not a client?"

"Client of what?"

The guy laughed. "Of who," he amended. Tenor voice, soft and melodic.

"Who?" I echoed, confused.

The girl finally relaxed. Her smile was wry. "She's clean." She touched my face, traced my cheekbone, and I was so startled I didn't move.

"Name?" the guy said, approaching.

I don't know why I said it. I hadn't planned to lie, but some instinct kicked in and said, *Be someone else.* "Morgan."

The two of them exchanged a look, hearing the fakeness.

The guy circled me, not menacing, merely . . . appraising. Baby blues scanned my body without lingering or smoldering with want. The way you'd look at a horse, an animal you meant to buy and use.

I knew what my body did to men. This one wasn't fazed.

"Age?" the girl said.

"Twenty-three. Today."

She smiled brilliantly. "Happy birthday."

First person besides Mamá to wish me a happy birthday, and it was a beautiful stranger about to pull me into some *Eyes Wide Shut* shit. How sad was that?

And how sad was it that I half hoped this might end up as some bizarre sex thing? Truth was, no one had made me come in months. Part of why I felt subhuman was the fact that I was young and horny and alone with my left hand every night. If Blondie here wanted to watch me fuck his smoking-hot girl-friend, I was down. And if she wanted to watch me bang him, fine. I'd even do them both. I wasn't picky.

I just wanted to be touched. So badly.

"Morgan," the girl said, "what do you do for a living?"

"Survive."

"Want to make some money?" the guy said.

They wanted to fuck me. Kinky shit, BDSM or something. I was lonely, but maybe not that lonely. They read the hesitation on my face.

"He'll leave," the girl said. "Just you and me. Five minutes of your time. Fully compensated."

What could a girl do to me in five minutes?

Everything.

"Okay," I said, surprising myself. There was a glimmer of knowing in her eyes. I didn't think she'd hurt me, but also I didn't much care if she did. Sometimes you get so sick of a familiar hurt you'd prefer anything else, even new pain, just for the sake of it being new.

The guy made a mocking bow and left the room.

"Take off your shirt," the girl said.

"I don't hook up till I get a name."

The smooth mask of her face broke into a smile. "Call me Frankie."

"Is that like 'Call me Ishmael'?"

"Take off your shirt."

Her voice hit my skin like a whip crack. I slipped my blouse off, trying not to laugh. God, Ellis. If only you could see this. If only you knew how pathetic I am without you.

Frankie's eyes ran over me expressionlessly. I always felt more nervous under a girl's eyes. We know each other too well, our gazes laser sharp, instantly zeroing in on flaws. I watched her take in the ink scrolling down my ribs and inside the low waist of my jeans. I avoided looking at the tats now, avoided my own body in mirrors. It had been so long since I'd let anyone look at me like this.

"Like what you see?" I said.

"Be silent until spoken to."

I bit my bottom lip deliberately, and she laughed.

"You've got spirit. I like that." She lifted an eyebrow. "Take your bra off. Seduce me while you do it."

Voyeurism, then. All right.

I maintained eye contact and raised my hands to my breasts. Unbuttoned the front clasp, slowly. "Do you like watching, Frankie? You do. You like to watch." The cups fell free and cool air grazed my skin and for the briefest moment I felt like myself. In control. The center of someone's world. "Look at me. Do you want to touch?" I slipped the bra off, flung it aside. Lowered my voice. "Do you want to taste? Do you want to kiss me? On my mouth, my body? I'd let you put your lips all over me."

I don't know where it came from. The knowingness in her eyes unlatched a kindred knowing in me. I'd never actually spoken to anyone like this. I stood naked from the waist up in front of a gorgeous stranger and felt—powerful.

"Touch yourself," Frankie said quietly. Her eyes were wet and dark as ink.

I cupped my hands beneath my breasts, never breaking eye contact. Imagined our limbs tangling, our skin juxtaposed, umber against bronze.

"Do you want to fuck me?" I said.

She touched my cheek again. "Put your clothes back on."

Instantly, the enchantment dissolved. I glanced at my bra across the room.

"What was this, a job interview?"

She just smiled, enigmatic.

Her guy friend reentered the room as if Frankie had silently summoned him. He pulled a wallet out and pressed a hundred-dollar bill into my hand while I was still straightening my blouse.

"Wait," I said.

The guy headed for the door. Frankie asked for my number.

I gave it to her, saying, "What just happened?"

"Go to this link. Use the code . . ." She paused, typing something on her phone. Her eyes flashed up at me. "Use the code 'morganiscute.' "

I stared at her text, bewildered.

"Hey." Frankie snapped her fingers. "Got it?"

"Yeah, got it."

"Have a lovely evening."

Then she was gone and I stood there rereading her text.

camwhorez.com/tiana

Oh, damn.

———

I flung a rock at the second-story window and listened for the whistle and crack, the rattle of glass. Nothing for a good long minute. In the distance the ocean murmured against the shore.

I flung another rock.

Turned out one hundred dollars would buy a fifth of Cîroc

and a cab ride to the East End of Portland, Maine, where million-dollar houses gazed over the water with a thousand blind eyes, blank and undreaming. I texted Curt to tell him I'd gone home with someone and turned off my phone. Couldn't throw for shit lefty so it took me a good dozen rocks before I hit the window again. But when a light finally came on, it wasn't on the second floor. It was the first. A silhouette eclipsed the golden glow.

"Come fucking talk to me," I yelled, slurring.

The silhouette remained still. The light flicked off.

I dug a new stone from the gravel path but before I could throw it, the second-story window flew open.

"What on earth are you doing?"

The rock slipped from my hand, the vodka bottle dangling from the other. "Ellis."

I couldn't see her face but I knew that tousled rake of hair. I'd run my hands through it so many times.

After a pause she said, softer, "Are you drunk again?"

I lifted the vodka. "It's my birthday."

"I know." In the ocean-brushed quiet I could hear her breathe, each exhale a small sigh. "Why did you come here?"

"Aren't you going to wish me a happy birthday?"

The window slammed shut.

I tumbled onto the lawn. It wasn't exactly my decision—my legs had gone on strike.

The front door opened and Ellis appeared, wrapped in a fleece blanket. She glided toward me, seeming to float over the lawn like some sea spirit. This all felt half-real: taking my clothes off for Frankie, showing up at Elle's drunk as fuck.

"Hi," I said sweetly.

"Oh god. You're wasted."

There was something wistful in her voice. It made me warm. Take care of me, I thought. "I'm twenty-three."

"Okay." Ellis rubbed her temple. "I'll call a cab."

"I can't go home. Don't have one."

"What?"

The bottle was uncapped but I rolled it carelessly, letting liquid crystal leak into the grass. "Got evicted."

She snatched the vodka and stood it upright. So like her. Proper, precise Ellis. Everything in its right place.

"What do you want, Vada?" Her voice was brittle. "You ignore my texts, then show up drunk and pick fights. What is this?"

"Technically, it's emotional abuse."

This is how much of an asshole I am:

Elle had been texting me. Every day.

I hadn't actually blocked her number. I couldn't do it. But I let her plead, and beg, and tell me over and over how much I meant to her, how sorry she was, how she wanted to change.

Then the texts turned angry. It wasn't fair, she said. We'd both made mistakes.

Then sweet again. Poignant. They came days apart. Weeks.

I'm sorry.

I wish you were here.

I just miss you.

When the texts got sparser I came to her house, drunk, to reboot the cycle. To keep her hooked.

"Is this funny?" Elle said. "Is hurting me a joke to you?"

"Everything is a joke. Especially pain." I curled my bad hand in the grass. It felt like grabbing a fistful of hypodermic needles. "Pain is fucking hilarious."

"I think you should leave."

"I don't know where else to go."

"Go anywhere else. Please."

I was so used to being hurt I barely felt it. A finger on a deep bruise, pressing a little harder.

"You don't want me anymore," I said, and laughed. "Nobody wants me."

Elle's phone emerged from the blanket. "I'll get you a hotel."

"Who's in your house?"

She turned her back and said, "Do you have any vacancies?"

"Who's in the house with you, Elle?"

"I'd like to rent a room, please."

Throwing money at the problem to make it go away. Just like her mother.

I scooped up the bottle and rose shakily to my feet.

"Vada," she said.

"Fuck your money. And fuck you."

Ellis followed me as I stumbled toward the street. She stopped at the edge of her lawn.

"Happy fucking birthday," I said, and took a swig off the bottle, and then, on impulse, smashed it on the concrete. It burst spectacularly, glass and clear liquor flowering into the freezing air. A perfect encapsulation of how I'd felt these past months, jagged and see-through and a complete fucking waste.

I bent to pick a shard from the sidewalk and she rushed to my side. "Do not."

"Do not what?" It felt so good, being childish. Making her care about me. Making her feel actual concern.

Her hand clamped onto my wrist. I dropped the shard.

And shoved her onto the grass, tackling her.

We'd fought before. Gone at each other savagely with nails and edged words. It was all so familiar: my hands fitting around the grooves of her throat, and hers under my shirt, raking my skin.

"Fuck," I said, my breath a cloud connecting us. "More."

Nails ripped down my spine. I was too drunk to really feel it but my grip tightened on her neck and she scratched mercilessly and then it was a real fight. We rolled through the grass, clawing, choking. At one point I bolted her wrists to the ground but somehow she ended up on top, holding me down. I writhed and she stayed on me, viciously agile.

"God," I panted. "Don't stop. Please."

I wrapped my arms around her waist. Pulled her body hard against mine.

Ellis wrenched away. I tried to drag her back but she was limp now and my bad hand twinged, fire lacing up my nerves. I slammed my palms into the grass. My hair hung in my eyes, a dark scrawl across this night, this ugliness.

"What do you want?" she rasped.

"You. Touch me. Hold me."

"No. You just want us to hurt each other."

I sat back on my heels, exhausted. Sad, stupid, ugly. All of this. My shoulder blades burned, the skin shredded as if someone had torn off wings. Vodka churned in my gut like a jumble of razor blades. *You're right,* I thought. *I want to be hurt. Because this is the closest I feel to you anymore, when you hurt me.*

"Go home," Ellis said.

"You are my home."

She kept her face averted but I saw the hiccup before a sob.

"Don't cry," I whispered.

"You need to leave." She refused to look at me. I saw the effort it took, the tense lines of her shoulders. "Please leave, Vada. And don't come back."

"What?"

"I can't do this anymore. I need a clean break."

"There's no break. Nothing's breaking."

"We need to. We've been dragging it out for months. All we do is hurt each other. Please, just let me go."

I stood up, teetering. "What are you saying?"

Elle didn't move and didn't go back to the house. She simply waited, letting me rage and burn out. Like always.

"Look at me, Ellis. Fuck you. Say it to my face."

Nothing.

I went to my knees beside her, touched her shoulder. "Don't do this. I'm fucked-up, okay? I'm sorry. I'll be better." I gripped harder. "Everything fucking hurts. I feel raw, everywhere. I'm sorry for taking it out on you. It's depression or something. I'll get help. But don't do this, okay? Don't cut me off. I need you."

Nothing.

"Elle, please. You're all I have."

Tears ran down her face. She remained silent.

I let go.

My teeth gritted till it felt like they'd snap, every bone in me poised on the brink of pulverizing into white powder. There was a pain inside that I could no longer express. I couldn't draw it anymore. I couldn't share it with her. It lay buried, trapped, echoing off its own walls and growing louder and louder, a scream I could never voice.

How do people go through their entire life with something like this inside?

But they don't. That's why Ryan got behind the wheel with a 0.20 BAC.

A pain like this must become violence. Toward another, or yourself.

She was right. I needed to go, before I hurt her more.

I staggered to my feet and ran through halo after halo of streetlight.

It was a long way back, and after crying and puking myself into dehydration I collapsed on a bench near the shore. I felt like some creature out of an Ernst painting, a patchwork monster, a furious unraveling of color, grotesque and absurd. Staining everything I touched.

I curled into a ball and tried to stop shivering.

It used to be us versus the world. Fast friends from the day we met, always guarding each other's backs. When I let my anger take control Ellis was there to soothe me, to gently pull at my reins. When someone took advantage of her naivete, her faith in the goodness of people, I shut them down without her even knowing. I'd sheltered her a little, but she deserved a little sheltering. Her heart was pure, open. Not shadowy and labyrinthine like mine.

But sometimes when you absorb all the hate and cruelty meant for someone else, it gets inside you. Feeds on your fears, your insecurities. Speaks in the voices of people you know, like your mother, and says, *Two grown women should not share one bedroom,* mija, and, *Vada, you'll never find a man if you keep living like this.* Sometimes you end up resenting the person you're protecting.

Somewhere along the way, it became me versus her.

The rest of the walk flickered in my head like a dream. Salt wind stung my face, white grains collecting like barnacles on my shoes. Exposing your open wounds to an ocean is pure masochism. Then the alcohol rose in me like the tide, drowning all the bad parts, and it felt so good to drown a little.

Someone was sitting on my porch steps.

My idiot heart soared and I thought, *Ellis,* but Max raised his head, and for a second I was so crushed it wasn't her that I was glad he knew how this felt. The stomach plunge of never seeing the person you're hoping to see.

"I finally did it," I said, leaning on the fence. "Bottom of the barrel. I'm officially homeless next week."

Max sat silently, backlit by the porch lantern.

My body kept growing heavier. I slid down to the frozen dirt. "Probably lost my job today, too. And I'm dropping out of school. And it's my birthday and Ellis said she never wants to see me again." My voice cracked on that last part. "Know how suicides give away all their stuff before they kill themselves? The universe did it for me. Now all I've got to do is find a razor."

Max got up. A bolt of morbid excitement shot through me. Come on, I thought. Hurt me. I deserve it.

Air trembled in his throat, like a death rattle.

He was crying.

My arms rose and we more or less fell into each other. Rigid, resistant, limbs entwining even as our faces angled away. But the contact thawed us and he stroked my hair, and I clung to him and let his sobs rock me, toss me, like waves. Fuel and woodsmoke. Fatherly smells.

"I'm sorry," I whispered in his ear. "It was a stupid joke. I'm drunk."

Still he didn't speak.

"I'm a jerk. I'm seriously an asshole, Max." I pressed my cheek to his shoulder. "I was an asshole even before the accident. A bully. Too scared to be myself, and now it's too late. Everything's fucked-up. I'm fucked-up."

Because God rolled the dice and let the wrong person live.

"It should've been me," I said. "I should have died instead of Ryan."

His body went taut. Blunt fingernails dug into the back of my skull. I didn't flinch.

"Don't say that. Don't you ever say that."

"It's true. He was better than me. Everyone's better than me."

Max pulled back to look into my face. The air fogged, thick with my vodka breath. "You're a good person, Vada. You took care of me when I needed it."

"I killed your son."

"Not you. You didn't do it."

"Huh?"

He helped me stand. He wasn't even drunk. "No more suicide talk, okay?"

"Okay."

"That's not you. You're strong."

"Okay."

"Do I need to stay here tonight?"

"I'm fine, really. Why are you here?"

He took an envelope from his coat. "Happy birthday."

"What is this?"

"I know you're struggling."

We both stared at the envelope, avoiding each other's eyes. "Max, I can't. I can't take your money."

"No strings. You don't owe me anything. Please."

You don't get it, I thought. I owe you everything. I took the most precious thing from you.

"I appreciate it, but I'm okay. My mom will help me out."

"Your mother's struggling, too."

"Let me worry about that."

Max shook his head. "Stubborn girl."

It took a while to convince him to go. Tonight I was the jumper and he was the lifeline. I smiled, lied, flirted till he felt awkward. Promised I'd text if I felt like hurting myself.

What a joke. *If I felt like hurting myself.*

That's what got us all into this mess in the first place.

A bar of moonlight split my room in two. I sat at my desk and flattened my hands to stop their shaking.

"Ellis, have you ever thought about killing yourself?"

I turned on the banker's lamp. Pulled a sketchpad from beneath a pile of art history books, a drawing pencil from the cup. Dull tip. It took a minute to find a razor blade and another to shave a point.

"Doesn't everyone?"

"But I mean, have you fantasized about how you'd do it?"

The last time I'd drawn was three months ago. I flipped past my final sketches, studies of hands, wrists, delicate bird-like bones. Blank page. The pencil looked like someone had massacred it with a hatchet, but there was enough graphite to work with.

I switched it to my drawing hand.

At physical therapy, they said my nerve damage was healing well except near the elbow, where bone had broken through skin. When you hit your "funny bone," what you're really feeling is the tingle of the exposed ulnar nerve being struck. Mine felt like that permanently. They test ulnar damage by having the patient grip a piece of paper between thumb and forefinger, then they pull the paper away. An uninjured person holds on easily. Someone like me crooks their thumb into a claw, desperately trying to hold on with the surrounding muscles.

I failed the test every week. It wasn't healing.

"You're lucky you're young," the physical therapist had said. "You have time to retrain."

"What the fuck is lucky about this?"

The medical questionnaire had asked what I'd done for a living before the injury. Did I expect this injury to negatively impact my career? Would I like assistance transitioning into a new job field?

I'd crumpled it (with my trainable hand) and flung it in the trash.

The PT had ticked a box on his clipboard that I assumed read DENIAL.

Now I propped the sketchpad in my lap, held the pencil in a

loose paintbrush grip. Much of drawing comes from the shoulder, not the hand. The hand is for fine detail; bold, smooth lines come from the whole arm. Even though my ulnar was toast I could compensate with other nerves and muscles—with vastly diminished control and progressively increasing pain.

When I pressed the onyx tip to the paper my arm drooped and a thick black scar tore across the sheet.

I had as much grip strength as a toddler.

I gritted my teeth. Try again. This time I managed to draw steadily for an inch before my hand weakened and the line zigzagged.

Try again.

"If I really wanted to die," Ellis said, *"I'd build in redundancy. Opiates and alcohol in a warm bath."*

"Wow. You're even nerdy about suicide."

"Anything can fail. Always have a fallback."

The page filled with a schizoid flurry of dark wires. Lines that could not connect to each other, out of sync, out of touch. An accidental self-portrait.

Desperately, I took the pencil in my left hand and tried again. Same result: childish scribbling.

Everything was still in my brain—how the human skeleton fits together, how ribbons of muscle furl and twist around bones, how light and shadow paint objects into three dimensions—but it was locked inside and I could not extract it and put it on fucking paper anymore.

"If you were actually going to kill yourself, how would you do it?" Elle said.

"I don't know. With whatever was nearby, I guess."

"You don't care how?"

"I care more about the note."

It was so like us—she was always hung up on *how*, when all I cared about was *why*.

"What would your note say?"

"Not really a note. A drawing."

"Of what?"

I ripped the sheet from the pad (with my trainable hand) and mashed it in my fist, tighter and tighter till it felt like my skin could absorb it, make it vanish.

"Of what I love most."

Of you.

(—Bergen, Vada. *One Thousand Ways to Say Good-Bye.*
Charcoal drawing on paper.)

The razor glinted on the desk, clean and bright.

Calling to me.

Put something else in your hands. Now.

I took out my phone. And there was Frankie's message.

I know. It's a cliché: life robs girl; girl sells body. But I didn't think of it like that. And I didn't think of it *affirmatively*, as me finding worth in my flesh despite losing the part I prized most, my primary hand. I didn't think of it as being sex-positive or even having much to do with sex at all.

I was just broke and sad and lonely, like everyone else on this planet. The Internet is life, and life is a bunch of lonely people making money off each other's longing.

I hurled myself onto the bed and flipped open my laptop.

Okay, cam girl. Show me what you've got.

————

The front page was a grid of images: pussies, asses, tits, mouths, a catalog of every fuckable orifice and cleft in full HD. Skin everywhere, pale peach and buttery gold and creamy brown. Few faces; the occasional tat or piercing became a substitute for identity. The bodies were in the middle of teasing them-selves and others with toys and fingers, spreading legs to the

lens, stroking breasts and cocks. The images had captions like
#cumshow at 500 tokens and *#anal play close-ups*. Most of the
cammers were girls, waxed and tweezed and lotioned till their
hairless skin shone, but a handful were boys, also polished.
They were ranked by popularity.

Tiana was number one.

Clicking her thumbnail took me to a page with a live webcam and a chat box. In the cam, Tiana/Frankie, still in her
white dress, sprawled across a canopy bed. Amber light drifted
through muslin bed drapes and diffused into a warm mist. Tiana
looked like a reposing empress, one knee raised to show the
shadow between her legs. She smiled down at her laptop screen.

The chat was full of things like this:

ImUrDaddy: spread ur legs more honey
ImUrDaddy: u look so hot
jiffylubed: how are you tonight bb?
AlphaBillionaire has tipped Tiana 200 tokens.
choclit_luvr: lets see dat pussy

Tiana's mouth quirked. "You're impatient tonight, boys
and girls."

Her hand trailed up her shin and caught the hem of her
dress, as if on accident. It rode up her thighs. She wasn't wearing panties.

choclit_luvr: FUCK YEAH BB
jiffylubed: exquisite.
ImUrDaddy: touch urself

She teased. When a user tipped her with tokens, more
skin appeared. Eventually the dress came off. She cupped her
breasts, dipped a hand between her thighs. Took her time.
Those hands moved over her own skin as if she were sculpting
it for us, creating herself out of nothing. Her viewers grew

wild. Trash-talked each other. Lunged against invisible leashes, barely civil. The more frenzied they became, the more languorous her movements.

No. She wasn't slowing down—I was just caught up in the hysteria with all the others.

At two thousand tokens, the page informed us, Tiana would perform a blowjob. The tokens ticked up. So did my pulse. Part of me prayed she'd blow the blond boy from the party. He was my type to a T—slender, viperous, his eyes hooded and knowing. Boys like that usually knew how to fuck, took it slow, made you come first. But another part of me felt a strange resentment. As if I deserved to be in that room with her. As if I were the one she called to every time she gazed deeply into the cam. I knew that on her side she was facing a black pinhole on her laptop, a lens into nothingness. There was nothing between us. Only light dancing down wires. But somehow it still felt like she was looking at me.

Which was exactly what every other Joe Blow was undoubtedly feeling.

The token counter flashed GOAL MET.

"Thank you, gentlemen. Ladies." I could swear she winked at the cam. She bent over, flashing bare ass and a slash of damp pink, and pulled a box from beneath her bed. "Biggest tipper gets the honors. Alpha, who will I fuck tonight?"

AlphaBillionaire: ty bb
AlphaBillionaire: big white please

Tiana removed a large peach-skinned dildo from the box.

ImUrDaddy: nooooooo suck the black one
tool1995: fuck u n***a ass bitch
[MOD]HenryVIII: *tool1995 has been banned from Tiana's chat.*
ImUrDaddy: lol owned

Tiana rolled her eyes wryly, winked at the cam, then put the sex toy to her lips.

———

When I looked up from my laptop the room was awash in dawn light.

All night I'd clicked cam after cam, one of those porn zombies who can't get enough, mindlessly devouring, growing hungrier the more I consumed. In the end, Tiana/Frankie was tame. There was something almost quaint about a girl sucking a dildo for hundreds of anonymous viewers. So uncomplicated, so obviously sexual. The deeper I delved into the rabbit hole, the less it was about sex. Somehow the cam girl who smeared her belly with ketchup and mayonnaise at a generous tipper's request seemed more vulnerable than the girls who vigorously fingered themselves while their tits bounced. Fetish work was so nakedly about control. About one person's particular pleasure.

I pay you. You obey me.

The code *morganiscute* unlocked a private section on Tiana's page. Videos of her doing virtually everything sexually conceivable: fucking toys, boys, girls, household objects. Photo shoots with ultra-high-res close-ups of her nipples and clit and toes, brown and pink pixels totally decontextualized into blobs of color, like abstract art. Mundane shots of her brushing her teeth or pulling on socks. Oddly, the mundane pics far outnumbered the sexier ones.

Was that a thing? Chore porn?

Maybe it wasn't solely about getting off. Maybe it was the illusion of intimacy, of sharing a life with this girl you jerked off to. Seeing her doing normal human things. Imagining yourself there beside her, brushing your teeth after you made her come.

I'd expected stuff like anal and bondage, every shade of kink. None of that fazed me. It was the sheer normalcy that made me uneasy. The raw, pulsing loneliness of it. I knew this world. I knew these hungry zombies with gravestone shadows beneath their eyes, emptiness aching in their palms. I was one of them.

Camwhorez.com operated on a token system. One token cost ninety-nine cents USD.

There was no info on the site about what percentage cammers took home, but even at a measly 10 percent royalty rate, Tiana would've earned two hundred bucks for two hours of work. My entire month's rent in one night.

"Numbers don't lie," Ellis said once. "Not like fiction. Or art."

"'Art is a lie that makes us realize truth.'"

"Who said that, some artist?"

"Some artist. Pablo something."

"Oh, shut up. I know who Picasso is." She looked at me fervently, imploring me to understand. "But that's the difference. Numbers can't lie. They're pure. Our faces, our names, they're all lies. They're fictions we invent to tell stories about ourselves."

"But you like stories." I twisted a lock of her hair. Long bangs, buzzed on the sides. As if she were two different people. "You like playing make-believe with me. Isn't there truth in that, too? In the ways we pretend?"

"That's different. That truth is full of shades."

"So is life."

"To us. But when you look at it under a microscope, life is just equations playing out. Geometry and physics. Numbers. Each one has one meaning. It's so simple and clear. So beautiful. It comforts me."

I smiled. "I love the way your mind works. It's so simple and clear. It comforts me, too."

"Are you calling me simple?"
"No, silly. I'm calling your mind beautiful."

(—Bergen, Vada. *A Beautiful Mind.*
Copic marker on paper.)

Truth in numbers. Who could argue with two hundred
bucks a night?

Maybe it really was that simple.

You pay me. I obey you.

———

On Monday I walked into the coffee shop and stood in the doorway, soaking up the light. Ceiling crisscrossed with timber beams,
exposed brick walls. Once upon a time it had been a warehouse
full of men in brine-stained overalls with arms like marine rope.

Strange, to look at something and know it's the last time
you'll see it.

I wondered what Max said the last morning he saw his son.
If he regretted it now, something petty, thoughtless. An omit-
ted *I love you* because of course he did and it was awkward to
keep reminding the kid. No *I'm proud of you* or *I know your life
isn't easy* or *I'm sorry I wasn't a better father.*

I knew exactly what I'd said to Elle before the headlights
flared in the rearview like a supernova.

I'm sorry I'm sorry I love you.

Tanya gave me a cagey look when I stepped behind the
register. She wasn't scheduled today.

"Someone call off?" I said, reaching for my apron.

No answer.

Curtis poked his head out at the sound of my voice. "Vada.
Come see me in my office."

I'd shut my phone off when he wouldn't stop calling all
weekend. So this was the inevitable, then.

"No."

"We need to talk about—"

"No," I echoed, louder. "If you're going to fire me, do it here. In front of everyone. Where you can't put your hands on me, for once."

Heads swiveled from the order line. Tanya darted a shocked glance at us. Curt reddened.

A customer walked over and strode right behind the counter.

"Excuse me," Frankie's blond friend said in his mellifluous voice. "There a problem here?"

Frankie sauntered up behind him, planting herself at my side.

I could have kissed them both.

Curtis eyed the guy edgily, possibly wondering if he was a jealous ex. "Sir, I'm afraid I have to ask you to—"

"The thing is," Frankie said, propping her palms on the counter, "maybe I misheard, but I could swear the young lady just described sexual harassment by a superior."

Her friend shook his head. "And then you were going to fire her? That's—what's the word—"

"Extortion," I blurted, my heart skipping.

Frankie *tsk*ed. "And in front of all these witnesses, too."

"Not smart," the guy said.

"Not smart at all," Frankie said.

Curt looked from him to her to me. "This is a big misunderstanding. I never meant—"

"How about you take some time to reflect," the blond guy said, "and give the lady the day off?"

"Paid time off," I added.

Frankie caught my eye and smiled.

My boss mumbled at the counter, head down. "Okay. We'll see you tomorrow, Vada."

Dumbass. Don't use my real name.

The three of us strolled out into cool ocean air and cobblestone streets glazed with mist.

"Holy shit," I crowed once the shop door closed. "What are you guys even doing here? You realize you just saved my job?"

Blondie gave me a shrewd look. "Don't thank us. If you got fired, you could get unemployment."

"I don't want unemployment. I want to work."

"Pride comes before a fall, Vada Bergen," Frankie said slyly.

I stopped in the middle of the sidewalk. They went on a few paces before turning.

"Who are you?" My fists and calves tensed. "Did someone send you?"

"Huh?" said the guy.

"Are you from the insurance company? Am I under investigation?"

They glanced at each other.

"You in some kind of trouble?" Frankie asked.

It seemed ridiculous, suddenly. *Trouble.* Trouble would be a price on my head, a hit. All I had was a bereaved man seeking closure over his son's death. Closure I had good cause to prevent.

No one is after you, I thought. You're just paranoid, Vada.

The blond guy peered up the street. "You afraid of your boss?"

"No. Never mind."

"This is no place to chat," Frankie said. "Join us for breakfast? We're not criminals, I swear."

"Just criminally good-looking," Blondie said.

Frankie rolled her eyes.

Portland's morning rush was in full swing. Flannel coats streamed around us, the weather-beaten faces of laborers mixing with pristine white collars. You could read their lives in their hands. The dockworkers' were callused, rope-burned, cracked. Golem hands, tough as stone.

We headed to a pub at the end of the wharf, entered through a swing door. No patrons at this hour. Sawdust hung in still nebulas within shafts of sun. We sat on high-backed stools near the kitchen and watched a cook open a crate of fresh-caught fish.

Frankie scrolled her phone while the blond guy spread his hands in welcome.

"We haven't officially met. I'm Dane."

"Vada. Which you already knew, apparently."

"We e-stalked you," Frankie said.

"Gotta vet the candidates," Dane said.

Frankie counted off a finger. "Mistake number one: didn't use a disposable email address, 'recuerdo.el.corazon@gmail .com.'"

"That's 'memory, the heart' in Spanish," Dane said. "I looked it up. Some painting. Total nightmare fuel."

"So uncultured," Frankie said. "But at least he's cute."

He ignored her slight. "We found your real name. Then all your social media accounts. We know where you work, go to school, who your friends are. Even found your mom and sister."

Frankie flipped another finger. "Mistake number two: didn't use a proxy."

"A proxy hides your tracks online," Dane said. "Makes you anonymous. People can't tell where you're connecting from."

"I know," I said. "Shouldn't you stalkers know my best friend is a coder?"

Frankie raised an eyebrow. "Your best friend didn't do a great job teaching you online safety."

She had, though. I'd grown careless on purpose. I was so sick of being lost I just wanted someone, anyone, to find me.

"Okay," I said. "What else did you learn about me?"

Two women survive fatal car accident. Man, eighteen, who died in crash was well above legal blood alcohol limit.

Dane shrugged. "The past is the past. All we care about is who you are now."

"Can you follow instructions?" Frankie set her phone on the bar. "Can you exercise discretion in heated situations? Can you handle new experiences which may disturb and unsettle you?"

"Am I joining a cult or a cam site?"

"The site I linked you to," Frankie said, "is no longer my employer. They're my competition."

"You quit?"

"Broke out. I was their biggest star, and they paid me peanuts. I stopped doing private chats. Wasn't worth the time. I made more in free chat off tips."

"We thought we could do better," Dane said. "So we became entrepreneurs. Rented a studio. Bought top-of-the-line gear. Now we're signing the talent."

That's where I came in. Fresh blood, naive. They'd exploit me the same way this site had exploited them.

But I needed cash and a place to crash, fast.

Dane stroked a thumb across his lower lip. In the dimness his eyes glittered like sun skipping off ocean chop. His face fascinated me, aesthetically. Every angle was oblique, deflective. The shift of the sea was in it. Emotion crested for a second and was gone.

"Sell me on it," I said.

"Great work environment." Dane laced his hands behind his head. His jacket rode up, revealing chiseled abs and V lines. "Excellent views."

I snorted.

"You make your own schedule," Frankie said. "Work at

your own pace. All necessities are provided—room, food, clothes. We take care of you. And our royalty rate is the most generous in the industry. To make this much solo, you'd have to be a celebrity."

"What's the catch?"

"Our clients have very particular tastes."

"What she means," Dane cut in, "is they're kinky bastards."

"And not your garden-variety kink," Frankie said. "We're talking extremes. Gray areas. Boundary pushing. There's an EMT on-site at all times."

"It's not for everyone." Dane scrutinized me dispassionately. "You need to be willing to face your dark side every night, and not fall into it."

"Intrigued?" Frankie said.

I nodded, slowly.

"Good," she said. "Very good."

"Now," Dane said, the hint of a curve in his lips, "sell us on you."

—SUMMER—

-4-

Incoming video call from gag4me.

I clicked ACCEPT and a window opened. On one side was me: tungsten floodlights toning my skin a soft copper, chest tilted toward the webcam. My body all lithe lines in a dark bra and jean shorts. Sultry half pout firmly pasted in place. On the other side, a black rectangle held my reflection. Clients rarely turned on their own cams. It cost more.

gag4me: good evening morgan

"Hey, baby." I untucked one leg and stretched it across the bedspread, my fingertips skimming the inside of a thigh. Hoodie Allen's "No Interruption" thumped in the background, a murky hip-hop heartbeat. "Should I call you 'Gag,' or would you prefer something else?"

gag4me: can u call me daddy

I dropped my head a little, batting my eyelashes at the cam. "Yes, Daddy. Is this better?"

gag4me: perfect
gag4me: your a bad girl arent u morgan
gag4me: u need to be punished

I gazed directly into the lens. "I'm sorry, Daddy. I don't know what gets into me."

> gag4me: i know whats getting into u
> gag4me: turn around

And so it went.

I turned. The chat transcript scrolled on my phone beside the pillow. I ran a hand over my ass and when he said to spank myself, I did. For ten dollars a minute, I'd do anything on my list of approved sex acts. And some not on the list.

"Daddy, it feels so good when you spank me. Is it supposed to hurt?"

> gag4me: oh now u done it
> gag4me: u need to learn your lesson
> gag4me: take out daddys cock

In the nightstand, within easy reach, was a cache of my most-used toys: dildos in various skin tones, a vibrator, and several men's ties.

I took out a peach cock and stroked it for the cam. "Like this, Daddy?"

> gag4me: yea
> gag4me: perfect
> gag4me: suck me

This part had taken a while to get right. Sucking a silicone dick did fuck-all for me, aside from knowing someone out there was getting off watching. But when I closed my eyes and remembered things—a guy I'd once met in a bar who'd gone down on me in his backseat, my nails gouging the leather, leaving ten tiny half-moons—I could perform. I imagined that guy standing at the edge of my bed, unzipping. I imagined giving as good as I'd gotten. Kissing his head slowly, circling it with my tongue. Taking him in an inch at a time. Sucking him deep and pulling back, giving him the slightest scrape of my teeth.

> **gag4me: your a good little slut**
> **gag4me: take your clothes off**

I put the toy down, opened my jean shorts. Wriggled out with my legs in the air, ass to the cam. Hooked my thumbs in my thong and tugged.

> **gag4me: oh u bad girl**
> **gag4me: did u wear that for me?**

"Yes, Daddy. I was hoping you'd punish me."

> **gag4me: take it off**

I was naked so often these days it didn't feel momentous. Brief chill on my skin, the thrill of that cold finger of air between my legs, then nothing.

"Do you want to fuck me, Daddy?"

> **gag4me: it wouldnt be right**
> **gag4me: but i want u so bad**
> **gag4me: finger yourself while i jerk off**

My eyes glazed over, another memory taking hold. A soft hand between my legs. Night, gauzy sheets, skin whispering against skin. Fingers parting me, one to either side of my clit.

Every day, a million-plus girls the world over fuck themselves live on the Internet for money. What set girls like me—like all of Frankie's crew—apart is that we took it to the next level. My profile page didn't just show a tatted-up twentysomething cupping her tits. It showed my signature item: a necktie slung around my throat, pulled tight by my fist.

In kink, this is known as breath play.

gag4me: look at my cock bb

"It's so big, Daddy. So big and hard. It must be torture. Can I help you release?"

gag4me: get the tie

I slid my free hand into the drawer, grasped a silk men's necktie. Oxblood. The deepest of reds.

In my wardrobe I had dozens more in various patterns and hues. This was my favorite. It looked like a vein. When I slipped the loop over my head my libido finally kicked in, my heart stuttering to life. I cinched tighter and my thighs tensed. The finger I was mechanically grinding against started to feel like an actual part of my body rather than a medical instrument.

gag4me: tell me to come on your face

"I want you to come on my face, Daddy."

gag4me: be daddys good little slut
gag4me: choke yourself

Neck flung back, tie taut. Silk dug into my carotids, my pulse twitching through the thread, the floodlights, the music, the whole world throbbing in sync. My lungs were full of dead air. Every blood cell rushed to my head, the body's automatic attempt to save the brain. The brain will actually drain limbs and organs of precious blood to buy itself a few more seconds. When Ryan's skull smashed open on the asphalt, his body poured red ink right out through that hole. Ellis once told me that near-death experiences are really just a short-circuiting brain releasing a final burst of electricity. For one moment, right at the end, a sort of hyperconsciousness activates. Every neuron fires in a barrage of rainbow light. You feel everything.

Near-death is the only time I feel anything now.

My eyes were closed. Or maybe I was blacking out already. Two fingers inside me, one fist on the noose. Limbs light as the air I could no longer breathe. All sound condensed into a heavy drone, filling my head like the ocean roaring out of a nautilus shell. Something tugged me upward. The lightness of my own body, so light it could no longer anchor itself to this earth.

I was going to come. You're supposed to wait for the client to say when, but fuck, fuck, I was going to come.

In a vague way I sensed my arm spasming, pulling the tie tighter. If you catch the climax before it reaches crescendo you can prolong it. The trick is to keep breathing.

Except it's hard.

It's so hard.

To stay.

In this world.

———

I stared up at the glimmering brocade of golden Christmas lights weaving around the rafters. I'd passed out and woken up. It felt like a new day.

I loosened the tie with a tingling hand. My whole body felt fuzzy, blurred.

I pulled my laptop over from the edge of the bed.

gag4me: wow bb
gag4me: that was AMAAAAZING
gag4me: ty for a great time
gag4me: see u soon
gag4me left the room.
Session ended. Total: 14:43.

Fifteen minutes of masturbation while I strangled myself with a tie. One hundred and fifty bucks. And all I had to do was die a little death. On webcam, for a stranger.

I couldn't tell if I'd actually come or not. Autoerotic asphyxiation plays havoc with the divide between pleasure and oblivion. And what's the difference, really? Either way, it's an annihilation. A small rehearsal for the grand exit that's coming someday.

How can I stand masturbating for voyeurs half a dozen times per night? Because I'm addicted to losing myself. I'm the original Suicide Girl. I destroy myself on cam night after night and men (and sometimes women) watch me and come.

I shut my laptop lid. I'd made nearly one K tonight.

My room at the studio—which I never thought of as "the studio" but, like everyone else, just the house—took up the entire attic. My cam setup occupied one corner: floods fitted with umbrellas to generate soft, even light, a bed decked in eggshell-white sheets, salvaged lobster trap nightstand crammed with photography books, prints tacked to the wall. Clients sometimes asked about the prints. *Did you take those photos, Morgan?* Yes. *Why are they all of broken things?* Because I'm broken. Everything I look at looks broken, too.

I'd just slipped into pajama pants when the door banged open and a blond head ducked in. Dane.

"You okay?"

He'd been monitoring my cam—someone always monitored during breath play so I didn't accidentally kill myself—and he'd seen me sign off. He knew I was fine. Just another excuse to come talk.

I gave him a droll look and crossed the room.

My real bed was a narrow twin wedged into the dormer window nook. I sprawled on it and pulled my knees up. The glass gleamed like a black mirror. Night cloaked Chebeague Island in a dark so deep and vacant it was less like darkness than outer space. Ocean fused with sky and even when I laid my forehead on the pane, there was nothing out there. In Maine, the abyss doesn't lie beneath. It's all around you.

Dane drifted nearer, studying my body. I still wore only a bra and sleep pants, tats exposed, spilling over my ribs and down one hip and up one arm. Most were from my myth obsession phase: gryphon, minotaur, chimera. I'd drawn the mockups; Hector, my old boss, had inked me. For no particular reason, they were all on my right side. I liked the asymmetry.

The last tattoo I'd ever inked was on an old friend. She'd had me draw a girl's red-nailed hand, fingers clawed, skin sprouting black fur. "It's for my little wolf," she'd said.

Typically I discouraged lovers' tats. Pick someone more permanent in your life. Child. Parent. Best friend.

"You killed it today." Dane leaned on my desk. "Blew everyone else out of the water. Let's celebrate."

"The day's not over yet," I said, my breath ghosting onto the glass.

"Take a break. You'll burn out."

"That's the idea."

He came to the edge of the bed. In the window our faces rippled and warped, as if underwater.

"Your spot's not in danger," he said. "You'll be number one again this month."

His Henley clung to his chest and the wiry muscle coiling around his arms. Dane was lean in a serpentine way, a lazy grace in his body that could snap into hardness unexpectedly. I'd seen him work. He was one of us, a cam boy who jerked off for a mostly male audience. I'd watched him come on his belly. Watched him suck dildos while he stroked his dick. His eyebrows rose, prayerful, a humbled openness transfiguring his face when he came. An almost innocent beauty.

"I'm not worried about my spot."

"The money?"

I shrugged.

"Then what's in this for you?"

"Anesthesia." I pressed my palm to the cool glass. "The more I work, the less I feel."

Dane's reflection locked eyes with mine. Two phantoms gazing at each other in a dark mirror.

"Take a walk with me," he said.

A break from fucking inanimate objects might be nice.

I followed him downstairs past three flights of closed doors, slivers of light knifing along the edges. Behind each door a body was wet with lube and oil and maybe even actual human fluids. On the other side of a screen, somewhere in the world, another body responded.

A group of cammers hung out in the kitchen, laughing riotously as they passed around a bottle of Southern Comfort. Someone called for Dane to stay, but he merely waved. I felt their lingering eyes as we stepped outside.

Our house was a few hundred feet from the water. No moon tonight, but the Milky Way furled overhead, a pale twist of stardust stained with orchid and indigo dye. We picked our way across the sand, the house glow fading at our backs. I'd never really heard silence until I moved to Maine. The soft crash of the waves receded into white noise and became part of the emptiness, an emptiness so pure, so weighted and intense that it pressed against my skin, gripped me, held me, an absence become presence.

On nights like this, the silence was indistinguishable from my heart.

Dane skirted the rocks near the tide line and came to a halt. A shadow fluttered away from him. Then he bent over, and I realized he was stripping.

"The water's freezing, you know."

No answer, but I sensed his grin.

He tossed his jeans aside and dashed off, and I followed. I dropped my pants, kept my bra on. Dane howled when he hit the water and thrashed wildly, a bomb of spray exploding around him. I jumped in on his heels and screamed. Even in the depths of summer, the ocean up north is always cold.

We kicked and flailed and stirred up our blood. Dane swept an arm and sent a wave over my face, and looked very pleased with himself until I dunked him. Our legs locked, using each other for purchase as we wrestled, and in the icy water the warmth of his skin was a shock. He didn't really fight. His hands lingered on my shoulders, my ribs, feeling me.

I pushed away.

Still couldn't swim, but I'd learned to float. On my back, facing the vast black lens of the sky, I began to detach from myself. The cramp in my hand and the numbness between my legs felt distant, insignificant. I was as small to the universe as the stars were to me. The Milky Way looked like a scar, a half-healed wound letting the light bleed through.

"Where do you go?" Dane was close, but I couldn't see him. As he spoke my ears dipped underwater and his voice went ultra-deep. "When you leave the house at night."

"You've been watching me."

"I'm fascinated with you."

My wet skin prickled.

On nights I couldn't sleep, which was often, I'd take the skiff out. From Chebeague to Peaks Island was a good five-plus miles. Depending on the current, I could row it in under two hours. Then a short walk from the shore to Max's house. By the time I got back home near dawn, my body had evolved past pain to some uncharted territory where I could slice my palm open on the gunwale and not even realize it till I saw the red mess on my clothes.

If my PT knew about this I'd be lectured from here to kingdom come.

"I go for walks," I said vaguely. "To clear my head."

"I could clear your head."

"I am seriously overfucked these days, Dane."

"Not the way you should be."

I kicked myself upright, spitting salt water.

Dane stood close behind me, his hips at the waterline. His chest dripped with crystal beads, slick with starlight. He was a gorgeous man, and not for the first time I felt that telltale knot low in my belly. A different arousal than I felt when camming. Not because he was flesh and blood while my viewers were merely grains of light on a screen—it was the unpredictability. The unscriptedness. I didn't have to play a role, wait for him to tell me what to do. I could step forward right now, wrap my arms around his neck, put my lips on his.

"Morgan." The water shivered, that black mirror breaking as he moved closer. "You want this, too. I see it when you look at me."

"What you see," I said, not moving when his body stopped centimeters from mine, heat bridging the space between us, "is your own reflection. Not me."

I turned and waded toward the beach.

Dane followed slowly, giving me time to dress. I waited on the rocks. He pulled his jeans on over wet briefs, watching me out of the corner of his eye.

"There's a meeting Friday," he said finally. "Frankie wants to expand. She's bringing in some people to talk about it."

"Who?"

"Some web guy and some sales shills."

"Okay."

"I want you there."

"Forget it," I said, standing. "I'm not getting into some power struggle between you two. I'm here to work."

"It's not because I don't trust her. It's because I trust you."

"You don't even know me."

"I know me. If I see my reflection in you, it's because we're the same."

Now I gave him the side-eye. "So I'm a shady player with commitment issues?"

"And a sexy smile."

"Don't even start. Did you miss the sign saying 'Emotionally Unavailable'?"

"Big words. I read slow."

Grudgingly, I smiled. Dane smiled back, all boy-devil mischief. My heart gave one hard knock to remind me it was still there. We trekked together up the beach, his gaze on me the whole time, and I thought, *If only you were someone else. If only you were that someone.*

―――――

Dane thought I'd gone to bed. I texted him **good night, player** and set my phone aside. Then I opened my laptop and switched on the proxy.

We scouted other cam sites religiously, to poach talent and sniff out trends and generally be ruthless motherfuckers. Frankie sussed the competition; Dane and I were too busy jerking off on cam. She'd become the de facto boss even though Dane was an equal partner in the company. It didn't concern me.

The only thing that mattered was that I knew which sites catered to which fetishes.

It took only ten minutes to find her. "Ariel" was Canadian. I caught a trace of her accent, the curve in her vowels. Her profile described her as a "kinky-ass bi nerd girl." Short auburn hair and Buddy Holly glasses and a hoop nose ring. In her photo gallery she masturbated with a vibrating Xbox controller. *Doctor Who* and *Firefly* posters plastered the walls.

young_rae-z: what kind of games do you play
Dahlz: Read her bio.

sweet_ophelia: do you do breath play, bb?

young_rae-z: who made you mod dahlz

Dahlz: Who taught you how to read? Oh right, no one.

Ariel stretched, her nipples poking through her sheer tee in hard studs. "I play lots of stuff, Young. Right now I'm on a *Diablo III* kick. You guys like *Diablo*?" Her voice was nasal, cynical. "Yeah, Sweet, I do breath play."

I clicked the PRIVATE CHAT button.

When the video stream loaded, Ariel's smile had changed, no longer ironic but sultry. Her voice slowed. She looked into the lens, establishing eye contact even though she couldn't see me.

All the usual cam tricks. I smiled.

"Hi, baby. What can I do for you tonight?"

sweet_ophelia: hello, Ariel

sweet_ophelia: are you comfortable choking yourself?

"Sure, I can do that for you, baby."

sweet_ophelia: thank you

sweet_ophelia: can you call me Morgan, please?

"Of course, Morgan. You're so polite."

sweet_ophelia: and you're beautiful

sweet_ophelia: your eyes are amazing

sweet_ophelia: the perfect shade of green

Just like hers.

"A sweet talker. I lucked out." She laughed, low in her throat. "Do you want to tell me about yourself?"

sweet_ophelia: no, bb

sweet_ophelia: I'd like you to be quiet now

sweet_ophelia: and take off your shirt

I leaned back in my chair, my thighs spreading. One hand inside my pants. My breath came fast.

sweet_ophelia: squeeze your tits
sweet_ophelia: good
sweet_ophelia: now put your hands around your neck

———

Dane took the yacht out Friday morning to ferry our guests over from the mainland. In the house, Frankie barked orders at the crew, prepping the dining room for her conference. I grabbed my camera and sneaked out the back door.

Fuck that corporate bullshit. I intended to remain a worker drone mindlessly serving the queen bee. The less I had to think, the better.

Chebeague was a small wooded island ten miles off the coast of Portland, with a year-round population of three-hundred-something souls. Those who wanted more quiet and isolation than the mainland offered, a place to feel away from it all without really being away. Open beach stretched from our front steps to the ocean, but behind the house was a thick quilt of pine, so lush and deep you could walk a dozen feet and feel transported into myth. In the trees the light turned eerie green, pollen sparkling like gold dust. Nymph shadows flickered at the edge of vision. The branches thrived with birds like nerve impulses, swallows in royal and peacock blues, orioles in goldenrod, flashes of intense color. Underfoot the earth was damp and fragrant as coffee grounds.

I followed a deer trail to the coast. Even on the brightest summer days the ocean was a weary gray-blue, an aluminum sheet dented by the sun. Our neighbor islands were dark smudges in the mist. From above, Casco Bay looked like a shattered emerald strewn along the coast of Maine. We were too far from the mainland to hear the city—out here it was only the shriek of seabirds, the sweep and sigh of waves. A distant bell when the ferry docked.

On the stone below me, a seagull pecked at a mound of bloody flesh. There wasn't enough left to tell what it had been when it lived. I slithered down the rocks, slow and steady, snapping photos. This was the kind of shit I lived for now. Things coming apart. Insides, stuffing and stitching. Undoings.

The gull spooked and flapped off. I got in close for a macro shot of mangled meat glistening in the sun. Not sure, but that small red lump might be a heart.

The hair rose on the back of my neck. I slowed my breathing until my pulse echoed in my ears.

Red, wet meat. Like Ryan's broken skull, gray matter bathed in blood. Like the bone jutting through my skin as my arm went numb, forever.

Look at it, I told myself. Stop being a little bitch. Face it.

Face what you did.

I felt like I was going to puke.

Breathe.

Waves on stone. Spray and fizz. Far off, a bell and a foghorn. Eternal, unchanging.

Instead of backtracking through the woods, I made my way down to the shore and followed it around the island, a slog through wet sand. My running shoes filled with muck and I was sweaty and the sun was directly overhead by the time the house came into view.

I needed to talk to someone. I didn't care about interrupting Frankie's meeting. What would she do, fire her highest earner?

I just needed to talk. To get out of my own head for a minute.

I flung open the French doors and stormed into the dining room. Everyone turned.

Frankie sat on one side of the table, black curls in a springy nimbus around her head, eyebrows raised. Dane slouched beside her, and then our lawyer, tapping on an iPad. Across from them sat a handful of guys I'd never seen before, in slacks and collared shirts. And at the foot of the table, right in front of me, was—

My chest went tight as if all the air had been sucked out of the room.

"Nice of you to finally join us," Frankie said.

Dane waved me over, pulling up a chair.

If I hadn't barged in I could've backed out, but it was too late now. I sat down. Their stares weighed on me, one heavier than all the others combined. The last person I wanted to see. Sitting five feet away. In my house. In my life.

"This is the girl I was telling you about," Frankie said. "Our highest earner, Morgan. Morgan, this is *blah, blah, blah*—"

I heard nothing, saw nothing except that face. The one that stared back, reflecting my shock. Wide eyes the color of sun filtering through leaves, a green haze speckled with gold.

"And this," Frankie said, "is—"

"Ellis Carraway," I finished, my voice flat. "We've met."

Here's how the meeting went.

FRANKIE: So. Expansion. We're opening new houses.

DANE: I'll be heading up our first branch.

VADA: [Glares at Ellis.]

ELLIS: [Stares at the table.]

FRANKIE: And I want to experiment with new tiers of service. Private group sessions, subscription plans. Can we add that to the existing infrastructure?

ELLIS: [Still facing the tabletop.] Sure. But it's better if you start with a clean slate. I had a look at your code. It's a mess.

FRANKIE: Does it matter?

ELLIS: [Shrugs.] You want to build new levels atop a house of cards. Eventually it'll crash. Then you'll have to rebuild anyway, and your business might be offline until you do. Huge waste of resources.

FRANKIE: Okay. We'll do it your way. Clean slate.

VADA: She's going to redo the entire site? *That's* a huge waste of resources. It works fine as is.

ELLIS: [Finally looks at Vada.] Sometimes you think it's working fine as is, when it's really falling apart.

VADA: So you want to raze it to the ground. Destroy everything and rebuild it to fit *your* vision, not ours.

ELLIS: If you build on top of a collapsing foundation, it won't last anyway.

VADA: Maybe it isn't meant to last. We're not even sure it's what we want long term. But you want us to commit everything. Risk it all.

ELLIS: So think it over. You shouldn't commit to something you're not really serious about.

VADA: And you shouldn't push us to take the next step before we're ready.

FRANKIE: [Glances at Vada, then Elle.]

DANE: What the hell are they talking about?

FRANKIE: Enough. We've heard both sides. Let's vote. All in favor of a rebuild?

[FRANKIE, DANE, and the LAWYER raise their hands. VADA folds her arms and scowls.]

FRANKIE: The *aye*s have it. Morgan, your petulance is noted.

DANE: [Snorts.]

VADA: Do you even know what that word means, Dane?

DANE: Does it mean you're kind of a bitch?

ELLIS: [Covers her mouth, hiding a smile.]

FRANKIE: Darlings. Save the foreplay for the clients. Now,
let's talk search engine visibility. How can we . . .

———

The discussion continued while I sat there and seethed, not
parsing another word till people scooted their chairs back and
said their good-byes. Dane touched my arm. I eyed his hand
as if it were a leech.

"I'm taking her to the mainland," he said, nodding at Ellis.
"The boys have their own ride."

I started to stand and he gripped tighter.

"Come with."

"No chance."

"Don't you want to catch up?"

I didn't know where to begin with that. Instead I said, "You
told me you were meeting 'some web guy.' "

"I thought 'Ellis' was a guy."

I groaned. My shoes felt full of quicksand. I was still disgusting from the hike.

"I need a shower," I said. "And I've got stuff to do."

"More important stuff than seeing your best friend?"

I'd avoided looking at her, but now I forced myself. She
stood at the edge of the room, tall and lanky and awkward,
shifting her weight from foot to foot. She wore a gingham
button-up with skinny jeans and black Chucks. As I watched,
she spun a long bang around one finger, over and over, until
it wound so tight she gave a start. Nervous habit. Sometimes
she'd done it with my hair, not realizing.

My heart clenched.

"Come on," Dane cooed. "Don't be so stubborn. Besides,
do you really want to leave me alone with her? I'm a predator."

"You're as dangerous as a teddy bear."

But I ended up on the yacht anyway, Dane in the upper-deck captain's chair, me and Ellis at the stern rail.

The boat was old yet in good repair, a gleaming white fang cutting smoothly through the water. Dane coasted along slowly. Giving us time to *catch up*. In my head I went back to last night and held him under till he stopped struggling.

Elle kept shooting glances at me, but averted her face when I glanced back. Wind whipped her shirt and traced the outline of those thin bird bones. Against the ocean blue her hair looked redder, the only living thing in a drowned world. A freighter in the distance gave a mournful bellow, like whalesong.

"What?" I said.

"Nothing."

"Then stop staring at me."

Her hands curled around the rail. "This is all so—it's so weird."

"Yeah, must be weird seeing someone you never wanted to see again, right in your fucking workplace. Wonder how that feels."

No response.

Foam trailed in our wake, scarves of air rustling through the water.

"You're a cam girl," Ellis said finally.

"Are you judging me?"

"It just doesn't seem like you."

"It's not." I smiled. "I'm not me anymore. You don't know me."

"I guess not, 'Morgan.'"

My smile fell. I called out to Dane, "Can we hurry the fuck up, please?"

His aviator sunglasses flashed. He caressed the wheel, un-hurried.

I couldn't take this. I headed down to the cabin and paced to the bow, not seeing any of the leather furniture, the polished wood and glass. I felt like I couldn't breathe, and my first instinct was to go down, not up.

Elle followed. I knew she would.

I rounded on her and said, "Don't take this job."

Out of Dane's sight, we both let the pretense of ambivalence drop. Her jaw locked, rouge rising into her cheeks.

"I need it," she said. "I'm broke, too."

"Did Mommy's money finally run out?"

"Stop it. Stop trying to push me away instead of talking it through."

"What's there to talk about? You made it pretty clear what you want."

"I was hurt. I was trying to make the pain stop, same as you."

I tried to smirk but it came out more of a sneer. "Gee, sure hope your *pain* stopped, because everything stopped for me. My heart. My entire fucking world."

Ellis winced, her hand half rising in supplication. I should have left then, but I could never walk away from a fight. Something in me craved damage. To myself, to others.

"You were treating me like dirt," she said plaintively. "What was I supposed to do?"

"It's called depression, Elle. It sorta happens when you kill somebody and lose everything. Sorry I wasn't a model human being while I was depressed."

"Before then. It was before then, too."

I rolled my eyes. "I've already seen this episode. Spoiler alert: it ends with us realizing we hate each other."

"You hate me but you're calling yourself Morgan? You let guys call you that while you get off? Strange way of hating someone."

"Well, I've changed. You wouldn't want to know me anymore."

"You haven't changed that much. You're still a total bitch."

Despite myself, I laughed. So rare to hear her swear. I was really pressing her buttons.

My laughter made something flicker in her eyes. Something soft.

I looked away. "This job is a mistake. You shouldn't be here."

"Why?"

"We're just going to hurt each other again. You were right about the clean break."

"No, I wasn't. I've been miserable and lonely and depressed. Just like you."

"You don't know shit about how I've been."

She stepped closer. We were practically the same height, and for once she stood straight, meeting me eye-to-eye. "You looked so tired, so hollow, but when you saw me your eyes went bright. Like you were waking up."

"It's moot. I'm not the person you knew. She's gone."

"You still have her face, and her voice. I missed them so much."

Every word chipped into the walls inside me. "Listen, Ellis. I'm a cam girl now. A well-paid Internet whore. I do filthy, fucked-up things for money, and I like it. I'm not your princess anymore. Take me off the pedestal."

"It's still you. Just a different part of you."

"Stop being so fucking understanding. It's exhausting." My good hand curled in and out of a fist. "You were right to move on. I was an asshole. Still am."

"I didn't move on."

"Then who was in your house?"

She shook her head. "We haven't seen each other in months and that's what you want to know? Not if I'm okay, but if I've replaced you?"

"Did you miss the 'I'm an asshole' part?"

"You're still doing it. Pushing me away because you're scared."

"No shit I'm scared." I leaned closer. It took monstrous self-discipline to keep my hands still. To not put them on her. "You know what I learned in all these months? That I built my whole fucking life around you. My entire adult life. Five years. I'm totally lost on my own. You know how terrifying it is, to be that dependent on someone?"

"Yeah, I do. I was that dependent on *you*." Her hand floated toward me again, grazed my forearm, my fingers. "You're all I had."

"I made you miserable."

"I'm miserable without you, too. We both are."

I would've killed for something to hold. A beer, a cigarette. Her. "I begged you. I never beg anyone, but I begged you for another chance. And you let me go. It fucking broke me." Stay hard. Stay cold. "Go home, Elle. Go find another job. Go live in your nice house with your new *friend*."

"You don't give up on someone you love. I learned that from you."

The meanness in me rose, and I let it loose.

"All you learned from me," I said, "is how to be a fucking doormat."

Her eyes glossed with tears. If she started crying I was going to cry, too, because I didn't mean this. I hated hurting her. But I couldn't do this again. Not when I still hadn't put all the pieces of me back together.

To my surprise, she said, "Fuck you."

Then she started laughing, that sweet voice turning bitter.

"Vada, you're so full of it. You lash out when you're hurt and scared. I know you. You didn't become some total stranger just because you're camming. And this?" She pressed her palm to the center of my chest. "This is probably the hardest your heart's beaten in months. The most alive you've felt."

I swatted her hand away, but she grabbed my wrist.

"You're right. I can be a doormat sometimes." Ellis leaned close enough that I could feel her breath. "But at least I'm not a coward."

I was weak. I was weak and I touched her, because my hands were shaking so hard I thought my bones would crack, that I'd crumble inside. They snapped to her shoulders. Before I could stop myself I shoved her to the cabin wall, knocking her breathless. She grasped the neck of my shirt but I held her down.

"It's so fucking easy for you," I hissed into her face. "You know exactly who you are. Exactly who you want."

"It's not that simple."

I thumped her shoulders against the wall. "Who the fuck do you think you are, calling me a coward? Because I don't fit into some neat category? This relationship has always been easy for you. You never struggled with it."

"You don't know what I struggled with."

"Not this. And I hated it. I hated how *disappointed* you were when I got scared. I hated the way people assumed things about me. Sometimes I even hated you, too."

Air rushed through her bared teeth and she twisted my collar, pulled my face closer, and I knew it was going to happen again, just like that night.

Then Dane was in the doorway, giving a time-out whistle.

"Hey," he said. "No blood on my carpet. I just had it steamed."

We stumbled away from each other. My limbs tingled, numb with adrenaline.

Ellis hung her head, glanced at Dane, then whirled around and left us in the cabin.

"What the hell was that?" he said.

I smoothed my shirt and gave him a dry smile. "Just catching up."

Incoming video call from BigDeezy.

ACCEPT.

"Hi, baby."

BigDeezy: clothes off

Okay then. All business.

I took them off dutifully, but without rushing. Tossed my hair, slid my palms up my chest to cup my breasts and massage them. "What should I call you, Big?"

BigDeezy: Mark

"Hi, Mark." For a second I thought of that B movie *The Room* and tried not to snicker. "Are you feeling naughty tonight?"

BigDeezy: get on your hands and knees
BigDeezy: ass to the camera

He knew what he wanted.

I positioned myself, glancing back over my shoulder. Ran a hand over my butt and gave a light slap. On-screen I looked like every generic tan piece of ass ever, a pink slit of pussy, anonymous. Interchangeable.

BigDeezy: jiggle it
BigDeezy: faster
BigDeezy: put a tie on
BigDeezy: pull it from behind
BigDeezy: moan
BigDeezy: louder

Camming was usually more complex than this. Men wanted to get off, obviously, but if they *only* wanted to get off there was an Internet full of free porn out there. What camming offered was companionship. A dialogue. Interaction. Even if it was illusory, it fulfilled some social need.

Men like Mark didn't want companionship, though. They wanted a living doll. Something to pose and fuck and discard. It was more a power fantasy for him than an erotic one.

These strictly pornographic sessions depressed me. Mark was never impolite, but he was utterly impersonal. It was a relief when the chat ended.

My next request popped up immediately.

Incoming video call from RicanLover.

Any ethnic reference in a username gave me pause. Clients were usually respectful, even appreciative. Once a guy paid to chat in Spanish for an hour and told me about his extended family in San Juan. He called me Boricua and said I was a dusk flower blooming. He paid me to get him off, too, of course, but it was nice, unexpected, that little wire of human connection, a bright filament threading across the digital void.

But sometimes they just wanted an outlet for their darkness. I could always cut the session short if it was some creep. ACCEPT.

The client wasn't one, but two guys. They'd paid to transmit video to me. Broad chests in lettered hoodies. Frat bros, both grinning in a dimly lit bedroom. One clutched a can of PBR.

"Hi guys," I said. "Two for one. Lucky me."

They chuckled, nudging each other. They mumbled, but their mic didn't pick it up clearly. Their eyes shone.

I could see they'd need some coaxing.

"You boys look excited." I ran a hand over the bra I'd put back on. "I love sexy college men. Do you want to double-team me?"

"You speak English?" Beer Can said.

A hitch in my pulse. Don't judge yet. "Yes."

"Cool. So do we."

They laughed again.

Bad vibes.

I scrutinized the room. Pinup posters. Red Sox pennant. University of Massachusetts sweater hanging on the back of a chair.

Bingo.

I smiled. "So you guys go to UMass? That's cool. Do you have friends at Harvard? MIT?"

"Hey," Beer Can said, leaning forward, "we're not paying you to talk."

The other guy—Lacoste, I mentally dubbed him, spotting his polo collar—jostled his friend. "Sorry," he said to me. "He's been drinking. We'd like a show, okay?"

I played up the striptease, feeling them out, but they were quiet now, respectful. Off came the bra. When I squeezed my breasts together and groaned, Beer Can took a long sip. His eyes stared over the rim, mesmerized.

Lacoste smiled. "You're fucking hot."

"*Caliente*," Beer Can said, and giggled.

Lacoste elbowed him. "Hey . . . Morgan. I was wondering something."

"What's that, baby?"

"Do you have, like, other outfits?"

"I've got plenty. What are you looking for?"

"Like a . . . maid's outfit."

Beer Can snorted.

"A French maid?" I said cautiously.

"Sure, whatever."

"Yeah, I've got one of those. You boys mind hanging on a minute? I'll play something to get you warmed up."

They nodded, all grins.

I launched a video clip for them—me deep-throating a

dildo—and went to my wardrobe. By the time the clip ended I was dressed in a white-laced black babydoll and knee-high stockings, sitting on the bed.

"Oh, *fuck* yeah," Lacoste said. "Damn, that's hot."

I struck poses—bending over to the floor, rubbing an imaginary speck of dirt off the bedpost—and let myself zone out, feeling as if the costume did the work for me. Like it was the body, not me. Every now and then I touched the bracelet on my wrist like a lucky charm.

"Hey . . . Morgan."

Lacoste perched on the edge of his seat, watching me avidly. Beer Can sprawled back spread-legged, his erection jutting against his track pants.

"Yeah, baby?"

"I was wondering if you could . . . man, this is going to sound weird." Lacoste cleared his throat.

"Go ahead. You can ask me anything."

"It's kind of personal."

"No judgment here."

"All right. When I was a kid, growing up, my parents had a maid. Named Luisa." He shifted in his chair. "She was hot. Really hot. I used to fantasize about her."

I looked at him encouragingly.

"Can I call you Luisa?"

"Sure."

"Cool. So like . . . I used to jerk off to you, Luisa. In my bedroom. While you were downstairs vacuuming."

I leaned over and ran a palm across the mattress as if pushing a vacuum.

"Fuck yeah. Just like that." Lacoste sucked air through his teeth. "I'd squirt in my socks, right before you did the laundry. So it would get on your hands."

"Naughty boy." I rubbed a hand between my thighs.

Lacoste began to rock in his chair, as if touching himself. Beer Can watched me silently.

"Luisa?" Lacoste said.

"Yeah, baby?"

"Would you like to come . . . clean my house? And watch me jerk off?"

God, some men. "Sure. I'd like that."

"Yeah?" Lacoste rocked faster. "Would you watch me jerk off into a sock?"

"Sure, baby."

"You would?"

"Of course."

"And then would you let me slap you in the face with it? Could I slap you in the face with my come-filled sock, you spic whore?"

Lacoste leaned back from the laptop and snapped a sock at the screen. Beer Can burst into high-pitched laughter.

Red.

I saw actual, literal red.

"What the fuck is wrong with you?" I grabbed the laptop, wishing it were him. "Huh? This is what gets you off, spewing racist shit at a woman?"

"Woman?" Lacoste said. "Woman? Do you see a woman?"

"Nah," Beer Can said. "Just an island monkey sticking her ass up to get fucked."

"God, look at her face," Lacoste said.

"You pathetic sacks of shit." Run up the clock. Pay me to rant at you, dumb fucks. "You're a joke. Fucking privileged white boys, intimidated by women. You think I haven't heard shit like this before? Get the fuck off my planet."

"Whoa, whoa," Lacoste said. "Calm down, *mamacita*. Or we'll come over there and calm you down. You like getting double-teamed, right?"

"In the real world, you could never touch a woman like me."

"In the real world, I pay sluts like you to do what I want."

"You think paying me gives you the right to spew this fucking garbage? You think you can buy a license to abuse a human being? You're the fucking cancer in this world. Entitled little shits like you."

"Where do you live, Luisa? I'll pay you to suck my dick. No lie." He pulled out a money clip, a fat wad of bills. "Then you can wash my socks."

"You're paying me right now to make an ass of yourself."

Beer Can smirked. "We can find you."

"No, you can't, you fucking troglodyte."

"We're tracing you right now. We're coming for you, Luisa."

DISCONNECT.

I sat back on the bed, fuming.

There was no danger of being found. Before I started camming, Frankie coached me on safety and anonymity. No identifying objects in the room. No sports team or college memorabilia. Never mention any place you've gone to school or worked. And on the off chance someone might recognize me on the street, I had a region ban in place. No one in the state of Maine could view my cam.

There was no physical danger. Only psychological.

The first rule of camming, Frankie said, was to protect yourself. Always be safe. You are the product, the service, the whole business. Value it. Value your time, yourself. Don't compromise for a few extra bucks. They were never worth it in the long run.

But I always learned things the hard way.

———

Each stroke of the oars painted silver moonlight across the ocean. My mouth was salty from brine and my own sweat.

Hair in wet coils like kelp. Dip, pull, lift. As long as I kept rowing, the pain couldn't settle. Be a moving target.

I hit a sandbar, the skiff wedging firmly into place, and jumped out. My shoes filled with seawater. Plenty of starlight to see by, and a shim of moon.

His house was the highest on the hill. Well after midnight, it still radiated gold and warmth into the island dark. I leaned against a tree trunk, watching.

Max was restless. He never stayed in a room longer than half an hour. Often he paced, or played musical chairs with himself, as if, like me, he couldn't stay long in one position before the pain grew unbearable.

But tonight I watched, and watched, and saw nothing. All the lights were on, hurricane lamps on the porch, candles in a bedroom. Not once did his silhouette cross them.

A disturbing thought entered my head.

If he was lying in a warm bath with his veins open or swaying from a garage rafter, I'd be the only person in the world who'd know.

I hiked uphill.

The house was hedged with bushes, grass grown wild. I waded through a sea of spines and thorns. Garage door open, nothing inside but boxes, the remains of eighteen birthdays and Christmases. Max spent hours touching the dumbbells, the electric guitar, things coated with dust and the oil of his son's skin. I knew that ritual. I kept a duffel bag full of Elle's old T-shirts, heady with camphor from vaping. I could close my eyes and inhale and feel the warmth of her body again, a breath away from mine.

He wasn't anywhere on the first floor. Open rooms paneled with white wood, empty save for candle-thrown shadows. I tried the rear door. Unlocked.

I froze at the crack of a branch.

The yard swam with dark but a shape moved against it, a deeper darkness.

"Looking for me?"

He walked into the corona of light. Still scruffy, thinner now than when we first met, tanned. Frayed tee, salt-bleached jeans. Something glinted at his side.

I waited, motionless, as he came up the steps.

"Max," I said tensely.

We both looked at his hand. At the gun that hung there, as if forgotten.

"Oh."

He checked the safety and tucked it into his jeans. I exhaled. Max patted my good arm.

"You look beat. Want a beer?"

"God, yes."

I waited on the porch, sprawling in an Adirondack chair frosted with mold. At my feet rusted garden tools lay abandoned. Weeds crept through the wood slats. This place was a graveyard.

Max brought two bottles of Shipyard and took the chair beside mine. We clinked and drank.

"Thanks for not shooting me," I said.

He rolled his shoulders. "Sorry about that."

"Didn't know you were into guns."

"It's for home defense." He took a long sip, staring out into the trees. "The police just returned it. They had it in an evidence locker."

I swirled my bottle, frowning.

"I went out to shoot, but couldn't bring myself to fire. It's the last thing he touched."

We glanced at each other. The name drifted between us, unspoken.

Ryan.

All this time I'd spent avoiding Ellis, I'd been growing close to Max Vandermeer.

He didn't work anymore. He lived on savings, passed time tinkering with his yacht or pacing the house, wearing the wood floors velvety. I caught hints of his old life. Blueprints for boats. Samples of fiberglass and metal. Shipbuilding engineer. He'd made enough money to own a mansion on a summer tourist island. Once there was a woman in the house, and I'd rowed away without a word. I never saw her there again. The Ex-Girlfriend.

My psychiatrist had wanted me to process my losses, to heal. I didn't want to *process* anything. I'd kept my eyes closed and my wounds open and dumped my shrink. Max was my therapist now, and I was his.

He told me about the islands: how Peaks, where he lived, used to have theaters and hotels lining the gaslit boardwalk, until one by one the buildings burned down. In World War II it became a military bunker, with a huge gun battery built to shoot down enemy ships. But the guns were never fired and then they were taken apart, and in the decades since, the island had edged back toward wildness.

Like you, I thought, studying him. His beard was all gold and bronze brambles, his skin sun-chapped, rough. Sometimes when I looked at him I remembered a man bringing birthday presents when I was little. A dash of blond hair, an elusive, slinky laugh. A silhouette in the door, always leaving.

I wondered if Max still glanced up when a shadow fell across the floor and thought, before he remembered, *Ryan*.

"Ever feel like he's still here?" I said.

"Every day."

I flexed my bad hand. My phantom hand, I thought sometimes. There but not really. Like Elle was still here, but not really. Not part of me anymore.

"Do you talk to him?" I balanced the beer on my knee. Rowing wrecked my dexterity for the day. "Sometimes I talk to her. Out loud, like a crazy person."

"That's not crazy."

"It is when I answer for her."

He eyed me, concerned. "Something happen?"

"She's back. She got a job where I work." I kicked a foot against the railing. "It's like a dream and a nightmare both come true. Every night I've prayed for this, and when it happens the first thing I feel is resentment. Anger, honestly. There's something wrong with me."

"It's not wrong. You can miss someone without missing the way they hurt you."

"Did Ryan hurt you?"

He took another sip.

"What did he do, Max?"

"Signed up for the Marines. Despite all my pleading and begging. You'd never know it from the trophies, but he hated playing ball. Could've had his pick of minor league teams. He threw it away to get shot at in the desert."

"Why?"

"Destructive impulse." Max was watching me now. "Sometimes people set themselves up to be hurt by a situation, instead of hurting themselves directly. To absolve the blame."

I peered into my bottle. "If he really wanted to be a marine, you should've supported him. Even if you didn't believe it was for the best."

"I couldn't support my son throwing his life away."

"You sound like my mom."

"Then your mom loves you."

I put the bottle down, hard. "Part of loving someone is wanting them to be happy, even if it hurts you."

"You're right. You're right, of course. I suppose that means I was a bad father."

"That's not what I meant."

He drained his beer.

"Max, I didn't say you were a bad father."

Now his eyes held a too-bright luster. Shit.

He stood and so did I.

"I'm sorry, I didn't—"

He flung the screen door open. And I did something I'd never had the balls to do.

Followed him in.

"Wait. Max."

He strode through the house and I chased and when he stopped suddenly in a dark hall, we collided. His arms locked around me. My back touched the wall.

"Wait," I said again, in a different tone.

Warm breath on my face, beery. He was much stronger than he looked and I smelled the sea on him, salt water and sun-wrought sweat. I'd hugged him before but it was always brief and reserved. Not like this. I breathed fast, my chest touching his. Heat seeped into my skin. And crazily, I felt something. Something I should not be feeling for this man.

"Let me go," I said.

He took a step back. "I'm sorry. I thought—maybe I'm not ready for this."

Talking about Ryan, I thought, or *this*?

No. *This* was not happening.

I turned and fingers grazed my shoulder blade. I stood there not breathing as his hand ran lightly up my neck and cupped the nape.

It was so strange, I realized. He was the first man who'd touched me this way since Raoul. And that was years ago. Entire years of my life.

"Max," I whispered. "What are you doing?"

His hand fell. A candle flickered somewhere, skimmed the edges of our faces with fire.

"I'm sorry," he said again. "I'm not thinking straight."

"It's okay. I'm not, either." I shifted my weight, uncomfortable. "We're both emotional right now. And slightly drunk."

"I didn't mean to upset you. I know you prefer women."

I cringed. "What? No."

"You and Ellis—"

"That's nothing. It's just . . . it's whatever." Now I felt totally off-kilter. "Look, I should get going. Let's not make this weird."

I didn't want to think about this. The way it felt to be touched by a man.

Max watched me walk toward the kitchen. His eyes were different on me now. Not fatherly.

When I reached the door he said, "Hold on. Please."

He stepped into another room, returned with a folio. Flipped through papers. I watched the muscle curl and knot in his arms and made myself look away.

"This might not be the best time, but I wanted to go over this with you. You had a chance to look at these yet?"

"At what?"

He laid the folio on the table. "The black box reports. From the cars."

My eyes went to the papers, then back to his face, slowly. "No. Why would I? Why are you?"

"Got a lot of spare time. And a lot of need for closure." He shrugged. "It gives me a reason to stay sober. But there's something off."

"What?"

Max gazed at the table. "If you tell me, I won't hold it against you. I promise you that."

Shit.

"Tell you what?"

"Who was driving your car."

"I was, Max. Like I told the police."

"That's what you said." He tapped a sheet. "But these say something else."

Our eyes met. The air between us pulsed like an invisible heart.

"I've never lied to you," I said.

"I believe you, Vada. But I don't believe you've told me the whole truth."

This was my chance. The window would never be this open.

If you tell me, I won't hold it against you.

Except Elle was back, and I wasn't sure I was ready to throw everything away now.

"I have to go."

"Vada—"

"See you around."

I stepped onto the porch. Let the screen door slam, took the steps in one leap. When my shoes hit the dirt I started jogging, and by the time I reached the road, it was a full-out run.

5

This is what happens when you lie. Lies grow thin and steely and hard and become bars. Bars become a cage.

Ellis was probably awake. Huddled in her hoodie, typing away in the wraithlike glow of her laptop. I smoked a joint in a hot bath and stared up at the pine plank ceiling, thinking.

I could've let myself out of this cage. But I chose to stay. For her.

I slept for a few hours and woke unrested. Everything was soft and heather gray, a pencil sketch of a day. Rain coming. Frankie and Dane were heading out on the yacht, and I cornered her on a stone jetty while he coiled rope.

"Can we talk?" My voice was a croak.

Dane raised his eyebrows at us.

"Alone," I said.

Frankie wrapped herself in her cardigan, warding off the chilly spray. "You look hungover. Get some sleep."

"I just need to talk to you. Please."

I must have looked haunted enough to convince her.

"Morgan's doing the run today," she called to Dane. "We need some one-on-one time."

He headed over. "Girls' day out?"

"Something like that."

Dane frowned when he saw my face. "You okay?"

"Come on." Frankie took my arm. "Before he talks his way in."

We boarded while Dane stayed behind to help us cast off. I hauled up the stern and bow lines, pulled the fat boat fenders from the water. He watched me till I climbed to the helm.

Frankie reclined in the captain's chair, all in white, a dimple at one side of her mouth that I thought of as her *well, well* look. Against her clothes and the boat her skin shone burnished brown. My hands ached for my camera, to capture contrast, the clean edge between hues.

I sat beside her. Wind washed my hair over my face.

"What's on your mind?" she said.

"Don't hire Ellis."

Her eyebrows lifted over her Ray-Bans. "Why?"

"There's bad blood between us. It'll be a disaster."

"I like you, Morgan, but I can't let your personal drama dictate my business decisions."

"You can find a million other coders. You won't find another cam girl like me."

"Is that a threat?"

"No. I meant—I'm asking as a friend, okay? Please."

We cruised for a bit, the rush of water like silk tearing. Frankie had taken me under her wing. Taught me the tricks of the trade. How to tease and prolong, get paid for anticipation as well as delivery. How to sculpt a persona. How to protect myself. My first night on the job she'd unpinned a gold barrette from her hair, a wire butterfly. She'd placed it in my palm.

"Do you know what this is?"

I shook my head.

"This is Tiana. I used to do live theater. Onstage, you're in costume. You wear someone else's face, someone else's life. It's easier to separate yourself from the character. But on cam, there's no bar-

rier. *We're bare-ass naked, at someone's beck and call. Completely vulnerable."* She touched the butterfly in my hand. *"So this is my trick. My costume. When I put this on, I'm Tiana. Anything that happens will happen to her, and it stays inside this. When I take it off, I'm Frankie. Understand?"*

It was strange, I thought later, that her trick was similar to how people separated themselves from their bodies when terrible things happened to those bodies. When a man held you down and unbuckled his belt. When a mother raised a stiff palm. As if you could just decide that bad things would happen to someone else, someone who wasn't really you.

But I took her advice and found a bracelet Elle had given me, silvery and fine as a spiderweb. I put it on every night and became Morgan. In a way, it felt like a fetter. And in a way being shackled felt good because it meant I couldn't drift any further. I couldn't get more lost.

"Is this about the trouble you're running from?" Frankie said now.

My head snapped toward her. Dead giveaway.

"You're trying to protect Ellis from it, aren't you?"

"I just don't want her around me."

"Dane said you nearly tore each other's throats out on the boat."

"It wasn't like that."

"I think it was. But Dane is a man. He doesn't see what's really going on." Frankie drummed on the wheel. "You two had a thing."

"I don't want to work with her, okay? That's all."

"Actually, I think you'd work great together."

My mouth fell. "Seriously?"

"I watched you lock horns. She's the dreamer, you're the doer. Good pair. If she gets fancy ideas about the site, you can keep her grounded." Her smile flashed, an arc of opal. "Besides, I haven't seen you that animated since we met. Something lights up in you when you're near her."

"Yeah, like a bomb."

"I already promised you'd be her liaison. Show her the ropes. I don't have time and Dane will be in Boston. You're my top choice." She glanced at me over her sunglasses. "If you can handle this, I'll make you a partner."

Promotion.

Most of what I'd earned so far was paying off my student loans. More money meant I could return to grad school without worry. Or not, because what the hell would I do with an MFA? Teach budding young artists about the world I'd been severed from, the world I could only observe instead of touch? I didn't even know what to do with the extra money I earned now. I rarely bought anything. The things I really wanted couldn't be bought.

I frowned suddenly. "Wait, Dane's going to Boston?"

"He didn't tell you? That's where we're opening the new house."

That bastard.

"Guess I'm not important enough to tell," I muttered.

Her eyes lingered on me. "Or maybe he doesn't know how to say good-bye."

Frankie had contracts to sign in downtown Portland. All those fancy foil-stamped documents about girls riding dildos and boys pulling on cock rings. Any of these lawyers in their crisp Armani and asshole roadsters could log on tonight and beg, *Let me come on ur face.*

The rain thickened, coming down in sheets of silver tinsel.

Frankie took me shopping, undaunted. She'd done this when we first met, bought me airy negligees and vaporous thongs, things so sheer it seemed any moisture would dissolve them, like spun sugar. Now we hopped from boutique to boutique, filling bags with designer denim, organza tops, strappy heels, more makeup than I could use in a year. She was spoiling me. I could've bought this stuff myself but these were gifts, and I'd learned quickly as a cam girl that all gifts carried a price. When she held a pair of garnets against my ear, I pulled away.

"Happy birthday," Elle had said, pushing a small box into my hands.

"You did not."

"I did. Open it."

"You don't have the money for this."

"Shut up and open it."

Inside, on a bed of velvet, lay a pair of ruby earrings set in sterling. The settings were molded into threads of cold fire.

One day we'd gone window-shopping and pretended to buy all the things we couldn't afford. Tried on clothes at high-end stores till they kicked us out, got spritzed with a potpourri of perfume at fragrance counters, talked a jeweler into taking the ruby earrings out of the glass case and reluctantly holding them up against my head. The jeweler said they looked lovely. Ellis said they looked like drops of blood bursting into flame. That night I painted a phoenix tearing its own wings apart. My brushstrokes were wild, paint licking up my arms as if fire were bleeding onto me, or from me. When I put the brush down, Elle dipped it carefully in the red and dabbed each of my earlobes.

"You remembered," I said softly, letting reminiscence fade.

She turned my head and put an earring in, gentle. Then the other side. The graze of her fingers made me shiver.

"Do they look lovely?" I said, smiling.

"You do."

She never told me where she got the money. But eventually,
I knew.

(—Bergen, Vada. *Happy Birthday, Baby.*
Oil on canvas.)

Frankie was giving me a strange look.

"Zoned out," I said. "I'm starving. Call it a day?"

We went to a hipster clam bar near the wharf. Frankie ordered a flight of red wine, then another, and by the time the steamers were served I was grinning stupidly, tipsy.

"I have no idea how to do this," I said.

She raised an amused eyebrow. Her face said *watch me.*

Frankie popped a shell with one hand and pulled out the clam, peeled the dark part off like a stocking, dipped the meat into the broth and melted butter and then finally lifted it, dripping gold, to her mouth. Her tongue flicked out to bring it inside slowly.

"Holy shit," I said.

She licked a glaze of butter from her lips. "Think you can do it?"

"Show me one more time."

"Only if we go private, baby."

We both laughed.

By my third steamer I was doing it like a pro, sucking the juice before it could trickle over my chin, gesturing with my wineglass like I wasn't on the brink of dropping it. Being around Frankie made me feel sophisticated, her urbane air rubbing off. She was an econ major with a solid background in high culture, and when I talked about Frida Kahlo or Paul Klee she knew who I meant. "Describe it," she'd say when I mentioned a painting, and I let the wine take rein over my tongue and told her how Kahlo was a raw cry, how her colors burned into the canvas like blood still hot from a vein, how she captured the way that pain, chronic pain, felt like a nightmare that started when you woke up, and it made everything surreal, every ordinary object a torture device, every mundane chore a labor sentence. It both impeded Kahlo's expression and intensified all she experienced. That's what made her great, I explained. All art comes from pain. She was closer to the nerve pulp than most of us. But every stroke of the brush, every lyric, every word whispered between human beings resulted from the pain of being alone. In our haunted heads, our imperfect bodies. Islands carved from clay and bone, our skulls like shells full of mist.

Frankie stared at my hands. "That's how it feels for you?"

"I have good days and bad days."

"Can't you have surgery?"

"Already did." Today was a good day, and the wine buffered any twinge of discomfort. "Messing with it more might make it worse. I could lose all function."

Sun speared through the rain, skewering the droplets crawling down the windows. Frankie tilted the cabernet in her glass.

"I never guessed it was that bad by looking at you," she said.

"You probably see a hundred disabled people every day and don't realize."

"Never thought of that."

"Most people just want to pass quietly in society. No preconceptions, no prejudices."

"You're preaching to the choir. People look at me and immediately see *black girl*." Frankie smiled, dimples popping. "Not the girl, or the person. But my blackness. Then comes that pause, you know, checking if they're being racist or rude or whatever. Like they're saying, very politely, 'You're not like us. You never will be.'"

"Exactly. They're othering you."

"I'm sorry if I've done that. Or not accommodated your needs."

"When I need help, I'll ask. Assuming I need it makes me feel othered." Except I never asked for help, even when I legit needed it. My dumb stubbornness. "If I've ever made you feel that way, I'm sorry, too."

"Oh, please." She whisked a fingertip over my forearm and the hair there stood on end. "Look at your gorgeous color. Where's your family from?"

"Mom's Puerto Rican, Dad's Swedish. You?"

"Nigerian, Brazilian, and English. And I swear, if I hear 'chocolate, caramel, and nougat' one more fucking time, I will murder someone."

"You mean you're actually a person, not a Milky Way bar?"

She grinned. "You get me. And I get you."

I took a long draught of wine. "Why'd you buy me all this stuff? Are you seducing me?"

I'd said it jokingly, but her smile grew sly, almost carnal.

"I like you, that's all." Frankie pushed a clam across her plate with a lilac nail. "You remind me of a younger me. Feisty, fiery. Chip on your shoulder. This business is tough, and it's easy to see other women as enemies. But we're the only real allies we've got."

"Tell me about it."

"You've had to fight for everything in your life. You deserve some goodness pro bono. A rising tide lifts all boats."

"Maine's getting to you, Frankie. Next you'll grow a beard and stroke it while staring out to sea." She laughed, charmingly, and I dared to ask something personal. "Why'd you get into camming? You're like, superhumanly beautiful. Top model material."

"Modeling is a joke. There are millions of pretty faces out there. If you want in, you've got to fuck your way through talent scouts and photogs. Think the casting couch is only in Hollywood? It's in fashion, too. It's everywhere we sell our skin. And when men are the gatekeepers, they make us pay with our bodies to get in the door. But camming's different. No gate. Anyone with an Internet connection can do it. Now we've only got to fuck ourselves."

We both giggled. We were slightly drunk.

Then her gaze slid past me. "Speaking of the casting couch. Isn't that your old boss?"

Shit.

Curtis sat at the far end of the butcher-block bar, hunched over a tin plate of fish and chips. He was still all skin and bones and shaggy hair. When our eyes met, he nodded.

"Let's get out of here," I said.

Frankie called for the bill. But the rain was brutal, and as we waited for a cab Curt sauntered over.

"Vada?"

I frowned as if trying to remember who he was. "Hey."

"Hi. You look—wow, you look great."

All those days hiking and rowing had toned and tanned me even darker. Less alcohol, more fresh air. Less thinking. Self-improvement, I guess.

"How are you?" he said.

Last time I'd seen him, I'd been desperate enough to fuck him for money. Trade my body for a small extension of my crappy lease on life. And now I'd made it my profession. Whoring it up for the entire Internet.

Frankie slid an arm around my waist, as if sensing my embarrassment. Frankie, with her master's degree and scalpel blade of a brain, who took no shame cashing in on her looks till she could do what she really loved: run her own business.

If she didn't feel embarrassed, why the fuck should I?

I made a living doing something on my terms. On my time, at my comfort level. Without letting anyone touch me. And I made more money online than I ever would have in the real world.

My eyes rose to his. "I'm good."

For the first time in ages, I actually meant it.

"That's great. That's really great. Hey, if you ever want to catch up—"

Our cab pulled to the curb, a yellow blur in the downpour, and Frankie and I strolled out together, arm in arm, leaving Curt there with his mouth hanging open.

———

We waited out the storm on the yacht, Frankie reading an e-book while I stared at the roil and wrath of the sea. My shoulder twitched involuntarily, mimicking drawing. I used to love attacking paper with a stub of charcoal, racing to capture motion before it stopped. Catching that in-between flicker where a movement hung breathless and timeless and forever. It was getting dark before we cast off, a plush velvet fog lying over the water, so thick I tried to scoop it up with my hands, like marshmallow. Once we launched there was only pure white in every direction. Heavy slabs of silence bordered us on all sides, magnifying the slap of water on the hull, our small human noises. Frankie glanced at me and for a wild moment I thought, This isn't real. She's Charon, ferrying me to the underworld.

Then the pier materialized out of nothingness, a pair of loons ruffling and gliding off in the lavender twilight. Dane stepped through the haze and my heart lurched in a pleasant way. Frankie left us to handle the boat.

We worked side by side wordlessly. Dane threw me a line without warning and I caught it; he knelt to help me tie it down without prompt. When I slid on the mist-filmed deck he put a steadying hand on my back. The imprint seared into my skin, a warmth silhouetted against the chill.

We were walking up the pier when I yanked at his shirt-sleeve, stopping him. An iron lantern bathed us with warm manila light.

"Morgan—"

"You didn't tell me," I said, moving closer. "That you're leaving."

He put a palm against my cheek. "Didn't want to worry you."

"Worry me. You can't just leave without saying anything."

"You're going to miss me."

"Whatever. No. A little."

"You will," he said, stroking my face, and abruptly I broke free and stalked away from him.

"Morgan."

Fuck, fuck, what was this? Confusion. Loneliness, manifesting as physical want. Like with Max. Dane was not someone I wanted a relationship with. Someone I'd fuck, yes, sure. But nothing beyond that. Nothing real.

He caught my arm and I spun around and hurled myself at him. For a second we gripped each other, equally stunned, then one of us started the kiss and we both fell into it.

His lips were soft and tinged with bitter earthy beer, and he kissed me gently, one hand behind my head, the other on my waist. I wrapped my arms around him like I'd imagined the night we swam beneath the stars. His body was hard and alive, so alive, moving against mine, pulling me to him so tightly every movement he made rippled through me like water. Our mouths opened, slow and sinuous, tongues curling and my legs parting and his hips pressing between them. I was ready for this. I'd been fucking myself all day, every day for the past four months, and the first warm body against mine made me wetter than I'd ever been on cam. Dane's erection pressed into my thigh. I could imagine already how we'd fuck: he'd let me get on top, give him a show, then hold me in place and give it to me hard. If we could just get from here to the house without slowing down, without losing focus—

The fog swirled around us like ghosts.

I pulled back.

"Morgan," he said, reaching for me.

"You're leaving." Hands in my hair, frantic. "I'm not fucking you right before you leave."

I'm not losing someone again.

"What if I stay?"

"You can't actually do that, can you?"

"No."

I paced away, tense, then returned calmer. Touched his chest and felt the rise and fall beneath my palms.

"I don't want to miss you," I said.

Dane covered my hands with his. "I'll miss you. Whether or not we hook up."

I pushed him playfully. Fake lightness. "You'll meet some gorgeous Boston girl and forget all about me."

"No."

"Or a gorgeous guy. One of your clients. A true gentleman. He'll sweep you off your feet, beat some culture into your thick skull."

Dane laughed. "Come with me."

"Frankie needs me here."

"You don't need Frankie."

"Are you splitting?"

"Wasn't planning to. But if it means I can hold on to you . . ."

"Dane, don't be stupid." I stepped away. "We're the wrong people at the wrong time. We weren't meant to happen."

"Maybe I'll ask your friend with the La Roux hair, then."

"Ellis?" I said in disbelief.

"She's cute. And she thinks I'm funny."

"You are so barking up the wrong tree."

Dane cocked an eyebrow.

I lifted my face to the wet sky. "This is a good time to say good-bye. Before we really know each other."

"It would've been better before you kissed me."

"I had to know what I won't be missing."

"How was it?"

"Not bad for our first and last kiss."

He smiled, and I let him sling an arm around my waist and walk me to the house. We parted on the porch and I kissed his cheek. He brushed mine, sweetly.

"Go break a million hearts," I said.

"But never yours."

When Dane was gone I sat in the shadows at the corner of the porch, knees to my chest. It was like this every time I got close to someone. Painful. Impossible. Because it was never right. Never what I really wanted.

Mist broke into fingers, long and wispy, curling around me, taking hold. Pulling at me. Tearing. Like my ghosts.

———

Late the next morning I woke up horny. I hadn't gotten off last night, but now I was focused and distilled and ready to make some money off the ache between my legs.

Clock check: the UK was getting off work for the evening. I took a soft-focus selfie—sleepy smile, faded Union Jack tee—and wrote, *Free show at noon Eastern. Come one, come all.* Posted it to my social media accounts and left my cam live while I hit the shower. When I sat down again in a towel, a hundred-odd viewers were waiting.

manchester91: there she is

sexy_stepbrother: welcome back bb

beautifulbastard: girl u look fine
beautifulbastard: I want to be that towel
beautifulbastard: and soak u up
beautifulbastard: like the Brawny man
sexy_stepbrother: lol
manchester91 has tipped Morgan 100 tokens.

Getting paid just for sitting down. I smiled. "Thanks for spreading the word, guys. I see some regulars. How are you, Manchester?"

manchester91: great bb, how was your shower?

"Just got out, and I'm still dripping." I looked into the cam and tried not to laugh. "But you boys are going to make me even wetter, aren't you?"

I lay back on the bed, let the towel fall, and got to work.

Another shower after, more leisurely. Eyes closed, water pounding at my face. I pressed my palms to the tile and lowered my head. A line of scarlet heat scrawled up my right arm. Fuck. One of those days.

I threw on shorts and a tee and was toweling my hair dry when I walked into the kitchen and Ellis looked up from her laptop.

We both froze. She blushed.

"Oh," I said. "You're here already."

She snapped the lid shut and stared at the table.

I grabbed coffee and a yogurt, totally cavalier, and sat across from her. Dull platinum sun poured at her back, a humid fog of light. I watched her as I ate. Super tomboy today: rolled-up cargos, plaid shirt, her hair doing that cute thing where her bangs swept upward. She adjusted her glasses, rubbed a smudge off her phone. Anything to avoid looking at me.

"So, what'd you think?" I said at last.

"Of what?"

"My show."

The blush deepened. "Excuse me?"

"You can't blush and then feign ignorance. I know you, Elle."

For a second she met my gaze and something sparked, but then she looked away again. "It was . . . good, I guess. I have no idea."

"Was it hot? Did it turn you on?"

"Can we talk about why I'm here? Frankie wants you to show me around."

I licked the last bit of lemon yogurt from the spoon and smiled. "This is the kitchen. Where we eat. Hungry?"

Ellis wasn't amused. She kept her head bowed, eyes lowered, and I started to feel guilty for goading her, then resentful for the guilt.

"Let's get this over with. Come on."

I walked her through the first floor of our sprawling Queen Anne mansion. Odd-angled rooms printed with wild zebra stripes of sun and shadow, gabled windows, French doors, halls that bent and doubled back and didn't quite seem to line up, as if the house were a slowly spun kaleidoscope. Frankie had let me decorate and I'd matched the eclectic architecture: sleek Eames chairs, tables made from whitewashed driftwood, wrought-iron lanterns grandly crumbling into rust. On every wall I'd hung prints: Klee's pixelated mosaics of color, Kandinsky's schizophrenic geometry. Elle glued herself to my side, staring.

"This is so you," she said. I don't think she meant me to hear, but a tiny wick flared in my heart.

I walked ahead, leaving her to catch up.

The second and third floors were all bedrooms, doors closed. Cammers. Most of us slept during the day, waiting for clients to come home from work and eat dinner with their families or their TVs and then shut themselves in dark rooms with bright screens. The attic lay at the top of a rickety staircase, and when Elle felt the boards give, she stumbled. I caught her, pulling her close. We stared at each other.

"Easy," I muttered. But I held on till she found her footing again.

"So this is your room."

She nudged past me. Curiosity always got the better of her awkwardness.

Elle inspected the desk first, traced fingertips over my camera and handmade softboxes. Clothes hung from a beam of the slanted roof and her hands drifted through satin and silk, stirring them like a breath. She scanned the camming bed, squinted at the photos of broken things. Then over to my real bed across the room. I came up behind her, slowly.

I'd peeled each photo from Mrs. Mulhavey's guest room and transplanted them here. Creased now, frayed from the obsessive stroking of fingers. Elle's face and mine. The way we used to smile before we killed a boy and ruined each other's lives. My love and longing scarred the paper clearer than any ink.

She glanced at me and I met her gaze.

Our eyes held for a second, then we turned away.

"I'll show you the site," I said.

We settled at my desk.

"So. This is how camming works."

I showed her how clients bought tokens, tipped us, purchased photos, videos, personal merchandise—worn panties or unwashed socks or used razors—how we banned problematic users, handled special requests for Snapchat and other apps. Some of it baffled her—"They actually buy your *dirty socks*?" she exclaimed, and I laughed—and Elle took notes, absorbing my every word. In the middle of explaining, I realized how utterly natural this felt. Familiar. Warm. We slid back into our roles so effortlessly when we stopped thinking about how we'd hurt each other.

Ellis cleared her throat. "Vada?"

That name snapped me out of it. Nobody but Max called me that anymore.

"I'm working tonight," I said, standing. "We can finish tomorrow. Need a ride to the mainland?"

She stared at her phone, avoiding eye contact. "I'm, uh, staying on the island, actually."

"Where?"

"There's a place in the woods I'm fixing up."

My eyes narrowed. "You are not talking about the tree house."

Elle shrugged sheepishly.

Deep in the woods, a few hundred yards from here, was an old one-room cabin built on stilts and the thick arms of an ancient oak. I climbed up there once: abandoned, the wood rotting, soft and barnacled with moss like a sunken ship. Some sea coffin tossed up onto land.

"You can't stay there."

"Dane said it was fine."

"Dane's not the brightest crayon in the box. That thing is falling apart."

Her eyes flashed up to mine. "That's why it suits me."

What the hell could I say to that?

"Do you want me to—" I began, but she grabbed her laptop bag and darted down the stairs, quick as a bird. "—walk you out," I finished to the room, and sat down, feeling like the air around me, the vacant chair. Empty.

———

#Cumshow at 1,000 tokens.

One hour in, and I'd already hit seven hundred.

Seven hundred dollars for sixty minutes of lying on my bed, teasing myself with a silicone dick. Making fuck-me eyes at the cam, pulling on a tie, moaning the screennames of the men who tipped me. In the next hour I'd fuck this dildo and fake an orgasm and go back to reading that Dalí bio or tinkering with my digital photos or brooding at the window, wondering what Elle was up to out in the woods.

But for now, customer service.

iwatchusleep: damn bb you are TNT

iwatchusleep: you're gonna make me blow

SixPackCoverModel: boom

iwatchusleep: haha

BigManOnCampus: my cock is so fucking hard

BigManOnCampus: I want to fuck the shit out of your tight little pussy

[MOD]UnicornTears: *BigManOnCampus has received a warning. Total warnings: 1.*

    1 warning = 5 min mute | 2 = temp kick | 3 = PERMABAN

    ~Keep it FUN and BEHAVE!~

aussieboi: no1 cares about ur cock

I smirked at the screen. "You can tell me about your cock in a tip note, Big Man."

Viewers could message cammers privately if they tipped a minimum of twenty tokens. Once, a guy tipped me seventeen times in a row to describe himself getting off. Why he didn't just pay for a private chat, which would've been cheaper in the long run, was a mystery. Insecurity, perhaps. Maybe he couldn't handle the pressure of my undivided attention.

Or maybe he was just bad at math.

I clutched one tit hard and opened my mouth, gasping.

ero_sennin: can I see your tats plz bb?
aussieboi: check her photos m8
ero_sennin: I know but I want to see her ass ^_^
SoBlue has tipped Morgan 100 tokens.

"Thank you, Blue. Ero, is this better?" I rolled to my left side, ass to the cam, ink exposed. A beep signaled an incoming private message. I glanced over my shoulder.

[PM from SoBlue]: i'd like to take you private.

"Sorry, Blue. No private tonight. Just enjoy the show, baby."

aussieboi: dont be greedy
aussieboi: shes on every nite
BigManOnCampus has tipped Morgan 20 tokens.
[PM from BigManOnCampus]: I want to shoot my hot cum in your mouth

"You're a dirty boy, Big Man. You can tell me more in another tip." I flopped onto my back, legs spread to the cam. "Just a few more tokens. I'm so fucking wet. I can't wait to come for you boys."

ero_sennin: come on guys!
ero_sennin: almost there . . .
SoBlue has tipped Morgan 179 tokens.

The token counter ticked up to 999. I laughed. "Thank you again, Blue."

[PM from SoBlue]: i will pay you $1000 if you go private with me for an hour.

I'd heard lines like that a million times. Viewers would push you as far as you'd bend. Horny guys promised the moon and stars in a basket. Just like RL.

"You're a big talker, Blue, but I told you, no private. Now, one more token and this girl's getting fucked."

SoBlue has tipped Morgan 1,001 tokens.
iwatchusleep: OMFG
aussieboi: m8!!!
aussieboi: did ur finger slip??
SixPackCoverModel: that's what she said
iwatchusleep: lol
[PM from SoBlue]: i'll pay $1000 more if you stop the show.

I sat bolt upright, my shirt falling back over my breasts, the toy tumbling out of my lap. He really did just tip me a thousand and one bucks. I stared at the screen for a second, then put my hands on the keys.

[PM to SoBlue]: if you're serious, my paypal is morgan.xxx@gmail.com

Rich guys had done crazy shit for me before. One of them bought me this MacBook, fully loaded. Another sent a whole Marc Jacobs ensemble—dress, jacket, shoes, handbag—that cost as much as a fucking car. It had belonged to his ex-wife. He got a kick out of watching me come in it. "She never could," he confided.

Extreme generosity was rare, but not unheard of.

And it was always gifts. They wanted the control. They wanted to see me wearing the clothes they'd bought, typing on the laptop they'd paid for. They wanted to extend their reach into my real life, touch my physical body, the only way they could: with gifts.

No one had ever offered me cold hard cash.

My viewers grew impatient, asking about the cumshow, but I ignored them and grabbed my phone to text Dane.

MORGAN: this client offered 1k to go private
MORGAN: he already tipped me like 1300
MORGAN: this is crazy
MORGAN: do you think it's safe

My phone vibrated in my hand, and I jumped. Not a text. An email confirmation from PayPal that $1,000 USD had been deposited to my account.

I set the phone down shakily.

> **iwatchusleep: bb, we gonna get a show or not**
> **aussieboi: lets see you ride it**
> **[PM to SoBlue]: send me a private chat request**

I waited, my fingers curling and uncurling over the keys.

Incoming video call from SoBlue.

ACCEPT.

———

Cam window: me on one side, disheveled, flushed; his side, the ubiquitous black rectangle. His mic was muted. I stared at the chat box for an endless minute, watching the status bar informing me that *SoBlue is typing . . .*

> **SoBlue: hi.**

I laughed, the tension breaking. "What took you so long? Hi, baby."

> **SoBlue: i tried out some suave lines.**
> **SoBlue: but every time i look at you my mind goes blank.**
> **SoBlue: and all i can think is . . .**
> **SoBlue: hi. hi. hi.**
> **SoBlue: like an excited puppy.**

He was cute. I sat back on the bed, pulling the laptop between my legs. All I wore was my tee and a thong.

"Hi hi hi to you too, Mr. Big Spender. What can I do for you?"

SoBlue is typing . . .

I watched the ellipsis fill and reset and fill again, over and over, as he chose his words.

SoBlue: i just want to talk.

"You sure? You seem pretty flustered. I could do something about that." I ran a hand down one thigh. "What do you want to talk about?"

SoBlue: you.
SoBlue: close your legs.

Those legs tightened. Domination turned me on. I never let men in my real life dominate, but here the right edge of aggression could make things so much easier. Some nights I was little more than a sex therapist, assuring timid men that it was okay, no judgment, no shame.

I tucked my legs beneath me. "Is this better, Blue? Can I call you that?"

SoBlue: yes.
SoBlue: now.
SoBlue: tell me about yourself, morgan.
SoBlue: who are you?

I leaned in, breathed deep. Cleavage boost. Strange, how ridiculous these cam tricks seemed right now. Once you're paid it's all revealed for the absurd skin circus it is. "I'm twenty-one." Every cam girl was either eighteen or twenty-one. "I'm in college for photography." MFA dropout. "I love the outdoors, hiking, camping." I loved torturing my body till every nerve burned and I groaned like the beast I was, passed out from exhaustion before I shored the boat, woke to fish nibbling at my toes and sand in my mouth. "I've never had a serious boyfriend." I'd been in love once. "I've never been in love." And it wrecked me.

> *SoBlue is typing . . .*
> SoBlue: i don't believe you.

"About what?"

> SoBlue: anything.
> SoBlue: try again.
> SoBlue: tell me something true.

"It's all true, baby."

We'd never know what was real and what wasn't about each other. That was the beauty of our shared fiction.

> SoBlue: here's something true.
> SoBlue: you're sad.
> SoBlue: tell me why.

For the first time, I drew a blank in front of the camera.

I'd heard it all. The objects men wanted to put inside my body. The ways they wanted to touch me, fuck me, defile me. The names—*slut, spic, cunt, whore, bitch, honey, mommy*—and the people I stood in for—ex-girlfriend, sister, stranger, boss. They acted out fantasies with me that they couldn't in the real world. Followed me off a bus and dragged me into a dark alley. Locked a classroom door and bent me over a desk. None of it fazed me, because none of it was real. We were both characters. Only our loneliness was real, and for ten dollars a minute I'd pretend to care.

But sometimes they really just wanted something human. Someone to talk to. Those guys were the hardest for me.

I faked a laugh, throaty, reckless. "Why do you think I'm sad?"

He didn't dignify that with a response.

I glanced at the clock. Fifty more minutes.

I could log off whenever I wanted. I already had his money.

SoBlue: do i make you uncomfortable?

I started to speak and then, on impulse, typed instead.

Morgan: I'm not sure what you want from me
SoBlue: i just want to talk.
Morgan: you want to talk about real things
Morgan: that's not what I do
SoBlue: too kinky for you?
SoBlue: i could describe my big veiny cock if that makes it easier.

I laughed again, genuine. "It sort of does, yeah."

SoBlue: why is that?

"Because then I know what you want."

SoBlue: it's simple.
SoBlue: i want you.

A thousand other men had said those words to me. This time I felt exactly how heavy they were.

"Who are you?"

SoBlue: i'm just a lonely guy on the internet.
SoBlue: who's in love with a lonely girl.

It's funny. Boys call us mushy and romantic, but they almost always declare their love first. Girls are the ones who hold back.

"You're silly, but sweet. You want real talk? I'm sad because I've completely fucked my life up." I wrapped my arms around my knees. "But that's such a cam girl cliché. Let's talk about something else. Like the color blue."

Then I told him something true.

A long time ago, there was no word for the shade of the sea and sky. People described them instead as moods, temperaments: fierce and volatile, or melancholy and pacific. In Homer, the sea was "wine-dark." In other classic texts it was a degree of gray. No one knows, really, why the ancients couldn't put a word to that hue. It was colorblindness not at a physical but an intellectual level, an inability to describe what we saw because we lacked the language to conceive of it as separate. The sea was a vast goblet of wine. They looked right at it and saw juiced grapes and the fluid in their veins.

Scientists studied isolated tribal societies to see if the phenomenon still occurred in the modern era. And it did. Those with simpler languages called the sea a shade of black or red, a primal color. It wasn't important enough—not like blood or nightfall—to give it its own name. Their brains became wired to see it as a subsidiary of another color, glossing over the hue and instead focusing on its emotionality. But people with more complex, technical languages, those rife with hues and hex codes and Pantone swatches, are trained to see color in a different way. We all see blue, but some of us see blue as an inflection, a mood, of black or red, while others see blue as its own creature.

"A lot of artists," I said, "have been obsessed with the color blue. Yves Klein got so crazy about it he painted canvas after canvas with nothing but pure ultramarine. They named a new color after him. He had models roll around naked in blue paint and throw themselves at blank canvases. He called them 'living brushes.' That's how intense it was for him."

SoBlue: you're an artist.

"Photographer."

SoBlue: more than that.

SoBlue: you speak about art sensually.
SoBlue: you're a living brush, too.

"I've dabbled."

SoBlue: don't be modest.
SoBlue: let me see your art.

I waved at the wall behind me. "Voilà."

SoBlue: not photos.
SoBlue: i want to see something that came from you.

My first instinct was innuendo—*I washed that off in the shower, baby*—but instead I gnawed my lower lip, not even caring how unattractive it looked. I kept staring at that black rectangle and thinking how, a thousand years ago, it would have been the same blue as the sea.

"That was the past. I don't paint anymore." Then I let my temper fly, a small barb. "Don't ask about it again."

Blue didn't respond.

It shocked me to see that the hour was up. It'd felt like mere minutes.

"Why did you pay so much to listen to me ramble?" I said.

SoBlue: i've thought about you all day.
SoBlue: every day.
SoBlue: for a long time.
SoBlue: tonight i just . . .
SoBlue: needed more.

"So you've been watching me. Are you one of my regulars?"

SoBlue: i wouldn't call it regular.

"What would you call it?"

SoBlue: obsession.

It wasn't unusual. The entire point of camming was to coax viewers into a frenzy of infatuation. Make them want more, and more, and put a price tag on each piece. We became obsessed with them, too. We fell in love with their infatuation. It's hard not to love the way someone loves you. The entire industry was a device to bring two lonely minds together in a digital nowhere, put two disconnected obsessives inside the same small box and let our explosive yearning generate money.

In a way it wasn't so different from art. It bridged the void between minds, let us feel something together, ten tokens per minute. Sometimes I thought, Money isn't filthy or cold. It's the only way we can be human with each other anymore.

SoBlue: morgan is thinking . . .

I smiled. "I wonder what you think will happen. Between you and me."

SoBlue: i'm not thinking beyond this moment.
SoBlue: i'm completely in it with you.

His words made my chest expand in a strange way. Partly just the breath in my lungs, partly something unnameable.

"Tell me about yourself, Blue."

SoBlue: our hour is up, morgan.

First rule of camming: protect the product. Value your time.

"You've already paid me a ton," I said. "I don't mind talking more."

SoBlue: if you could see how my face just lit up, you'd laugh.
SoBlue: i'm like a little boy on christmas.

I laughed anyway. "You're kind of cute."

SoBlue: i'm excessively cute.

"Don't be modest. Let me see how cute."

SoBlue: clever.
SoBlue: you like me, morgan. admit it.
SoBlue: you don't want to stop talking.

"You make me laugh. It's been a while since a client's done that."

SoBlue: "client" sounds so cold.

"What are you then? My Romeo? My—"
I'd started to say *Prince Charming* and felt a stab of guilt. Here I was flirting my ass off with some guy, while Elle was alone out in the dark woods.

SoBlue: not quite that tragic.

I sprawled on my side, switching to typing.

Morgan: sorry, bad thoughts
Morgan: where were we?
SoBlue: let's see.
SoBlue: what are you wearing?
SoBlue: no. we've established that.
SoBlue: the question is, what am i wearing?
Morgan: bet I can guess
SoBlue: please try.
SoBlue: this should be good.
Morgan: you're too anal-retentive to be a boxers guy
SoBlue: why do you say that?
Morgan: no misspellings, perfect punctuation
SoBlue: i'll take it as a compliment, then.
Morgan: you're also too much of a hipster to be a briefs guy

SoBlue: this seems more like character judgment than an erotic guessing game.

SoBlue: why am i a hipster?

Morgan: your pathological disdain for the Shift key?

SoBlue: fair point.

Morgan: so, Blue

Morgan: I think you fall somewhere in the middle

I raised a knee, not too provocatively, just teasing him a bit.

Morgan: you've got an edge in you

Morgan: a little ego, a little swagger

Morgan: but you're too smart to be one of those caveman chest beating types

Morgan: you're a boxer-briefs guy

Just the way I like them.

He didn't respond for a second and I said out loud, "Am I right?"

SoBlue: you're right.

SoBlue: but i bet you can't tell me the color.

On impulse I said, "Red."

SoBlue: i'm torn between being aroused and alarmed.

"My next guess was Superman undies."

SoBlue: funny you should mention that . . .

"Oh my god. No."

SoBlue: yes.

SoBlue: owned. never worn.

SoBlue: i'm saving them.

"For what?"

SoBlue: for the girl of my dreams.

SoBlue: who's waiting to be swept off her feet by a suave anal-retentive hipster wearing superhero skivvies.

I lay back on the bed, laughing. "What grown man admits he owns Superman underwear?"

SoBlue: one who's very comfortable with his masculinity.

You are, aren't you? I thought. You don't give a shit what I think. You're not one of those try-hard guys desperate to prove how alpha you are.

You just paid me enough to get my attention. And then you were yourself.

There's nothing sexier than a man who's comfortable being himself.

I gazed at the cam, my eyelashes lowering. "Blue."

SoBlue: morgan.

SoBlue: you have that look in your eyes.

"What look?"

SoBlue: like you want to get off.

"Do you?"

SoBlue: in my mind, this whole time . . .

SoBlue: my hands have been all over you.

SoBlue: every time you move, every time you breathe, i can feel it.

"That's fucking hot." I slid a hand over my thigh, toward the inside. "Let me get you off. Both of us."

SoBlue: i want you.

SoBlue: so badly.

SoBlue: but not yet.

"Don't be shy, baby. Are you hard?"

SoBlue: no.
SoBlue: now stop.

Spit stuck in my throat. I sat up straight. "Are you for real? I *want* to do this for you."

Do you not realize how rare that is, dumbass?

SoBlue: this isn't business.
SoBlue: i'm not your client.
SoBlue: don't give me a show.

"Who exactly do you think you are?"

SoBlue: let's not end on a bad note.

"Well, being sexually frustrated kind of sucks. Which I'm sure you know, since you drop thousands of bucks on cam girls. I can't believe a client is turning *me* down."

SoBlue: i'm not your fucking client.

There we go. I'd found his button.

I dragged the laptop closer.

"You are, though, Blue. You might be funny and cute, but you paid me to talk to you. Don't forget that."

SoBlue: when was the last time you truly connected with someone?
SoBlue: when you didn't feel completely alone?
SoBlue: i saw it in your eyes.
SoBlue: it was tonight. with me.
SoBlue: i may have paid you, but i gave you something, too.
SoBlue: don't forget that.

My pulse vibrated so hard it made my hands shake. Who the fuck did he think he was? Paying me a couple thousand bucks didn't mean shit. He had no idea what kind of relationships I'd had. What they'd meant to me. What they still meant.

When I wrapped my hands around Elle's neck I felt a deeper human connection than I ever had with anyone else. It might be sick and unhealthy, but it was real. I felt it in my marrow. My blood.

This? This was words on a screen. Nothing.

"You know nothing about my life," I said. "Nothing about my loneliness. But I know all about yours."

I moved my cursor over the DISCONNECT button.

"Thanks for reminding me why we don't get personal with *clients*. Have a nice night."

Click.

Morgan left the room.
Session ended. Total: 1:31:16.

6

Ellis was in the kitchen again the next morning. This time two coffee cups stood on the table. She eyed the farther one, then looked up at me.

I sat grudgingly. "Caffeine: my one weakness."

"You also have a weakness for gummy bears."

"Okay, two weaknesses. I'm still supervillain material."

"And what about gel pens?"

I narrowed my eyes. "You know too much, Ellis Carraway. I'll have to destroy you."

She lowered her face, but I caught a slight smile. A brassy red lock strayed across her forehead and I clutched the mug, battling the urge to touch her hair.

It was so easy to forget the bad blood when she was right there, across the table, sitting in the morning light. It could've been a year ago. No time lost at all.

"So what are we working on today?" I said.

"Actually, Frankie's going to—"

On cue Frankie walked into the kitchen, radiant in white chiffon. She rubbed my shoulder in friendly greeting and nodded at Elle.

"Ready, Miss Daisy?"

Ellis blushed.

"She's kidding," I said. "She likes putting people on edge."

"I'm a professional provocateur," Frankie said.

I raised an eyebrow. "Is that what they call stripping on the Internet now?"

"Sassing the woman who writes your paycheck. That's bold."

"Did you just say 'sass'?"

Frankie flipped her sunglasses down, Deal With It style.

"Where are you guys going, anyway?" I said.

"To take over the world. But first, legal meetings."

"Well, knock 'em dead."

Elle rose to leave, then paused beside me and murmured, "Bye, dorkus malorkus."

I tried to be cool. I really did. But she gave me that crooked, sweet girl-next-door grin that I could never resist, and I said, "Bye, nerdus maximus."

"You look pretty."

My stupid sappy heart mopped this up. "So do you."

"Oh my god," Frankie said. "Too cute. You two. I can't."

I sat there after they left, the coffee forgotten, feeling mixed-up and conflicted and inexplicably warm.

Then Jasmine, a petite, cherubic cam girl who did BDSM, came downstairs in just her panties and a pair of nipple clips and I returned to my room. Dane had finally answered my texts.

DANE: sorry busy night
DANE: did u do it?
MORGAN: yeah
MORGAN: we just talked
MORGAN: and he paid me
DANE: damn
DANE: ez $
MORGAN: the best kind

I sprawled on my bed in a drizzle of honey sun.

DANE: be careful
DANE: guy gives u $
DANE: wants to meet irl
MORGAN: he didn't say anything about that
DANE: he will

I thought of Blue's parting words. *I may have paid you, but I gave you something, too. Don't forget that.*

Yeah, but I don't owe you shit, buddy.

I asked about Boston but Dane had errands to run. I could pass the time with another surprise cam show, but it didn't appeal. Nor did reading, sunbathing, taking photos, or getting off purely for my own gratification. I paced my room, nervy, agitated, feeling like Max.

Get out of the fucking house, loser.

Last time I'd seen the tree house, rain had been falling right through the roof. Today the woods were full of sunlight, clear beams glittering with dandelion seeds and pollen like jewel dust. The air was pungent with sweet summer rot. I climbed the split-log staircase winding up the old oak. The door had no lock. Few things did out here.

Inside was a single large room. Tree branches thrust up through the floor and exited through holes carved in the roof. Kitchenette, couch, loft with a bed at the top of a narrow staircase. Ellis had swept out the drifts of leaves and scrubbed the pine boards pale. Her neatness and precision were everywhere: dishes aligned razor-straight on the sink counter, blanket folded crisply on the couch.

"This is so you," I said aloud.

All this bare wood needed color, life. I'd bring her something. Housewarming gift.

Wait, why am I gifting someone I want to leave me alone?

"Because," I said, "I'm the queen of fucking denial."

I walked to the window. On the table she'd stacked a pile of small logs, too tiny to give much heat. Besides, it was summer. Who needed fire? So Ellis: overprepared but impractical.

"All you do is hurt me," I said, hefting a log and smacking it into my palm. "And I keep coming back for more. Why do you keep hurting me, Vada?"

I answered, "Because I hate the way I feel about you."

"Why do you hate it?"

"Because it screws up the whole way I see myself. It makes me feel crazy."

"Well, you are crazy. You're standing in a tree house talking to yourself, psycho."

Time to bounce.

I retraced my steps, searching for clues that someone had been there. When my phone buzzed I knocked a glass off the counter but caught it like an ace, lefty.

"Hello?"

"Where the hell are you?" Frankie sounded riled. The hair on my arms prickled. Frankie never got upset.

"Went for a walk. What's wrong?"

"Get back to the house immediately. We have a situation. Ellis is freaking out."

She hung up on me.

It wasn't until I got home that I realized I'd left one thing different. I'd forgotten to replace that log atop the stack.

———

Frankie crossed her arms and said, "Who is Max Vandermeer, and why is he stalking you two?"

I glanced at Ellis beside me on the couch. Glasses off, eyes red. She sniffled into a tissue and my hand floated toward her, then fell.

"He's not stalking us," I said wearily. "There was an accident."

If you tell a story enough times, it sounds like fiction. You don't feel that visceral throb of resonance with the person who is you, who did the things you did. She's just a character. Vada and Ellis on an icy winter road. Flaring headlights, bursting glass. Three white dragon tails of breath. Then only two. Later, a haggard man who holds you and cries, who wants to be close to you because you're haunted, because you carry the ghost he loves. His hands touch you differently one night but you don't tell anyone. You pretend everything's fine. Even when your feet feel heavier every day, when the air smothers like a pall. When you feel something pulling you under but can't escape, because it's pulling from inside.

"I don't understand," Frankie said. "His kid was the drunk driver. Why is he harassing you guys about it?"

"It's not harassment," I said. "He wants closure, and he's looking for it anywhere he can."

Ellis gripped the couch cushion. "He said there are 'strange findings' in the black boxes. They don't match our reports."

"It doesn't matter," I said.

"They could reopen the case—"

"They won't. Relax."

She eyed me askance. "Why are you defending him, Vada?"

It was jarring to hear my real name in front of others. "I'm not. But I had to deal with him when you were gone. When you *abandoned* me. So I'm the authority here."

Ellis averted her face.

"Is this going to be an ongoing problem?" Frankie said. "I can refer you to a good defense attorney."

"It's fine, really. I'll handle him."

"You understand why I dislike strange men yelling my colleague's name on the street, right? Anonymity is a precious thing. It protects us."

"I know. I'm sorry."

Ellis took a shaky breath. "It's all because of me. I'm a liability."

Frankie frowned. "Liability?"

"She's upset," I said. "She always blames herself."

"No, it's true. It's my fault. I was the one who—"

I put my arms around Ellis and yanked her to my chest. I had to shut her up.

"It's okay." Over her head I gave Frankie an apologetic smile. Look rational. Look calm. "We'll get a restraining order or something. He won't bother you again, Elle. I promise."

She trembled in my arms.

"It's okay. It's okay, baby." My right hand was hidden from view and I traced her ribs, the curve beneath her breast, gentle. Her breath caught. My voice lowered. "Let me take you home."

The light was failing, a rusty stain seeping through the trees, like cooling blood. A thousand leaves whispered little lies underfoot. I let her walk ahead so I could see what she reacted to. What she noticed. When she froze in the tree house doorway, I stepped behind her and threaded my arms through hers. Stronger now, sinewy from rowing. I pushed her past the beam of bloody sun that cut across the living room and into the shadows and stopped, holding her against me. My hands cupped the thin cage of her ribs, felt her heart flitting madly at the bars. My own pulse beat hot and tight in my belly.

The last few times we'd been this close, we'd been hurting each other. But not now.

"Vada," she whispered.

Control yourself.

I released her, crossed the room. Faked a stumble and knocked the log pyramid off the table, hiding the misplaced one. "Shit. Sorry."

"I've got it." Elle nudged me aside. "Light a candle? Matches by the stove."

I pulled a candle from a cupboard and lit it. When I brought the shivering yellow light over, Ellis looked up at me strangely.

Had she told me where the candles were? Fuck.

"Need some help?" I said.

"Someone was here."

"No one was here. We're in the middle of nowhere."

"Max found me in the middle of nowhere."

I set the candle on the table and touched her shoulders. "You can't talk to anyone about that night. Especially not him. Let me do the talking, okay? We have to stick to the story."

"The story," she echoed. "The story we're telling each other."

I let go and tumbled onto the couch. An oak branch snaked to one side of the table, and the flame flickering against it made long, clawing shadows on the wall, the scratching of a black nail. "Are you punishing yourself, Elle? Is that what this asceticism is about?"

"No."

"Then why are you living in the woods?"

"I wanted to be near you."

I winced, and looked up at her, and couldn't bear it anymore. "Come here."

She threw herself into my outstretched arms and I hugged her fiercely. Our first real hug since I was in the hospital, so tight I felt the tendons in my arm pull like barbed wire. But I didn't relent. I'd dreamed of this. This was exactly how it felt in my dreams: so sweet it hurt.

After a while I realized she'd gone still and I'd pressed my face into her hair and was just breathing her scent, that autumn spice, leaves turning, grass crackling. Her heart drummed fast against mine. I disentangled myself, sprawled on the opposite side of the couch. She drew her knees up tidily.

"Are we okay?" she said.

"I don't know. But this is better than hating you."

"Did you really hate me?"

I gazed at her across the couch. "Hate is when you love someone but wish you didn't."

Candlelight danced in her lenses. She faced me unflinching. Elle had a hard time looking people in the eye, but not me.

"Max won't bother you again," I said. "I promise."

"How can you promise that?"

"I just can."

They were paying too much attention to us. I was designated drink-watcher that night, and I spotted the creepers right away: two clean-cut frat boys in Ralph Lauren who ignored a club full of sorority girls to beeline straight for us—my nerdy bestie, our tatted-up Aussie friend, Blythe, and me in paint-splotched work clothes. Not your typical bro bait.

These guys were up to no good.

Blythe was already hammered. "So which one of you blokes is the bottom?" she said, and Ellis, polite as always, tried to apologize till Blythe kissed her in front of everyone, open-mouthed. We were all shocked. I looked away, feeling weird. Like something clutched at me from the inside, claw-nailed. Something you might call jealousy. Ralph #1 caught my eye.

He smiled, but it was a shark's smile.

I put Blythe in a cab, and told off Ralph #2 when he tried to climb in with her. Sleazebag. When I walked back into the club, Ralph #1 was pulling the oldest trick in the book on Ellis.

He dropped his wallet to the floor, credit cards sliding out. As she bent to retrieve it, he tapped a packet of powder into her drink.

"We should get going, too," I said. "Mind walking us to the train?"

I flirted the whole way. He boarded with us. When we left the station I insisted that we switch cars, sending Elle across first. The frat boy followed, and I yanked him back onto the coupling between cars. He teetered off balance. I levered him over the edge by his collar. Wind screamed and streetlights smeared past in neon ribbons.

"Look down." I pushed his head forward. "See this? If you ever lay a finger on her, this is how I will kill you."

(—Bergen, Vada. *The Things We Do for Love.*
Colored pencil on paper.)

"I've never let anyone hurt you, Elle."

"That's true. You're the only one who hurts me."

Something sharp pricked my gut. "I should go. Don't talk to anyone else about the accident. Come to me first."

"Why don't you tell Max the truth?"

"I did."

"Then why don't you tell *me* the truth?"

I got up and stalked toward the door. Elle darted after me, and when I knocked her away she made another grab, rougher, and we stumbled against the wall.

"What are you doing?" I hissed, pinning her to the planks. "We've been through this before. It doesn't end well."

"It doesn't end, ever." She trailed her fingers over my throat, my wild pulse. "I know you still feel this."

"Of course I feel it. I'm not totally dead." I shoved her hand off. "But it fucking hurts. And I'm tired of pain."

"Then stop fighting."

"Fighting what?"

"Us."

Ellis grasped my face and kissed me.

My mouth hung open against hers, gasping. Shock. Every nerve lit and overloaded and popped and for an instant it was like the moment of impact, glass floating all around me, a shrapnel cloud of shattered light. Then my hands shifted to her jaw and I kissed her back, hard. She tasted like cigarette vapor, cool and herbal. It used to drive me so crazy. It still did. My thumbs bracketed her mouth and I pulled her lips open, took the top in mine. Ran my tongue inside, roughly. I tasted spearmint and sage and her, just her, a clear sweetness like a mountain stream. I pressed my body to hers to the wall. Slim bones, the thrash of blood and breath beneath translucent skin. Her want all tangled up in rage and fear. My hand slid under her shirt, found the tattoo on her left ribs. The one that matched mine.

If you're going to get one, I'd told her, get one that'll mean something when you're older.

Get it for someone you'll love forever.

She kept kissing me and I couldn't stop. My body rebelled. I wanted this so much, even knowing where it would lead. Knowing I'd wake in her bed, a lace of bare limbs and soft skin, hair knotted, hearts heavy. Knowing she'd bury her face in her hands while I dressed and left.

I jerked away, breathless.

"Don't stop," she said.

"I can't do this."

"Why?"

I started to speak but I really just wanted to kiss her again, softer. We drifted from the wall to the couch and I leaned on the armrest and brushed my lips over hers. An open kiss, breathing into each other's mouths. Slower, lighter. Eventually so slow and light it stopped being a kiss at all, and I looked up into her face.

"I can't," I said again, weakly.

"I missed you."

I touched her cheek. "I missed you, too. So much."

Her bangs tumbled into her eyes, hanging above that wine-red mouth. Her eyelashes were a fringe of fire. She gave me a mournful, longing look that twisted me up inside.

"This is why we fight so much," she said. "Because we're fighting this."

I kept trying to let go but my hands locked to her skin and she kissed me again, this time slow, intent, raising my chin and raking my hair back. Ellis kissed with that charming meticulousness that was so *her*, moving over every inch of my mouth and parting my lips and curling her tongue around mine softly and insistently till I tasted her everywhere, till I felt totally filled in, completely kissed, completely hers. Then her teeth sank into my bottom lip and I gasped and she tilted her head, watching me come undone.

This felt right. No matter how fucked-up things got, this always felt right.

Being in her hands.

"I want you back," she breathed.

"As your friend, or this?"

"Everything. You were my everything, Vada."

This was the problem with being so close. Friendship became codependence. Codependence consumed. When you possessed every piece of someone's heart and soul, it was only natural to want the flesh, too. Skin, bone, blood.

I grazed my lips over her cheek. "I have to go."

Out in the night woods I sank to my knees, hands over my mouth, holding in something wild, bestial. In *The Wounded Deer*, a buck with Kahlo's face kneels on the floor of a withered forest, his body pierced with arrows. His eyes are calm, focused on something far off. In the distance the turquoise sea glistens while he bleeds.

I bit my palm. Didn't cry out. An owl watched me with coin-bright eyes, pitilessly.

———

Need to avoid real life? Drown yourself in work.

I'd disappointed my regulars this week, so I made up for it with hard-core shows. No build-up, no tease. I started with the tie around my neck, face aflame with broken blood vessels, all the life in me surging to the surface of my skin. Afterward I'd check stills from the video captures and see a stranger. A necklace of bruises around her throat. A glaze in her bloodshot eyes.

But there was something else there, too. Ironically, in the pics where I looked most corpse-like there was a flash of fury, of desperation. Of life.

Blue didn't attend those shows. I looked for his name, or a variation. Someone called cyan_of_doma lurked one night but when I googled it, I got some video game character. Ellis would've recognized the reference. *Never heard of* Final Fantasy VI? *You need some culture, Vada. Staring at paintings all day will rot your brain.*

She came and went to the house but I never ran into her. Mutual avoidance.

"Everything all right?" Frankie said, checking in on me.

"Yep."

"Jasmine says you've been doing breath play all day. Take a break."

"I'm fine."

"It's not a request, Morgan."

So I turned off my cam and lay in lukewarm water in the bathtub, testing how long I could stay under.

The thing about not breathing is no one tells you how addictive it is. That tingling rush, the buzz in every neuron as they eat through oxygen stores and reach for more and find nothing. It feels like a billion minuscule teeth digging into your brain. A shimmering wave of needle pricks starting in your lungs and skittering up your brain stem like a silvery centipede and spreading over your whole scalp, numbing you like a drug.

Yes, I was in love with my best friend. So fucking what.

That's all in the past.

We fell apart. Broke each other's hearts and screwed up our friendship. Now I'm adrift, unmoored without her. I keep treading water, looking for land. All I can see is endless blue.

People knocked on the door, calling, "Morgan? Are you okay?"

But they didn't really mean *Are you okay.* They meant *Should we call 911. Should we find someone whose job it is to care. Who gets paid for it.*

What a strange world where we pay people to listen to our problems, and pay them to fuck themselves while we watch, and pay them to save us.

Three days after the kiss, he came back. No private message. The email arrived first: **SoBlue has sent you $1,000 USD.** When the chat request followed I hit ACCEPT immediately, and didn't even mind that it felt like a life preserver tossed to someone drowning.

————

SoBlue: hi.

I stared at the black feed on his side for a while. Then I typed, **Morgan is thinking . . .**

SoBlue: what is she thinking about?

Morgan: everything

Morgan: my stupid fucking life

Morgan: how I hurt everyone I love

Morgan: how I've wanted to talk to you again

Morgan: and how sad that is

SoBlue: why is it sad?

Morgan: you only said hi once

Morgan: you're not as excited as me

SoBlue: you have no idea how many times i've jerked off to you these past three days.

SoBlue: it's downright superheroic.

I rolled my eyes, but smiled, too.

SoBlue: i've thought about you. incessantly.

SoBlue: analyzed every word i said to you.

SoBlue: edited the script in my head so i sound much smoother.

SoBlue: in my version it ends with me saying i want you.

SoBlue: but i want a connection first.

SoBlue: any two people can get each other off.

SoBlue: i want it to mean something.

SoBlue: for both of us.

This guy. He wanted to know me as a person and I just wanted to use him. Like we'd flipped roles.

Morgan: sorry I got defensive last time

Morgan: I've been on edge these days

SoBlue: i like that you're prickly.

SoBlue: it's real.

Morgan: what do you want to do tonight, Blue?

SoBlue: just talk.

SoBlue: tell me why you're on edge.

I sat back with my legs crossed. Still in shorts and a sleeveless tee. "Are you a shrink in real life?"

SoBlue: not even close.
SoBlue: but i'm a good listener.

"Okay. I'm prickly because I've been . . . fighting. With my best friend. Things are weird between us. They've always been weird, honestly, but sometimes it gets more . . . intense. This is intentionally vague." I narrowed my eyes at the cam. "I can't let you into my real life. You know that. It's a safety thing."

SoBlue: i can read it in your face.
SoBlue: you look like you're battling something.

"Pretty observant for someone who's not a shrink."

SoBlue: i can't help it when it comes to you.
SoBlue: i drink in every detail.
SoBlue: what are you and your friend fighting about?

"It's hard to explain. She wants me to be someone I'm not sure I am. She doesn't realize how scary that is for me."

SoBlue: have you told her you're scared?

"Kind of." I frowned. "Well. Okay. No."

SoBlue: well. okay. why not?

"It's complicated. Her parents were horrible to her. She's really struggled to accept herself." Great, here I was defending Ellis to Blue. "I'm scared of facing the same thing. My mom loves me, but not this part of me. She wanted me to be something else."

SoBlue: what did she want you to be?

"A princess. The Disney kind."

SoBlue: but you turned out to be a rebel princess.
SoBlue: like leia.

"God, you and Elle would get along so well." I caught my mistake too late—her real name. Idiot. Divert him. "You don't have to do this, you know. Send me huge amounts of money. I like talking to you. You can pay the normal private rate."

SoBlue: how romantic.
SoBlue: run away with me.

I laughed. "Why money, by the way? You're the first rich guy who just sends me cash."

SoBlue: various reasons.
SoBlue: for one, you deserve it.
SoBlue: you work hard.

"Taking my clothes off isn't hard work."

SoBlue: no.
SoBlue: letting yourself be vulnerable in front of strangers is hard work.
SoBlue: what you're doing is a type of performance art.

I laughed again, darkly.

SoBlue: i'm serious.
SoBlue: the other reason it's cash is because you're not a child.
SoBlue: those men who dress you like a doll are afraid of you.
SoBlue: they're afraid of women.
SoBlue: your sexual power over them.
SoBlue: they want to control you.
SoBlue: i want to free you.

"You do, huh? Like Han Solo freeing Leia from being a sex slave?"

SoBlue: that analogy is impressively on point.

"Yet here I am, your captive instead of theirs."

SoBlue: you don't have to be here.

"Taking payment without rendering service is unprofessional."

SoBlue: i'm not paying for service.
SoBlue: and i don't care about the money.
SoBlue: spend it. donate it to charity.
SoBlue: it's yours.

"Come on. Nobody's that selfless. Even altruism is motivated by some kind of subconscious self-interest."

SoBlue: i thought my ulterior motive was obvious.

"Enlighten me."

SoBlue: if you're talking to me, you're not talking to anyone else.
SoBlue: you're all mine.

I shivered. "So it *is* about control. You want me all to yourself."

SoBlue: i'm not noble.
SoBlue: i don't want anyone else looking at you this way.

"How are you looking at me, Blue?"

SoBlue: like nothing else exists.
SoBlue: like i'd tear the world down just to touch you.

In my head, I saw him. Leaning over his laptop, the cool glow tracing his jaw, the skein of tension running along it.

And I felt guilty, that this lonely guy had fixated on this unavailable girl.

So I did what I do best.

"Listen, this is fun, but I have personal rules about clients.

I don't get involved. This is my job." I shrugged. "I cam for other men. I get off with them. I'm not yours. The only person I belong to is me."

It was pure bravada, but the more I sold it to him the more I could sell it to myself. I didn't need anybody else. Not Ellis, not anyone.

SoBlue: i believe you want that to be true.
SoBlue: but part of you wants to belong to someone.
SoBlue: and i want it to be me.

"You're paying me, Blue. I'm performing for you. It's an act. I'm an actress."

SoBlue: it's never real?

"Sometimes I fantasize to get in the mood. Like method acting. But that's just . . . mental lube. It's an aid, not genuine."

SoBlue: do i make you feel anything real, morgan?

My breathing sped up. I stared at the screen for a moment, then typed.

Morgan: this feels different
Morgan: you're different
SoBlue: how?
Morgan: you don't demand I get you off
Morgan: you don't pose me like a doll
Morgan: but I still feel how much you want me
Morgan: it's infuriating
Morgan: you're the biggest clit tease ever
SoBlue: how poignant.
SoBlue: two sexually unfulfilled people, torturing each other.
SoBlue: dancing around it dizzyingly.
Morgan: you're a sadistic bastard

Morgan: what are you getting out of this?
SoBlue: i want to see how long you can go.
Morgan: until what?
SoBlue: until you beg me to fuck you.

I pushed back from the keyboard, riled. "I have the power. *You're* paying *me*."

SoBlue: you're right.
SoBlue: let's try shifting the balance.

"What does that mean?"

SoBlue: it means this.
SoBlue: you have your money.
SoBlue: enjoy your night.
SoBlue left the room.
Session ended. Total: 35:44.

———

I stared at the screen for a good minute after he logged off, dumbstruck.

Then I started to laugh.

You sweet, sadistic bastard.

My night was mine.

This week of literal wallowing meant my room was a sty of dirty clothes and lowball glasses sticky with whiskey like caramel. Time to clean. I opened the windows to let the night breeze in, heady with brine and rust, elemental. Starlight winked on the water like fish scales. On my way back from the laundry room my foot hit something crinkly on the attic steps.

A bag of gummy bears. No note.

Ellis.

I clutched it to my chest, my heart going fast.

Max was digging into the accident reports. He didn't believe my story. He'd tried to talk to Elle alone, knowing she'd buckle without me to guard her back.

If he went after her again, he'd find me square in his path.

Our last meeting played over in my mind. The gun, and his hands on my body. He wanted closure. Maybe he wanted something else, too.

That gun, though.

Why had it been in police evidence? Why did Ryan have it that night?

Something happened, something Max wouldn't tell me. Something that made him feel like a bad father.

For the first time since the accident, I googled Ryan Vandermeer.

When people die today they don't disappear, leaving only their best legacies, their highlight reel. Now we leave behind an epic mess of the mundane. Drunk texts. Offensive Facebook comments. Dick pics. Hate memes. All the splintery, slimy flotsam of a life, the stuff that used to be swept out to sea when we died, forgotten.

Now it remains. And you can collect it like driftwood and piece together a life.

Did you know your son was depressed, Max?

Ryan's Twitter didn't contain much. Mainly he retweeted others, but the retweets were telling: angsty lyrics, moody black-and-white photos. Quotes about self-loathing and despair.

His Twitter name matched a Tumblr full of photos.

I recognized Maine: long, empty roads running naked to the ocean. Pines so still they looked almost fake, painted in. Profound silence in those photos, a strangled, breathless quiet.

Over time he switched from landscapes to macro shots: broken bottles glinting in the weeds, bullet holes peppering a road sign. Rust so thick you couldn't tell what it had once been eating: a railroad spike, a chain link, a key.

Body parts.

Hands at first: lithe and long-fingered, rivered with veins. Gripping, clenching. Fists. Then the arms, and then the cuts in the arms, thin hashes from wrists to elbows, bright red ribbons against white skin.

His skin.

Boys who self-harm are at a higher risk of suicide than girls, because cutting is seen as a "girl problem." We expect boys to lash out and girls to turn inward, on ourselves. Gendered violence. We ignore the signs in boys, more worried that they'll bring a gun to school, or refuse a girl's *no*.

I saw a pain boiling so deeply not even cutting himself open relieved the pressure.

Artists were no strangers to self-harm. Van Gogh sliced his ear off. Petr Pavlensky's whole career revolved around self-mutilation: he sawed through his earlobe, sewed his mouth shut, nailed his balls to the ground. In a way, tattooing was similar: a rite of pain that forever altered the body, our skin a living canvas. My scars were called "art." Ryan's scars were just scars.

He'd captioned some of his photos with fragments of thoughts, feelings.

who am i
i don't recognize myself
all i see is a stranger

And the most telling, and most cryptic:

there's a bomb inside me, waiting to explode

There was something wrong with Ryan before Ryan ever got in that car. And Max was trying to hide it. Shift the guilt to someone else. If he found a scapegoat, he'd pounce in a heartbeat.

I knew this because I knew he was like me. Expert blame deflectors. Masters of denial.

And he was eyeing Ellis as a potential target.

If he thought I'd let that happen, he had no idea who I was.

You can fight for your ghost, Max, but I'll go down fighting for mine.

———

I peered into the green gloom, then pushed the door open and called, "Burglar here. Anyone home?"

A ruff of ginger hair poked up from the loft bed. There was something of the *O RLY?* owl in Elle's just-woke-up face.

"Rise and shine, little bird." I lifted the bag. "Breakfast."

Suspicious squint. Her head disappeared.

I'd set the coffee table and sat on the floor by the time Ellis climbed down, all bedhead and confusion, wearing only a tee and men's tight undershorts. So disarmingly cute. She eyed the food, then me, with astonishment.

"What is this?"

"Bagels and lox and Americanos. Sit."

"Where'd you get it?"

"Hiked up to the café." I offered her a paper cup. "Olive branch?"

"Vada, you don't have to—"

My bad hand wavered. The cup began to tilt and she took it just in time.

Goddammit. I couldn't even apologize right.

"Okay," Ellis said softly. "Olive branch accepted."

We ate in silence while the sun rose, a line of Day-Glo orange torching the horizon. Sunlight streamed through the leaves like stained glass, dappling the cabin with patches of rose and gold. Smoked salmon melting on my tongue. Wood creaking in the breeze. It calmed me, the smallness and peace of this moment. We'd had so many moments like this, me and her. A breakfast spent sitting quietly in the sun. A smile from a train window that stuck with me all day. They gathered in my mind, bright grains of sand shoring up against a dark wave.

As we finished our coffee I said, "I want to show you something."

I sat beside her on the couch. She shifted her bare leg away from mine.

"There's some stuff we didn't know about Ryan. Stuff that might be important." I switched my phone on. "These will be hard to look at, but I need you to."

I showed her his photos. The tame ones first. Then the bloody ones.

Ellis covered her mouth.

"He was a cutter," I said. "This was going on for months, at least."

She stared at the screen. "Do you think he was trying to kill himself that night? Like, intentionally drunk driving?"

"I don't know. But some weird shit's happening here."

Our gazes flickered toward each other. Then she touched me, briefly, tracing the heart of my palm. Just once, but it lingered in my skin like the buzz of a tattoo needle.

"There's something else," she said. "Tell me."

"Promise you won't get mad." Before she could consent, I said, "I've been going to see Max these past few months."

Her mouth fell and I realized how it sounded.

"Not like that. Nothing skeezy."

"But why at all? Vada, what are you doing?"

"I needed someone to talk to. And so did he. His girlfriend left him; he rarely sleeps. He just works on his boat or sits around obsessing." I looked away from her face, self-conscious. "I could relate."

"I see. All that time I was texting you, begging you to respond, and you were talking to *him*."

I thought of Blue. "Sometimes it's easier to talk to a stranger."

"Well, I'm glad you found somebody." Her voice was dry and cool. She stood and paced away from me. "What have you been *talking* about?"

I almost snapped, *What about you and whoever's in your house?*, but the absurdity stopped me. She'd said she hadn't moved on. When we'd kissed, I believed it.

"Nothing important. Until last time, when he unveiled those reports. Elle, he's going to find things that'll cause trouble for us."

"What things?"

"Discrepancies." A beach-glass dreamcatcher hung from the branch above us, and when the sun shot through, it sprinkled our skin with aqua confetti, like sea spray. "But there are discrepancies in his story, too. The last time I was there he had a gun."

"Oh my god."

"He didn't threaten me. But he said strange stuff. Ryan had the gun the night he died, and the police took it. Then Max said he was a bad father and clammed up."

Elle frowned, spooling her bangs around one finger.

"It's weird, right?" I said. "Why would they take the gun?"

"Criminal evidence."

"But there were no charges in the accident."

"Maybe he'd already used it. Or planned to."

We stared at each other, our minds whirring.

"Something happened to Ryan," I said. "Before that night. All of this points to something really bad."

"What does it have to do with us?"

"Max won't let this go. Trust me, I know him. He has nothing but this. He'll obsess." Just like me, obsessing over what's gone. "He'll keep digging till he finds closure. And if he does, I could go to jail."

"Why?"

"I lied to the police, Elle."

She sank to the couch, eyes wide and imploring. "Tell me exactly what happened that night."

"You weren't driving, I promise."

"Don't lie for me."

"I'm not."

She was holding on to a breath, scared to let go. "I remember things, sometimes. Little pieces come back at random. Vada, I remember getting in the driver's seat."

I put my hand on her knee, and she didn't pull away. "You did. But I made you get out."

"Is that our story, or the truth?"

"Both." My palm slid higher, unambiguously. "Art is a lie, remember? And all communication is art. We're never entirely honest. It's not possible."

"Do you really believe nothing's honest?"

"This is. Feeling." The heat of her skin drew at mine. My hand ran up her thigh to the hem of her tight boxers. "I missed you, Ellis. So much. *Eres mi todo.*"

You're my everything.

Her eyes half closed. "Don't start with the Spanish."

"Why not?"

"Your voice gets this little growl in it. Like a cat."

I gave her my best Cheshire grin. "*Esta gata te quiere, pajarito.*"

On a sun-scoured L train platform in Chicago, the concrete reflecting heat like foil, three Latinos hassled a girl, talking loudly in Spanish about the "red birdie" and flicking their tongues at her and meowing. She got the gist. She clutched her messenger bag to her knees, trying to hide her long bare legs.

*I walked up to the group of guys, smiling. "Hey," I called.
"Hola."*

*The ringleader, handsome, all stubble and sharp jawline,
smiled back.*

"¿Qué tal, mami?"

"Déjala tranquila o te arrancaré los cojones, cabrón," *I
said.*

*His eyes bugged. His friends burst into laughter, wild and
yipping. He hustled them away, elbowing them when they glanced
back at us.*

*The redhead gave me a quizzical smile. "Thanks, I think.
What did you say?"*

"Just told him to leave you alone."

She seemed dubious. I sat beside her on the bench.

"We have a class together," I said. "I'm Vada."

The girl stuck her hand out. "Ellis."

I looked at it, laughed, shook. "Got a business card?"

*"Oh, sorry. Not on me. But I can give you my—" Then she saw
my face and blushed. "You're making fun."*

*I laughed again, warmer, and she lowered her gaze shyly, but
a smile crept over her lips. Her face had an elfin androgyny, fey
lines filled in with a soft bloom of watercolor. Orange-red hair
raked around her face like flames. She was tall and reedy, sylvan.
Instantly I was dying to draw her.*

"What did you actually say to that guy?"

"'Leave her alone or I'll rip your balls off, asshole.'"

Ellis's mouth dropped.

"Think he got the message?" I said.

*"Yeah. Probably. Jeez." She laughed, fluting and sweet. "Can
you teach me that? How to swear in Spanish?"*

I grinned. "Sí, mi pajarito rojo."

"What does that mean? What you just said."

"I'll tell you, but you have to promise me something."

Her eyes flashed, nervous, thrilled. "What?"

"Let me draw you."

(—Bergen, Vada. *My Little Red Bird.*
Watercolor and ink on paper.)

Ellis framed my face with her hands. "Why did you leave last time?"

"It was too intense." I combed my fingers into her hair, leaning closer. "But when I was alone I couldn't breathe. Everything feels like drowning except you. You're my oxygen."

"We have to talk about this. For real."

"Can we not and pretend we did?"

"Yeah, sure. Because normal people talk about their relationship, and we're obviously not—"

I cut her off with a kiss.

It was light, halting, because I wasn't sure it was okay, only that looking at her made my chest ache, made me feel the stark hollowness in my lungs, that place where I was unfilled. But once her mouth was on mine, warm silk parting against my lips, I was certain. This was right. This was air and light and life. I pushed her against the couch, kissing her harder. My hair tangled across my eyes and my knee slid between hers and I wanted every inch of our skin to touch, to totally connect. Her legs tightened around my thigh. She pulled me close but held my face, stopping. Ran her fingers against my mouth. I kissed them, felt her heart slamming like a sledge beneath mine.

"What are we doing?" she whispered.

"Not fighting it anymore."

"Not like this, Vada. I want this, but it has to be real. And you're not ready."

"You started it last time."

She slipped out from under me and got to her feet. Flushed, palms upraised. "Let's call a truce."

I sat up calmly. "A kissing truce?"

"An everything truce. Tabula rasa. Start over."

"We can never really start over, Elle."

She turned solemn. "Well, let's try. Let's be friends for now, and see if we can even get along."

"I thought you wanted more."

"I do. But not the way it was. We have to do better."

At that moment I just wanted the old us. I wanted to go back to how things were before that night. When we went to art exhibits and comic cons, rode trains across the city so we could sit shoulder to shoulder and scuff our sneakers and talk, moved in together because not seeing each other every day was unbearable. Then we hooked up with people we didn't love so we could break up and console each other, cuddle on the couch in pajamas and watch Netflix all day, as friends. Just friends. The pretense wore thinner until one day, we stopped pretending. Then we were best friends with benefits.

That was my naivete. There was a reason it didn't work out.

"Okay." I stood and cupped her shoulders. "Just friends. But you're still my prince, always."

The look in her eyes made me shiver. It seemed so sad.

We couldn't really go back to square one. Couldn't undo our closeness. It was mixed-up forever, one part friendship, one part something else. So I put my arms around her, and though she stiffened she let me hug her, then returned the embrace, softening. No words needed. Just her head on my shoulder, and her cheek to my cheek, and her heart against mine.

-7-

No sign of Blue for days. It bothered me more than I cared to admit.

I idled in my chat room, half-assing a striptease, waiting for him. These other guys with their monotonous, simplistic needs began to bore me. *Show me your pussy. Pull the tie tighter. Moan my name when you pretend to come.* So mundane. I felt like an animal in a cage being stared at by other animals, all of us anonymous, mindless, interchangeable.

I used to take comfort in the mindlessness. In switching my brain off and going to town. Now I zoned out, thinking of a boy who made me feel different. Who made me laugh and feel smart and sexy and irresistible. He wanted to fuck me, but he wanted my mind, too, in a way that was both unsettling and exhilarating. These other guys didn't come close.

My viewer count dipped. They sensed my disinterest.

Finally I logged off and went downstairs. Ellis sat alone in the dining room, the pale blaze of her laptop painting only her face and hands, like some apparition reaching out of the darkness. I touched her and her knees banged the table.

"I need your help, spaz," I said.

"With what?"

"Reconnaissance."

She squinted. "Is this about Max?"

"Nothing gets past that big brain of yours. Come be lookout while I poke around."

"Inside his *house*?"

"Objections?"

"He has a gun. You don't break into the house of a gun owner."

"He's not going to shoot us. I'd bet my life on it." I squeezed her shoulder. "Max is looking into those reports for a scapegoat. He doesn't want it to be a suicide—he wants to blame someone else."

And he knows, I thought. That I'm holding a secret.

But so was he. If I found his out first, maybe I could keep mine.

Elle's brow creased.

"Just trust my gut on this," I said.

In the skiff she tried to convince me to turn back. I rowed steadily, ignoring her protests. But a few hundred feet out, my right arm lit up like a live wire and I had to stop and grit my teeth and listen to Ellis count my breaths. *In, hold. Out, hold.* I bit the inside of my cheek to keep from crying, filled my mouth with the sweet tang of pennies. Don't see me like this, I thought. Don't see me diminished.

Then we sat side by side and rowed in tandem. Somehow, it was perfect: my strength, her dexterity, our hands and hearts falling into one rhythm.

Peaks Island rose before us, a black skull protruding from vexed water. Whitecaps skittered over the surface like agitated thoughts, swelling, smashing, dissolving into sizzling foam. Off in the distance lighthouses trailed skeleton fingers across the sky. We dragged the skiff up the shore over seashells and glassy pebbles. Something bolted through the trees, a zipper of noise ripping through the underbrush and dying as abruptly as it began. We stared at each other, the whites of our eyes glowing palely.

"Just an animal," I whispered.

In the woods she took my hand. The darkness had that hallucinatory Ernst quality where shadows swirled and twisted and everything became a face if you looked at it too closely. Elle's hummingbird pulse fluttered against my palm.

We split up at the house. I called her phone and left the line open.

"There's a light on." I circled to the west. "First floor. Living room, I think. Try to look in from the porch."

"Okay."

"Car's here. So's the boat. He's either inside or on foot."

Scrapes and creaks from the phone. "Laptop in the living room. But I don't see him now."

"Stake it out. Maybe he went to the bathroom."

"Okay." Her voice was breathy, nervous.

Max's forty-foot cruiser yacht stood parked on a trailer behind the garage. I climbed the stern ladder and monkey-walked down the gunwale till I reached the garage roof. Then I scrambled up the shingles, fingertips skidding over asphalt tiles. Below me the ceiling timber moaned. I crouched beneath a second-story window.

"Vada? You okay?"

"Yep. How's the stakeout?"

"No sign of him yet." She paused and I heard the frown in her voice. "There's something weird about . . ."

I set the phone down on the windowsill, dug my nails beneath the frame, and heaved. Pain fired up my shoulder like a gunshot. Grimace. Breathe. Again.

". . . sort of creepy. Maybe we should . . ."

Again. The frame screeched.

"Vada? Are you there?"

Finally the sash flew upward, rattling. I snatched my phone and slipped into the house. "Sorry. Putting you on speaker. Be quiet a sec." I flicked on the flashlight app.

Before me was a teenage boy's bedroom: captain's bed with tartan quilt, a row of baseball caps on pegs, band posters—Queens of the Stone Age, alt-J. Wicker hamper frothing over with dirty clothes.

Going on eight months, and Max still hadn't touched them.

I snapped pics, then went to the desk.

"Vada—"

"Shhh." Ryan's phone was nowhere to be seen. In a drawer I found a laptop with a sliver of charge left. I flipped it open but it asked for a password. Of course. Two accounts populated the log-in list: Ryan and Skylar. "Elle, can you get files off a hard drive if the laptop asks for a password?"

"Yes, probably. But listen, there's something—"

Her voice was too loud in the stillness. I turned off speaker-phone. "Hold on a second."

Quick search of other drawers: no phone, no photos, nothing but school notebooks and assigned paperbacks. Max had already gone through it all.

"Can you hear me? Vada?"

"What's up?"

"We have to go. Where are you?"

I tilted my head, listening. Feeling the darkness. Tasting it. Stagnant summer air, vibrating with suppressed energy, like the inside of a hive. "Second floor. Ryan's room."

"Get out. Get out of the house *now*."

The skin on my back stretched canvas-tight. "Why?"

"His laptop. It's showing webcam feeds. There are cams all over the house. *He's watching us.*"

Through the floors, the buzzing air, I sensed the shift of weight. Of movement.

I tucked the laptop under my arm and ran for the window, floorboards squealing under my heels. Then I was outside and sliding down the shingles, kicking tiles loose, chips flying, skin grating off my ankles and knees. At the roof's edge I leaped, blind, onto the boat below. I struck the hull and buckled and rolled over the prow, hitting the ground hard, but kept rolling, absorbing the shock. The laptop spun across the dirt. Hands gripped my shoulders and I clawed at them wildly.

"It's me, it's me."

Elle hauled me to my feet. I fetched the laptop and kept running for the trees.

We crashed through the brush and froze, stumbling together. Ellis put her hands on me. Shadows stirred around us, black dye swirling in darkest violet.

"Did he see us come to the house?" I said.

"I don't know. What did you take?"

"A laptop."

"Great. Grand larceny."

"Worry about it later." Below my knees I felt a crawling, festering heat, abrasions meeting air. "We need to get out of here."

This time she took my hand and led me through the woods. When I stumbled she caught me, braced an arm around my waist. We skirted lit houses. At the shore she pushed the skiff out solo and made me get in to avoid the salt. Then she shucked her button-up shirt and tossed it to me.

"Clean those cuts. I'll row for a bit. The current's with us."

"Ellis—"

"Come on. While I've still got adrenaline."

She made good on her word, taking us out swiftly. She rowed till her arms trembled, her hair and tank top pasted to her skin, gluey with sweat. Red strands trickled over her temple like blood. Once we cleared Peaks she let the oars collapse. For a while we drifted, the water enameled with starlight and hurling itself at the hull before shattering like ornaments, jet and chrome disintegrating into glitter.

I joined her for the final leg, and when we finally reached the shore of Chebeague we were both exhausted and silent. We glanced at the beach house, shook our heads. Staggered through the trees to the big oak. In her kitchen she boiled water and I let her clean me up because looking at the peppery flecks of asphalt ground into my skin made me dizzy. Memories surged to the surface like kicked-up sediment. The reek of gasoline and tequila. Headlights splintering the rearview. Glass and bone sticking through human meat.

"Vada," Elle said, "stop looking. Drink this."

Vodka, crisp and icy as glacier runoff. I gulped it down and felt like I'd swallowed a frozen sword. It soothed me.

The abrasions weren't that bad. I was being a baby. It was just tough to look at my own blood. I kept thinking, What will I lose this time?

Ellis dropped sopping crimson towels in the sink without batting an eyelash, like some wartime nurse.

"You're sort of a badass," I murmured.

"You're sort of crazy. But brave."

"Recklessness isn't brave."

"Recklessness makes you act. Bravery is following through."

We eyed each other a moment, thinking of other things. Other times I hadn't been brave.

She left to fetch supplies from the beach house. I drank more vodka and thought about how a man with a gun scared me less than telling my mother I'd fallen for my best friend.

Ellis returned with clean clothes, spare hard drives, and a plan.

"I'm going to clone the data from Ryan's laptop. Then we're putting it back. Well, I'm putting it back. While he's out of the house. You have a different role."

"What's my role?"

She eyed me grimly. "You're the decoy."

———

I stayed the night at Elle's. By tacit agreement—I glanced at the couch; she pulled some pillows down from her loft bed—I curled up and let her work in the kitchen while I dozed, fuzzy-brained and lead-limbed with vodka. Sometime in the wee hours my phone pinged with an email.

> thinking of you. like i do every night.
>
> you and your friend.
>
> i'm jealous of her.
>
> of anyone who sees you off cam.
>
> anyone who touches you.
>
> i think about your skin. obsessively.
>
> i want to be inside it, like your ink.
>
> and deeper.
>
> i want to feel you. i want to fill you.
>
> are you thinking of me, morgan?
>
> —blue.

of fucking course I am, I began, then realized sending it from my phone would reveal my IP, my geolocation, and I trashed it.

I peeked over the couch. Ellis sat on a kitchen stool, shoulders hunched, working on the laptop. Candleglow bled through her seersucker shirt as if she wore a fairy wing, turned the flyaway wisps of her hair into little filaments of electric light. Guilt churned in my gut, hot and queasy.

Here I was, thinking filthy thoughts about my Internet crush, while Prince Ellis, my real friend and maybe-whatever, sat ten feet away, fixing my mistakes.

Vada Emery Bergen, scumbaggiest friend ever.

In the morning I found Elle sprawled across the counter, sleeping. I tucked her in on the couch. She struggled to speak through yawns.

"Max is meeting me for lunch," I said. "You've got time. Go back to sleep."

Most of my abrasions were superficial and already scabbed over, ruby filigree lacing my skin. The worst I'd suffered was a plum-black bruise on one thigh. In the kink camworld, bruises and scabs were commonplace.

I sat beside Ellis and brushed her hair from her eyes. "Poor tired thing."

She mumbled something unintelligible.

In another lifetime, I'd have grabbed my notebook and pencils and sketched her. The sleeping prince in her forest cottage. Now I could only trace her bones with my fingers, etch the lines in memory.

Recuerdo, el corazón.

I kissed her forehead and left.

Max had responded to my text with a time and place in the Old Port. I took the ferry to the mainland. On the way over, I watched the waves.

Ellis explained to me once how light is both a particle and a wave. Think of what happens if you drop pebbles in water, she said. Their ripples overlap. Some cancel out, some double up. Colliding ripples create an interference pattern, a dizzying web. But light was both the pebble *and* the wave. It was a point and also a probability. The same way she was both a friend and more than a friend and when we collided, we made an interference pattern.

The Old Port on a late-summer morning: fishing boats thronging the wharf, nets full of sun-sequined bass and traps swarming with lobsters, all those feelers and claws writhing, insectile. Cooks haggled with fisherfolk and threw live animals into trucks. The air was so wet and briny it seemed obscene. Like if I dabbed at it with my tongue, it'd be a lewd act. I loved Portland like this: rough hands dredging up shellfish and clams and all the weird pale meat of the ocean, that bizarre underworld spilling into the hard sun. Tourists flooding on and off ferries, the water a perfect Yves Klein blue. I sat on an iron stanchion and watched the catch come in, listened to the thud and slap of meaty tails on the dock.

Capturing this used to be my life. All those nights I'd stayed up while my hand cramped, my shoulder a ball of agony, feverishly drawing because a vision was in me and would not forfeit possession of my body till it had emptied every last demon ounce of itself through my fingers—gone. Now all I could do was take a photo, flat and hyperreal, devoid of imperfection, of guts and pain and nerve. Of me.

I got to the café early and chose a corner seat.

Max arrived soon after, and while he stood in a hot white bar of sun at the door, I stared. He wore a tailored summer suit sans tie. His tan turned his eyes searing blue.

"Vada," he said warmly. "You look beautiful. May I?"

I nodded, not trusting my voice. He sat and ordered two beers, smiling the whole time.

"It's funny," he said, rolling up his shirt cuffs. "I was about to ask you to dinner. You beat me to the punch."

"This isn't a date."

"Date?" His smile turned patronizing. "You're a bit young for me."

"I wasn't too young the other night."

He held my gaze. "I'm sorry about that. I crossed a line."

"What line?"

"We're friends. I'd like to keep it that way."

"Friends don't secretly record each other, Max."

"Friends don't break into each other's houses, either."

Well, shit.

The waitress set two sweating amber bottles on the table. Max raised a toast.

"To a beautiful day, and a beautiful woman with her whole life ahead of her."

The bottle shook in my hand. I put it down without sipping.

Max watched me as he drank, his eyes glimmering like the sea refracting sun. I waited till the waitress took our orders before I began.

"Look. I thought we *were* actually friends, Max. I opened up to you. Trusted you. Was this whole thing some sick game? How long have you been recording me?"

"A few months."

Nausea twisted in my belly. "Why?"

"First, it's a home security system. I have a lot of valuable assets on my property."

"Why were you recording me?"

He reached across the table. When his hand covered mine I was so shocked I let him. Light touch, but enveloping.

"This may sound strange, and I don't expect you to understand. But when you're around, I feel like a parent again, in some ways. As if my life isn't so pointless."

"Parents don't record their kids for jerk-off material."

His hand lifted. "It's nothing like that. All I wanted was to hear your voice." His eyes drifted past me. "It's good to hear a familiar voice sometimes. The house is so quiet now."

Our food arrived. I felt too unsettled to eat, but made myself take a bite of the lobster roll. Tangy lemon butter, sweet meat breaking on my tongue. Memories flooded back. When we first came to Maine, Elle and I had gone on a lobster roll rampage, trying them at every diner we could find. She made a chart and graded them. Such a nerd. I teased her, and sketched her in ballpoint on napkins stained with Saturn rings of ale. She saved the napkins. She saved every sketch I ever did of her.

"Are you that vain?" I said, mocking.

"I'm fascinated by the way you see me."

"How is that, pajarito?"

She spun the napkin around. "Look."

It was a quick thumbnail sketch, the shadows hatched with tiny crosses. Her head turned in profile, her short hair and sharp jaw making her boyish.

"When you draw me, your hand sees this. But your eyes see something different."

"What does that mean?" I said, but she took the napkin and pressed it into her notebook, leaving me in the booth, bewildered.

(—Bergen, Vada. *Nighthawks in Maine.*

Ink on paper.)

Max sipped his beer and said, "You stole Ryan's laptop."

"Don't know what you're talking about."

By the time he got home, it'd be back as if we'd never touched it.

"I won't press charges. Maybe Ellis can crack the password." He smiled. "I'm not good with technology. I'm a mechanical guy. I understand moving parts."

"I really don't have the slightest idea what—"

"You've always been candid, Vada. I admire that." He sloshed the beer in his bottle. "Don't put on a show for me."

Those words. Those words didn't belong in his mouth.

"Listen," I said, "I came here to tell you I'm not okay with this shit. I don't care what you do to me, just leave Ellis alone. She doesn't remember the accident. If you have questions, you ask me. But my answers aren't going to change."

"I don't want to question you. I want to protect you."

"Huh?"

"I was in your shoes once. Someone lied to me about something very important. It destroyed my world."

"What are you talking about?"

Max reclined in his chair, sighing. "Vada, ask yourself why you're defending a liar."

I blinked.

"Tell me your girlfriend's full name."

"I don't have a girlfriend," I said automatically.

"Okay, 'friend.' What's her full name? Humor me, please."

"Ellis Morgan Carraway. Why are you—"

" 'Ellis Morgan Carraway' didn't exist until five years ago. There isn't a single record of her."

Heat rose in me. "Now you're digging into her records?"

He crossed his arms. A whiff of cologne drifted toward me, cedars and sawdust. "If you were in my position, you would, too. You'd want to know everything about the last moments of your son's life."

"Her personal records have nothing to do with it."

"They have something to do with you, Vada. And the danger you're in."

"What danger? Are you going to sue us?"

"No one said anything about that. But listen to yourself." He cocked his head. "You instinctively defend her, instead of asking about the name. You're blind to it."

"To what?" I spit.

"Who she really is."

"This is ridiculous. Five years ago she was a minor. Of course there are no records."

"Not even a birth certificate."

"That means nothing. Her parents are religious zealots. They could've—"

"Who are her parents? Their full names."

I shifted in my chair. "Why are you asking me? This is all on Google."

"You don't know. You've never actually searched it, have you? You took her word." He spread his hands. "I hired an investigator in Chicago. Her father is Klaus Zoeller, her mother is Katherine Brennan. She has no blood relations named Carraway."

Adrenaline coursed through me, the cold tingle in my hands and feet making me feel invincible. Like I could tear the wooden table apart. "You hired someone to go after Elle. In what reality did you think I'd be okay with this?"

"I saw the signs. I knew you were blind to it, so I entertained a hunch. And I was right."

"This is betrayal, Max. You betrayed me. I'll fight tooth and nail before I let you touch her."

"Listen to yourself."

"You have nothing." I gripped the table's edge, feeling no pain in my right arm, for once. "You can't pin anything on her. You'll have to go through me first."

And I still had cards up my sleeve. Including the ace. My last resort.

"I'm not the threat, Vada," Max said softly. "Look at the big picture. Really look."

Again I thought of Elle spinning that sketch around, saying, *Look.*

"*Occam's razor,*" she said once, "*isn't exactly what people think. It doesn't say that the simplest solution is the correct one. It says that when you're making a guess about something, make the fewest assumptions possible.*"

Her favorite book was *The Great Gatsby*. For her eighteenth birthday she went to New York, to see where Nick Carraway and his friends had lived. To the libraries and museums, because she was a nerd. The Morgan was her favorite—it looked like something out of Harry Potter. And of course she went to Ellis Island, because obviously.

Obviously.

She'd made her name up.

"What's her real name?" I said.

"Why don't you ask her? And while you're at it, ask why she had a DUI charge under that name."

My mouth dropped.

We'd told each other everything. Every stupid little story, every pixel that made up the whole portrait. I felt it in my bones. I knew her, heart and soul.

Except the name she was born with, and this.

I fumbled a bill out of my wallet, slapped it on the table. "I have to go."

Max caught my elbow as I stood. Firm, but not painful.

"Think about what I said, Vada. I care about you. I don't want you to fall prey to a danger you refuse to see."

I dug my nails into his forearm. "Think about what *I* said. No one touches her. Not while I'm still breathing."

I left him there and stormed onto the street.

―――――――

The house on the promenade was dark, all the windows onyx mirrors, like laptop screens. Weeds knotted the lawn and the roses hedging the porch had grown feral and fangy, vaguely carnivorous. I got out of the cab and stared up at the second floor, hit hard with vertigo.

This used to be ours. Mine and hers.

meeting's over, I texted Ellis, and turned off my ringer.

The mailbox was stuffed with assorted spam and, for a Mr. Brandt Zoeller: a bill from a hospital in Naperville, Illinois; a letter from a Chicago law firm; a hunting magazine; gun and fishing catalogs.

Who the hell was Brandt Zoeller? Same last name as Elle's dad.

Was Brandt her brother? Cousin?

Why hadn't she told me about him?

My phone vibrated. I ignored it and padded down the porch steps and into the gangway.

"Occam's razor," I echoed. "That reminds me of Picasso's bulls. This series of sketches he drew. The first ones are very detailed, heavily shaded. You can see the strain of muscle in the bull's flanks, the hairs in its hide, the folds of fat. So much weight, so much palpability. Then the sketches become more abstract. Shadows dissolve. Three dimensions flatten to two. It becomes a cartoon bull, comical. And he keeps abstracting it further, to one dimension. To a wire skeleton. Just a few curves, a broad back and horns. And the crazy thing is, it still looks like a bull. It actually looks even more like a bull than the original because it's the essence of bullness. It's not a particular bull anymore but all of them. A symbol. A word in a brand-new language."

Simplify what you see until it's only bones, essence, soul. That's the only way to understand what something really is.

I climbed up the back porch, stepping rabbit-soft, and peeked in a window.

Hanging industrial lights, Expressionist lithographs, wireframe chairs. My touches. All still here. But now there was an army of beer bottles besieging the trash, a battered pair of men's running shoes. Crumbs dusting the table.

And in the hall, cutting against the periwinkle ocean haze, the silhouette of a man leaning out, gazing straight at me.

I froze dead.

"Emily?" he called in a deep voice.

Then he moved toward the door.

I stood there, mind racing. Meet him. Ask him: Who are

you? Who is she? Go behind her back on this, shatter the fragile chrysalis of trust we'd begun to rebuild.

Or let her tell me, on her own terms.

My phone buzzed. I jerked around and vaulted over the railing.

I ran madly through the yard, hopped the neighbor's fence, and scrambled through their garden to the alley. No backward glance to see if the man gave chase. On the brick paving I broke into a sprint and didn't stop till I was five blocks away.

Phone still buzzing.

"Hey."

"Finally." Elle sounded irked. "I've been calling forever. I'm at the ferry. Where are you?"

"Almost there. Sorry."

"Why are you out of breath?"

"Went for a run."

"Okay. Weird, but okay." Puzzlement, that lilting tone she took when she was trying to figure something out. "I'll wait for you."

I walked the last few blocks to cool down. Found her sitting on the pier, her hair ruffling in the hot breeze. I came up from behind and stood there a moment, watching her.

Who are you? I thought. Who is this stranger with my best friend's face?

I sat down, dizzy.

"There you are," Ellis said. "I was worried. Are you all right?"

"Fine. How'd your mission go?"

"Complete success. I jammed the cameras and put the laptop back. We've got a cloned drive, and he can't prove we stole it." She frowned. "You're quiet. Did something happen with Max?"

"No."

"Get any new info?"

You lied about your name. There's a strange man in your house.

"Nothing."

She tugged at a shoelace. Then she said, "Vada, were you on the promenade?"

"I ran by our old place."

She said nothing.

"Still renting it?"

"I sublet to someone." Her brow clouded. "You went to look, instead of asking me. You don't trust me."

My fists balled on the concrete. I couldn't hold it in. "You want to talk about trust? Okay. Why didn't you tell me about your DUI as a minor?"

Her eyes widened. "How do you know about that?"

"*That* is probably something you should've told me, Ellis."

Or should I say Emily? Emily Zoeller. Emily Brennan.

Whoever you are.

"It's not what you think. It was so stupid. God." She seemed about to cry. "I was like, sixteen. I drank one of those mini bottles of schnapps at a party. Then I drove someone home. Our taillight was out. I got pulled over and my friend made a scene, so the cop tested us both. I blew 0.01. But Illinois has a zero-tolerance policy for minors, so it counted as a DUI."

"That's all?"

"That's all." She eyed me sidelong. "How did you know?"

"Max told me. He's obsessed with us. He wants to know every little detail of our lives."

"Those records were sealed. How did he find out?"

"Online, probably. All it takes is one idiot blabbing on social media." And knowing your real name.

Ellis clutched her fists in her lap. "Maybe it's better that he knows. That all the truth comes out."

"What truth?"

"About that night."

"Don't get crazy ideas about confessing. You don't even remember it."

"But you do. You could tell him, Vada. I know I got behind the wheel."

I looked out at the water. "Why are you so eager to come clean? It's like there's something else on your conscience."

"Why are *you* so eager to protect me? It's like you're hiding something from both of us."

Clever little bird.

"Ellis." I turned my head. "We have to be honest with each other. About everything."

Sunlight flashed on the water like a blade slicing the tops off waves, bleeding liquid silver. Her pupils shrank and left only clear moss green. Her freckles were sun-dark, fetching. I knew her face so well. I'd never seen anything in it but sweetness, wonder, purity.

Now there was something else. When I looked at her through an artist's eyes, impartially, I saw it.

Fear.

"Remember saying you could trust me with anything? That you knew I'd never turn my back on you, no matter what?"

She nodded.

"Do you still trust me like that, Elle?"

She nodded again, slower.

"I trust you like that, too. There's nothing I'd keep from you." I breathed in, salt sharp in my throat. "There are some things I'm still trying to process. Things I haven't accepted myself. I can't talk about them yet. But there's no one I'd tell before you."

Her eyes skittered away from mine. "I have stuff like that, too."

"Promise me again. Promise we'll never turn our backs on each other."

"I promise, Vada."

"Ditto, Ellis."

No matter how many times I said her name, she didn't break. I wondered what would happen if I said *Emily*.

The ferry coasted up to the dock and we joined the people streaming on. We went to the top deck and stood against the rail, against the infinite blueness of sea and sky. The wind tore at our faces like fingers trying to pull away masks.

I put my hand on hers on the rail. Then she leaned into me, and I wrapped an arm around her, and we faced the salt spray and ruthless wind all the way home.

———

Ellis said it'd take a while to crack into the cloned drive. Time to kill.

I'd flaked out of work so much this week that one of my regulars sent a "breakup" email. The camworld is fickle, intense, and brutal. One day they love you; the next you're a "cum-guzzling gutterslut" who doesn't know the first thing about customer service and is "probably a dyke irl."

Do you ever wonder if porn creates a sense of entitlement in a certain type of person?

I don't wonder.

I had a tie in either hand, debating which color I should strangle myself with tonight—aubergine or pomegranate?—when my email pinged.

A thousand bucks.

Him.

———

"Hi, Blue."

I flopped onto a cloud of goose-down pillows. For the first time ever, I was camming from my real bed. Beside me the dormer window looked over the ocean and the spinning pulsar of a lighthouse, the firefly flares of ship signals. I'd slid the window open and a breeze flicked in, cool and ozonic, that smell of sparks that presaged rain.

> SoBlue: hi, you.
> SoBlue: this is somewhere new.
> SoBlue: where are you?

"My room. The part viewers don't see." I smiled cryptically. "You're the first."

> SoBlue: i'm a lucky boy.
> SoBlue: so this is where you sleep.
> SoBlue: gazing up at the night sky.

"It's like a planetarium." I tilted the screen to give him a better view, careful to avoid the photos on the wall. I'd tested lines of sight. I knew the safe zones. "The sky is so clear here, the stars looked etched in. Have you ever seen scratchboard art? It's cardstock that's been coated with black India ink and engraved with a stylus, so the drawing is all sharp white lines, like a woodcut. That's how it looks tonight. Etched." I stared through my reflection, the gold buds of Christmas lights in the rafters. "Is it nighttime where you are?"

> SoBlue: yes.

"So you're in the Western hemisphere."

> SoBlue: uh oh.
> SoBlue: she's getting warmer.
> SoBlue: soon there'll be a knock at my door.

"I'll show up prepared. Tie you up and torture you the way you've been torturing me."

SoBlue: by being winningly sincere and unbearably charming?

"And a total cock tease."

SoBlue: here's the fault in your plan:
SoBlue: i would greatly enjoy being tortured by you.

"I bet you would."

SoBlue: morgan.
SoBlue: hey.
SoBlue: you look sad tonight.
SoBlue: something's upset you.

I stared at the vacant rectangle of his cam as if it were human, a shadowed face, an extreme close-up of a pupil. As if at any second it would come alive and the vague thumbnail in my head—a blur of fingers, eyes glazed with cyan light—would become detailed, whole. Picasso's bull in reverse.

"Something I've been running from is beginning to catch up with me. And it might hurt somebody I care about."

SoBlue: your best friend.

"Yeah." I leaned back, sighing. "I just started scraping my life back together, and now it's falling apart again."

SoBlue: what kind of trouble are you in?

"Legal. Ethical. Moral."

SoBlue: that's a lot.
SoBlue: which one bothers you the most?

"Moral."

SoBlue: that's the one that really matters.
SoBlue: did you hurt someone, morgan?

The breeze whisked across my shoulders, and I shivered. "Yes."

SoBlue: intentionally?

"Depends who you're talking about. I hurt a lot of people. Him. And her. And me."

SoBlue: him?

"A bystander. Someone in the wrong place at the wrong time."

SoBlue: and "her" is your friend.

"Yeah. My friend." I laughed, faintly. "You can call her Red."

SoBlue: okay.
SoBlue: so you hurt the bystander, and red.
SoBlue: unintentionally.
SoBlue: because you were trying to hurt yourself.

I sat up, my spine ramrod straight. "I didn't say that."

SoBlue: morgan.
SoBlue: it's okay.

"It's not okay. That's not what I said. You're putting words in my mouth." Go on the offense. "Why are you fishing for info?"

SoBlue: because i can't stand seeing you sad, or afraid.
SoBlue: it tears at me inside.
SoBlue: i wish i could shoulder some of your burden.
SoBlue: let you rest for a while. breathe.

"I'm not some damsel in distress."

SoBlue: and i'm no prince come to save you.

"Good," I snapped back. "Because I've already got one of those."

SoBlue: do you?
SoBlue: strange.
SoBlue: you've never mentioned a man in your life.
SoBlue: never mentioned anyone else.
SoBlue: only red.

"There is no one else," I said impulsively. "It's her."

SoBlue: i thought so.

It felt oddly thrilling, to get it out. To him especially. I swept a hand through my hair, my tension draining.

SoBlue: tell me about her.
SoBlue: what is she like?

"Worried about your competition?"

SoBlue: didn't realize it was a contest.
SoBlue: i just want to know you.
SoBlue: and she's an important part of you.

I pressed a knuckle to my mouth, mulling. From the water came the eerie, mournful call of a loon, rising and bending into a haunting shriek at the stars. The call they made when searching for their mate.

"Be right back," I said.

I left the bed and pawed through a box beside my desk. When I returned I started to say something, then simply flipped open the sketchbook.

This was the last one from before the accident. Figure studies, but of only one figure. One pair of hands repeating again and again and consuming the book, an obsession, hazy sketches coalescing around them: a thin body draped in a bedsheet, the avian vertebrae, the slender crane neck. That rake of hair catching and burning the light in a thousand angel-fine fuses.

I flipped the pages slowly. When I reached the end and the furious scribbles tearing the paper, I looked into the lens and said, "This is what I did, Blue. This is how I hurt myself. I lost this."

SoBlue: the art, or the girl?

"Both." I lowered the book. My style was on the masculine side—bold lines digging into the paper, aggressive, unhesitating—and when I drew Ellis, it brought out her androgyny. "How do you know that's a girl?"

SoBlue: from context.
SoBlue: she must be red.
SoBlue: your obsession.
SoBlue: the way you're mine.

"I'm not—"
Footsteps thudded up the stairs, then a cursory knock followed by my door banging open.

"I just cracked Ryan's password," Elle said, bounding in. "You told me to get you as soon as—"
She cut off when I leaped from the bed and lunged at her.

"Oh my god. I'm sorry. I didn't know you were doing a—"
I grabbed her and cupped a hand over her mouth. Shook my head and pointed at the laptop. Her cheeks bloomed carnation pink.

Sorry! she mouthed when I released her.

I mimed walking downstairs. *Five minutes.*

Elle nodded, chagrined, and crept out of the room. I shut the door behind her and locked it, let out a sigh like I'd been punched.

There were messages waiting when I returned to the laptop.

SoBlue: where did you go?
SoBlue: is everything okay?

For a moment I stood there, my heart throbbing in my fingertips. A frisson of realization glided up my spine.

I sat down and typed.

Morgan: sorry
Morgan: I'm fine
Morgan: you know what?
Morgan: you just answered a question I didn't even know I was asking
SoBlue: what question?

So easy to talk to. So comfortable, familiar. I felt like I'd known him years, not weeks. In the back of my mind I'd wondered if—sometimes almost hoped that—Blue was Elle.

Strange, how it came as both relief and disappointment.

"Nothing," I said. "Something dumb."

SoBlue: who was that?

Fuck. "What?"

SoBlue: i heard a voice. not yours.

"Really. And what do you think you heard her say?"

SoBlue: things that didn't sound very legal.

"No idea what you're talking about. But I need to log off now, Blue. Thanks for—"

SoBlue: that was her.
SoBlue: my archnemesis.
SoBlue: red.

I had to laugh. "She can't be your archnemesis, Mr. Superhero. She doesn't even know you exist."

SoBlue: you never mentioned me to her?

"You're my little secret."

SoBlue: not sure how i feel about that.
SoBlue: but you can tell her about me.
SoBlue: it's only fair, now that i've seen her naked.

I made a face. "Those were artistic nudes. There was no frontal."

SoBlue: they felt intimate.
SoBlue: private.
SoBlue: the way you look at her . . .
SoBlue: it's not something anyone else was meant to see.

"Well then, welcome to our sordid little relationship. Want to be the third point in a completely twisted love triangle?"

SoBlue: i'll think about it.
SoBlue: morgan.

"Blue."

SoBlue: your art is excellent.
SoBlue: not just technically, but stylistically.
SoBlue: you have such panache, and you're still so young.
SoBlue: it's raw talent.

I waved a hand in dismissal, but his words set off a small thermonuclear blast in my chest.

SoBlue: you're gifted.

SoBlue: life threw you into the race miles ahead of everyone.

SoBlue: you never struggled to be competent.

SoBlue: you got a head start so you could be a pioneer.

SoBlue: you're special.

SoBlue: and you know all of this already.

"Look, if you're going to tell me I'm still an artist even though I can't make art—"

SoBlue: no.

SoBlue: but an artist makes art however she can.

SoBlue: have you read charles bukowski?

"I've heard of him."

SoBlue: he has a poem, "air and light and time and space."

SoBlue: about a young artist who's simplified his life.

SoBlue: sold his house, bought a studio with great natural light.

SoBlue: and now he's ready to Create.

SoBlue: with a capital C.

SoBlue: (see? i'm not allergic to the shift key.)

"Still a hipster. Liking Bukowski confirms it."

SoBlue: i'll let that slide.

SoBlue: so, charles says, art doesn't work that way.

SoBlue: if you're going to Create, you'll do it no matter what.

SoBlue: you don't need the studio. you don't need natural light.

SoBlue: you'll do it while you're chipping away in a coal mine.

SoBlue: you'll do it as a single mother on welfare.

SoBlue: you'll do it with half your body blown away.

SoBlue: you'll do it because you can't not do it.

SoBlue: the studio isn't really a studio.

SoBlue: it's the idea of readiness.

SoBlue: of preparedness.
SoBlue: it's an illusion.

In my cam I could see my frown, the reflexive resistance to what he was saying.

It has to be real, Ellis had said. *And you're not ready.*

I felt perpetually unready for my life.

Maybe that was the trick: accepting that readiness wasn't real, wasn't ever going to happen, and living anyway.

SoBlue: something changed tonight.
SoBlue: you showed me a piece of your true self.
SoBlue: i want to show you who i am, too.

My heart played a glitchy beat in my chest. "Send me a pic, Blue. I want to see you."

SoBlue: it'll change things.
SoBlue: right now you see me in a pure way.
SoBlue: no preconceptions.

"Show me *something*. Some part of you. God, send me a fucking dick pic if you want, I don't care. I just want to see you." I stared into the tiny cam lens. "I showed you my real self tonight. Show me you're real, too."

SoBlue: those eyes, morgan.
SoBlue: i can't say no to those eyes.
SoBlue: all right. one sec.

Calm the fuck down, heart. This could be anything. This could be a massive letdown. Maybe there's something that'll ruin it, maybe he's older than your dad, maybe he's Max, maybe—

A photo popped on-screen: a table covered with small

wooden figurines. Carved animals. Striped tomcat, pop-eyed frog, pig with a curly tail made from a single wispy wood shaving.

"What is this?" I said.

SoBlue: something real.

Another photo popped up, with more animals: pony, owl, rabbit. All chibi style, round-bodied and doe-eyed.

"Blue," I said, my voice dangerously saccharine, "these are painfully cute."

More photos followed, figurines in various stages of whittling. A whole menagerie.

"This is so fucking adorable. Shit, you're good. You have a sweet side. The cuteness is killing me."

Then I went still.

His hands.

In the final photo, he held a hunk of wood in one palm, a Buck knife in the other. Fair skin, braids of blue veins cording in his wrists. Long slim fingers, elegant and strong. Beautiful hands.

"Holy shit," I breathed. "Hi."

SoBlue: hi.
SoBlue: i'm real.

I ran a fingertip across his palm, ridiculously, before I remembered he could see me. Then I clicked SAVE IMAGE AS.

SoBlue: are you saving that?

"What do you think?"

SoBlue: i think you're going to get off to it later.

"Good guess, Freud." I glanced at the clock, remembering Elle waiting downstairs. "Shit. Blue, I have to go. I'll be back."

SoBlue: listen.

SoBlue: before you leave.

SoBlue: there's something i've been thinking about.

"Tell me."

SoBlue: i'm getting attached to you, morgan.

He'd said silly shit about love before, just like a hundred other guys, but this time felt different. It felt real.

"Guess what, Blue? I'm getting attached to you, too."

SoBlue: when we talk, i feel . . .

SoBlue: awake.

SoBlue: aware of the blood in my veins.

SoBlue: the breath in my lungs.

SoBlue: as if i was dead before.

SoBlue: it's all i look forward to anymore.

SoBlue: these pieces of you.

SoBlue: and it maddens me, to think of sharing them with anyone else.

"If you mean Red, she's not up for discussion."

SoBlue: not her.

SoBlue: we can share.

SoBlue: but the others have to go.

"What?"

SoBlue: i'll pay the same amount every night.

SoBlue: and you can do whatever you like.

SoBlue: spend your time as you wish.

SoBlue: on one condition.

I knew what it was, but still I said, "What condition?"

SoBlue: you don't cam for anyone else.

SoBlue: only me.

———

When I went downstairs, the dining room was empty. On a napkin, Elle's neat, angular handwriting:

I'm tired. Let's meet tomorrow. Sorry again.

Great. Now I didn't have Red *or* Blue.

I returned to my room and aimlessly browsed erotic Tumblrs, black-and-white photos with the heads and faces cropped. Skinny arms and lean torsos, grasping hands. Anonymous. Genderless. Desire reduced to its most elemental lines. My mind wandered.

I browsed my messages on social media.

we miss u bb
are you doing a show tonight?

I slung a tie around my neck and took some selfies, classed them up in Photoshop, but then I thought:

you don't cam for anyone else.

I deleted the photos. I crossed and uncrossed my legs. I got up and paced.

Finally I opened a new tab and joined Ariel's chat room.

She sprawled on her bed in bikini bottoms and striped knee socks, one hand inside her panties. Her glasses were white mirrors reflecting her laptop. She smiled lazily.

"Hello, Sweet. Nice to see you again."

sweet_ophelia has tipped Ariel 100 tokens.
Dahlz: Thank you for tipping.
young_rae-z: ass kisser
Dahlz: Pretty sure we'd all love to kiss her ass.

I slumped in the window frame, my head thudding on the glass. Wind stirred the treetops and made them toss and roll like a dark sea. In five minutes I could run through the woods and be at Elle's door.

"You want to take me private tonight, Sweet?"

I could pin her against the wall. I could kiss her till her reserve melted, till she pushed back, tore my shirt off, licked the rivulet of nectar running between my breasts, my sweat.

I brushed my belly. Popped the button of my jean shorts.

sweet_ophelia has tipped Ariel 500 tokens.
Dahlz: Sweet lord.
young_rae-z: ha
dizneeprinz: see how much we luv u Ari ;)

Ariel leaned toward the cam. Dark roots showed through her auburn hair dye. "You are being *very* sweet. It makes me so wet, baby."

Wildness tilted inside me. One part nausea, one part lust. This was how my viewers probably felt: ashamed to pay for this, but too horny to care. Loneliness would hit later. Now there was just the hot ache spreading between my legs, the chafe of stiff nipples against my shirt.

sweet_ophelia has tipped Ariel 1,000 tokens.
[MOD]Sebastian: *Congratulations, sweet_ophelia. You have set a NEW RECORD!*

I understood why wealthy people did this. Tipping a thousand bucks felt incredible. Like a good hard thrust midfuck. Like I was the one with the dick, and when Ariel's eyes widened and her mouth made a small O I thought, You like that, baby? Want me to fuck you harder?

I sat back, breathing fast.

What the fuck.

This was not her.

This was not the same.

What the fuck was I doing?

I X'ed the tab and was about to slap the laptop shut when a notification popped up. I'd left my cam app idling.

Incoming video call from TrueBlue.

Guess he couldn't sleep, either. But why change his screen-name?

ACCEPT.

I sat bolt upright in bed.

There was a video feed from Blue this time.

Dark room. Red leather couch against a black wall. Some framed geometric print above it, maybe an Escher. Subsonic bass pumped in the background like depth charges firing. The couch was empty.

My heart filled my throat and swelled, huge, choking.

A man walked on-screen and sat down.

Blond, he was blond, lean, shirtless, barefoot in jeans—

Dane.

"Jesus fucking Christ," I blurted. "You?"

"Happy to see me?"

I felt like my picture of reality had gone all Cubist, things not lining up anymore.

Dane hooked his arms over the backrest. Violet veins spidered up the insides of his biceps.

"This is impossible," I said.

"Yeah, I can finally afford to take you private."

"No, I mean, you. Being him." My mouth hung open. "You didn't have to spend all this money. You could've just told me. Why'd you mess with me?"

His jauntiness fizzled. "I feel like I'm missing something here."

"Why did you do this to me, Dane?"

"I'm sure I did something wrong, but you're gonna have to tell me what."

It couldn't be him.

It couldn't be.

They were too different. Blue was quick-witted, articulate, observant; Dane was a cute dumb puppy. Blue got off on words; Dane's interest in me was, for the most part, nonverbal. He wouldn't fork over a grand each night to talk about Charles Bukowski and Frida Kahlo. He'd want to talk dirty, jerk off, and log off.

"Why did you pick this screenname?" I demanded.

He leaned in and his eyes grew cartoonishly wide. Baby blue.

"Jesus." I sank back onto my bed. "Wait, why did you take me private? What is this?"

Dane flexed his chest, his pecs tightening. A sheen of peach fuzz shimmered over his skin. "Missed you."

"You missed your mirror. How's Boston?"

"Way less fun than it should be. What's all this stuff about money and screennames?"

"I thought you were him. My anonymous patron. He calls himself Blue."

"That's still going on?"

"Yes. Which you'd know if you ever read your fucking texts."

"Sorry, baby. I'm juggling a lot of balls right now."

"Gross."

"It's a metaphor. Am I doing it wrong?" Dane grinned. "How are you, really?"

"Losing my mind. Everything's getting crazier and crazier."

"Want me to come back?"

"And do what, flutter your eyelashes and charm my pants off? I'll survive."

"How's Ellis? You two enjoying that sweet pad with the sick nature views?"

I laughed. "Only you would call a shack made of matchsticks and gum a 'sweet pad with sick nature views.'"

"I can sell anything, baby."

"Sell me on believing things will be okay, Dane."

"Things'll be okay." His tone turned mischievous. "Listen to your girlfriend. She told me she's your voice of reason. Then she got this twinkle in her eye, like I do when I undress you in my head."

"You are so stupid."

"Are you denying it? I heard you have a denial problem."

"Shut *up*."

The word felt weird, but Ellis *was* pretty much my on-again, off-again girlfriend. We'd spent five years of our lives together, and even when we hooked up with other people, when we were more platonic than romantic, the only face I wanted to see before I slept each night was hers. I'd toss myself on her bed and tell her about my classes: the douchebags who smuggled tracings into Life Drawing; the girl who was legally blind and drew based on memory of where she'd touched the paper. When I was frustrated, uninspired, Elle taught me things. Once she told me about golden spirals, spirals that could turn inward infinitely, twisting tighter and tighter and always fitting perfectly inside themselves, never collapsing. Golden spirals were found all over nature, she said. In nautilus shells and the cups of rose petals and—she leaned close, her fingertip tracing the whorl of my ear—in us.

(—Bergen, Vada. *Every Time You Touch Me.*
Watercolor and ink on paper.)

"Anyway," I said. "It's nice to see your stupid face again."

"Mm-hmm." Dane's eyes flickered over me. "You've got that sex glow. Just finish a show?"

"No."

"You look fucking beautiful right now."

My dumb heart went wacky at this. "You want a show, baby?" I said, mocking.

"I want to do one for you."

He leaned back, the leather seat squawking. His abs furrowed. One arm dragged over the cushion, slowly, a sine wave snaking through the muscle beneath his skin.

"Dane," I said, all mockery gone.

He put a hand on his fly. His eyes were half-shut, sleepy with desire. "Let me do this for you."

I stared wordlessly at the screen.

My cam boy opened his fly, bit his lip as if it pained him to release the pressure. One hand slipped inside and squeezed. My legs pressed together in response.

"Take off your pants," I said, surprising myself.

He flashed that satyr grin. Stood, kicked his jeans off. His wiry body shone in the dim light. Those boxer-briefs did practically nothing to hide his erection.

"Touch your belly."

His hand brushed over his ribs, his abs. He stroked the clean V lines running inside the waistband of his Calvin Kleins. Against the fluorescent white cotton, his skin was the color of sand dollars.

"You look fucking beautiful right now," I said.

Dane laughed.

"Sit down. Take off your underwear."

He obeyed, and as he stripped he maintained eye contact with the webcam. I'd seen his cock before. I'd seen him jerk off. But my breath caught, because this time he was going to do it for me.

"Stroke it."

Dane took himself in one hand, his lips parting slightly

at his own touch. Every muscle in him tensed, every gnarl and knot swelling against his skin, his mouth so red it looked lipsticked and his eyelashes thick and long, and I thought, absently, of how I found myself drawn to androgyny in the human form. People who blurred the lines. He ran his fist up and down his cock, steady and slow.

"How does it feel?" I said.

"Wish you'd come here and tell me."

I nestled into my pillows. "Squeeze your balls."

His lips quirked. Dutifully he cradled them and squeezed. His cock was flush with blood, a drop of opal fluid beading on the tip. As he worked himself he kept glancing up at me, sometimes holding for several strokes, and I wondered how he was imagining fucking me. If I dominated him in his mind the way I dominated him now.

"Faster," I said.

Dane's fist pumped, jerking harder with each upstroke. Tension spread through him, deeper cuts of definition carving into his muscle, all his power radiating inward, toward the core of himself. *You don't cam for anyone else.* On a whim I placed my thumb over my webcam lens, blocking my video transmission.

Dane didn't notice for a few seconds. When he did and faltered I said, "Don't stop."

He shot another glance or two at the screen and then focused on his dick. Instead of the intimate ricochet of eye contact he seemed determined to finish quickly, get it over with.

"Slow down," I said. "Don't come yet."

I could tell it jarred him. He'd been jerking off to me but now the image was gone. It was like any ordinary private show.

My free hand slid between my legs.

Is it you? I thought as I ran a finger against myself, and a coruscating heat bloomed in my thighs, kindled the fine web of nerves threading up my spine. Could you actually be the man I've been talking to, only letting your true self free when you type? When I can't see you?

I stared at the hands working his dick. Slender fingers, almost elegant.

"Come for me," I said.

His strokes grew short and rough. He gritted his teeth, not the dreamy pretty-boy face he usually got when he came on cam but something pained, almost resentful. For a moment before climax he didn't look like he was in the middle of a sex act but an act of violence, of self-annihilation.

"Fuck," he said suddenly, and his head lolled back, his body shuddering, pearly come spilling over his fist and onto his stomach, a sticky mess of spider silk. He lay slack and listless for half a minute, then grabbed a tissue from off cam. Even though my feed was black he avoided looking at the screen.

My hand stilled. My body was taut as a tripwire. I barely breathed.

"Well," he said finally, "enjoy the show?"

"Yes."

Dane laughed, huskily. "Maybe next time you'll keep your cam on."

"Next time, huh?"

Is it you, Dane?

He looked dead into the lens. "That's right, baby. Next time it's your turn."

He gave me a small, knowing smile, and logged off.

VADA: are you awake?

ELLIS: Yes. Hi.

VADA: hi

VADA: sorry about freaking out earlier

ELLIS: No, I'm sorry for barging in. I feel like an idiot.

VADA: don't

VADA: it was an unplanned private chat

VADA: not your fault

ELLIS: Can I still feel like an idiot?

VADA: okay, but only if I can feel like one too

ELLIS: Why are you still up?

VADA: having a weird ass night

VADA: why are you still up?

ELLIS: Having a weird-ass night.

ELLIS: Plus, you know me. Every time I make a faux pas, I analyze it to death.

VADA: you make the best faux pas

VADA: remember when you got drunk at Umbra

VADA: and went behind the bar and tried to "help" the bartender

VADA: and they kicked us out

VADA: and threatened to call the cops

ELLIS: Oh my god.

ELLIS: How do you remember that?

VADA: I wasn't as drunk as you

ELLIS: You passed out in the taxi!

VADA: that was just a power nap

VADA: and do you remember when we went to the cat shelter

VADA: and you kept asking how many cats you could legally
adopt

VADA: in this really quiet, intense voice

VADA: and they escorted us from the building because they
thought you were going to experiment on them or something

ELLIS: If you're trying to make me feel better, this is the opposite
of that.

VADA: #sorrynotsorry

ELLIS: I wanted to adopt them all because they were going to be
put down.

VADA: I know

VADA: you big softie

ELLIS: Big psycho, apparently.

VADA: you're too good for this earth

VADA: we should send you back to Krypton

VADA: with the other supermen

ELLIS: Ha, ha.

VADA: Elle?

ELLIS: Yeah?

VADA: did you mean it, about not moving on?

ELLIS: Why do you ask?

VADA: I don't know

VADA: curiosity, jealousy, confusion, loneliness

VADA: take your pick

ELLIS: Remember when we threw the key into the ocean?

ELLIS: I meant what I said.

ELLIS: Now please tell me what you were doing at my house.

VADA: trying to figure out who Brandt Zoeller is

VADA: Elle?

VADA: hey

VADA: come on, don't just ignore me

VADA: I thought you wanted us to talk things through

ELLIS: Did you talk to him?

VADA: who is he?

ELLIS: I can't believe you're going behind my back.

VADA: I can't believe you're hiding shit from me

ELLIS: Really? You can't?

ELLIS: After you hid our relationship from everyone?

ELLIS: Made me feel like some kind of dirty secret?

VADA: that's not fair

VADA: I hooked up with girls before and everyone knew

ELLIS: Oh, so I'm special.

ELLIS: I'm the only one you felt compelled to hide.

VADA: fuck, what do you want me to say?

ELLIS: Something real.

VADA: it wasn't easy for me, okay?

VADA: my entire life revolved around you

VADA: and one night you decided to just walk out of it

ELLIS: It wasn't one night. It was every night.

ELLIS: Every night you dangled me on a string while you waited
    for someone better to come along.

VADA: oh, my bad

VADA: so I was supposed to know exactly who I was at age 22

VADA: and exactly who I wanted to be for the rest of my life

ELLIS: No.

ELLIS: But when someone lays their heart at your feet, you could
    at least have the decency to say you don't want it.

VADA: I didn't fucking know what I wanted

VADA: aside from not losing my best friend

ELLIS: Well, that happened anyway.

VADA: because you put all the pressure on me

VADA: you left me to decide our entire future

VADA: do you get that?

VADA: how you made it all or nothing?

VADA: either you wanted me entirely or not at all

VADA: that was an impossible choice, Elle

VADA: one I wasn't ready to make

ELLIS: Brandt is my cousin.

ELLIS: He has health issues and needed a place where he could recover.

ELLIS: My aunt offered to pay all our bills if I took him.

ELLIS: Happy?

VADA: why couldn't you just tell me that?

ELLIS: Why should I?

ELLIS: You won't tell me the truth about that night.

VADA: you weren't driving

ELLIS: I know you want to protect me.

ELLIS: But protecting me from the truth isn't a good thing.

VADA: Ellis, I promise

VADA: I didn't lie about that

VADA: and no one will lay a finger on you

VADA: they'll have to get past me first

ELLIS: I wish I could believe you.

VADA: want a selfie where I look all Xena Warrior Princess?

ELLIS: God.

VADA: you laughed

ELLIS: Vada?

VADA: yeah?

ELLIS: Have you moved on?

VADA: interesting question

VADA: let's examine the evidence

VADA: exhibit a: I have your pics over my bed

VADA: exhibit b: I've paid a small fortune to redheaded cam girls who look vaguely like you

ELLIS: Wait, seriously?

VADA: quiet in the court

VADA: exhibit c: my cammer name is Morgan
VADA: your honor, clearly I have hang-ups about my former BFF/
life partner/soulmate
VADA: the prosecution rests
ELLIS: You're such a dork.
ELLIS: Do you really have hang-ups about me?
VADA: si, mi pajarito rojo
VADA: I really do
ELLIS: Good.
ELLIS: Because I have them about you, too.

———

The next day we sat in her kitchen, poring over data from the cloned drive. Ryan Vandermeer's life read like a checklist of the All-American bro:

- Varsity baseball.
- ACT score: 20 (51st percentile).
- No college applications.
- Two arrests for alcohol possession as a minor.
- Application to United States Marine Corps (rejected).

"Huh," I said. "Weird. Max told me Ryan signed up for the Marines, but not that he was rejected. Wonder why."

"They'll reject you for anything. It could've been something like asthma."

"Yeah, but the rest? Cutting, arrests, shitty test scores? Something heavy was going on."

Ellis took a nervous hit off her vaping pen. "Those are symptoms. We don't know the cause."

"Or do we?" I tapped my fingers on the counter. "On Tumblr he said he looked like a stranger to himself. He felt like there was a bomb inside him."

She took another hit. She'd been going at it nonstop since I

showed up with food: fresh prawns for *asopao de camarones*—
Puerto Rican shrimp soup—and plantains to mash up for
mofongo. Now I pulled ingredients from paper bags, and
brand-new copper pots, shiny as mint pennies, and a bottle
of wine.

"What is all of this?" she said.

"Happy housewarming."

Her face softened. "Why are you so sweet to me?"

Our little phrase.

I looked away. My chest felt like an atrium full of small, ec-
static birds whirling around madly, smashing in puffs of bright
feathers, no regard for glass or each other.

Her cheer didn't last. She got up to pace, trailing a ghost
ribbon of steam.

"What's wrong?" I said.

"Max is digging into my life, looking for—I don't even
know. We're both under the microscope. How can you be so
calm?"

"Low blood pressure, little bit of weed."

"I'm serious, Vada."

In that case:

Guilt.

Fatalism.

Fatigue.

I knew what Max would find out about me. In a way I
looked forward to it, letting that weight roll off my back. Letting go and seeing if I'd sink or float.

There's a bit of a self-destructive streak in me. Nero fiddled
while he watched his city burn. I pressed harder on the gas
pedal.

People who create have to do a little destroying to stay sane.

"What about this Skylar person?" I said. "The other log-in
on the laptop."

"Dead end."

Skylar had deleted her data shortly before Ryan's death, and Elle couldn't recover it. This girl knew how to hide her tracks.

"What if she knows stuff? Like why Ryan was so fucked-up, and why he hurt himself?"

"Those are some big what-ifs."

"Got a better idea?"

Elle shrugged.

"She's our best lead," I insisted. "She was important enough to have an account on his computer."

"Why do you keep saying 'she'? 'Skylar' is gender-neutral."

"Her log-in icon is a high heel."

"Which proves what?"

"I'm not gender stereotyping. I'm making an educated guess based on statistical probabilities, Professor."

She frowned. "What if the name was Ellis? What would you assume?"

"I'd assume it was you."

"Boy or girl?"

"Just you."

Elle exhaled, her eyes focused on something far off. This was my chance, I realized. To ask about Emily.

"It's weird," I said. "Your parents never struck me as the type who like gender-neutral names."

"They're not."

"I guess people are full of surprises, huh?"

"They are."

She'd never introduced us. Her parents were toxic, pretty much convinced their gay atheist daughter was the Antichrist. *"But don't pity me,"* she'd said. *"I don't fear them anymore. I feel sad for them."*

I met her mother once. But I never told Ellis.

Me and my secrets.

There was no way I could prod more without setting off alarms.

"Put the wand down, Hermione," I said. "We're making lunch."

She was better with sharp things and I was better with fire, so she cut and I cooked. I started the broth and peeled prawns, clumsy but determined; threw in minced garlic and cilantro; swept chilies from the cutting board while Elle was still chopping; and she grinned to herself and I knew she was remembering things, as I was. All those nights back in Chicago when we'd cook by candlelight and invite our friends over. Blythe and Armin from school, Hector from the ink parlor. Blythe joked that we were like an old married couple, and Elle blushed, and later Elle and Blythe hooked up and I joked to myself that old married couples were essentially platonic anyway, and besides, it wasn't like I knew what the fuck I wanted.

I still didn't.

We set the coffee table with tin camping plates, poured Chablis into jelly jars. Laughed at how fucking rustic it was. City people out here on a rocky shard of earth floating in a cold ocean. It felt more like home than anything had in a very long time.

We raised our wine and paused, fumbling for a toast.

"To good friends?" Ellis said finally.

"To good friends."

Clink.

The cabin was heady with the scent of shrimp and spicy-sweet herbs. A water curtain of light moved across the table, gold and green spilling over us, pooling, running off. She'd taken the floor this time and left me the couch. I watched her hands, silver twirling through her fingers.

"Are you okay?" she said.

I should have burned my sketchbooks. Keeping them was sick. Like keeping the bones and teeth of a child, fragments of a precious thing, lost before it could reach its potential.

"I'm fine." I ate a spoonful of something red and tasted only the metal.

Elle got up and fetched the wine bottle and topped me off without a word. I touched her wrist as she poured and the ribbon of pear-gold silk twisted, broke into ragged threads. The splatter on the table looked like drops of liquid sun.

My touch could still do that. Make her tremble.

"Do you want to talk about it?" she said, sitting beside me on the sofa.

"Not really."

"When has bottling it up ever not backfired and exploded in your face?"

"I'm not bottling it up," I said, literally stuffing the cork back into the wine bottle.

She tried not to laugh. "Come on. You're supposed to be the one who's in touch with her feelings."

"I'm in touch with feeling stupid and whiny. Other people have it worse."

"It's not whiny, Vada. It's life-altering. You're allowed to freak out."

"Freaking out means accepting that I'm a freak. I'm still in denial, and I like it here."

"What are you afraid of?"

I made a fist with my bad hand and a razor thread pulled at my spine. "I'm not afraid. I'm resigned. This is it, Elle. It's not going to heal more."

"Are you taking pain meds?"

"I don't need them."

"I've seen you grit your teeth when you think I'm not looking."

"I don't fucking need them." I picked up my spoon and tried to hold it level. After a second my hand spasmed and drooped. "This is the problem. Not the pain. *This*." I tossed the spoon onto the table. "It's fucking *gone*. I'm as weak as a baby and I'll be like this the rest of my life. I can't draw, I can't do shit. All I have left is jerking off for random creeps on the Internet, like the loser I am."

She watched me awhile. At one point she grazed my bare arm, made me shiver violently. Then she stood.

"Let's do an experiment."

"This isn't the time. We haven't finished eating."

"It can wait. This is exactly the time, Vada. Trust me."

I sulked as she moved around the cabin, searching. Finally she returned with a pillowcase and placed it in my hands.

"Blindfold me."

"What happened to romance?"

"Just do it."

She took her glasses off and I tied a loose knot. My pulse skittered.

This was not the first time I'd tied a blindfold on her.

"Okay," she said, tilting her head this way and that. "Here are the rules: Lead me to the ocean. You may only speak in colors."

"What?"

"That's a pronoun, not a color."

I gawked.

"I can feel that look." She reached out, found my elbow. "Come on. You can do this."

"I don't even know what you want me to—"

Her hand traveled up to my jaw. She pressed her palm gently against my lips.

Her skin was so soft.

"Take me to the ocean. With your eyes."

Pajarito loco, I mouthed, and swiveled her toward the door. "Um . . . green?"

She stepped forward, and I followed. I darted ahead and flung the door open.

"Red. *Red*. Okay, green. Green, green, green . . . red."

Elle took halting steps onto the log stairs.

Jesus. This was going to end with a hospital visit.

Getting her to ground level nearly killed me. Traffic colors worked, to an extent: green for go, red for stop, yellow for caution. But when we reached the forest floor and the thick tangle of exposed roots that she needed to climb over, I blanked.

"Uh, you need to—"

"Vada."

"Goddammit. What are you trying to teach me, how to break your neck?"

Her cool glare radiated through the blindfold.

"Fine," I said. "Be a masochist. Green."

Her foot caught in the tree roots. I grabbed her before she fell.

How the fuck could I communicate how to climb?

Two squirrels scuttled up a tree, shredding bark. The air was alive with birdsong, trills and whistles and tweets, mutters, musings, a hundred voices spiraling into the sky. A trail of red ants boiled over the leathery tendrils at our feet.

"Red," I blurted. "Fire-ant red." What else crawled? "Caterpillar yellow. Spider black."

Ellis toed the roots, crouched, and picked her way over on hands and knees.

I laughed triumphantly, and she smiled in my direction.

"You're still insane," I said.

"You're corrupting the experiment."

"Green. Emerald City green."

The trail was mostly green, with patches of yellow and red

where I had to drag branches out of her path. I ran through all the basic greens—kelly, shamrock, clover, grass—but that got boring fast so I mixed it up: watermelon rind, Mountain Dew, zombie skin, envy. The Chicago River on St. Patrick's Day. Then we reached a rock ledge, and I parked her with a *cherry red* and began hauling branches to make a ramp.

I was in the middle of this when a fox pranced into the path, a limp dove dangling from its jaws.

"Ellis," I murmured, but if she removed the blindfold she'd probably spook it.

I had to show her.

"Red. Harvest red. A jacket of russet, and sienna, and umber." She didn't object to extra words, so I went on, "Soot-black socks. A vest of pure snow. And amber . . . buttons. Old, wise amber that holds the sun, and carries it into the darkness, like tiny lamps."

"Is it a fox?" she whispered.

The fox arrowed into the underbrush, leaves shimmering with light in its wake.

I smiled and touched her arm. "*Verde musgo.*"

"What's that?"

"The color of your eyes."

I walked her through the woods, taking time now not just to guide but to describe things around us—the arresting scarlet of a tanager, pulsing like a plush heart, and a cache of violets rich as twilight that I plucked and wove into her hair, and the bronze of my skin in the shadows, like a cast sculpture. The trees thinned and we crossed a silty beach and I made Elle sit on an outcropping. Sky and sea fused into blue haze.

"*Azúl,*" I said, kneeling behind her. "*Azúl infinito.*"

I untied the blindfold and let it fall.

Ellis squinted at the water, then up at me. Her smile was big and guileless. "My hypothesis was correct."

"What was it?"

"That you're still an artist. No one can ever take that from you."

Something was trembling in my chest, like a cupped leaf full of rain, tipping, starting to spill.

I touched her shoulder. Then I threw my arms around her and didn't let go because I was pretty sure I was crying. "I get it. You trust me. And I trust you too, Elle." Yep, that was a sniffle. "More than anyone in the world."

"Vada—"

"You've always been there for me. You're my prince, my—"

"Vada, I can't breathe."

I released. And hugged her again immediately, gentler, and she laughed but I spied tears in her eyes, too.

"Still think I'm crazy?" she said.

"In the very sanest way."

I pulled back to look at her.

Come clean, I thought. Start small.

"I want you to know everything. I want to be that close again. I've been talking to someone online, Elle."

"Who?"

"He calls himself Blue."

And I told her all about him.

As I spoke she angled away from me, frowning. Coiled her bangs around a finger and tugged till the violets fell out. That little frown wouldn't unknit itself.

Finally she said, "Why didn't you tell me sooner?"

"Guys have sugar-daddied me before. It's not that weird."

"He gave you a ton of money and you told him a ton of personal stuff. Like a paid informant."

"It's not like that."

She scratched a nail on the rock. "What does he know?"

"Not enough to track me down."

Elle's frown deepened.

"What?" I said.

"For all you know, it's Max."

"It's not Max. He's too young. He's like us."

"Right, because Max wouldn't act our age to get info."

That was not a pleasant line of speculation.

"Why did you tell him about me?"

"You're my best friend, Elle."

She kicked her foot irascibly. "I hate that you call me Red."

"Why?"

"Like I'm the opposite of *him*."

And then it clicked: she was jealous.

The epiphany shot a jet of helium into my heart. I leaned into her, and we looked out at the ocean. Water lapped the rocks and left a skim of foam, seaweed and wet lime mixing with Elle's autumn scent. For a moment I forgot myself, forgot the rules and our history and thought about pushing her flat against the stone. Holding her body down with mine so I could feel her breathe, feel her bones creak, her blood slow. So I could show her how I felt about her. How much she was a part of me.

My love is savage and rapacious. It isn't content to touch. It wants to be inside, crawl into the marrow, caress each vein until the cells are all mixed up and there is no you and me anymore, no secrets or shadows sliding between our skin. Only this endless devouring of each other. The ouroboros we call us.

Ellis shrugged me off. "Let's head back."

I trailed behind, spinning one of the violets between my fingers. She loves me, I thought, plucking a petal. She loves me not. She loves me. She loves me not.

She loves me.

———

We were drinking wine as the sun fell when we saw it. I almost spit and dropped my glass. Elle jerked back from the keyboard as if it had bitten her.

After hundreds and hundreds of Ryan's pics, we'd grown complacent. Selfies. Alt takes of photos I'd already seen on his Tumblr. Bad shots, blurry, overexposed, a newbie learning his camera. Even the cutting pics weren't shocking anymore.

This one was.

Ryan had a baby face, sleepy-eyed and pouty, skin smooth as cream. But it was barely visible beneath the bruises and cuts. One cheek swelled up fat and purple as eggplant. One eye was black, bruised shut. Puffy lips, cut and cracked in a dozen places.

Ellis tapped a key.

Pic after pic, all showing the same brutality: his face, wrecked.

"What's the date on these?" I said.

"Day before the accident."

"That's it." I clapped my bad fist into my good palm. "That's what made him drink."

Elle peered up at me. "That's speculation."

"Look at his face." I butted in and flicked through the other photos. Couple more bruise pics, then nothing. "Someone beat the shit out of him, then he tried to kill himself."

"You almost sound happy about it."

I wheeled away, paced a circle. "Things are finally starting to make sense. It's a relief."

The relief of blaming someone else for what happened.

"It's sick to feel glad that someone got hurt."

"I'm not *glad*, Elle. But he's a stranger to us. I can look at it objectively. We never knew him."

"We still killed him."

"Did we?" I pointed at the screen. "Or did the person who did *this* kill him? Because this is what made him drink, not us."

She poked glumly at the keyboard.

I sat beside her, laid a hand on her knee. "You don't seem surprised."

Shrug.

"You already saw these, didn't you?"

"I glanced through while I was copying files."

"And didn't tell me."

She hung her head, hair shading her eyes. "I just don't like where this is leading. We're going deeper down this rabbit hole without getting closer to understanding. It's only getting darker and darker."

But don't you see? I thought. If we're not the reason he died, then everything's okay. We can heal. Go on with our lives.

Forget all of this like it never even happened.

"I need closure, Ellis." Her leg tensed beneath my curling fingers. "I need to know why Ryan did this so I can put it behind me."

"We already know. He was depressed and his life was falling apart, so he drank."

"That's *how* it happened. Not *why*."

"You're looking for meaning in something meaningless. He was just in pain."

I flung my hands up. "My whole fucking life changed that night. I lost myself, and you, and my entire future. If I can't find meaning in that, how can I survive?"

"Is that really why you want closure?"

I didn't answer that. Instead I said, "Don't you want it to mean something, too?"

"I don't know what I want anymore."

My arm slipped around her. She was shaking. About to cry.

"Elle." I stroked the back of her head, the fine short hair there. It still smelled like violets. "Why are you acting like this?"

"It makes me sad."

"What does?"

"That someone hurt him for being the way he is."

I touched her cheek. "Is this reminding you of your parents?"

The glint in her eyes was answer enough.

"It's okay, baby. That's all over." I tucked her head beneath my chin. "You don't have to be afraid of them anymore."

"I'm not."

"Then what?"

Her arms wrapped around my back.

This whole thing was freaking her out. Her nervousness earlier, the white lie about the photos. That comment about the rabbit hole. Still convinced she was behind the wheel.

I couldn't blame her for being scared. But I had to know more, for both of us.

"Hey." I swabbed her tears dry. "No being sad. It's not allowed today. You know what today is?"

"What?"

"The best day I've had all year, because of you."

She finally smiled. Sweet and small, unassuming. I slid her glasses off and brushed the wet glaze from her lashes. I couldn't take my hands from her face.

"Stay the night," she whispered.

Electricity arced from my spine to my fingertips and collected there, buzzing. I was sure she could feel the static I trailed across her skin. I ran my thumb over her lower lip, and when her mouth opened and she exhaled into my palm I felt suddenly weightless, no bones or heaviness inside me, just a shimmering mist of nerves. I thought of Dalí's *Galatea of the Spheres*. A girl made entirely of translucent bubbles containing sea, skin, sky.

"What are we doing?" I said.

"Falling in love again."

Heat flashed in my belly, lightning white. "I thought we were trying to be friends."

"We've never just been friends, Vada." Ellis circled her hands around the back of my neck. "Let's not pretend anymore."

She was irresistible like this, all tousle-haired and unraveled. So rare to see her careless, overcome with want. With loneliness.

"This isn't a good idea," I said, stroking her cheek. "Rushing back into things."

"You like rushing."

"I know. It's weird being the voice of reason, for once." I grinned. "You are so pretty right now. All I want to do is kiss you. But I don't want to fuck this up again. I want my best friend back, Elle."

"You don't want me."

"Of course I do."

"No. You want your *sugar daddy*."

Sucker punch.

It's not that I wanted him instead. But Blue was going to drop another grand tonight to keep me off cam. While I was here, with her. It felt wrong. I knew it was mainly social conditioning—girls are taught that our bodies are currency, that we owe them to men for being nice to us, for giving unasked gifts to us, for not assaulting and raping us—and if Blue wanted to pay me to fuck my ex and further complicate our It's Complicated–ship, that was his kink. Thank God for low-maintenance clients.

But I also thought: It's not fair to him. He can't touch me like this. All he has are his words.

And his words make me feel something that I want more of.

Ellis saw my hesitation. Hurt blossomed in her face. She wrenched away, left the room.

"Elle—"

"It's fine. Go see *him*."

Ask me again, I thought, and I'll stay.

Ask me. Please.

But she didn't say another word.

———

"Hi."

SoBlue: hi.

I sat cross-legged on my bed, swishing a bottle of beer. Silence for a minute. "Bad day?"

SoBlue: no.
SoBlue: just feeling more ruminative than talkative.

A knot loosened in my gut. "Me too."

SoBlue is typing . . .

Then nothing. Erased.

"Can I make a request?"

SoBlue: shoot.

"Press Enter instead of Delete. Before you second-guess yourself."

SoBlue: ha.
SoBlue: deal. but you too. no self-censoring.

"I couldn't censor myself to save my life. It's a legit problem." I sipped golden ale that tasted like malted passion fruit. From my window the sunset clouds looked oil-painted, a soft scumble of cobalt and coral. A gentle Monet sky. I wondered if Ryan had ever sat in his window and watched the paint melt off the troposphere and trickle into the ocean. "I don't know what the hell I'm doing anymore. I keep getting into situations where I have to make some life-defining choice. When does that end?"

SoBlue: when life ends.

Shiver.

"Something really bad happened to me once, Blue. I almost died. Someone else did instead. And I keep feeling like God made a mistake, that he let the wrong person live. The person who's too afraid to even commit to her own life." I took a swig. "There. No self-censoring."

SoBlue: that can happen even when you think you know what you want.
SoBlue: someone i know used to be a star athlete.
SoBlue: golden boy. bright future.
SoBlue: but he had an accident and became disabled.
SoBlue: no more sports. whole life uprooted.
SoBlue: now he feels adrift, like you.

"Is he depressed?"

SoBlue: very.

"What keeps him going?"

SoBlue: pet projects, diversions, amusements.
SoBlue: but nothing truly fulfills him.
SoBlue: he's hollow.

Is he you? I wondered.

SoBlue: point is, nobody knows what to do with this life.
SoBlue: and the second you think you do, your life will flip upside down
SoBlue: like this:
SoBlue: (╯°□°)╯︵ ┻━┻

I laughed. "Emoji zen, huh?"

SoBlue: some of my most profound thoughts are emoji.

"We are such Millennials."
In the back of my mind I thought:
Or you're really good at faking it.

SoBlue: i feel ancient tonight.
SoBlue: like a . . .
SoBlue: redwood tree. or something.

"Are you trying to say you've got some massive wood?"

SoBlue: maybe i am.
SoBlue: maybe you should take your shirt off.

I set the beer bottle on the windowsill. My thighs tensed and a pull started low in my belly. We'd never done anything sexual before. I was still amped from Elle, my blood fizzing. I checked myself in the cam: hair tucked into a lazy chignon, my body draped with shadow. This wasn't my pro setup with floodlights and calibrated colors. But if he wanted that, he could've asked.

I grasped the hem of my tank and held eye contact with the lens until I pulled the shirt over my head.

Typically after an article of clothing came off, I'd flaunt the newly exposed area. Instead I just sat there in my bra, arms limp, feeling him look at me.

SoBlue: god.
SoBlue: you are so beautiful.

"Remember what you said, about seeing how long I could last?"

SoBlue: yes.

"This is how long. I want you to fuck me, Blue."

SoBlue: you.

SoBlue: you have no idea how i've craved those words.

SoBlue: touch your belly.

I did, remembering how I'd asked Dane to do the same.

SoBlue: stroke.

A breath escaped me involuntarily as I complied. I ran a palm up and down my skin, slow, feeling the taut satin he must be imagining. He didn't type for a while, so I let the hand stray. Up between my breasts, down between my thighs.

SoBlue: i can feel your softness.

SoBlue: all curves and silk.

SoBlue: open your bra.

On the upstroke I caught the clasp and flicked it open. When my breasts fell free I took one in my hand, ran my thumb around the nipple. My breathing grew pronounced, my breast swelling in my palm. I raised my chin, top teeth bared. That fuck-me look.

"Are you hard, Blue?"

SoBlue: like you wouldn't believe.

SoBlue: put the other hand around your throat.

SoBlue: just below your jaw.

I did it languorously, fitting it beneath the bone and gripping till the carotids throbbed, two wings of blood. My nipples hardened. I dug my thumb into an artery and exhaled slowly, slowly, like the last sigh leaving the lungs at death. A pleasant buzz percolated over my brain.

SoBlue: tighter.

"You, too."

SoBlue: i am.

SoBlue: i'm so fucking hard.

SoBlue: show me how you'd hold me.

My hand clamped and the head rush made my skull feel like a shaken bottle of soda. A vignette of fog gathered at the edges of my awareness, a dulling of all senses. I couldn't keep this pressure up for long.

SoBlue: how does it feel?

"Like falling asleep. It's fuzzy and strange but also . . . lucid. Dreamlike." My voice was gauzy, drifting. Letters swam on the screen. I squeezed my breast and felt only an abstract tingling, as if my body were not fully here but ethereal, in between worlds.

SoBlue: release.

Letting the blood flow again hurt more than cutting it off, and that was part of the rush. Pins and needles in the brain.

SoBlue: take your shorts off.

He wasn't giving me time to recover. Good.
Woozily I unbuttoned, slid out.

SoBlue: panties.

Those too. Then I was completely nude in front of Blue for the first time in private.

My head felt heavy and gimbaled, like a lantern in a ship, pivoting with the waves. Red had drained from the sky and now it was a deep hyacinth purple. The laptop lighting made me look like some creeper on Chatroulette. Between my thighs was only darkness.

"What are you thinking about?" I said, my voice thick.

SoBlue: my hand between your legs.

"Like this?"

I dragged my left hand up the inside of a thigh. Before I touched myself I could feel the wetness, and the thought that it was partly because of Elle and partly Blue turned me electric. In that moment when my fingertips traced my lips and every nerve sparked like a firecracker, I realized I had an image in my head: a tall, lean, fair-skinned man, hair and eyes of indeterminate shade. His hands I pictured clearly: those long elegant fingers, veins cording up his arms like fine blue vines spiraling up Grecian marble. Hands that typed with surgical precision, never misspelled. That would touch me that way, too. Laconically. Intensely. Not a single movement wasted.

In a real private show I'd have my pussy up to the lens, anatomy on display in absurd HD. In this show you couldn't even see it, just my hand delving into shadow.

And it was more erotic than any show I'd ever done.

SoBlue: inside.

I was so wet it happened almost before I realized I was doing it. My finger slipped inside and I groaned, a real one, no porn star fakery but an animal sound from low in my gut, full of agony and resentment because this felt so goddamn good and I didn't want it to end and also didn't want to endure it.

SoBlue: show me how she fucked you.

Everything in me stilled. "What?"

SoBlue: don't stop.
SoBlue: fuck your finger.
SoBlue: and show me how she fucked you.
SoBlue: the object of your obsession.
SoBlue: red.

Shock is an incredible sexual tool. It intensifies arousal. Blue knew what he was doing.

"Like this." I brought the other hand to my clit, carefully. It was hard to get off with both hands since the accident. One too gentle, one too fierce. "With her fingers. Inside me." My words unraveled into a gasp. Part of me was picturing Blue's hands, a stiff finger between my legs and his cock in the other fist, pumping slowly, matching pace with the way he fucked me. But part of me was picturing her. Holding me in our bed, kissing me sweetly, delicately, while she fucked me with two fingers, so tender we kept pausing to touch each other's faces, constantly stunned.

Cognitive fucking dissonance.

"It was intense, Blue." Slow down, slow down. Lightly. I took my finger deep and held still, teeth gritting at the tightness. Tension unrelieved by friction. "She used to do this. Drive me crazy till I wanted to hurt her for not letting me come. I'd wrap my hands around her throat and squeeze. Till we were both right at the edge, and everything became so clear. Clearer than when you actually come. Clearer than reality. It's like looking into the sun. You can't take very much of it. I'd beg her to finish and she'd say, 'You're so pretty when you come,' and I felt it, I felt beautiful in a way I haven't with anyone else. Deeper than my skin. My blood or marrow. She saw through all that like no one else does."

SoBlue: you see her the same way.

"I wish I didn't."

SoBlue: why?

"Because what does that make me?" My face lowered as I withdrew my finger, felt the stark loss, the need to be filled again, fucked, and I closed my eyes and shut Ellis out and thought of Blue. Slim straight hips, jeans unzipped. His cock hard and hot to the touch. "I'm bi, but I prefer guys." I penetrated myself again but in my head it was him, my back to a wall and my knees hooked around his waist. "I've been with girls before, but never seriously. Not like her." Broad shoulders, dense bone. His dick driving into me and filling me with heat. "Guys are different. The way you think, the way your mind works . . . that's what I fall for. That's what thrills me. With girls it's just sex. No romance, no fantasy. Not for me."

"I love you," I'd told her, "but this isn't my future, Elle. This isn't what I dreamed of."

"What did you dream of?"

"She's the only exception. And that's not how I see myself. Not as some—whatever. I'm not like that."

"Me in my mother's wedding dress. A cathedral full of sunlight. My family in a front pew, his family in the other."

"I don't know what to do."

I heard the incoming message pings from Blue, but I was lost in myself, in the fantasy of fucking him. The fantasy of riding his cock and feeling completely enveloped, his arms around me and his muscle and masculinity something solid, steadfast. Something normal.

"And you next to me, Ellis. As my maid of honor."

"Go to hell."

"Sometimes I wish I'd never met her."

SoBlue: you're close.

SoBlue: hold it back.

SoBlue: get a tie.

I stopped, though it almost made me scream. Dug into a drawer beside the bed and found a knotted argyle tie. Slung it hastily around my neck and tugged it snug.

Strangulation was a relief, a valve slowing my thoughts. But still the memory leaked through.

"I'd rather die than be your maid of honor."

"Stop being dramatic."

"We're perfect for each other. But you can't get over this stupid idea of a plastic bride and groom on your perfect vanilla cake at your perfect straight wedding."

"Sorry to disappoint you, Elle. Sorry my dreams are so fucking heteronormative. Sorry my skin is brown and I deal with enough shit for it and the idea of becoming even more marginalized exhausts me."

"That's not an excuse. You think my life has been easy?"

"You're a rich little white girl, so yeah. Doesn't really compare."

She turned to go and I made some sound of fury, wordless, raw, and hurled myself at her. We slammed into the wall. I put my hands around her neck.

"Do it," she spit in my face. "Tighter, baby. Come on. Like when you fuck me. Because this is the only way you're okay with us being together. When it hurts me the way it's hurting you."

(—Bergen, Vada. *How to Break a Heart.*
Watercolor on paper.)

SoBlue: are you thinking about her?

"No." I grimaced. "Yes. Fuck. Stop talking about her."

SoBlue: i can't help it.
SoBlue: i'm becoming obsessed, too.
SoBlue: she's the one who gets to see you.
SoBlue: to touch you.
SoBlue: to make you wet.

"I wish it was you instead."

I wanted to yank the words back as soon as I spoke, but they were out, irretrievable.

SoBlue: selfish.
SoBlue: all that matters to you is you.

"That's right. Now tell me how you'd fuck me."

SoBlue: with this long, thick cock, morgan.
SoBlue: that i'm holding for you.
SoBlue: stroking.
SoBlue: do you want it?

"Fuck yes."

SoBlue: good.
SoBlue: because i'm going to give it to you.
SoBlue: i'm going to bury it deep.
SoBlue: make you take it all and hold it inside.
SoBlue: make you feel me pushing into the core of you.

"God, Blue."

SoBlue: pull the tie tighter.
SoBlue: fuck your hand.
SoBlue: and feel me inside you.
SoBlue: until you ache with fullness.
SoBlue: until you don't remember ever feeling empty.

I rode two fingers and held the tie in my weak fist, trying not to let the pain come before I did.

SoBlue: i'm going to hold you up against a wall and fuck you.
SoBlue: make you take every inch of me.
SoBlue: make you ride me because there's nothing to hold on to but my body.
SoBlue: all you can do is take it.
SoBlue: feel it, morgan. feel my hips meeting yours.
SoBlue: feel me pushing inside.
SoBlue: into your tightness.
SoBlue: into your sweet wet cunt.
SoBlue: you can't stop this now.

SoBlue: me and you.

SoBlue: all you can do is get fucked.

SoBlue: take my dick over and over.

SoBlue: feel it go all the way in.

SoBlue: feel me touch the core of you.

SoBlue: the deepest, sweetest part.

SoBlue: you're so full it almost hurts but you like it that way.

SoBlue: you like riding the edge of pain.

SoBlue: you like knowing i'm so close to hurting you.

SoBlue: but not knowing if i will.

SoBlue: god, you're so tight.

SoBlue: so sweet.

SoBlue: i'm going to come.

SoBlue: i'm going to come inside you.

SoBlue: show me your face.

SoBlue: look at me.

I looked dead into the lens, my body tense, combustible, waiting for the spark to set it off, and he gave it to me.

SoBlue: good girl.

SoBlue: take me deep.

SoBlue: tighter, baby.

SoBlue: you're so fucking pretty when you come.

Holy shit.

I pulled the tie to prolong my climax, catching the explosion at its peak and drawing it out into a plateau, a flatline at the height of sensation, a still frame paused at the moment of the biggest firework bursting. In reality it was just deoxygenated blood and CO_2, but it made me feel superhuman, like I could tear myself apart, or punch through the window and pluck the stars out of the sky. A moment of pure power.

Then I blacked out.

It wasn't a full-on faint, because the next thing I knew my palms were mashing the keys, spewing gibberish onto the screen, as Blue typed:

SoBlue: morgan.
SoBlue: can you read this?

I sat up, clawing the tie away from my neck. Afterward I always hated the feel of the ligature. It was a binding now, a trap, not the key to freedom.

I nodded groggily and slipped my tank back on.

SoBlue: you scared me for a minute there.

"I scared myself."

SoBlue: are you all right?

"I'm fine. Really. That was just . . . intense."

SoBlue: yeah.
SoBlue: wow.

For some reason, it was hard to look at the camera. "Do you need to, like, clean up?"

SoBlue: yes.
SoBlue: be right back.
SoBlue: don't go.

Those two small words—*don't go*—struck me as ineffably sad. A lifeline between us, across a vast digital ocean. A thin shining thread spanning the darkness.

I thought of Ellis alone in the cabin. Blue using her words to get me off.

And how I liked him because he was like her, with one key difference: he was a real boy.

What a selfish piece of shit I was.

I almost closed the chat out of guilt but he came back before I grew a pair.

SoBlue: morgan.

"Yeah?"

He didn't type for a full minute, and somehow I sensed him staring at the screen, at the pixels that made up my eyes. The way you'd look into the eyes of someone you'd just made come so hard they lost a little slice of reality.

SoBlue: i wish i could hold you right now.

My lungs felt waterlogged. As if I'd been under without realizing. As if, in the place where there should be clean air and filtered blood, there was just a sunken wrecked thing, a shattered prow, trapped air bubbles in a small space velvety with sea moss.

"Good night, Blue."

I shut everything down and lay in bed, clutching a pillow to my ribs. Tighter, and tighter, and tighter, as if I could crush it into myself, into the watery hollow between my lungs that ached to be filled with another person's heartbeat.

-FALL-

–9–

Firelight flickered over the sand. They'd dug a pit for the clambake and the smell still lingered, seaweed and lobster and steamers, mixing with woodsmoke and the cold salty air. I held Elle's hand as we picked our way around beach chairs and steel pails, vapor whispering off the melting ice, a stray sun hat floating in a tide pool as if someone had dived in and shattered into a hundred starfish.

End of summer was different out here. The beach was effaced with fog, the earth sighing out its ghosts. A breeze flicked over the ocean and sank neat and sharp through my skin like a switchblade. I shivered and Ellis drew closer, slinking her arm around my waist. In Chicago it'd still be warm and muggy but here it felt closer to the end of all things. Wind whistled over the stony, jagged shore where islands snapped off and drifted and would, someday, go fully under. A disintegrating beauty, slowly sinking into haze and abyss.

Up on the hill Max's house glowed like a golden coal. He'd invited us to the Labor Day clambake. We'd gone but skulked in the shadows, watching. He made friendly noises at his neighbors, drank, went home alone. Under cover of darkness, we followed.

Ellis stopped just shy of the road, fussing with the Bluetooth mic pinned inside my blouse.

"It's fine," I said, brushing her hands away. "He won't see it."

"I don't want to give him any cause to shoot you."

"He's not going to shoot me. Relax."

"We can still renege."

"Nope. Once I commit, I'm like a cat. I sink my claws in and don't let go till I shred everything."

Ellis sighed. "Come back to me in one piece."

On impulse I leaned in, kissed her cheek. Trailed my fingers along her jaw.

"You look beautiful," she said. "For a dork."

"So do you. For a nerd."

As I walked to the house I wondered if Max was watching me on cam. I wore a midthigh skirt and a blouse with a deep neckline, subtle makeup. On the ferry ride I'd felt Elle staring, so I'd leaned up against the railing and let the wind have a field day with me. She'd blushed, but hadn't looked away.

It was strange. Part of what made camming bearable was that I loved being looked at by men. I loved the quiet, tigerish way their eyes followed me, as if just waiting for the bars to be lifted, the cage opened, so they could pounce. The intricacies of beauty were wasted on them. They never noticed uneven eyebrows or uncoordinated shoes. A tiger doesn't care what shoes you're wearing when it eats you. Dolling myself up had never been about impressing men—I did it for myself, and for other women. To make Frankie look at me and say, "Damn. I'd go gay for that." To make Ellis stare at me in a way that made a flame start low in my belly.

With Elle it was somewhere in between. She noticed the intricacies, but she was a tiger, too.

Like Blue.

My pulse quickened as I walked up the front steps. Max

had a gun and I was wearing a wire, sort of. But he'd invited me. He wanted to talk.

I punched the bell.

When the door opened he was still in beach clothes: dress shirt, cuffed twill trousers, boating shoes. His oxford was halfway unbuttoned, revealing light chest hair. It took a second for my eyes to travel to his face.

"Good evening," he said, smiling.

"Hi."

"Come in. Please."

I hesitated on the threshold. "Are you filming this?"

"The cameras are off, Vada."

We'd have that on record, if he lied.

Inside I walked slowly, observing. The first time I'd been in here I was flustered, hyped on emotion. This time I was ready.

The house was cozy, if cliché New England—lots of bare timber and whitewashed planks and striped fabrics—with industrial touches: drafting table and stool, steel swing-arm lamps. On the mantel and in the halls were family photos: Max and Ryan and a blond woman, then later, just the boys.

"What did you want to talk about?" I said.

"Anything. I've missed your company."

Right. "You want something."

He drew up beside me, the smile still in his eyes. "I know you don't believe it, but I worry about you. It's the paternal instinct in me. You said it wouldn't go away, and you were right."

I fought the urge to touch the mic, ensure it was hidden.

"Can I get you something to drink?" Max said.

"Okay."

He poured cognac into snifters at the bar in the dining room. I reclined against the table, watching.

"How's Ellis?" he said.

"Fine."

"Did you ask her about what I told you?"

I sipped, savored the licorice burn in my throat. "Yes."

"No, you didn't. Do you know how I know?"

I stared into my glass, considered bailing. Elle could hear every word we said right now.

"It's in your eyes, Vada. That flicker of doubt."

"Leave her out of this."

"Can she hear us?"

I made my face blank. "What?"

"Is she listening in? I want you both to know I have no intention of pursuing legal action against you. Put your minds at rest, please."

Despite myself, tension uncoiled in my shoulders. "Not like you could do shit to her, but okay."

"We can stop here." Max looked at me over his glass. "You let go, and I'll let go."

"Let go of what?"

He glanced at the neck of my blouse. Then he touched his chest, the same place my mic was hidden.

It took a second for me to parse what he meant:

He didn't want Elle to hear.

I shivered. Wanted to blurt, *Why?* But instinct guided me.

"You're creeping me out, Max," I said aloud, pulling out my phone.

"I'm sorry. I don't mean to make you uncomfortable."

I sent him a text:

write it down, but keep talking out loud

"You two missed a great clambake," he said, tapping his phone as he rambled about the steamers.

MAX: **She hurt you before and she's doing it again.**

MAX: **It pains me to watch this happen to you.**

VADA: how is she hurting me?

MAX: You see it, but you won't accept it until it's too late.

MAX: Don't make the same mistake I did.

VADA: what the hell does that mean?

But instead of replying, he put his phone away.

"Did you crack the laptop password?" he said.

Thin ice. Careful. "We found some stuff, if that's what you're asking. Photos."

Against Elle's advice, I'd filed for a copy of the autopsy, too. Autopsies were public records in Maine. Ellis thought it gruesome— *"We saw how bad it was, why do you want more?"*— but the more details we uncovered about Ryan, the more I wanted to know. The more something seemed so obviously wrong, right in my face.

And Max kept trying to make this about Elle. Deflecting.

So I said, "I saw the pics. The ones where Ryan was beaten till he was nearly unrecognizable."

He drained the snifter in one gulp.

"Who did that to him, Max?"

He filled his glass again, guzzled. I set mine down and moved closer.

"Was he gay? Is that what this is about?"

He laughed, brief and humorless. "You're loyal to the people you love. Even when they lie to you."

"Stop changing the subject."

"Walk away, Vada. We'll all be happier."

"Did you hurt him?"

His glass tumbled to the floor, cracking. His hand shot out and clamped onto my shoulder. I grabbed his wrist but he was stronger and held on, grinding my bones.

"I never hurt him," Max rasped. "Never."

His hand sprang away. I massaged my right arm, glaring.

"Stop this. Please. Let me keep my memories, at least."

This was exactly where I wanted him: vulnerable, unstable. Prone to spitting out truth.

Prone to hurting me.

"You went after my friend, Max. You started this."

"I was worried. I care about you. But I can't save you from it. It's going to tear you up, like it did to me. I'm sorry."

I bared my teeth and mouthed, *Leave. Her. Alone.*

He stared at my mic.

This cryptic shit was getting me nowhere. I moved closer again, undaunted, peering up into his face.

"I don't want to hurt you, or your memories, or anything. But I need answers. I can't move on otherwise. Give me *something*. Why did the cops take the gun?"

"They found it in the Jeep."

My eyes widened. "Was Ryan going after someone? Whoever beat him?"

"He'd never hurt a soul. That was Skylar, not him."

His lips curled at the name.

Bingo.

"Tell me what she did." I leaned nearer, pressed a hand to his arm. His heart boomed so hard it rang in my bones. "Tell me what was going through Ryan's mind that night. We both want the same thing, Max. Closure. And we can give it to each other, if you just help me understand."

His eyes gleamed, the color intensified like wet paint. So blue.

"There's no closure," he said hoarsely. "It's a lie. You keep yourself distracted, pretend you're making progress, but the wound never closes, Vada. It will never close."

He sounded like Ellis. The deeper I dug, the more reluctant they both grew. Max had pried into her past and she'd pried into Ryan's. Now both of them wanted to drop it with no explanation, no resolution. Just vague warnings about each other.

As if they were rivals.

Max stepped away from me.

Instinctively I lunged after him, caught his arm. Ran my hands down to his palm and turned it toward the light.

The back of his hand was a rich gold tan, but the inside was pale. I expected roughness from boat work yet the skin looked smooth. He jerked free before I could memorize it, compare it to the photo I'd saved. The hand that held those wooden carvings.

"Leave now. Please."

"Max—"

"I want to be alone."

Goddammit.

In a final act of defiance I drank the rest of my cognac, slowly. He stood with his back to me, shoulders hunched as if expecting a blow.

He didn't turn or move. Barely seemed to breathe. My eyes played over his body, and I wished with a gutting desperation that I could draw because drawing was how I remembered things, and I wanted to remember this. I wanted to hold those images side by side.

At last I left him and stalked out into the night.

———

The constellation of Christmas lights in the rafters filled the attic with a soft radiance. Ellis sat in the dormer window with her laptop as I paced, nursing a beer.

"Got another bite," she said.

I flopped onto the bed beside her.

We'd made fake social media accounts using the names and pics of kids from Ryan's graduating class. Then we messaged his old classmates. *This is Meg. I forgot my password so I made a new profile. Can you friend me again, please?*

Amazingly, it worked. If you even remotely impersonated someone, people often filled in the blanks themselves. *You're always forgetting shit, Meg. I told Steph & Kat to re-friend you too.* Each act of trust gave us more names, pics, info.

"This is phishing," Ellis said. "If we're caught, we could go to jail."

"We're not stealing their credit cards. We're just socially engineering them to tell us stuff so we can solve a hate crime."

She pushed her glasses up, frowning. "We don't know that there was a hate crime."

"Trust me, Watson. I have a nose for these things."

"'There is nothing more deceptive than an obvious fact.'"

"What's that from?"

"Really?" She sighed. "You're more Katie Holmes than Sherlock."

I pinched her bare thigh, and she kicked me away.

Once we breached the outer circles of Ryan's senior class, we scanned through pics and comments for mentions of him. He'd been a popular jock before senior year, when the gay rumors started.

Ryan is so fine.
Too bad he likes D in his A.
Just like you, ho.

Suspicion confirmed: Ryan was closeted, acting straight. At his winter formal, three days before he died, something big happened.

I CAN'T BELIEVE MY FUCKING EYES
[image removed]
Is this a prank? Is it for real?

omfg #eyebleach #cannotunsee
LOLOLOL EPIC TROLL
OMG is that RYAN???

But we still had no idea what.

Something shocking. Disturbing. Epic.

What could he have done in front of everyone? Kissed a boy?

Rumors flew that kids who talked about *the incident* got suspended, their college plans threatened. Discussion was driven underground, into private messages and invite-only groups.

Now we were trying to breach those inner circles and find Skylar.

I rolled onto my back, musing at the ceiling. "What if she was Ryan's beard, and got sick of playing his fake girlfriend? Maybe she outed him at the dance."

Ellis twirled a lock of hair, agitated.

"What?" I said.

"This feels cruel. They're so easy to manipulate."

"Because they're dumb." I snorted at our new "friend's" profile. "I could send her a pic of Beyoncé and she'd believe I'm her. If she goes through life this gullible, something way worse will happen someday. Better to learn this lesson early."

"She wouldn't believe you're a celebrity. She believes you're her friend because she trusts her friend."

"Maybe she trusts her friends too much."

Our eyes locked, and something electric crackled between us. I was so close to asking about her name again.

"How much trust is too much?" Elle said.

"When they can hurt you with it." I didn't break eye contact. "Good thing we're not hurting anyone, right?"

"Right."

It's going to tear you up, like it did to me.

What the hell had Max meant? Maybe I already knew this story: gay son, homophobe dad. It would explain why Ellis was loath to dig deeper, scared of reliving her own past. And why Max wanted to believe she was at fault in the crash. Blame the deviant.

Except he knew I wasn't exactly straight, either. He'd assumed Elle was my girlfriend from the start, and never called our relationship *unhealthy*, like Mamá. But maybe I'd made my case for being more-straight-than-not too well. Constantly dissociating myself. Reflexively denying it.

Like the coward I was.

I got up and cracked open another beer.

"Guess I'll go," Ellis said. "So you can talk to Blue."

No bitterness in her tone, only resignation. Blue was my nightly routine now. A thousand bucks, a soul-searching dialogue that made me laugh and think. Then we got off. Every night the tension built, our flirting intensifying, growing luminous, incandescent, imploding. I put the tie around my neck. He came all over his fist. Sometimes we kept talking after. In my head I ran my fingers through his hair, his legs twining with mine. The thought of his hard slender body, his deft hands, his self-deprecating humor and intoxicatingly gentle maleness got me wet again. Sometimes we'd go for round two.

He was the perfect guy. Almost ridiculously so.

Night after night I lay awake, staring up at these fake glass stars.

What's wrong with me? I thought. Why am I obsessing over him when Elle is right here, flesh and blood, real? What do I really know about him beyond what he wants me to believe? Her, at least, I know. Why couldn't I love her the way she loved me?

It *was* the same love. I knew that.

Ellis packed up her laptop and headed for the door and then stopped, came back, and pulled something from her bag. "These are for you."

Gourmet gummy bears.

Way to make this impossible, Elle.

"Well," I said, "now you have to stay the night."

"Why?"

"To help me eat them."

I was rewarded with the deepest blush ever.

Ellis wouldn't touch beer, so we raided the kitchen and found horchata in the back of the fridge, which I mixed with rum. Half an hour later we were lying on my bed with a pile of gummy bears spread on the quilt between us. Elle half-assedly played *World of Warcraft* on her laptop.

"What exactly are we looking for?" she said, shooting arrows at a lumbering ogre.

"Her." I sorted bears into a color wheel, red to blue. "You heard Max. 'He'd never hurt a soul. That was Skylar.'"

"We don't know if Skylar did anything."

"Maybe she put the gun in Ryan's car."

Ellis frowned. "You're making a lot of assumptions about this person."

"You have to make *some* assumptions about people, Elle. Otherwise you'll never get anywhere."

"You won't get anywhere by assuming too much."

Fucking Occam.

"So you think Skylar has nothing to do with it?" I said. "They just beat Ryan up for being gay? Is that still a huge deal here, in Maine?"

"It's still a huge deal everywhere. My own parents didn't see me as human. I was an aberration. Sinful. Defective."

I touched her arm, silently.

If we'd known each other as kids, it would've been different. I never would've let them hurt her. Sometimes I fantasized about it: packing our bags and running away, teen urchins living in the city. Broke but free. Happy.

"And it's not just homophobia." She unleashed a barrage of arrows, mowing the ogre down. "Some things go deeper. Like gender. Pink for girls, blue for boys. It's the very first category we're put into as babies, before we even know who we are. Messing with that is sacrilege. It goes against everything they assume to be true about people."

"Obviously I agree, but what's your point?"

"Some people get violent when you challenge their deepest beliefs. Like their religion, or their binary definitions of people. Maybe Ryan made them question those things. Things they assumed were universal truths."

The deceptively obvious.

Could he have been bi, like me and Dane? Could that have been worse, the refusal to be pigeonholed into Us or Them? From personal experience I knew people dealt poorly with shades of gray. When I was with Elle they saw me as gay. When I was with Raoul I was straight. Neither was true.

Sometimes I bought into the black-or-white mentality, too. It was easier, picking a side. Not fighting to be recognized as a fluid, nuanced individual, but simply accepting a premade label, a prefab identity.

I'd only felt like my real self with a handful of people in this world. Ellis was one.

Blue was another.

He was unlike any guy I knew. Other men might call him weak, beta, soft, but to me his tenderness only made his masculinity stronger. He wasn't afraid to feel. Men who express emotion have more balls than those who fake toughness. His softer masculinity fit my harder femininity. We fit each other.

When I'd looked at Max's hand, I could have been looking at the hand that made me come each night. The hand
that carved the wooden animal figurines now sitting on my
desk: cat, bird, snake. Blue sent them using a mail forward-
ing service. I didn't know the origin and he didn't know the
destination—something came from nothing, arrived at nothing. Ex nihilo.

If Ellis wasn't here, I'd touch them. These things that Blue
had touched. Made for me.

If Max was Blue, how the hell would I deal with that?

It frightened me. Exhilarated me. Made me a little sick.

"I need to kill something," I said. "Let me play."

She sighed and slid me the laptop.

I went to the log-in screen to choose a character. "Oh my
god, you nerd. All your characters are blood elves."

"Shut up." She tried to grab it back but I fended her off.

"Will you relax? Smoke a jay or something." I scrolled
through the list. "Holy shit, you have one of every class at max
level."

"So I play a lot. That's not a crime."

"No, it's a sickness. I bet these names are all lore-appropriate,
too."

"Don't pretend you know what that means."

"Believe it or not, I actually listen when you geek out on
me. But thanks for the vote of confidence." I frowned. "All
your characters are guys? No girls?"

"Girls get harassed."

"But they don't know if you're actually a girl in real life."

"Doesn't matter." She sifted through the gummy bears, fin-
ishing my sorting. "People treat you the way you present. One
of the 'girls' in my guild is a guy in real life. People send her gifts
all the time. They kill monsters for her, give her the best loot
drops. But they expect attention in return. If she neglects them,

they get mad. She got kicked from her last guild for starting 'drama' between two guys who had crushes on her. All she ever did was talk to them. There was nothing unsavory going on."

"'Unsavory.' Cute. It's like you haven't been grossly corrupted by a cam girl the past couple months."

"You do the same thing, cam girl. You play a role."

I clicked on an elf in shining armor. "Everything is a role. Right now I'm role-playing a blood elf paladin. When are we ever our real selves?"

"I'm real with you."

I looked at her across the bed. "Ditto, nerd."

Ellis picked up a blue bear and pinched it till its head swelled. "You're real with *him*."

"Can't it be both? You each see different sides of me."

"What if I want all of you? What if I gave you an ultimatum, like he did? No one else. Only me. You wouldn't do it."

Would I?

Elle stared at the bear and abruptly bit its head off.

I laughed. "You are being so Freudian right now."

For a while I putzed around in the game, killing drunken ogres. I looted a rare item and the tooltip said it'd sell for a ton.

"Elle, how are you on money?"

"Rolling in it. I have this system worked out for gaming the auction house—"

"I mean in real life."

She fidgeted. "Oh. I'm fine."

"That means you're not."

"Don't, Vada. Brandt's family is helping me with bills."

"You have that nice big house on the promenade and you'd rather live in a tree. You *are* an elf."

Ellis rolled her eyes.

"Why are you staying out here, anyway? It can't just be for me."

"It's easier to meet with Frankie when I'm nearby."

"Are you avoiding your cousin?"

"No."

"Do you not want me to meet him?"

She shrugged. "I just like it here. I like when things are simple."

"But you like me, and I complicate the fuck out of you. Explain that, Professor." I frowned, thoughtful. "If you won't take my money, you'll take my gifts. Only a jerk rejects a gift."

"Open your mouth."

My eyebrows shot up. "Is this about looking gift horses in the—"

"Open."

I did.

Elle scooped up a handful of red gummy bears and stuffed them in. "There. Now be quiet."

I choked, trying not to spit. Swallowed. Set the laptop aside. Then I tackled her.

"Oh, no. Truce, truce, truce."

"You have violated our peace accord for the last time, Ellis Carraway." I pinned her to the mattress, straddled her waist, and grabbed some gummies. "Now you must pay the ultimate price."

"What price?"

I leaned in close. "Eating the blue ones."

Elle made unhappy noises as I fed them to her one by one. She was too well-mannered to spit them out, but she glared, and bit me, which made me laugh and leave my fingers in her mouth, taunting. Then the humor dissolved. Suddenly I was acutely aware of her body between my legs, her chest heaving. The heat of her tongue on my fingertips. Her eyelashes lowered and she sucked two fingers in to the knuckles, and everything tied to my spine unraveled.

"You're drunk," I said, my voice husky. "We're just friends, remember?"

I pulled out but she held on, kissed my fingertips, my palm.

"Do it for me," she said. "What you do for him."

"You want a show?"

"No." She looked at me meaningfully. "Pretend I'm him. Not one of your clients."

Well, I was drunk, too.

I rose from the bed, holding on to her hand. Drawing her with me. I wasn't really sure where this was going till I pulled the chair from my desk.

"Sit."

Ellis sat obediently, gazing up at me. She still wore street clothes but I was in a cami and boyshorts. I grabbed my phone, queued a track on the room speakers—some slinky, sultry Jaymes Young—and turned back to her.

I'd done this on cam dozens of times. But my heart had never raced this way before.

Let's do this, alcohol.

I raised a leg and set my foot between her thighs. Instantly her demeanor changed—lower body tensing, upper relaxing. Resisting and submitting at once. I trailed a finger inside her collar, traced her clavicle around to the nape of her neck. Stroked the short hair there. She bit her lip, eyes closing a moment.

Touching her was like touching water. She responded instantly, fluidly, in a way that felt as if I painted myself into her. I swung my leg astride her lap, grasped her collar. Every time my fingertips brushed her throat I felt her pulse collide with mine. I undid her first shirt button, sketched the V of skin, then the next and sketched lower. Stopped at the top of her bra and instead lifted her glasses off. Without them she looked even more androgynous. When I drew close studies of her face, you couldn't tell her sex. Sometimes a very pretty boy, sometimes a very dashing girl. A canvas you could fill with anything.

She was shy at first, but I finally convinced her to pose for me. She sat in a bath of pink-gold afternoon sun while my hand and eye traced her. My strange, bashful sylph. The light inflamed her hair and brought color to her skin, a blush of apricot in cream.

I set my pencil down.

"Did I mess up?"

I smiled. "You're doing great."

We'd been roommates for months. I knew she'd dropped out of high school. I knew she had an IQ of 161, though she resented her parents making her take the Mensa test. I knew she was gay.

I knew she had a not-so-secret crush on me.

I got up and crossed the room. Drawing made me a little drunk, the normal inhibitions—don't touch your roommate's face, don't ask her to take her clothes off—seemingly arbitrary. I perched on the windowsill and pretended to gauge the failing light, running my fingers over her cheekbones. You are so beautiful, I thought.

"Can I move?"

I laughed. "Yeah, you can move."

Elle's shoulders sagged. She adjusted her glasses. "Sorry. I'm too twitchy for this."

I took the glasses from her face and slid them into my shirt pocket.

"Hey."

"Hey what? You don't need to see." I pulled a bang free and framed her face with it. "I have an idea. But you'll hate it."

Those lucent peridot eyes stared up at me. "What?"

"I want to draw you"—I let the strand fall—"nude."

I was sure I knew the answer already. Sure I knew her shyness,

her reservation. But she stared back without blinking, then said,
in a quiet, brave voice, "Okay."

(—Bergen, Vada. *What Falling Feels Like.*
Oil on canvas.)

"You're so beautiful," I whispered now.

Our eyes met. My blood burned beneath my skin, excitement rippling over me like a film of cool silk.

I rolled my hips against her, our bare legs grazing, soft as sin. Her hands went to my back and pulled me closer. I unbuttoned her shirt the rest of the way, let it fall open. Skin to skin. This body I'd drawn so many times I knew it better than my own. This body I'd held so many nights I hated to sleep alone anymore. Our limbs twisted together and I ran my hands over her ribs, her breasts, her throat. She touched me back with featherlight fingers, wing tips flickering against my skin.

"Does he touch you like this?" She cupped my ass, pulled my hips to hers, and I groaned and rocked into it.

"He can't."

"Because he's not real." Ellis held me tightly now, looking up into my face with that smoky squint that undid things in me. "He doesn't make you wet like I do. He's just words on a screen. This is real, Vada. Us."

All the blood in me rose to meet her skin. I was drunk and turned on like fuck and I lowered my head to kiss her, but she put her hands on my face, holding me back.

"We're just friends," she said. "Remember?"

It had been like this that long-ago afternoon, too. I'd taken her shirt off and my hands wouldn't leave her body and then hers were on mine. I'd straddled her lap like I did now, twined myself with her, and simply breathed. And even though I was insanely horny and wet, it felt perfect to stop there. Right at the wild trembling brink. Before we kissed, before anything else.

In the kink world they call it edging. Taking yourself to the shivering edge of climax and pulling back before you come. Stop, wind down, start over. Again and again until discipline shatters. Blue loved it, loved jerking off while he watched me fuck a silicone cock until I was about to explode, then told me to pull out. Wait. Let desire rage and cool. Start again, angrier, meaner. Desperate.

You could do it with intimacy, too. Hold her in your arms and put your hands on her body and stop before you hit the edge. Run full-tilt for oblivion and pull back at the last second, over and over. It was a way of having something without having it. Of having someone. And I'd done it to her so many times because I was just lonely, it was just closeness. We were just friends.

The lie we kept telling ourselves.

Ellis slid both hands into my hair and stared into my eyes. I let her have her way, let her press her lips to the cords of my throat, my collarbone, not quite kissing. Let my body sink against hers, my face in the curve of her throat. Hair tangled, hearts aligned. Beating together. Perfectly synced. She stroked my back as if drawing me, shading in the bones and hollows. Filling me with her shadows the way I filled her with mine.

"How does it feel?" she whispered.

Just as quietly, I answered, "Real."

In the morning my bed was empty. The old ache surged till I rolled over and saw Ellis sitting in the window seat, staring into the misty milk-white light. She wore a T-shirt of mine and balanced her laptop on her knees. When she gave me a small, serene smile I fought a crazy urge to drag her back into the bed.

"Hi," she said. "We've got a lead."

"Hi. Wait, what? Show me." I levered myself up on my bad

hand and my head filled with neon red. My arm gave out. I flopped back onto the mattress. "Fuck my life."

"Is this going to be a bad day?"

"Feels like it."

Elle helped me dress. It felt wrong, letting her do this not because it was sensual but because I physically could not do it without pain. Jaw clenched. Body bristling. I stared at the wall behind her and pretended it was a game, just role-playing. The wounded fighter. The valiant whatever.

I needed caffeine before I could process new information. Down in the kitchen she poured coffee while I waged a losing battle with the frustration colonizing my face.

"Talk to me," Ellis said. "I know you need to vent."

I yanked open the cutlery drawer and grabbed a handful of teaspoons in my good fist. Spread them on the counter before her, the silver jingling musically.

"Ever heard of the spoon theory?"

"No?"

"This is me." I counted out ten spoons and shoved the rest aside. "Like a video game. This is my life bar. These are my hit points for the day."

"Okay."

I picked up a spoon lefty. "This is what it costs me to wake up, when it feels like a shark is chewing my hand off." I flung the spoon into the sink and it banged on steel.

Elle watched me warily.

"This is taking a shower." I flung another at the sink. It missed, skidding over the counter and onto the floor. "Getting dressed." Another. "Eating breakfast." One more.

She didn't blink.

I nudged the remaining six together. "This is what's left of me when I start the day. This is how much of me I have to give." I slumped on the counter, suddenly fatigued. "Six spoons, and everything I do will cost more. When I'm out, that's it. I can't pull the zipper on a hoodie, or buckle a seat belt, or cut my meat for dinner. I can't hold still without being in pain. And tomorrow might be worse, so maybe I should've saved a spoon or two today, as a buffer. I never know." I flung the drawer open, swept the rest back inside. "It's always in my head. How many I have left. How many it costs to do something. It's like doing taxes for my body, constantly. And the counting itself costs a spoon. And feeling shitty about feeling shitty costs another."

"Is there anything I can do?"

"Invent a time machine."

"As you wish, Your Highness." Elle gave me a rueful smile, and I softened inside. "Have I ever made you feel bad about this? In any way?"

"No. You always treat me like me. And I love you for that."

Her lips parted but before she could speak, Frankie walked in.

"Good morning, ladies." When her eyes settled on me something ticked in them. "Can we talk alone?"

"You can say anything in front of Ellis."

Rose bloomed in Elle's cheeks. Frankie shrugged.

"It's about the private sessions."

Fuck. Blue. "Yeah?"

"You've barely earned a dime for me all month. You don't work the room anymore. No tips. Just these private shows with a guy who's paying you on the side. But you're still living here, using my bandwidth, my equipment, my security. And that makes me feel, well, *used*."

"It's a temporary thing. I have a—motivated client."

Frankie leaned on the counter, folding her arms. "I'm not a hard-ass. What you do on your own time is fine, as long as you fulfill your contractual responsibilities. But you haven't been working for me. You've been working for yourself." She raised her palm and a gold ring flashed, a loop of sun. "If you feel the contract is unfair, we can discuss it. Perhaps renegotiate some terms. But I need to know where your head's at. If you're thinking of striking out on your own—"

"I'm not." I avoided looking at Ellis. "I let it become too personal. I'm sorry."

"Morgan, you know better than that. Clients are clients."

"I know." Clearly not.

"This needs to stop. Not just for me. It's for your own good, darling."

I rotated a coffee mug on the counter. "So you need me to cam publicly?"

"Yes."

"What if my client doesn't allow that?"

"Drop the client."

"What if I pay you a percentage of what he pays me? Then you're still getting a big cut. That's fair, right?"

"It's not just about money. I've shaped our brand around you. On the traffic you drove to the site. You were my number one cammer all summer. Our reputation rests on you, Morgan." Frankie sighed. "In the last month traffic's been down thirteen percent. The only change is you."

"Okay. What's my deadline to fix it?"

She laid a hand on my arm. "No ultimatums. You're an adult, and a friend. Just take care of it."

Somehow that was less comforting than a simple deadline.

"I've got to run," she said. Then her gaze flicked between us rapidly, taking in our messy hair, Elle wearing my shirt.

"What?" I demanded.

Frankie pursed her lips as if holding back a smile.

When she left I faced Ellis. She had that too-innocent look that meant she was trying not to smile, either.

Great.

Even when I *wasn't* sleeping with my best friend, people thought I was sleeping with my best friend.

I lifted my mug. "So, what's our lead?"

———

Sergio Iglesias. Twenty-one. Bartender up in Bar Harbor this tourist season. About to head home to Boston.

Alleged ex-boyfriend of Ryan Vandermeer.

"This is pretty much our only hope," Ellis said, "because now our cover's blown."

One of our fake profiles was outed. Word spread about someone poking into Ryan's past. In an apt Maine idiom: they clammed up.

"Then we're going to Bar Harbor," I said.

Ellis and I eyed each other a moment. We both took a deep breath.

But I said it first.

"I'll drive."

———

We headed northeast through trees turning shades of vermilion and cantaloupe, a wildfire frozen in a single still frame, the flames caught midleap against a hard blue sky. I took coast roads, threading along the ragged rocky shore. The last time we were in a car together was the night of the accident.

I hadn't really driven since then, boats notwithstanding. And it felt so good being back behind the wheel that in less than ten minutes, I was speeding. Just a touch. Everyone speeds, anyway. I was smart about it.

"Detective, I didn't have a single moving violation in seven years."

Ellis was edgy. I switched on the radio and she switched it

off. We drove up ocean roads splashed with crisp champagne sun, the air cool and tinged with the sweetness of dying leaves, and I started singing Chester French's "Nerd Girl" to cheer her up. It was pretty much her theme song.

She flipped the radio back on.

"Is that commentary on my voice or song choice?"

Elle turned the volume up.

I laughed. She scowled, but I saw the tug of a smile.

We were cruising up a two-lane highway, approaching a semitrailer in the oncoming lane, when it happened. An SUV darted out to overtake the semi. It barreled straight at us, easily going sixty, the driver instantly panicking and veering left. Elle shrieked something unintelligible. The truck edged to the right to avoid our imminent collision.

In my head, it played out in cinematic slo-mo. The SUV peeled one way and the semi the other and I angled smoothly into the opening zipper of space between them. I hit the horn with my bad hand, too weakly to even trigger it. We slipped between two roaring walls of steel, coming out unscathed and untouched on the clear blacktop beyond.

"Oh my god, oh my god," Elle was saying.

All three of us pulled onto the shoulder, signaling that we were okay—the trucker concerned, the SUV driver rattled. I waved back, totally calm.

Then I looked at Ellis and unbuckled my belt. "We're okay," I said, wrapping my arms around her. "Hey, look at me. We're okay. Everything's okay."

She would not stop shaking.

"Are you going to be sick? Do you need to get out?"

"No." She hugged me so hard I could barely breathe. "Oh god. I'm so glad it was you."

"Glad it was me what?"

Elle pulled back to look at me. "Driving."

I held her for a long moment. The way she said it made me wonder.

Are you finally starting to remember?

We were quiet the rest of the way to Rockland, where we stopped for lunch on the harbor. But neither of us was super hungry so instead we walked down the long granite breakwater, a stony finger stabbing deep into the blue heart of Penobscot Bay. In the distance the tiny sails could have been stuck on toy boats. I took photos of smashed whelk shells and algae braided like mermaid's hair while Elle perched on the edge of the breakwater, vaping, staring at the horizon.

"Did you know," I said, sitting beside her, "that this whole state is a giant Winslow Homer painting?" A wave rolled in and burst on the rocks at our feet, needling us with sharp spray. "It's still being painted. If you sit here too long, they'll add you in. Then they'll have to title you. *Blood Elf on the Breakwater*."

Ellis smiled. The steam she exhaled tore into liquid clouds, infusing the air like white ink.

"Still freaked about that car?" I said.

"No."

"What's eating you?" I bumped her elbow. "You've been different lately. I think you don't really want to do this."

Her eyes flashed to me, then away.

"See? As an artist I notice these things. At least, someone called me that once. She probably had no idea what she was talking about."

Elle blew minty steam at my face. "I told you, it depresses me. And it's scary, too."

"What is?"

"The way people treat each other." She flipped the pen deftly over her knuckles. "The way they treat those who are different."

"You worried we'll run into some gay-bashing *cabrónes*? I'll handle it. If you haven't noticed, I'm kinda ripped from rowing. Come at me, fuckboys."

She laughed. "You've been different lately, too. More like your old self."

"Obnoxiously alpha female?"

"You've got your confidence back. It looks good on you, Vada."

How fucked-up was it that my confidence came from dumping the blame on some poor suicidal gay boy and jerking off for some stranger on the Internet?

By the time we reached Bar Harbor upcoast the sun had slipped below the trees, skeleton fingers of shade dipping into the ocean and pulling the world under. Ellis was calmer. When I floored the gas to pass someone she held her breath but didn't freak. My right hand lay on the console between us, and after a while hers joined mine, her touch soft as a new brush. We glanced at each other. Sunset flooded the car, raising all the blood and warmth in us to the surface, tinting the chrome to brass and gold. For a second she kept stroking my fingers absently, then blushed. But she didn't take her hand away.

God, fuck. Fuck, what was I feeling? Something vast and powerful stirring in my chest. Like an ocean swell. A massive wave rising over my heart, beginning to bear down.

We checked into our hotel on the harbor. I'd booked a suite with a bay view, hardly glancing at the price. A year ago my pulse would've skipped. Now I had enough cash to put a down payment on a house, or invest in a business.

It was intimidating. I felt like a kid. Could I just feed my money into a machine and twist the dial and get something that'd make me smile, please?

On the harbor, lanterns lined the piers, golden rings scalloping the dark water. A luxury yacht glided past, glimmering like a jeweled dagger as it cut through the night. Tiny paper-doll people moved on deck.

"Think they're happy?" I said as Ellis came up beside me.

"Right now someone's leaning on the railing, looking at us, wondering the same thing."

"Think we're happy?"

No answer. Her eyes were far away.

"Okay." I crossed the room, flicked a lamp on. "One of us should go and one stay. Two girls walking into a mostly male gay bar is way too conspicuous."

"I agree."

"Good. So I'll go."

"No, I will."

We faced off.

"Ellis, his name is Sergio Iglesias. I've kinda got a lock on the Latino thing."

"And he's gay, and works at a gay bar. And you're not. But I am."

"So you're going to walk into a bar full of gay men and be like, 'Hi, I'm the cute token lesbian, please confide in me'?"

"No. I'm going to walk into a bar full of gay men *as* a gay man."

My jaw dropped. "What?"

"I can pass."

"Elle." I moved toward her, half smiling, trying not to seem condescending. "You're not *that* androgynous."

"Yes, I am. You're not looking at me like they will. You're seeing our history, our baggage. They'll just see me."

I stopped, taken aback.

"He'll open up more to another man. No offense, but you'll come off as a fruit fly, Vada." She grimaced apologetically. "I can do this. I'll show you. Just . . . wait here."

She grabbed our duffel bags and disappeared into the bathroom.

I collapsed onto the king bed, feeling oddly winded.

We'd come all this way and now I was being sidelined.
And Elle judged me for not seeing her as she really was. And
I missed Blue.

And damnedest of all, I wanted to talk to someone I never
turned to when I was feeling down.

I brought up my phone contacts. Hovered over the name.

Tap.

She answered after one ring. "Is this intentional, *mija*, or is
it a butt dial?"

I laughed. "It's not a butt dial. *Hola, Mamá.*"

"Oh, your sweet voice, *cariño.*"

Hers trembled, and I felt the instant prick of tears starting.
How the hell did mothers do that? From zero to
gut-wrenching guilt in three seconds.

"I can't talk long," I said, switching to Spanish. "I've got
plans tonight. But I just—I missed you."

"That is all I wanted to hear from you, sweetheart. Those
words will make me smile for months."

"Keep twisting that knife, Mamá."

"What does that mean?"

"Uh-huh." She knew damn well. "How's Ariana?"

"Devastated. Her young man had wandering eyes. The
engagement is off."

Surprise, surprise. "Sorry to hear that."

"She's seeing someone else already. I told her she should
start taking some college classes, like you."

"I'm a dropout. A failure."

"No. You're taking a hiatus. How is the freelancing?"

I'd lied to her, said I was doing freelance photography for
cash. Her heart would shatter if I told her I was a cam girl.

"It's okay. I'm saving up money till I figure out what I want to do with my life now."

"Good. Smart girl. Like Ellis. And how is my *flaca*?"

"She's . . . fine."

"You patched things up?"

"Yeah, we did."

"*Cariño*, listen. There's something I want to say to you."

Oh god. "You really don't have to—"

"No, please. I've been thinking about it, and praying. God does not make mistakes, Vada. Only we do."

"Okay . . ."

"If someone makes you happy, that is not a mistake. Falling in love is not a mistake. God made you how you are. Everything good comes from Him."

"Elle doesn't believe in God, Mamá."

"I know. I love her anyway. And I love you, no matter who you are, or who you love."

Everything went all shimmery and bright. I closed my eyes for a second.

"I'll let you go, sweetheart. Be safe tonight. Have fun. And call your mother more often. Then the knife won't twist so much."

When we hung up I lay there clasping the phone to my chest.

The bathroom door opened. I sat upright.

Ellis—someone—stepped out and walked toward me.

This person looked like my best friend, at first. But little differences started pinging my consciousness. Hair styled in a quiff, the cut that had looked cute and punkish on a girl becoming suave and rakish on a boy. Shoulders set squarely, head held high but relaxed. Slow, deliberate movements. Sustained eye contact. Even the way this person breathed was different—it came from deep in the diaphragm, the core. This person looked so much calmer and more confident than my best friend. So much more centered.

I stood and said, ridiculously, "Ellis?"

"Hi."

Her voice was lower, but not in an affected way. It came from the gut.

"Holy shit," I said.

I moved closer, circling, evaluating. Glasses off, revealing all the angles of her face. Slight squint, flattened lips. Hints of hardness. She wore slim jeans and a button-up shirt, tucked in and belted. Elle was ultra skinny to begin with, narrow-hipped, but now there was no hint of breasts, either. I ran a hand right across her chest and she didn't flinch.

"Where are your boobs?" I said, trying not to laugh.

She answered in that smooth, low voice. "Under two sports bras. I'm kind of hot."

I stopped in front of her. "You are kind of hot."

No blush. She merely looked me in the eyes with a glimmer of satisfaction.

I touched her throat, the faint shadow sculpting her Adam's apple. "Is this my makeup?"

"Yeah."

"How are you so good at this?" I leaned out a bit, taking in the whole package, and gaped. "Oh my god. Are you packing?"

She tucked a thumb into her pocket. "I'm a perfectionist. Does it look fake?"

"No. It looks legit. What is it?"

"Pair of socks."

I laughed, but in awe. "You are blowing my mind right now. What do I even call you?"

"Ellis."

Again there was a strange moment that felt like a revelation, but also something I already knew. Like what she'd said about me driving earlier.

"Of course." I stepped back. "I can't believe you did this with some hair product, a couple of bras, and a pair of socks."

At last she cracked a smile. "All the world's a stage."

When she smiled at me—a smile I'd seen thousands of times in my life—my heart fluttered in a weird new way. Because I wasn't seeing my best friend, Elle. I was seeing some handsome, slender, sensitive-looking guy named Ellis smiling at me. A guy who could stand next to someone like Dane and completely pass.

This was way too much for me to process.

"You okay, Vada?"

"Fine. Want a ride to the bar?"

Her phone buzzed. "My cab's here."

"Your cab?" I eyed her askance. "You knew this would work. Going in drag. Why didn't you mention it till now?"

"It seemed simpler to show you."

And then to bounce, before I could ask questions. Before it could sink in.

I turned away, pretended to do stuff on my phone. "Text me if anything gets skeezy. I'll wait up."

"You sure you're okay?"

"Yup."

I peered into the hall and watched her leave. From the back the illusion was flawless. That was not the girl I knew.

That was a guy.

I walked from the patio down to the sea, the whispery sweep of waves like jazz brush drumming. Strands of tinsel moonlight floated on the water. The anxiety and unease in me all gathered into an ache at my elbow and I felt as if I could fire bullets from it, or set it on fire, or rip it out of the socket. Wasn't sure whether I wanted the badness out or if the badness could stay as long as I escaped. Pain makes a body a prison, the same way desire does.

So I did something stupid.

This was bumfuck tourist-trap Maine, near the Canadian border. Whatever cell tower my phone triangulated to, it was hundreds of miles from my actual place of residence. And I was a little past caring anyway.

I sent an email to Blue.

I'm having the most surreal night
come talk to me before my brain melts

There. Done. He could trace the IP and see that I was in Bar Harbor if he wanted.

Not like my life could get any crazier.

I knelt on cold rocks at the water's edge, my face flecked with stinging spray. In less than a minute he replied.

Skype?

no, private chat on my site
meet me in 5 mins

As long as he went through the cam site, the region ban would block Maine IPs. Not foolproof, but better than nothing.

Could I really picture Max going to the trouble of constantly masking his IP, then chickening out when he had the chance to touch me, in his house?

Could I have pictured Ellis as a convincing guy before tonight? My visualization skills had obviously gone rusty.

"You know," Ellis said once, "rust is just oxidation. The same chemical process as fire. Oxygen interacts with steel, electrons drift from one element to the other. So really, rust is a slow fire. Isn't that weird? Water causes something to burn."

Back in the hotel I put the burglar chain on the room door and opened my laptop.

He was waiting.

SoBlue: hi.
SoBlue: how long has it been?

"Three days."

SoBlue: is that all?
SoBlue: only feels like three eternities.

"Miss me?" I said, my legs sprawling to either side of the keyboard.

SoBlue: not a bit.
SoBlue: and the fact that i've been jerking off to you nonstop means absolute zilch.

I sank against the pillows. "Bad boy. While you're over there painting the walls white, I'm learning self-restraint."

SoBlue: bad girl.

SoBlue: such vulgarity.

SoBlue: it's hot as fuck coming out of your mouth.

SoBlue: but tell me what was melting your brain, before you melt mine.

I looked at his black rectangle. Then at the girl on my side: dark hair raveling around her shoulders, long brown legs spread. Beautiful but interchangeable. Another cam girl.

If I wanted him to be real, I had to be real, too. Not just this face and this body, but this heart.

"Blue," I said, "I think I'm falling in love with two people at the same time."

SoBlue: i see.

I would've killed to hear his voice then, gauge his tone. Jealous, indifferent, intrigued?

"And the scary thing is, I'm not sure I really know either of them. Not the way I thought."

SoBlue: one of them is red.

"Yes."

SoBlue: something happened tonight.

SoBlue: tell me.

"This will make me sound like a total asshole, I hope you know."

SoBlue: i'll probably still like you anyway.

"Probably?"

SoBlue: this will make me sound like a total asshole, but . . .

SoBlue: i'd like you even if you were a monster.

SoBlue: who frowned at puppies.

SoBlue: and tipped over wobbly kittens.

SoBlue: and thought comic books were for children.

SoBlue: and had a complicated pseudo-sexual relationship with her best friend.

I laughed, immensely relieved he framed it that way first. "Okay."

SoBlue: this goes back to that night, doesn't it?

SoBlue: when the bad thing happened.

SoBlue: that you don't talk about.

"Yeah, it does. And now I'm going to talk about it."

I told Blue the official story—designated driver; ice on the bridge; tragic collision—and then I told him the aftermath. How I lost Ellis, dropped out of my MFA program, became a cam girl, found Ellis again. How I got close with Max. How he flipped on me, tried to turn me against Elle.

I looked into the cam lens as I spoke, imagining different faces looking back. Max. Dane. Curtis. Even Brandt, whom I'd never met.

Names have power. They change the way the world sees you.

One man called himself Blue, and made me see him differently.

"Tonight," I said, "Red cross-dressed and went stealth at a gay bar so we can learn who beat the shit out of a dead kid and solve a possible hate crime. This is my actual life."

SoBlue: red cross-dressed?

"Yeah. Like, convincingly. Very convincingly."

SoBlue: your voice goes strange when you mention her.

SoBlue: not the dead kid, or the father.

SoBlue: red is the one who bothers you.

"It's weird. It's just weird." I grabbed a pillow and wrapped my arms around it, like a buffer. "Want to hear something fucked-up? When I saw her as a guy, I felt, like, turned on. And then I got depressed, because what if that means I'm actually homophobic? I have no problem with guys, but girls make me all conflicted."

SoBlue: feeling conflicted doesn't make you homophobic.

"If I hate the part of me that likes girls, it does."

SoBlue: do you hate it?

"I don't know. But moving halfway across the country to get away from it is a big sign, right?"

She was waiting outside my art history lecture one afternoon. The instant I saw her, I knew who she was: tall and willowy, her hair a fall of autumn leaves tumbling around her face, shades of russet, carrot, straw. An older version of Ellis.

She touched my shoulder warmly. Her eyes remained glassy and cool. "My name is Katherine. Do you know who I am?"

"I think I do, yeah."

"Can we talk?"

She took me to a coffee shop and put five dollars' worth of cappuccino in my hands. She drank plain green tea.

"Is this the part where you pay me to never see Elle again?" I said.

Katherine smiled as if holding a knife blade between her lips. "No."

"If you think you have any hold on her, you're out of your mind. She's done with you. I'm her family now."

The smile grew thinner.

"She told me everything." Night after night Elle and I stayed up talking till the sky turned pink and tender. I heard the whole sad story. Distant father, manipulative mother. Church every

week. Running away from de-gaying camp ("conversion therapy"). "Counseling" with a priest who said fucking girls meant she
wouldn't go to heaven. Ellis told the priest she was glad because
she'd hate to spend eternity with her mom. I'd fantasized about
meeting her parents someday, and now it had fallen into my lap
like a gift from God. "You should be prosecuted for child abuse,
Katherine. You're a monster."

She turned her mug with the tips of her fingers. "Imagine you're
a mother, and you watch your child suffer, day after day, when she's
too young to understand why. Would you want to stop the pain?"

"That's your logic? That's like mercy killing."

"Sometimes we have to hurt the people we love to spare them
a greater hurt."

"You caused more pain than anyone." I downed my drink in
a big gulp. "Ellis is the best person I've ever met. The smartest,
kindest. The most compassionate. Every day I'm grateful she got
away before you psychos destroyed her."

Katherine drummed her fingers on the mug rim. "I see what
she likes in you. Tough life, hard attitude. Classic bad boy, but
with a woman's heart."

My face went warm. "Don't even. You don't know either of us."

"You think we've been cruel, evil fairy-tale parents." She took a
leather folio from her purse and pushed it at me. "Look."

Bank letterhead, columns of numbers. "What is this?"

"She refuses to take a dime of our money. We know she's been
struggling. I hired someone to watch her, to make sure she doesn't
starve or get assaulted on the street. That's how cruel I am." Katherine tapped a number. "She wouldn't accept our help, so we set up
a trust in her grandmother's name. Drew up convincing-looking
documents. A surprise inheritance. Nothing to do with us. She
took it, but donated the bulk to charity. What little she kept she's
been spending on bizarre purchases. Jewelry, dresses. Things she
never cared for."

Automatically, I touched the ruby earrings I wore. Katherine's eyes tightened.

"I'm not here to pay you off, Vada. But I know you want her to be happy. She wants you to be happy, too."

"So what the hell do you want?"

"To give you a letter of recommendation. I'm a patron of the arts, and I have pull with several admission boards on the East Coast. Choose a graduate school, and I'll ensure you can go." She closed the folder. "Alone."

(—Bergen, Vada. *This Is How I Lose You.*
Pencil on paper.)

"I took her mom up on the offer," I said. "My family's broke. I've fought for everything I have. But honestly, part of me wanted to get away from Red, too."

SoBlue: you wanted her out of your life?

"No. The exact opposite. I wanted her *in* my life, in every way, just . . . not in some kind of official relationship. And she hated that." I sighed. "Not that it mattered, because I couldn't leave without her. I was halfway through packing when I broke down and begged her to come with. Funny thing was, she was planning to follow me anyway. So we left together. Her mom was pissed. She throws money at Red sometimes, trying to woo her back. But Red won't leave me. For a while it was nice, being here on our own. I thought I could do it. You know, be with her, officially. Then things got all messy and fucked-up again."

SoBlue: why not an official relationship?

"Because I really didn't want to sit down and have the 'Am I a lesbian now?' talk with myself, okay? I'd never even had a serious boyfriend. How could I know what I wanted yet?"

SoBlue: i don't think liking girls is what bothers you.
SoBlue: it's falling in love with one.

"It was never an issue before. I knew I was bi, but—maybe I internalized this from my mom, but I always thought of being bi as something that would turn off when I married a man. Then I met Red and my head filled with all these crazy thoughts. Like, 'What if I end up with a girl instead of a guy? What does that make me?'"

SoBlue: the same person, in love with a girl.

I squeezed the pillow. "You are so male. It's so fucking simple for you."

SoBlue: it really is that simple.
SoBlue: no matter who you are.

"That's not how girls work, Blue. Our minds are different from yours."

SoBlue: you have some hang-ups about gender, morgan.

"Please. Red is the biggest tomboy, and it never bothered me. Like, wears men's underwear and gets male haircuts and stuff."

SoBlue: you don't have a problem with masculinity.
SoBlue: your problem is with femininity.

This seemed totally absurd, so I just stared at the screen, baffled.

SoBlue: look, i don't want this to come off as mansplaining.
SoBlue: but i think it's red's femininity that disturbs you.
SoBlue: you're fine with the masculine side of her.
SoBlue: that's why you liked her cross-dressing.

SoBlue: you probably like being read as a straight couple in public.

SoBlue: it's when you think of her as a girl that you freeze up.

SoBlue: and start making it about you.

SoBlue: "what if i end up with a girl?"

SoBlue: "am i a lesbian now?"

"Okay, Dr. Blue. What does it all mean?"

SoBlue: you see things in a binary way.

SoBlue: feminine or masculine.

"Rojo o Azúl."

SoBlue: red or blue.

SoBlue: clever.

SoBlue: it's not surprising.

SoBlue: spanish is a heavily gendered language.

SoBlue: and language shapes culture.

SoBlue: maybe you've absorbed some ideas about gender without realizing.

I frowned.

Pajarito rojo. Little red bird. *En español,* the feminine forms of adjectives almost always end in *a,* not *o.* I never questioned why I used masculine forms with her—it just seemed to fit better.

SoBlue: are you having a linguistic epiphany?

"Shut up. So what's your diagnosis, doctor?"

SoBlue: mild femmephobia.

SoBlue: it's a real thing. you can look it up.

SoBlue: treatment plan:

SoBlue: stop being such an asshole.

I snorted.

SoBlue: and stop being so tough.

SoBlue: let your guard down sometimes.

SoBlue: i think your own femininity scares you.

SoBlue: makes you feel weak, when it shouldn't.

SoBlue: it's part of your strength.

SoBlue: you got into camming because it lets you control your feminine side, and how people react to it.

SoBlue: lets you explore it in a safe, compartmentalized way.

SoBlue: take that to the real world.

SoBlue: your real self.

"How are you more of a feminist than I am?"

SoBlue: what can i say.

SoBlue: i'm in touch with my feminine side.

"You are, aren't you?"
And it's sexy as fuck.
Who the hell are you?

SoBlue: there's that look on your face.

SoBlue: you want to tell me something.

"Good eye."
At this point he knew enough details of the accident that he could find me anyway. But I wanted it to come from me, willingly.

"Blue, my real name is Vada Bergen. I live in Maine, near Portland. I'm twenty-three."

SoBlue is typing . . .

Nothing. No send.
"You promised you'd hit Enter for me."

SoBlue: why are you telling me this

"Because I want to be real. My boss told me to stop the private chats with you. I can't be exclusive anymore."

SoBlue is typing . . .

"Press fucking Enter, Blue."

SoBlue: vada don't do this

My heart leaped, seeing him write my real name for the first time.

I typed my phone number into the chat.

"That's my cell. You can call it, text it, whatever." I was shaky but the more I revealed, the calmer I felt. "I want to meet you. In real life."

SoBlue: stop.
SoBlue: you're off-kilter tonight.
SoBlue: it's the catharsis. it makes you feel high.
SoBlue: you don't mean what you're saying.

"I mean it with my whole heart. Meet me."

SoBlue: vada.

Again my breath caught.

SoBlue: this isn't right.
SoBlue: you're conflicted about your friend.
SoBlue: you're forcing yourself into making a decision between us.

His words struck hard.

"Don't you get it, Blue? This is over. We can't be exclusive anymore. And I don't want to lose you. I want to meet you and see if this is real." My body tensed. "Tell me your first name."

SoBlue: this is a mistake.

"Tell me your name."

SoBlue: i can't.

"Why?" I said, but I knew.
Because I already knew him.

SoBlue: i don't want to lose you, either.
SoBlue: but i will.

"Man up, Blue. Show me who you really are."

SoBlue: you already know who i am.

I swallowed. Tried to speak but my voice failed. Instead I typed.

Morgan: when I think about you
Morgan: I think of this painting by Magritte
Morgan: called The Lovers
Morgan: a man and a woman are kissing
Morgan: but their heads are covered by cloth
Morgan: they're kissing through it
Morgan: but they can't see or feel each other
Morgan: that's us, Blue
Morgan: hiding our true faces
Morgan: touching each other through this digital veil
SoBlue: you see the veil as obscuring.
SoBlue: i see it as freeing.
SoBlue: we can be ourselves without preconceptions.

It can't be you, I thought. You can't be the person I think. I'll prove it.

Morgan: this is the last night you get to see me like this
Morgan: it's over
Morgan: our little online romance
Morgan: you gave me an ultimatum once, so here's mine
Morgan: either meet me irl or we're done

SoBlue: i'm not ready.

Morgan: readiness is an illusion, Blue

Morgan: remember?

SoBlue: this will change things between us.

SoBlue: irrevocably.

Morgan: I don't care

Morgan: do you really feel something for me, or not?

Morgan: because I feel something for you

Morgan: if you care about me, prove it

Morgan: no more secret online bullshit

Morgan: meet me

Morgan: let me see your face

Morgan: let me hear your voice

Morgan: show me that you're real

Now I was in Ellis's shoes, pressing someone to choose. To commit.

Thanks for the karmic payback, universe.

SoBlue: vada.

SoBlue: okay.

SoBlue: okay. we can meet.

A tingling wave washed through me. I slumped against the headboard, tension ebbing.

"No bullshitting," I said. "No putting this off."

SoBlue: when?

"Next weekend," I said on a whim.

SoBlue: where?

I thought of Dane. "Boston."

SoBlue: okay.

"Okay."

I felt like I'd been holding my breath for hours. I was light-headed.

SoBlue: i have one condition.

"You're putting a condition on *my* ultimatum?"

SoBlue: yes.
SoBlue: it's non-negotiable.
SoBlue: you'll understand when you hear it.

"So let's hear it."

This time, he surprised me.

SoBlue: i want you to bring red.

———

Warmth moved against my face. I blinked into the too-bright light. Ellis sat on the edge of the hotel bed, brushing my hair back.

"What happened to waiting up?" she said.

"A forty-ounce."

She smiled. "I drank too much, too."

"Kiss any cute gay boys?" I pulled her closer. "You smell like a Diesel store."

She laughed and pushed me away but I held on. Somehow we got tangled up, rolled across the mattress till we lay side by side. Still in her guy getup. Through the blur filter on my brain I thought: tell her, tell her, tell her.

"Did you find Sergio?"

"Yeah." She kept combing her fingers through my hair. "He's really nice. We talked a long time. He wanted to open up to someone."

"What'd he say?"

"Exactly what we expected. Ryan liked boys."

"That's it?"

She shrugged.

"There has to be more."

"He got bullied. Even Max couldn't stand it."

I frowned. "Max isn't homophobic. He's never had a problem with me."

"It's different when it's your own kid. Trust me."

True enough. Mamá didn't bat an eyelash at my best friend being gay, but my casual hookups with girls kept her up at night.

"So what happened at the dance?" I said.

"Ryan probably came out."

"But how? Did he kiss some guy? The way people were freaking out—"

"Vada, what are you hoping to find?"

"I don't know. The final puzzle piece. Something that makes the whole picture make sense."

"You always want things to be epic. Sometimes even a tragedy is just ordinary."

Lamplight skimmed the side of her face, the clean line of her jaw, the angled hollows. Her lips were soft and lily pink, girlish. Eyes narrowed, framed by long lashes. In her boy clothes she seemed like someone entirely strange and entirely familiar at once.

"Why are you looking at me like that?"

"It's like I've never seen you before, Ellis."

I pushed her down to the bed. Her shirt smelled like musky cologne and crisp autumn woods and her, just her, and I couldn't get enough. I drank her in. At some point the hand resting innocently beneath her back pulled her shirt loose, sought skin, and the mouth breathing against her ear kissed it, her lobe hot between my lips. Then it was really happening.

Legs intertwined and shirts riding up, bellies touching, soft on soft. She pulled my hips to hers and I groaned into her neck. I slipped my tongue into her ear, breathed so she felt the heat through my saliva, then the flash of coolness. She arched against me, grabbed my ass in both hands.

"I want you," I whispered. "I'm ready for this."

We twisted across the bed till she rose over me, pinning my wrists.

"Why now? Why all of a sudden?"

"It's not sudden." My left arm was stronger than hers and I jerked free, looped her waist, pulled her closer. "It feels like stones being laid on my chest every day. Small, and only a few each time, but I can barely breathe anymore. I need oxygen. I need you."

"Did something happen?"

"Will you just fucking kiss me?"

She took my face between her palms. Her mouth was bittersweet, amaretto and crème de cacao. She kissed lightly at first but when I bit her lip and opened wider she thrust her tongue inside, her body tensing, coiling against mine. So fucking hot when she was aggressive. She held me down, kissed me so hard and deep my mouth felt fucked. With my free hand I squeezed her ass, the back of her thigh. Slid between them. Gripped the crotch of her jeans.

Ellis went still, breathing hard. "Vada."

"What?"

"Are you thinking about me, or him?"

Idiot, drunken me hesitated.

She disentangled herself. Left the bed.

"Ellis, wait."

I caught her at the bathroom door. She tried to slam it in my face but I slapped my weak palm against it, crying out in pain.

"Oh god," she said. "Sorry. Did I—"

I shoved her into the bathroom. Bashed the light switch and flicked the fluorescents on. This time I was the tiger in the cage.

I was on her before she could react, my fingers fumbling at shirt buttons. I popped one on accident and the rest on purpose.

"Take your fucking clothes off," I said.

"Why, so you can see how much of a girl I am? So you can be disappointed?"

"I want you to fuck me."

"You want Blue to fuck you." She raked her hands through her hair. "This is like that night all over again. Nothing's changed. Nothing's changed at all."

You do remember, I thought. But how much?

She glanced wildly around the bathroom, panicking. Settled on the shower. Stepped inside.

"What are you doing?" I said.

"Making this feeling stop."

Ellis wrenched the water on, ice cold. She gasped but didn't recoil.

"You're crazy," I said. "Get out of there."

Her hair turned blood-dark, smashing against her eyes. Her clothes twisted heavily around her limbs.

"Ellis." I moved closer. "Goddammit."

I stepped in with her, shuddering when the water hit. It felt more like electric shock than cold. My shaking arms rose, hands skidding over her wet face.

"What are you doing?" she said, echoing me.

"Being crazy with you."

If there's a better definition of love than mutual benevolent insanity, I haven't heard it.

My tee and panties were instantly soaked. I put my arms

around Ellis, craving the heat of her body. She looked at me a moment and then kissed me again, less desperate, more a gentle inevitability, a slow fire. In the end, Atlantis didn't drown. It sank beneath the waves and burned into red ash.

Ice water jetted down on us but all I felt was her. Warm skin gliding against me. Wet hair splaying across our faces, catching in our mouths as we kissed. She pressed me up against the tiles, her hands in my sopping shirt, on my breasts. Thumbs brushed my nipples. One hand ran down my belly, between my legs, and I parted them for her, my limbs curling around her helplessly like closing petals when she pressed into that heat. She touched me through my panties. Gripped my jaw and raised my face, made me look at her while her finger pushed harder, harder, then inside. When I cried out water filled my mouth, steely, tinged with rust. She tilted my face into the stream, fingered me through wet cotton. I pulled her mouth to mine but she broke the kiss.

"Did you talk to him tonight?" she said.

"Yes."

"Did you tell him it's over?"

I didn't answer and she put a hand on my breast, pinched the hard nipple through my shirt. I let her. I took her finger deeper. I wanted this so much, so much.

"Answer me."

"No. I didn't." My head rocked against the wall. The only thing that was over was this. "I asked him to meet me in real life, Ellis."

No surprise in her face. She closed her eyes, leaned into the crook of my shoulder. Water steamed on our hot skin.

"Baby," I said softly, touching the back of her head.

Her hands fell away. She was shaking. Crying.

I turned off the water.

A swift chill swept over us. I gathered her into my arms,

this limp, lost little bird. We stood there, dripping wet and unmoving. Something hot spooled down my face. I hugged Ellis tighter, though she didn't respond.

I was a fool to fear this. To hold out for something less frightening, less risky, because all that meant was something less real. This person in my arms was one hundred percent real, breathing and shivering and crying, alive.

But I was still afraid. Still holding out for another prince, not the one in my arms.

———

Silence on the way home. The ocean was on my side of the car. Ellis stared into the pines.

When I stopped for gas before Portland, she got out and sat on the curb, watching traffic streak past. I filled up the tank and went to sit beside her.

Neither of us said anything for a while. I took a long exposure photo, taillights threading through the dark forest, glowing red veins unfurling into the twilight.

Ellis turned to me. Her mouth was grim, eyes shadowed.

"I'm going with you to meet him," she said. "And I'll drive."

———

The island postal carrier knew me by sight. She shook her head when I came jogging down to the mailbox.

Dammit. Still no autopsy report on Ryan.

You could tell a lot from the bruise patterns left by a person's hands. Whether they belonged to someone male or female. To the father, or the mysterious girl who'd touched that gun.

I needed to know how Ryan had been beaten. If it had been one person or multiple. What size hands.

Ellis barely spoke to me that week. At best I got sulky, monosyllabic retorts. Aside from confirming place and time,

Blue was scarce, too. Dane was excited to see me, but Dane got excited about pro wrestling and NASCAR.

I took the week off camming. Sat up late, alone, turning the tiny wooden animals in my hands. Obviously I was the cat, *la gata*, and Ellis was *el pajarito*, the little bird. So Blue saw himself as the snake.

La serpiente.

It made me shiver.

I walked to the tree house through drifts of citrus-colored leaves, lime and lemon and orange, crinkling like wrapping paper. The air had a dry bite, a hint of ash and bone dust. Ellis was coming down the steps as I went up.

"Where you headed?"

She stuffed her hands into her mackinaw. "To check on Brandt."

"I'm coming with. I'm going stir-crazy here."

Her eyes narrowed.

"What?" I said. "You're coming to Boston but I can't see my old house?"

"Fine."

We walked in silence to the ferry landing. Halfway across the bay, she finally spoke.

"Brandt is self-conscious about his appearance."

"I won't say anything."

"He's noticeably disfigured, Vada."

I glanced at her. "What happened?"

"It made the news in Chicago, actually. He went to our college. Some kids from Kenosha jumped him, beat him up. You know how intense their football rivalry is. He was the star recruit. Now he can't get through a day without popping pills constantly."

"Holy shit."

"He doesn't like talking about it."

"Point taken."

On the mainland all the paint had drained out of the world and soaked into the trees. Leaves rained from the sky, persimmon red, marmalade orange, dancing around our feet and swirling in midair and splattering across the streets in wild, fiery brushstrokes. My fingers froze. I took Ellis's hand as we disembarked, and she didn't let go. The heat between our palms pulsed like a heart. When someone jostled us on the ramp she gripped tighter, and I went warm all over.

At Commercial Street she turned for the East End. I pulled toward the Old Port.

"My cousin's waiting."

"He'll survive for an hour. Trust me." I tugged. "Let's do an experiment."

"What experiment?"

"If I tell you, it'll corrupt the results, Professor."

We wandered through the Old Port, past plate-glass windows full of local arts and crafts, lighthouses and lobsters stamped on fucking everything. A candy shop sold Maine blueberries that burst in your mouth like sun squeezed from an azure summer sky. I refused to give Ellis any till she let me feed her by hand. At first she balked, glaring, but after a while she gave in, and when her teeth touched my fingertips I held them there a moment too long. Juice splashed when she bit, tinting her lip purple. I pointed to the spot and watched her try to lick it off, laughing, then finally pushed her against a shop window and said, "I'll get it," and kissed her.

People passed us on the street. The cool fall breeze scattered my hair across my face. All I felt was warmth. Pure warmth.

When I pulled away, Ellis looked stunned.

I played it off, acting goofy, trying on ridiculous hats, posing with statues. I pecked a ceramic mermaid, smirking. We passed a narrow cobblestone alley and Ellis dragged me into it. I started to ask if she'd seen something neat but she pressed me against a brick wall, lifted my face, and kissed me. Not a second's hesitation. I grabbed the lapels of her coat for leverage. Inside I was nothing but water and sand, my bones made of soft coral. All the submerged things.

We stopped, breathing into each other's mouths.

"Remember?" I said, my hand sliding into her coat, against her ribs. "Do you remember the first time?"

Another rainy April afternoon in Chicago, water pouring over the city like melted pewter and nickel, gray and cold. I got off the L and shambled toward the exit. Two-mile walk home in this. Story of my goddamn life.

As I clicked through the turnstile, I saw her. Ellis, peering at the crowd as it streamed past, an umbrella tucked in the crook of her elbow.

"You're here," I said, flinging my arms around her. "I could kiss you. Actually, I will. Brace yourself." I planted one on her cheek, then started laughing.

"What?"

"Your face is experiencing chromatic inflammation."

She got mad when I pointed out her blushes, so of course I did it even more.

"I'm beginning to regret this."

"Hey, who else kisses you just for being you?"

I pulled her out into the rain, and she opened the umbrella just in time. People flowed around us. Elle turned toward the bus but I drew her on, down Division.

"Let's walk home." I slid an arm around her waist and heat flared up my veins. "It's not so bad now."

Her ribs pressed against mine. I felt the breath she took. "Okay."

On that day we'd known each other a year and a half and were card-carrying BFFs. Over hundreds of train rides and drawings and late nights, she'd opened up to me. Steadied me. Grounded me. She was there when my own family wasn't, and vice versa.

I could not imagine my life without this person.

The streets shone, coated with a mirror glaze of rain. Traffic lights leaked across the blacktop like spilled neon paint. We walked down Division, our steps slow, her arm circling me, and I thanked God I'd forgotten my keys and panic-texted her because this—this was worth it.

We passed a strip mall and I stopped. She followed my gaze.

"Gelato?" she said skeptically.

"Yep."

"But I'm cold."

If I kissed you, I thought, you wouldn't be.

And then:

Why the fuck am I thinking about kissing my best friend?

I headed for the café. She ran after to keep the umbrella above us. We pooled our money. Only enough for one person.

"You pick," she said.

"No, you. Come on. I dragged you here."

"I want you to be happy."

"I'll be happy if you're happy."

This went on for another minute until the server said, "You can do half and half."

Ellis got pistachio and I got mango. Mine tasted like whipped clouds drenched in sunlight. My eyes fluttered closed. Elle laughed and I scooped up a spoonful, extending it across the table.

"Taste."

Her gaze fixed on mine as she opened her mouth. When her lips closed on the spoon I couldn't look away. So red, a rich carmine red, as if she'd drunk blood.

"I want to taste yours," I said, and knew exactly how dirty it sounded.

She set a spoonful in my mouth. I didn't taste a damn thing.

The rest of the walk home was a haze of rain and neon, glowing bokeh confetti, red and yellow and green. We didn't touch now and when our hands grazed accidentally we both gasped, then pretended we hadn't. Stop it, I thought. She's your best fucking friend. We'd had so many close calls, tiny intense moments, our eyes meeting as our legs tangled on the couch and what had been innocent seconds ago now felt like being electrocuted for crimes we hadn't yet committed. But it passed, we laughed, she spun a finger in her hair and I smiled and thought, You just like that she likes you. It's nothing more than that.

So why the fuck couldn't I stop thinking about that spoon in my mouth, after it had been in hers?

When we turned onto our block I stepped out from the umbrella. Rain hit me like a waterfall.

"Vada—"

I took off running.

She didn't catch me. It wouldn't have mattered. I was soaked immediately, shivering as I catapulted up the stairs and ran all the way to the third floor before I remembered I didn't have my keys, because I was the forgetful idiot and Ellis was the faithful friend, always there for me. My fidus Achates.

I was calm when she reached the landing. In a way, the inevitable is calming. The if is gone. All that remains is the when.

We didn't speak. It was long past that anyway. Her hair was stringy and rain-dark, her shirt pasted to pale skin. She'd walked the rest of the way without the umbrella, to put us on even footing. Both soaked and shivering.

Sometimes someone says "I love you" so clearly that adding the words would only ruin it.

I don't remember who moved first. I just remember her arms around me, and her face in my hands, and the feeling that I couldn't spend another second of my life not kissing her. So I did. Now I tasted it, creamy pistachio, sweet like a spring forest. And a tinge of metallic rain. And her, just the way I'd imagined she would taste. I couldn't stop kissing her. Not when she fumbled at the door lock, or when I pushed her up against my bedroom wall and began to unbutton her shirt. Or even when all that remained of me was a blur of hue and light, a watery painting of a girl, dripping onto the floor in pools of rain tinted a million different colors.

(—Bergen, Vada. *Just Like I Dreamed.*
Watercolor on paper.)

Ellis laid her palm over my right ribs.

We always knew we'd get matching tats. Every day at work I'd seen cautionary tales—cheesy quotes, cliché platitudes—and vowed we'd be better. Weirder. Quirkier. We'd pick something only two people on earth would understand. A memory so vivid it would rip us straight out of the present no matter where we were.

Mine: a spoonful of pistachio gelato, melting, painterly streaks trailing down my ribs. Hector did a perfect job copying my drawing. Hers: a spoonful of mango. I'd inked her myself.

My art, my ink in her skin, forever.

"I remember everything," Ellis said. "Was that the experiment?"

"There was no experiment. I lied. I just wanted to hold your hand a little longer."

She stepped away, shaking her head. But she looked infinitely pleased.

I tried to picture Blue here instead. It was impossible to imagine anyone else in her shoes. There was no one like her.

As we walked I snapped photos, her jacket and hair vibrant against the leaden sky. Metal and rust. We angled toward the wharf, to the cyclone fence hung with locks, and searched in tense silence till we found it. The brass lion's head. *VB + EC* carved into the patina.

"I used to come check on this guy," I said, rubbing the lion's nose. "Every day. I convinced myself that when you were finally over me, you'd take him down."

The wind lashed her hair across her face. "Does this answer your question?"

We were both quiet on the way to the promenade. She padded up the porch steps while I stood on the lawn, remembering. A year ago I'd walk into our house and find her curled on the sofa with a comic book and hot cocoa, an extra mug waiting. I'd leave my scarf and boots on and pull her outside. Come with me, Elle. The sun is falling and the water looks like paint on fire. Come see.

"Vada?"

I pointed. "I used to sit in that window and watch you go for runs. There's the hallway with the floor that creaked at night. You'd wake up and make me check for ax murderers. And there's our old bedroom." I looked at her. "We didn't pretend anymore. No more separate rooms. Remember?"

In the distance, the sorrowful clang of a ferry bell, the see-saw screams of gulls. Here, a dull ache in my right arm and the center of my chest. And somewhere far away, a wrecked car rusted in a scrapyard and a gravestone grew lichen in a cemetery near the sea.

I walked past her, into the house.

Inside: big and open, rafters exposed, red iron staircases, track lights. Ellis said I liked it because it looked like a gallery. All over the whitewashed brick, in pops and splashes of color, was something that stopped me dead.

My art.

Paintings. Drawings. Tattoo plans. Casual sketches, pencil-smeared and water-stained. Even the ballpoint napkin doodles. Everything I'd left behind or given her over the years.

I moved through them, feeling detached from the body beneath me.

It was like looking at my own work and a stranger's at the same time. Definitely my style: jagged lines, dark and bold but breaking unexpectedly, splitting into fragments, as if I was so unstill I couldn't see the world as solid. Watercolor washes bled through ink drawings, dripping down the paper. Wildness. Rage. An intensity I could only capture by hinting at how much I *couldn't* capture, how I fought with brush and pen until they turned on me, shattered my lines, splattered paint.

When I reached the most recent ones I felt clammy, sick. It shifted from the fantastical—phoenixes and chimeras, weed-fueled weirdness—to human realism. Blythe dancing alone in a club, the only one in full color amid a sea of shadows, my tats alive on her arms. Armin in the DJ booth, one hand raised as the crowd gazed at him in rapture. Raoul, the only boy I'd semiseriously dated, flying kites with his kid brother, and Hector hunched over a customer with the needle, and strangers and one-night stands.

And Ellis.

Over and over. Five years of her.

My best friend. My world. My everything.

I stood in the middle of a stranger's life work. My arms hung slack, hands useless.

Ellis came to my side. "What are you feeling?"

Crazy urges. About kerosene, and a match.

"Anger," I said.

"At me?"

"At *me*. For taking this away from myself."

She started to say something and a creak sounded from upstairs, the noise that used to terrify her at night.

"Emily?" called a man's voice.

"Be right back." Ellis squeezed my arm. "Don't burn the house down."

Reading my mind, like always.

When she returned I'd slid to the floor beside the fireplace. Either the house was freezing or I was having some kind of episode. I huddled against my knees, shaking. Ellis knelt beside me and took me in her arms.

"Baby, it's okay."

Not really. Not when I was sitting in a mausoleum filled with ghosts, specters drawn by some cocky, arrogant girl who knew she was good, knew she could draw like the devil, knew she had a big bright future waiting and all the time in the world to grow into it.

I wanted to scream at that girl. Smug idiot. These are the last things you'll ever create. The last things you'll communicate to the world.

Why did you let fear control you? Why did you let it hold you back?

Ellis lifted my face, brushed tears away with the heel of her hand. "Vada."

"Emily."

She went very still.

"I've known since summer," I said. "I'm sorry."

She released me, sat back on the floor. "You didn't say anything."

"I was waiting for you to explain. It doesn't matter."

"Yes, it does." She swallowed. "Why didn't you tell me you knew?"

"Why didn't you tell me your real name?"

Her jaw flexed. "It's not my 'real' name. My real name is Ellis."

"Why did you change it?"

"Because it wasn't me." The muscle in her throat rippled. "It was someone else. Someone my parents named. Someone my parents made. This is the me that *I* made."

Her eyes were wet. Great.

"Ellis, I'm sorry. It doesn't matter. But why didn't you tell me, in all these years?"

"Because I'm *not her*. I don't want you to see me as *her*."

I started to speak but movement caught my eye.

A man stood on the stairs.

"That's Brandt," Ellis muttered, helping me stand.

"How rude. Are you not going to introduce your . . . friend?"

That voice, deep and playful, like the vibrato of a double bass. He was blond and broad-shouldered, but lean. Handsomer than I'd imagined: vulpine jaw, wry features, same dashing squint as Ellis. A Zoeller thing, apparently. Scars distorted his face, white jags of lightning pulling at the skin. His nose had a slight crook where it had once been broken.

"Hi," I said, staring.

"Hi."

Brandt smiled, revealing a gold molar. It was oddly disarming. If anything, the scars accentuated how too-perfect that face must've been before.

He slung his arm around Ellis and ruffled her hair. She elbowed him and he faked a pained gasp and when she apologized, he ruffled her hair again. They could've been twins.

"So this is the legendary Vada Bergen," Brandt said. "Now I see why my cuz is so wet for you."

"Oh my god," Ellis said. "Boundaries, Brandt."

"Sorry. You ladies care to join me in a drink?"

"You're underage."

"Relax. Vada doesn't look like a narc. She looks like she's fun at parties."

In the kitchen he took two bottles from the fridge. The opener was exactly where I remembered, and I glanced up at Ellis, my chest tightening.

"Are we having a tender moment?" Brandt said.

I snatched the bottles from him. "Are you twenty-one?"

"Busted. Twenty in April."

"Which day?"

"Eleventh."

"Mine's the tenth," I said, and popped the caps. "Okay, you can drink with supervision. But don't turn me in."

"Your secret's safe with me, Ms. Bergen."

Heat crept up my neck. I looked away.

The three of us wandered back into the living room gallery.

"You're really good," Brandt said.

I shrugged and he shrugged one shoulder, imitating me.

"I don't know shit about art," he said, nodding at a portrait of Ellis with her crooked, beguilingly boyish smile, "but anyone who makes Emily look that hot has talent."

Ellis covered her face with her hands.

"She *is* that hot," I fired back. "But thanks for the kudos. Means a lot, coming from a Philistine."

Brandt grinned.

Ellis said, "I'm going to the bathroom. Then we're leaving."

We waited quietly till she was out of the room.

"Your cousin's name is Ellis," I said. "Stop calling her Emily."

"I grew up calling her Em. Easy to slip."

"You didn't slip. You did it on purpose the first time you saw me here, too. This summer. I know you remember."

"Why would I do that?"

"Because you're a troublemaker." I leaned on a sofa. "Tell me about your disability."

"What disability?"

"You favor your left arm."

Brandt tilted his head. "Sharp eye."

"How much function do you have?"

He raised his right shoulder, grimacing. The elbow didn't bend. "It's like a parasite. Hanging off my body. Sucking me dry."

"How'd it happen?"

"I got what I deserve." Brandt laughed. "You can't run forever. The past always catches up with you."

My throat went thick. "Do you know who did it to you?"

"Do you know who did it to you?" He gestured to my right arm. "You favor your left, too. We match, Vada."

Observant.

I took a long sip, eyeing him. This wasn't anything. He was just trying to provoke me.

A bored kid, going stir-crazy in his house, like I was.

"I've dealt with depression," I said. "You can't will it away. If you need someone to talk to, I've been there."

"You want to be my therapist?"

"No. I'm not even sure I want to be your friend."

Brandt smirked. "Brutal. I like it."

"Listen, I care about Ellis. A lot. If you're part of her life, you're part of mine. But I don't tolerate people who hurt her. No matter if they're blood relatives."

"So I've heard." He lifted his bottle. "You're very protective of your personal punching bag."

I actually felt the words hit, right in my solar plexus.

Brandt's eyes gleamed. Same green as hers, but his were cold, unblinking. Reptilian.

"We should get going," I said, pushing off the couch.

He moved into the kitchen doorway.

"What are you doing?"

No answer.

I stepped around him and he touched my arm. My hand snapped to his.

"You don't want to fuck with me," I said. "And you *especially* don't want to fuck with Ellis."

"Feisty."

I grabbed his other arm and twisted it in the socket. He hissed in pain.

"Not feisty," I corrected. "Dangerous."

Tears sprang to his eyes. I released.

"Vada. Stay, please. I'm so fucking bored." He slouched in the doorway. "You two are always off playing lesbian Martha Stewart. No one can hold an intelligent conversation. Jerking off southpaw is giving me RSI. My mind is lonely."

His words and his voice resonated with me, familiar.

We had more in common than I cared to admit.

"Pro tip," I said. "Don't ever physically accost a woman. We're much more likely to stay when it's our choice."

His head bowed.

"Is everything all right?" Ellis said, coming down the hall.

"Yep." I gathered our bottles to toss in the trash.

"Those go in the recycling," Brandt said.

Ellis frowned. "Since when are you environmentally conscious?"

"I've always cared deeply about the Earth. I want it to be pretty for the day I assume control."

The recycling bin was near overflow. I rinsed the bottles and dropped them in, nudging aside wood chips and shavings.

"He's right," I said. "Apparently he composts."

"Portland chicks dig sensitive tree huggers. Right, Vada?"

"That's the other Portland."

"My bad. What kind of guys do you dig?"

"The kind who aren't douchebags."

"How about the kind who aren't guys?"

Ellis looked at him, then me. "Let's go before it's dark."

Was I actually flirting with her cousin? Fuck.

Brandt walked us to the door. He made Ellis promise to visit again soon, and wheedled me to join her, and for a moment I almost felt sorry for him. He really was lonely. As Ellis trotted down the front steps, Brandt brushed my coat sleeve. I stopped.

"I'd never hurt her," he said. "She's all I've got left."

"Good. She's all I've got left, too."

When I was halfway across the porch he called, "That's not true."

I glanced back.

"You've still got a great ass," he said.

———

On the last day before Boston, the air crackled with static.

I rowed out with Ellis beneath the gray sky. We shared a joint, lay on our backs in the skiff and stared up at rain clouds, watching our smoke rise and twist above us like nebulas, and I thought, *Tomorrow, everything changes. Reality splits. In one universe, I choose Blue. In the other, Red.*

"What are you thinking?" Ellis said.

"I feel like Neo picking a pill. Hashtag weed thoughts."

We both sat up, hugging our knees, sneaker toes touching. The boat rocked, a stray wave slopping over the gunwale and dousing my calf. I shivered.

"You?" I said.

"I was thinking about this Japanese art called *kintsugi*."

"Did you see this in an anime?"

"No. Shut up." She pushed my toes away, but I pushed back. "*Kintsugi* is a pottery technique. When something breaks, like a vase, they glue it back together with melted gold. Instead of making the cracks invisible, they make them beautiful. To celebrate the history of the object. What it's been through. And I was just . . ."

I pushed her toes again. "Just what?"

"Thinking of us like that. My heart full of gold veins, instead of cracks."

I stared. "That's beautiful, Ellis. Where'd you hear about it?"

She smiled sheepishly. "Death Cab for Cutie."

Ellis said she wanted to show me something at the cabin. We rowed back and trekked through the woods, through a sea of dry leaves fluttering around our shoes like golden paper cranes. Up in the tree house she had a log fire burning in the wood stove, and in the last good light she'd set up an easel, a primed canvas, and a tray of paint. I stood in the doorway, dumbstruck.

She uncapped a tube of green acrylic, raised it to my face.

I hadn't smelled anything like this in almost a year. It hit like a drug. My eyes watered from the faint plasticky scent, the gesso on the canvas. I edged away, dizzy, tumbled onto the sofa.

"Vada?"

When she touched me I grabbed her waist, crying.

"It's okay, it's okay." She pulled my coat off, wrapped her arms around me. "I'm sorry. We don't have to do this."

"Is this another experiment?"

"No. It's just something I always wanted to do."

"You wanted to paint with me?"

"Yeah."

I let go. Scrubbed hot saline from my cheeks and stood.

At first I didn't dare touch the canvas. I showed Ellis what to do: mix colors on the palette, keep the paint wet, apply and blend. She rolled her sleeves up, fastidiously avoided spattering her clothes. Unacceptable. I dipped a finger in red and dragged it down the front of her shirt.

"Now that you're dirty," I said, dabbing paint on her cheek and chin for good measure, "you can fucking relax."

Her eyes went wide. I laughed.

Ellis didn't have a subject—she just put colors down, glee-fully watching them interact, like a kid playing with a chemis-try set. Yellow and red turning into mandarin orange, blue and green becoming Atlantic teal. My throat burned at the scratch of bristles on canvas and the muddy rainbow swirling in the water cup. But I made myself take it. I can do this, I thought. I can feel this even though I can't really be part of it anymore. Through you.

Ellis tried to paint a line across the canvas with cautious, self-conscious strokes, but it kept going wonky.

"Why do I suck at straight lines?"

"Because you're not straight?"

"Neither are you."

"Those damn bisexuals, always getting the best of both worlds. Who do they think they are?"

She rolled her eyes. I laid my weak hand on her wrist.

"You're trying to control it from here. It's too close to the brush." I ran my hand up her arm, slowly, over fair skin sprin-kled with freckles and paint. Up to her shoulder, her collar-bone. "Do it from here."

I kept my hand there. When her arm moved I felt the smooth pull of threads beneath the surface. My palm slid over her neck, her back, feeling the delicate loom of muscle moving against my fingertips.

"If I could give this to you," she said, "I would. I'd give anything to make you happy."

I hugged her from behind, burying my face against her shoulder. "You make me happy."

For a moment Ellis was still. Then she turned and cupped my jaw and I thought, Kiss me.

"You're totally clean," she said, sounding puzzled.

She smeared turquoise on my cheek.

"Hey."

Royal purple next.

"Very funny."

Jade green.

"Ellis—"

We both grabbed the palette.

Then she flipped it onto my shirt and it was all-out paint war.

Ellis had the advantage of surprise and squeezed a handful of red paint into her palm before I caught her. It splattered all over both of us, bright as blood. My hand slipped and hit the canvas and left a dripping scarlet print. We both stared at it, impressed, then lunged for more. I fought her for the blue tube and it burst in our hands, shooting everywhere as we screamed. Yellow spilled on the sofa. Green slathered the window. In the middle of absolutely wrecking Ellis with paint I got more on the canvas, too, and suddenly there was an unspoken cease-fire as we both attacked it, Pollock style, flinging paint with our bare hands. Exhilarated, I popped tube after tube and hurled it half-blind, hitting the wall and floor as much as anything. Who fucking cared? This glorious mess was *me*. This was the color and energy and motion that had been locked in me for a year, finally breaking loose.

I fumbled in the tray, finding only empty tubes. My fingers and toes tingled. Crazed, breathless. We both looked like we'd faced a paintball firing squad.

"Holy fuck," I said.

Ellis closed the small space between us and kissed me, so hard I rocked back on my heels. I tasted paint, spearmint, salt water. Our arms wrapped around each other, and the numbness at the edges of me spread until all I was sure was real was the bell toll of my heart, a vague sense of blood ringing through my veins. I kissed that sweet pink mouth again and again and pulled back to look at her.

"It's on your glasses."

She tossed them onto the coffee table.

Down to the couch, her beneath me. Dabs and dashes of paint everywhere, on skin and clothes and upholstery, as if this were a van Gogh close-up and if you stepped back far enough, it would condense into a clear image. My hair fell around her face in a cup of shadow and she tucked it behind my ear.

"This is how I remember you," she said. "Just like this."

"Covered in paint?"

"That, but also the light in your eyes. The fire."

I laced my fingers through hers. "I think we're lying in Process Yellow."

"Want to move?"

"I'm not letting you go anywhere."

Ellis gave me that aw-shucks tomboy smile, ever so slightly crooked, and I couldn't help myself. The words were out before they hit me.

"I love you," I said.

We both stared, a little shocked.

"I love you, too."

We'd said these words a thousand times. But right now it felt like the first.

It was too intense for a kiss, for the way I wanted to touch her. Too pure to let some ephemeral thrill dilute it. Too perfect just like this. I guess she felt the same because she simply held me, so tight each breath we took made it hard for the other to breathe. Skin colliding, bones smashing, twisting together, crashing into each other. As close as we could get. This could be the last night I hold you like this, I thought. And I don't ever want to let go.

–||–

It rained all morning. The road was a ribbon of chrome winding through deep, dark forest, the broken coast shining like shards of metal covered in oil. Wind whipped foam off the water, thickening the air with mist. An empty fury that was all breath.

Ellis drove the rental car. I fought the urge to reach out, put a steadying hand on hers. She was good, if overcautious. I was good but reckless. That's why we fit so well. Balanced each other out.

"There's something I need to tell you," I said. "About Blue."

She frowned at the highway, the oncoming headlights scribbles of gold gel on the asphalt.

"He asked me to bring you. It was his sole condition for meeting, actually."

Ellis kept staring straight ahead. "Why?"

Because I'm torn between the two of you. Because looking at you side by side will break me, and I'm not sure which half of my heart will be bigger.

"I don't know," I said.

"What if he wants to kill us both?"

"Really? Is this a Lifetime Original?"

"What do you actually know about him?"

"I know he's not like that."

"What is he like? Since you're the expert."

Her tone was cool, taunting. I wanted to say *He's like you
with a dick*, but I didn't rise to it.

After a while she glanced over, sober now. "If it's Max, and
he's decided he can't live with the pain anymore . . ."

"Max wouldn't do that."

"How do you know?"

"Because he's had the chance to hurt me." And the chance
to take advantage. I looked out the window. "He never has. We
have a connection, Ellis."

We fell quiet. Rain came down hard, bouncing off the
blacktop like flashing coins. After a while I laid my hand
lightly on her leg. Not in an erotic way, but not platonic, either.
Merely familiar. I felt her tense up, then relax. We listened to
the rain shredding the sky, all those threads of mist fraying
into water.

Boston is almost a smaller, statelier Chicago, but instead
of a neat grid its streets are a drunken spiderweb. I got us lost
twice even with GPS. Neighborhoods scrolled past: cobblestone lanes and redbrick row houses, gas lamps leaking yellow
fumes of light into the rain. We crossed the Charles River, its
pewter skin stippled with raindrops.

Dane met us at a café a few blocks from the official meeting
place. He ran out with an umbrella in either hand. Always the
gentleman.

Indoors I threw my arms around him, squeezing hard.

"She missed me," Dane told Ellis when I let go.

"Shut up." I mussed his hair. He wore tight jeans and a fitted leather jacket, no inch of muscle undefined, and that puck-
ish smile I'd actually, yes, sorta missed. "Been raising hell?"

"Been raising lots of things, baby."

Ellis laughed.

"Don't encourage him," I said.

Dane winked at her. "You keeping out of trouble, Red?"

We both did a double take. Ellis recovered smoothly.

"Morgan never listens to her voice of reason. That's why we're here now."

"Come on," Dane said, motioning toward a table. "Let's strategize."

I left them to check myself in the bathroom. Last chance before meeting him face-to-face. As soon as I exited eyeshot, I pulled out my phone.

one more hour
my hair is frizzy from the rain
and I'm pretty sure Red hates us both
but this is actually happening
how will I know it's you? what are you wearing?
—Vada

I set my phone on the counter and touched up my lip gloss, tried to tame the frizz. Understated makeup. Blue already knew me glammed up. No pretension today.

My phone vibrated.

you'll know me when you see me.
i'm nervous, vada.
but when i think of holding you in my arms, all the fear falls away.
and all i feel is you.
see you soon.
—blue

I pressed the phone to my chest, inhaling deeply.

"Vada?"

Ellis stood behind me, watching me in the mirror. I slipped my phone into my jeans. She stepped close, caught my hand against my thigh. Her eyes were sad.

"This really is what you want," she said softly.

"I don't know what I want. That's why I'm here."

Our gazes locked in the mirror. For a moment I saw us as characters, not ourselves: a redheaded prince and a black-haired princess, neither of whom could rescue each other, in a story without a happy ending.

"Dane's waiting," I said.

"We could walk out of here right now."

"Ellis."

"We could go home. Or anywhere. Just me and you, Vada."

I averted my face, but clasped the hand at my side, twisting my fingers in hers. "You are my home."

"Then why are we here? What do you want?"

"I don't know." Something like this. Me and you, without the fear.

She untangled herself, pulled free. "I tried. But I was never enough for you."

"Don't."

"I loved you the best I could."

"Don't make me fucking cry, Ellis."

Eyes shut. Breathe.

When I opened them again, she was gone.

I turned on the water and listened to it for a while. Let it soothe me. Part of me had been born on a windswept prairie, but part had been born here, on this jagged, sea-lashed shore. The rawness and loneliness of New England resonated inside me like a tuning fork. The ocean was in my blood. I came here to escape who I was and only ended up finding myself again.

"You okay?" Dane said as I joined them at the table.

"Yep. So, plan?"

"Red says you don't have visuals of this guy."

I thought of the figurine photos. His hands. "Nothing that would actually help. He's fair-skinned, not old. All I know."

Ellis flicked a paper packet across the table. She and Dane were playing sugar hockey.

"That describes ninety percent of the people in this room," she said.

"He told me I'd know him when I saw him." I intercepted the packet. "That can only mean I already know him."

"Or he's someone famous," Dane said.

"Or he's lying," Ellis said.

I flipped the packet to her. "Occam's razor, Professor."

"What's that?" Dane asked, and for a second Ellis met my eyes, almost smiling.

"Assume I've seen him before," I said. "He's probably light-haired. Lean build. Blue eyes. Somewhere between his twenties and forties."

Dane reclined in the booth, hands knit behind his head. "Sounds like your type."

I kicked him under the table. Ellis flicked the sugar packet at his chest and it made a little *thwap*.

Again we almost shared a smile. Then she said, "He might be armed."

"Give me a break. We're meeting at a coffeehouse in the middle of the day. It's not going to turn violent."

"Unless you dump him in front of everyone."

"You're being ridiculous. I can go by myself if you're that worried."

I stood and they did, too.

"Morgan." Dane touched my arm. "We just want to keep you safe. Right, Red?"

Ellis sighed.

"Look," Dane said, "I'll be there the whole time. I'll come and go in different disguises."

"Disguises?"

He took Ellis's glasses and slid them on, grinning.

"I'm Clark Kent, baby."

He was so goddamn cute I couldn't stay mad. "Fine. No heroics, though. If stuff goes south, I'll give you a sign."

We hashed out the remaining logistics until Ellis went outdoors to vape. When she was gone I turned serious.

"Is it you, Dane?"

"What?"

"Clark Kent. Red. Our kiss. The show you gave me." My hand darted across the table, seizing his like a viper. I turned his palm up. "Are you Blue?"

"I guess you're gonna find out, huh?"

My heart hung in my chest, untethered.

Dane squeezed my hand and let go. "I wouldn't mess with you, Morgan. You and me had a spark. We let it die. That's that. Besides, I've been busy with the studio. No time for romance. Last couple months, we pulled in more revenue than Frankie's house."

Because I hadn't been camming. Because of Blue.

A suspicion flickered in my mind.

"Would you ever hire someone to . . . *distract* me?"

He raised his eyebrows. "You looking for an escort? I know some guys. I'm offended you didn't ask me first, though."

"No, you bozo." I had to laugh. "Never mind. And who do you know?"

"Some guys."

"Some guys. Right."

He winked.

Like me, Dane was primarily attracted to the opposite sex, but he hooked up with men, too. I wondered if he'd ever fallen in love with another man. If it made him question whether he was really bi. And I hoped he wasn't playing me, because I needed a friend who understood what this was like.

Dane checked his watch. "Ready to meet the man of your dreams?"

"I have a feeling I already have."

The walk to the café felt surreal. My head floated a dozen stories up, observing from a bird's-eye view: the city gleaming with an oil-paint glaze, cars and feet flowing through the warrens of Boston. Two people walking to a café. Two stories, one about to begin, the other to end.

Ellis and I went into an upscale hipster coffeehouse, all unstained hardwood and riveted steel. Track lights twinkled in the crisp air like champagne bubbles. We took a table on the mezzanine and I emailed Blue.

I'm here

Two syllables. The sound my heart was making, over and over.

When I looked up, Ellis was watching me. Our hands joined under the table. I hung on for dear life.

Thank you, I mouthed.

No response. But she was hanging on to me, too.

Below us Dane walked in, bought a latte, and sat near the window.

This was it.

The meeting was set for two p.m. At ten till I was a mess, breathing fast, my heart kicking down my ribs like a wild bull. Every time the café door opened I nearly leaped from my seat. Two o'clock came and went. Maybe his plane was delayed. Two fifteen. He got stuck in traffic. Two thirty. Dane left.

Ellis watched me more than the door. Her thumb moved over the back of my hand, steady, a little metronome of sanity.

Three o'clock. I stopped refreshing my email every thirty seconds.

Dane came back in wearing a track jacket, and glanced up before buying a bear claw and sitting beneath us.

I took a deep breath. "Blue bitched out."

Ellis said nothing. My pulse slowed enough to distinguish it from hers: hers was still fast, nervous.

She liked things scheduled and organized. Settled. This was chaos.

where are you, Blue?

I checked the weather. Plane delays. Road accidents. Someone died on the Maine Turnpike that afternoon. Water lying like silver silk on the macadam. Tires that couldn't bite through it. Skid, smash. No seat belt.

Buckle up, kids. Unless you're so tired and beaten you'd rather die.

At half past three I bought lattes. By four, the pale light flooding through the windows dimmed and faded. At four thirty I went to pee.

I'm leaving at five
where the fuck are you?

As I left the stall, my phone buzzed in my hand. I was so startled I nearly threw it.

vada.
don't be angry with me.

Guaranteed way to piss me off.

you're not coming, are you?

I was afraid to move, my entire being focused on this tiny phone screen.

The next email came while I washed up at the sink.

i saw you, with red.

holding her hand.

you looked right at me. through me.

i watched you together.

and i knew it was wrong.

coming between you two.

vada, i felt something real for you.

i still do.

but your heart belongs to someone else.

it's wrong of me to ruin that.

what i've done is wrong.

i hope someday you can forgive me.

yours, always,

blue.

Everything in me was going a hundred miles an hour. Then it hit:

you looked right at me.

He was *here.*

I ran out of the bathroom, crashing into someone on their way in. Mumbled apology. Blurred lights, a swirling cacophony of voices. I dashed beneath the mezzanine and looked up.

Ellis stood, peering down. "Vada?"

"He was here."

I stumbled through a couple at the door and onto the street.

Commuters flooded past, umbrellas up, small pearls and crystals of rain rolling off and shattering on the asphalt. A taxi pulled away from the curb and I chased it into traffic but when I grabbed the door handle, a shocked woman's face stared out. Mist collected on my skin. Any man that passed could have been him. Fine, pale hands. That's all I knew. Aside from the way he'd made me feel, the way he'd laced his fingers into my heart and unraveled it. Was that what I'd have to do? Pry my ribs open and see whose hands fit, whose fingers were stained with the same red inside me?

I walked up and down the block, peering into every face. Looking for Max, or someone I knew. Anyone. Only strangers. Then Ellis and Dane appeared like angels, one on either side.

"What happened?" Dane said.

Ellis clung to my arm, eyes wide.

"He stood me up. That fucking asshole stood me up. He was here. He saw us, and bailed, like a little bitch."

People on the street side-eyed me. I wanted to snarl, *What the fuck are you looking at? Haven't you ever seen someone getting their heart broken?*

"Why?" Ellis said.

I shook my head. "I'll explain later. I just—I want—"

Across the street, a bar sign glowed warmly through the rain.

"I want to get shitfaced."

———

Three White Mexicans later—tequila, Kahlua, and horchata— I felt a lot less shitty about this whole stupid scenario.

Dane matched me with Moscow mules. Ellis was still on her second amaretto sour, but she was easily the drunkest.

"Let's play a game," she said.

The bar bustled, sweat sparkling in the air, Ed Sheeran crooning "I'm a Mess" on the sound system. Scents of fish and chips and vinegar wafted from the kitchen. Ellis and I sat crammed in a small booth, Dane straddling a chair across from us.

"What's your game, Red?" he said.

"Never Have I Ever."

"It's a trick," I said. "She always wins. She's pure of heart."

Ellis gave us an airy look. "It's okay if you're not up to the challenge."

The later it got, the calmer and more confident she got. It curdled in my gut, knowing she was relieved I wasn't spending the night with a stranger. Because Blue bailed. Not because I'd chosen her.

Dane signaled a server, and Ellis ordered eight shots of Johnnie Walker Blue. Dane whooped. I put a hand on her arm.

"Do you have any idea how expensive that is?"

"Yes."

"Don't order it just for the sake of irony."

"I'm ordering it because it's expensive *and* ironic."

"You can't stand whiskey. You're going to puke it all back up."

"Unless I beat you."

I folded my arms. Ellis raised an eyebrow, defying me.

"Red's throwing down," Dane said.

I met her stare for stare. "You're on."

When the shots arrived she arranged them in two neat rows.

RULES OF NEVER HAVE I EVER:

1. Someone says, "Never have I ever" done something.
2. Anyone who *has* done that does a shot.
3. If no one drinks, the first person does a shot.

"Three shots and you're out," she said. "Last man standing wins."

"Who's first?" I said.

Dane shrugged. "I vote Red. Let's see how dirty she plays."

"You don't know what you're getting into," I warned. "Her IQ is probably a multiple of yours."

"Be nice," Ellis said.

"Floor's yours, brainiac."

She eyed us coolly. "Never have I ever kissed everyone at this table."

Shit.

I delayed a few seconds, poker-faced, then grudgingly picked up a shot. Liquid smoke and hot toffee. My chest burned.

Ellis and Dane gaped at each other.

"You kissed him?" she said.

"You kissed her?" he said.

I groaned. "I fucking told you. She doesn't play fair."

"I need details," Dane said, and Ellis said, darker, "So do I."

"Nope." I banged my glass on the table. "And if you two ever talk about it, I'm disowning you both. You're up, Dane."

He looked at me, then her, his eyes glittering. "Never have I ever fucked anyone at this table."

Nobody moved. Then Ellis and I reached for shots at the same time.

Dane crowed with glee.

"You are such a *guy*," I said, and slammed mine.

Ellis wrinkled her nose and downed hers. She looked poisoned. I was two deep, plus the other drinks, and getting giddy. I brushed my fingertips over her throat, tickling.

"You just drank thirty bucks like it was toilet water."

"Oh my god. Could you please not."

Dane watched us avidly, his hands steepled.

"I'll admit it, Dane. You're a natural. But I've got your number." I smiled. "Never have I ever received anal sex."

His eyebrows rose.

He picked up a glass.

"Who was he?" I said, intrigued. "Older, younger? Was he good?"

Dane did the shot and set the glass down. "Which time?"

I giggled. Ellis studied us, her game face on.

"She's so cute when she's all thinky." I traced a finger around her ear, along her jaw. "My pretty little prince."

"If you're that drunk, I will graciously accept your surrender."

"Never." I slapped the table, rattling the glasses. "To the death."

Ellis looked regretfully at Dane. "I'm sorry, but: never have I ever jerked off to everyone at this table."

"Aw, come on."

We both laughed at him.

"Payback's a bitch," I said.

Dane did another shot.

"But the question is," I said, "did you fantasize about us separately, or together?"

"Let's head to your hotel and I'll reenact it for you."

Ellis turned bright red. I wadded up a napkin and threw it at Dane.

We all laughed, drunk and careless and happy, and I realized with a pang that I hadn't thought of Blue for a while. The splintery, cracked place in my sternum felt blunted. It was mainly the alcohol but for a second I wanted to hug them both, hard. I slipped my foot behind Ellis's, linked my ankle with hers. She gave me a private smile.

Dane watched us, not salacious now but thoughtful.

"Your turn, ol' blue eyes," I said.

"Never have I ever been in love with someone at this table."

I stalled. "Not even a little?"

"Sorry, baby. Infatuation doesn't count."

Ellis reached for a shot. I took the one next to hers. We glanced at each other.

"I lose," I said.

We threw our shots back simultaneously. When I lowered my face, she leaned in and kissed me. Once, sweetly, on the lips. It burned through me in a flash of wildfire. Dane didn't comment—he didn't even look aroused. He just smiled at us.

What the hell am I doing here? I thought. Why did I come a hundred miles for some stranger when she made me feel like this?

I leaned in and kissed her back, not sweet. Fierce.

When I stopped for breath, dizzy, Dane was gone.

"He went to the bathroom," Ellis said. Shy-eyed and flustered, adorable.

"Want to get out of here?" I said.

"Shouldn't we wait for him?"

"He'll understand."

In the taxi I sent him a text.

MORGAN: taking a cab to the hotel

MORGAN: meet up tomorrow?

DANE: u bet

DANE: but who won the game??

MORGAN: you did

DANE: hmmm u sure?

DANE: ur taking the hottie to your room

DANE: in my book thats a win ·

I laughed, and held my phone away from Ellis when she tried to see.

DANE: let me know if u need backup

DANE: I can show u that fantasy red asked about

MORGAN: you're a pig

MORGAN: I'm blocking your number

DANE: ;)

DANE: have a nice night baby

Ellis wrestled for my phone, convinced Dane was mocking her. We sprawled across the backseat and I tickled her elbows and knees till she pulled my hair and we collapsed together, laughing, then falling quiet. Streetlights swept over us, amber into violet into amber.

The things I want to do to you, my prince.

Sixteen floors up, Boston was a diorama of tiny toy cars and boats, miniature lights, electric filigree. I'd paid a mint for a suite overlooking the harbor, with its own private terrace. In the twilight the gilt and porcelain looked palatial.

"This is like some fairy tale." I stepped outside. Cold, the wind tangy with brine. "None of this seems real."

Ellis leaned on the railing, gazing at the water. "I know."

"You seem real. Are you?"

She didn't answer.

I moved behind her, slid my arms around her waist. Kissed the bare nape of her neck, hot lips on cool skin. Exhaled into her short hair. There was something both masculine and feminine about her, or neither. The androgynous beauty of youths in myth, the type gods would chase and try to defile, until some other god took pity and turned them into a flower, or a tree.

"What are you doing?" she whispered.

"Mythologizing you." My mouth moved against her skin. "You're my favorite subject, Ellis. Your body. Your mind." I laid a finger at the center of her chest. "Your heart. I miss drawing you. Sometimes my hand moves on its own, a muscle memory. I dream of it. I dream of you in colors that don't exist."

Her back arched, her body molding against mine. My palms scaled her ribs till she pressed them still.

"You're drunk, Vada."

"Don't think I mean it?"

"We came here to meet your Internet boyfriend."

Instantly my mouth went sour. I released her, walked to the other end of the terrace.

"I'm glad he didn't show," I said.

My own words startled me. I repeated them.

"I am glad. Fuck him." I wrapped my fists around the railing as tight as I could. The left was strong, the right watery, ghostly. I'd kill to crack my knuckles. My bad hand always felt like this, one good crack away from being fixed. "We never should've come here. This whole time, I've been chasing a mirage. A phantom. Because I'm—" Can I actually say this to her? Right now I think I can. "I'm afraid."

"Of what?"

"You. This. Us."

She came up beside me, guarded. "You've said that before. What do you really mean?"

Salt air in my throat. Blue ocean beyond, licked by the gold flames of harbor lights.

"I mean it terrifies me that the love of my life is a fucking girl." I didn't look at her. I spoke to the dusk sky. "You want honesty, right? Well, here you go. I have stupid irrational hang-ups about you. About how people look at us. About how they'll see me as *this*, a girl with another girl, without caring who I really am. That there's more to me. They'll see a label, not a person."

"There's more to me, too. Sometimes you don't even see it. You see the labels you've put on me, instead of what's really here."

"You're right. I—" God, time to cop to how shitty I am. "Ellis, I liked Blue because he's like you, but a guy, okay? Because that's how fucking deep it goes for me. I wanted someone easy. Someone who wouldn't make me question so much about myself, about what's really inside me. In my head you've always been the exception to the rule."

"What rule?"

"That I'll turn out normal someday." I gripped the railing

with all my might. "I'm sorry if that makes me a shitty person. It scares me, that I might never love anyone else like this. Makes me wonder if I've been lying to myself about who I really am."

"Maybe I'm lying to myself, too."

I glanced at her. "How?"

"Sometimes it feels like something inside me is waiting to explode."

Ryan's words.

"Who am I, Vada? Who do you see?"

"Ellis Carraway. My best friend."

"Just your friend."

"There's no word for what you mean to me."

"Do I embarrass you?"

"Are you nuts? You're the smartest person I know. I brag about you all the time. And you're cute as hell. So cute I kissed you in the Old Port, on the street. And in that bar in front of everyone."

"That was kind of balls-out."

I grinned. "Reckless Vada."

"No. Brave."

We eyed each other in the deepening twilight. Lights popped on along the wharf, little yellow kernels.

"I don't want to just be friends anymore," I said. "The only problem with our relationship was me. My stupid hang-ups. My fear."

"I won't be your second choice."

I took her hands, brought her fingers to my mouth. Warmed them with my breath. "You're everything I want. If Blue showed up right now, I'd tell him to fuck off."

"Even if he was really hot?"

I answered earnestly, my throat tight. "You're the most beautiful person I've ever seen."

"Is this because we're drunk, or is it real?"

"I think both. Look."

I let go of her, gave her space to breathe. The navy satin of the harbor fanned below. Skyscrapers towered over it, a palisade of steel.

"Not exactly van Gogh, right? Too clinical. But see that?" I pointed. "The stars are still there. They fell out of the sky and drowned. They're underwater now, sparkling beneath the surface. Ruby, sapphire, amethyst, topaz. More colors than ever before."

"How do you see things like this? These drowned stars."

You, I thought. I see them because of you.

"Ellis, you totally have a type. I'm an artist, Blythe's a poet. Next you'll fall for an interpretive dancer."

"There won't be a next."

Knife, twist. "I lied about lying, about the experiment. In the Old Port. Do you want to know what it really was?" I didn't wait for her answer. "I wanted to see how it'd feel, being your girlfriend."

I sensed the hitch in her breath. "How did it feel?"

"Exactly the same as being your friend. But a lot nicer, because there was kissing."

Ellis hung her head, not hiding her smile very well. "Can I say something?"

"Can I kiss you after you say it?"

"Yes. Please. But listen." She made herself meet my eyes. I saw nervousness there, but no fear. "You said it scares you, that you might not love anyone else this way. But it doesn't scare me. It makes me happy, Vada. That I have someone I *can* love like this."

Right at that moment my silly drunk heart was an overfull paint can when a brush jams inside, color slopping over the rim, running everywhere.

I took her glasses off. Harbor lights danced over our skin. "You're getting kissed now."

But she beat me to it.

We both had alcohol on our lips, a whiff of burnt sugar and cream. My back curved against the railing. Ellis leaned in and kissed me gently, daintily, precise little brushes across my mouth. Her hands framed my face, angled it so she could kiss me exactly where she wanted. The way I'd position paper when I drew. I gave myself up to her. Let her cradle the back of my head, her lips softly shading mine in.

"I want you so much," I murmured into her mouth.

I pulled her across the terrace into the dark suite. She pushed me against the glass doors. More boy than girl now, this slender, pretty boy, smoky-eyed and tousle-haired, lifting my face to kiss me again and again. Her hands were all over me, pulling my hips to hers.

"Fuck me," I said.

I tugged the top button of her shirt.

"Do you really want this?"

"Do you want to feel how wet I am?" I dragged her hands lower, but she stopped me.

"Look at me. Do you want me, or a boy?"

I circled her waist, held her tight to my body. "You. Just like this. You're kind of a boy, aren't you?"

Her heart crashed against mine. "Do you want me to be?"

"Yes." I grabbed her ass, brought her knee between my legs. "Fuck me like a boy, Ellis."

She put her mouth to my ear. "Like Blue?"

"Like you."

She took my blouse off in a smooth pull, unclasped my bra. Held my wrists to the glass in one hand while the other slipped beneath the bra cups. Teased my nipples hard. Then took one between her lips, sucking till I could not feel where my spine ended, only this cord of electricity crackling from my skull to the tips of me, firing out wild trails of sparks. My hands fell free, raked into her hair and knotted. Held her to my breast as she circled the areola with her tongue till I couldn't take it anymore and pulled her up to face me.

"Let me see you," I said.

She let me unbutton her shirt now, slowly. The weak useless hand that fumbled and the strong awkward one. When I struggled, she guided my fingers. I used to do this so suavely. I used to be so confident. Invincible.

Ellis waited, patient.

"I'm sorry," I said.

"Don't be."

Her shirt came off, and the tight tee beneath. I dropped my bra. Our bodies met again, skin on skin. Her shoulder against my cheek, moon pale, freckles spilling down her arm like a fall of sand. I counted the ridges of her spine with my fingers and pulled her closer, crushed my breasts to hers, our lungs fighting to occupy the same space. I wanted her inside me. I wanted her deep, in the marrow, the bitter redness.

We tumbled onto the bed and lay side by side, kissing, until she rolled astride me and held me down. She kissed me everywhere, her hands on every exposure of skin, tracing my tats with her fingertips, nails, tongue, to the point where I could barely register any individual touch but felt her desire wash over me in a sweeping, impressionistic wave, the blurry underpainting of lust. We undid each other's jeans, slid them off. Nothing left between us. I pulled her face to mine and moaned, unabashedly throaty, carnal. Ellis moved against me, steady and hard, rolling her hips, and I wrapped myself around her and gripped that tight little ass and made her grind on me, spread her wetness all over my leg, till she pushed my legs apart. One hand between them, one on my throat. She kissed me when she touched me, traced my clit with a finger and ran her tongue inside my upper lip, and all the resistance in me dissolved. I'd never felt like such a girl as when she touched me. So soft and open, my body pliant, transparent like tulle, responding to the barest brush of her fingers. I'd slept with a lot of boys, but none made me feel this feminine. None knew how to touch me like this. Because Ellis knew exactly what this felt like. How the lightest glide against my tongue, my nipples, my clit felt like a spark racing down a fuse. How suggestion could be more powerful than direct stimulation. But I wanted it direct now.

She felt what I needed. We'd been together so long, we just sensed things.

The finger tracing me slid inside, then another, and I gritted my teeth because touching an ache feels so fucking good you almost don't want the pain to stop. I rocked against her, unable to hold back.

"Fuck," I said. "I'm close."

Ellis looked down at me. Tucked my hair behind my ear. Touched my mouth, fingers running down to my throat.

And then grasped it, tight.

Some noise rose from my diaphragm, beastly and crude. Animal pleasure.

Choking yourself is one thing. You control it, fine-tune it, but the pleasure is in the control. Being choked by someone else is exhilarating precisely because the control is gone.

"Tighter," I whispered.

Shadows seeped inward, vignetting my vision. The darkness seemed to glitter blackly.

"Baby, fuck me," I said, and she did. Two fingers inside me. One hand on my throat.

The first time I'd done it, it was instinctual. I'd been fingering her on the sofa, kissing her neck, feeling the artery pulse against my lips like a red butterfly trapped beneath the surface, and as she got close something dark reared up in me, bitter and unkind. I knew when she came and clutched me helplessly that I'd melt, I'd fall in love with her a little more, and I resented it, the whole thing, this beautiful friendship that went too far and couldn't go back, that would crash and burn and destroy the life I'd built around her. I wanted this love to hurt her, just a bit, the way it hurt me. I wanted to hurt her. My hand slid around her neck. Her eyes opened wide. We were fully, mercilessly in that moment together. Afterward we didn't talk about it, but it became part of us. It happened when we were upset, when we couldn't solve a problem any other way. We both did it. Ellis was reluctant at first, but the more I failed to be the out-and-proud girlfriend of her dreams, the more okay she seemed with this fucked-up manifestation of our tension. And then it started happening so often that sometimes I wasn't sure if we actually wanted to fuck or just to hurt each other.

Something hardened inside me. I rode her fingers, groaning when she pulled out and ran her palm against my pussy, wanting so badly for the pressure to burst. When she slid in again I raised my whole body to hers, her nipples grazing mine, her skin slick. Our lips brushed, her hair feathering my face. Then she pulled out and released my throat at the same time.

"God, *fuck*," I said. Head rush, sick and giddy. "Make me come. Stop fucking torturing—"

She stuck her wet fingers in my mouth.

I gasped, which made it easier for her to slide deeper. After the initial shock I closed my lips around them. It'd been so long since I'd tasted myself. Warm and clear, a slight tart sweetness. So fucking feminine.

"How does it taste?" she whispered. "You always tasted so good."

I pried her knees open with my own. Brought my hand to the heat between her legs. Ran a fingertip inside as I swirled my tongue around her fingers. She groaned.

"You're so pretty with me in your mouth." She slid in farther. "Do it, baby. Suck me off."

I stared up at her. Light struck part of her face, the chiseled jaw, the ridge in her throat.

And for a wild moment, I thought of Blue.

Not in her place. Not the way she feared. But *as* her. This androgynous girl with her hand in my mouth, telling me to blow her.

Holy fuck.

I licked her fingers and pulled them out, kissed the tips, took them in again, my eyes on hers. The other hand stroked her clit. Ellis cupped the back of my head like a boy would. We tangled together, legs linked, my wetness spreading as I rode her thigh. Every time I sucked her in and looked up plaintively, she rocked into my hand, hard. It made my head spin. This felt like fucking a guy and a girl at the same time. This felt crazy. All around us was a watery haze, shadows wavering, wisps of light floating like jellyfish in the thick, fluid air, and I had the sudden sense that I was actually under the waterline, my mouth full of ocean. The struggle for release was like fighting a drowning. I could feel it so close, dry air and clarity just overhead. Her body wound with mine, her nipples stiff against my breasts, her wet soft skin unbearable against my pussy. I intensified as I would with a boy, showing him how badly I wanted his cock. Deep-throating him. *Her.* Ellis made a fist in my hair. Force me, I thought, force me, fuck my mouth, and she did, her fingers thrusting to the back of my tongue, but I was a good girl with a well-trained gag reflex and I took it like a pro. Ellis heaved against me, saying, "God, *God*," and I kept giving it to her steady and rode her leg and came, pure air breaking over me, my head above the surface. She took her hand from my mouth. I inhaled, oxygen drugging my blood. That first crystalline breath. Ecstasy.

We curled against each other, panting. I stared at the ceiling, the play of reflected light. Lifted an arm and slid my hand up the wall to feel it. Air, just air.

Ellis looked at me through mussed hair, mouth swollen, squinting. So lovely. I touched her face, slid a hand through her hair and ruffled it.

"What do you see?" she said.

"You." I twirled a lock around my finger. "My prince."

Her eyes half-shut, as if looking at something bright. "I wish I could draw. I wish I could show you how you look to me. You're so beautiful, Vada."

My heartbeat echoed in my fingertips.

We kissed for a while, soft and slow, pausing to touch each other, to run skin against skin, lace fingers, look at ourselves entwined. I couldn't tell the taste or feel of my own body from hers. It was all one thing, just us.

When she shivered I pulled the quilt up and Ellis nestled in my arms. I love you, I thought, watching an imaginary zodiac spin over the walls. I love you more than anything. I'm sorry I ever made you doubt that. Because this feels right. It's the first thing that's felt completely right since the night our lives tore apart.

This feels like breathing again.

———

I woke in a stillness flocked with velvet shadows in tones of cornflower and mauve. Ignored my phone and the chill and leaned against the headboard, the sheet twined around my chest, watching Ellis.

Light sleeper. She stirred soon after, her shoulders peeking from the sheets. When she blinked I ran a finger across her collarbone, eliciting a shiver.

"Hi," I said.

Ellis didn't answer, but she had that *oh my god this actually happened* look.

I laughed. "*Yo sé eh.*"

She pulled the sheet over her head.

At first she was shy, hiding until I wrestled her down and kissed her. We were a total mess, half-hungover, feral from sex, and I didn't care. I kissed the hell out of her till she stopped being self-conscious, till she took me in her arms and kissed me back, breathless. A red sun rose and warmed the room. I pulled her atop me, gazing up at her.

"What are you thinking?" she said.

"That I could look at your face forever."

Her breath caught, and so did mine. I hadn't really thought about the words. I just said what I felt.

Ellis smiled, playing it off. "You like me, dork."

"Nope. Way too nerdy."

"Admit it."

"Dream on."

"You want to look at me forever."

"Only because it'd take that long to count your stupid freckles."

"You can't freckle-shame me. I know you think they're cute."

I shut her up with a kiss. Sweet at first, laughing against each other's mouths, but soon it turned intense and led to lip-biting, hair-pulling. "Okay," I said, pushing a knee between her legs, "you're not cute. You're hot as fuck."

It was a dream. All of it. Fucking each other as the sun poured molten gold against our backs. Perching on the sink and chatting with her as she showered. Interrupting her every five minutes with a kiss, a goofy smile, a piece of my heart. Finally dragging ourselves out of the room and ambling through the fog-haunted city, our breath hanging in veils of chiffon, pretending to peer in shop windows when I was really just watching her reflection. Hands linked, images tumbling through my head like kaleidoscope bits. If someone came up right then and shot me through the heart I was pretty sure a rainbow would splatter on the bricks. I took her to a comics shop and told her to buy as much as we could carry, and her eyes lit up. She kissed me, which made two teenage boys stare and break into grins. Then she led me down the aisles as her pack mule, shoving graphic novels into my arms. I didn't care. I was doped up on this, smiling dazedly at everything.

Oh my god. This *was* actually happening.

I was in love with my best friend. Hopelessly, completely in love.

No more hiding. No more denying and downplaying it. Fuck what other people thought. I didn't care how we looked, how they'd label us. I only cared what she felt. If two people could make each other smile and laugh and forget all the pain and darkness in the world for a moment, why should we feel ashamed of it?

Why had I been so scared of this, of being happy with her?

As payment for the comics I pulled her into a boutique to try on random things and demand her opinion. Ellis loathed clothes shopping. But she sat enrapt in the changing room, her pulse swelling in her throat. Only her eyes moved, locked on me. Finally she followed me into a stall and pushed me up against the door. My clothes piled on the floor. In the mirror across from us I watched a redheaded boy fuck me. One hand covered my mouth, muffling my gasps.

Dane met us across the channel. We bought soft pretzels from a street vendor, walked along the harbor taking pics. Joke porny group selfies for Frankie and sweet ones for ourselves. When Dane snapped pics I kissed Ellis unhesitatingly, then looked him in the eyes. Some part of me wanted to see something there—a flash of resentment, regret. Any clue. But he only looked happy for us.

Before he left, Dane kissed my cheek and murmured, "Now I get why you turned me down. You and her were meant to be."

"You big sap," I said, but something bright brimmed inside me, uncontainable.

Ellis and I stayed to watch the sunset. In its own way Boston is haunted—not with silence and loneliness like Maine, but with history. Blood soaked deep into the soil, cannonballs sunk low in the muck. We'd fought here bitterly for independence. I could still sense the bared teeth, tattered sails, the fiery arcs of flung torches. That fight was still in us, in our roots. And I wondered if it was still in me.

If you're really an artist, I thought, you'll find a way to make art however you can, like Bukowski said. With half your body gone. With soot and a cave wall. With your own blood.

Something settled heavily in my chest, like a book closing.

I thought of Blue somewhere out there in the lights twinkling across the harbor. Alone in a hotel room, watching the tiny people below. So far away from it, the warmth of skin and breath. From everything real.

Then Ellis took my hand, our fingers dovetailing, and all I thought of was her.

We watched the light fade behind the city and drove back through the black night, home.

—WINTER—

Snow fell on the beach, coating shells and the stony shore in fine white felt. All the colors softened as if too much water had mixed in. In winter Chebeague Island seemed even more isolated, a snowflake adrift in the great green-black abyss of the Atlantic.

I slid the box up the boat ramp with my toe, carving a trail through the snow. Ellis had told me she could carry them all. I wouldn't allow it. As if I'd let her show me up.

But as soon as I'd left her line of sight, I'd bitched out.

Most of her stuff was already on the yacht. Frankie let us borrow it to move Ellis back to Portland. Too cold in winter to stay in the cabin. Plus, there was us. Me and her.

Some of my stuff was on the yacht, too.

I hadn't told Frankie yet that I planned to retire from camming. Didn't want to leave her in the lurch. I wanted to come to her with a new business plan, and seed money.

And I was almost ready.

Back at the cabin I found Ellis sitting on the bare floor with her laptop, typing rapidly, frowning.

"Are you raging at someone who just pwned you?"

"It's Frankie," she muttered.

"Frankie pwned you?"

"Stop saying 'pwned,' dork. She's worried about the site."

Last month they'd discovered a bug in the cam site code. Ellis had worked round-the-clock to patch it, but repercussions kept echoing. A change here meant a cascading series of changes there, there, and there. She stayed up late, tapping away in the blue screenglow, code flying across the void. Sometimes I curled up and watched her work, wondering if my creative process was as cryptic and arcane to her. An entire universe unfolding inside her head, invisible to me.

Sometimes it reminded me too much of *him*, and I had to leave the house and walk along the shore, clear my mind. Ellis would find me there and fall in step, silent. She'd take my hand. And everything would be okay.

For a while.

I asked once if she could analyze Blue's IP logs. Maybe he'd been careless. All it took was one time, one rash log-in attempt from an insecure location, and I'd know. Peaks meant Max, Boston meant Dane. I even skulked at my old coffee shop, swathed in a scarf and beanie, watching Curtis. If I could just look him in the eyes, look at his hands. Why hadn't I paid more attention to his hands?

Blue never contacted me after Boston. I'd emailed him, messaged him on various sites. The emails bounced. The messages didn't deliver.

User does not exist.

As if he'd never been real.

"No," Ellis had said to my request. "That's a breach of privacy. Frankie could fire me for it." Her voice wavered. "I thought you let him go, Vada. I thought it was us now."

"It is, baby." I put my arms around her, my lips to her ear. "It's just closure. I hate not knowing why it happened."

"We don't always get closure. Sometimes we have to make our own."

So I tried. Very hard.

And I was almost there.

"We're pretty much done," I said, kicking Ellis's boot. "Couple more boxes and the mattress. No thanks to you."

"You're the reason there are so many boxes to begin with."

"Can't help it. I enjoy humiliating you with gifts."

"I don't think that's the spirit behind gift-giving."

"Let me give you the gift of silence," I said, setting her laptop aside and tackling her to the floor.

I kissed her, my whole body lighting up when we touched, my skin glowing like a paper lantern. Crazy, how wild she still drove me. As if we'd started all over again with limerence and lust. As if she were someone new. I cupped her face and gave her my patented Cheshire grin.

Ellis laughed. "Will you—"

I kissed her again, slower, running my tongue between her lips till she opened her mouth. Pulled back to make a flicker of eye contact, heat filling my head, then wrapped my tongue around hers. We were still in our coats. No fire in the hearth, the cold breathing through the wood. Her mouth scalded me. I kept kissing her deeper, trying to reach the point where we shared one breath, one set of lungs, one everything. She broke away.

"We have to—"

I kissed her again. She stopped trying to speak and used her mouth for more important things. Like me.

Somehow we managed to climb to the loft bed before all our clothes came off. By then Ellis was in control, kissing my breasts and throat and making me feel that weightless submission that came when I lay on my back in the water, palms upturned, mouth open to the sky. We burrowed under the bright white quilt and she put her face between my legs, painting me with her tongue. After, I reciprocated, our hands clasped, crumpling the quilt like crepe paper. It wasn't always rough and intense. More often now it was this tenderness, touching each other as if something fragile hung between us and we both wanted to protect it, keep it from shattering. I thought of those broken bowls glued back together with gold, more beautiful once they'd been broken. When she came I kissed her softly, adoringly, amazed that this was mine, this beautiful person, that letting go of my fear could feel like this.

You can fall in love again with someone you're already in love with. It's like waking from a dream within a dream and finding another layer, the colors more vivid, the light more lucid, the fantasy more real. Being in love is an endless loop of waking to reverie.

We lay side by side, tangled in a spell of blankets and warm skin.

"*Estoy tan feliz*," I murmured.

"Me too." Ellis smiled, one side of her mouth higher than the other. Every time she did that a little bird zigzagged madly inside my rib cage. "I wish time would stop right here."

"It does, you know." I spun a finger in her hair. "When someone makes a sketch, a song, a poem, it stops. The moment repeats forever inside that piece of art."

"Then draw us."

"Not yet."

"Why not?"

"I'm a big old scaredy-cat."

My hand fell. Ellis caught it, raised it to her cheek.

"You've already done the bravest thing. You told me what you've been holding back."

But I hadn't.

Then she kissed me, and for a while I forgot all my fears. There was only color and texture. White sheets folding around us like camellia petals, bare arms intertwined, red hair and near-black spread across the pillow. Like that Toulouse-Lautrec painting of the two girls in bed. A perfect moment.

Ellis nestled her head under my chin, and I said, "It's almost been a year."

We both brooded about it lately, a somberness lodged in our bones, weighing heavier the closer we got to the anniversary. Less than a week to go now.

"I wonder what Ryan would've done with this year," I said. "It's not right, that I'm here and he's not."

"Don't say that."

I traced a finger over the low ceiling, raw pine. The same thing they'd made his coffin from. Inside lay the urn holding his ashes. There was something perturbing about the cremation, as if Max couldn't bear for the body to exist a moment longer than necessary. "I wonder what he really wanted to be. Marine. Musician. Photographer."

"Maybe he just wanted to be himself."

"That's sad. Not even having that before you die."

I felt her tense against me, and kissed the top of her head. If I could shield her from every homophobic asshole out there—the kind who beat up gay kids at school dances, the kind who told their child to pray the gay away—I would.

Maybe it was enough to hold her hand in public.

Maybe if Ryan had had someone like that, he'd still be here.

"It could've gone the other way," I said. "It could've been us in the water and Ryan lying awake right now, wondering who we were. All of this is so ephemeral." I stretched out my right hand and candlelight cast witchy shadows from my fingers. I brushed Ellis's hair out of her eyes. "You don't even realize all the things you can lose."

"You won't lose me. I promise."

In my head I wrote the dialogue we didn't speak.

No matter what I tell you?

No matter what.

"Ellis."

"Vada."

Could she feel the craziness happening in my heart right now? Fuck.

"I don't ever want to lose you again. I don't ever want to wake up without you at my side."

It took a second for her to process it. She twisted around to look up at me.

"What do you mean?"

"I mean I want to look at your stupid freckles forever, okay?"

I was light-headed, blood pressure dropping from the words I'd just let loose into the universe. Her face was a mix of shock and wonder. Then she threw her arms around my neck so vehemently I actually did start to black out a bit.

"Baby, you're choking me. Not in a good way."

She pulled back, covered my mouth and face with kisses, and I gave up trying to breathe and let it happen. In my head I sketched her: hair in wild thistles around that elfin face, eyes lit up like I'd never seen before. Like the kid in her must have looked right after her first kiss, or when she aced a test and got the highest grade in the class. Like she'd just been given the whole world.

———

All that remained was the bed. Ellis was carrying the last box to the boat as I paced through the empty cabin, remembering. Paint still splattered all over the wood, a furious rainbow. We'd dragged the couch back to the beach house. An empty rectangle outlined where it had sat, and I knelt there, tracing the hollow.

My weight tilted a floorboard. Something white flashed beneath it.

Weird.

I leaned harder and the board corner rose. Below was a letter.

Mail that must have fallen, gotten trapped. I pulled it up with a nail. Torn envelope.

From the Office of the Medical Examiner. To Ellis Carraway.

Wait, what?

I'd let her complete the request form because she was better at that stuff—my lefty handwriting was shit, and I'd just end up doodling on it anyway. But we'd listed me as the recipient.

I pulled out the sheets inside.

Autopsy report: Ryan Francis Vandermeer.

What the actual fuck?

Footsteps on the log stairs.

On instinct I slid the report back into the envelope and dropped it beneath the floorboard. Ellis walked in as I stood.

"Hey," I said, too brightly.

"Hey yourself. Brandt's on the next ferry."

Her cousin had a legit boating license. We figured it'd be good to bring him along. Plus I needed some bonding time with him, since we'd all be living together soon.

I said nothing, staring at her face, my mind turning over and over.

Ellis moved closer. "You okay?"

"Just spacey. Having sex in the middle of moving day was probably not our best idea."

She blushed and lowered her eyes. Which gave me the chance to move from the hot spot.

I tried to process this, to phrase a conversation starter. Ellis, why? Even if it had fallen there, been mislaid, it was open. She'd read it. Never mentioned it to me.

Before I could begin, my phone buzzed. A text, from the last person I expected.

I need you.

I stood there staring at the screen.

"Who is it?" Ellis said.

"Max."

She frowned. "What does he want?"

"To see me."

"Why?"

"Don't know." I pocketed it before she could look. "Didn't sound serious, but who knows with him. Can you and Brandt handle the yacht?"

"Sure." Ellis touched my arm. "I should go with you, though."

"It's fine."

"Vada." She cupped my face and peered into it. So observant, so sensitive. Sometimes she seemed to know what I felt before I did. "What's wrong?"

I realized what she must be thinking: All that talk about forever. Cold feet, second thoughts.

"Nothing, promise," I said, and kissed her before she could ask more, and though my mind was going a million miles an hour a part of me surrendered to her, lost itself, my heart giving a flutter like a startled bird. I kissed her till the jittery energy in my body became focused and intense, then made myself stop. "I'll take the ferry. See you tonight at my place?"

Ellis nodded, flushed and breathless and so winsome I could almost forget, for a moment, that she'd hidden something from me. Something she knew I wanted, desperately.

Because why would she do that? To spare me? But she was the one who'd been reluctant to look, not me.

What had she seen?

"Love you," I said, smiling, as I walked out the door.

———

Snow fell on the ferry ride, the sky growing cottony and thick. By the time we docked I could barely see my hand before my face. I knew the path by memory, up the hills into the knotted heart of the island where tree roots reached centuries deep, clutching at rock that had been thrown here by glaciers. In Maine, like in Kahlo, the world was stripped close to the nerve.

It was dark when I reached the house. Snow-dark, light reflecting off the dull pearl underbellies of clouds. I scrambled up the porch and banged on the door, shaking powder from my coat.

"Max?"

No answer. But it was unlocked.

I went in cautiously, still calling for him.

The house smelled of leaves and dust, the peppery tang of ice. Lights off. Far cry from the last time I was here.

I walked past the bathroom twice before I came back, slower, peering into the shadows.

"Max?"

He sat in the tub, boots braced on the wall. Glass glinted, moved in an arc. He was drinking.

I found a candle and lit it on the stove, brought it to him.

This time I saw the gun.

It sat on the rim of the tub, dark blue steel shining softly. All the light seemed drawn to it as if it were hungry.

"What are you doing?" I said, sitting on the toilet lid.

I smelled him from here. Whiskey and a musk of sweat and sandalwood, like he'd been working in the woods. His hair was tangled. Fine stubble covered his jaw.

An empty bottle of Jim Beam lay in the tub with him, a half-filled one on the floor.

"Max, how long have you been drinking?"

He finally looked at me. Glazed eyes. "How long have you been lying?"

My spine went cold. "What?"

He drained the glass, reached for the bottle.

I snatched it away. "What the hell's going on? Why'd you text me?"

"I'm lonely."

His voice creaked like old wood. His head tipped forward, hair falling in his face. Even with how drunk and surly he was, I felt a wild urge to touch him.

No person should feel this alone.

I lowered myself to the floor. Gingerly, watching him, I pushed the gun away, lifted his hand to the tub ledge and laid mine over it.

I didn't have to ask about the booze. Anniversary week.

"You should get out of Maine," I said. "Go somewhere else, till it's over."

"It's never over."

"Why do you have the gun?" My hand tightened. "If I have to sit here on suicide watch, I will."

"Don't worry. Too much of a coward to do it that way." He laughed, unpleasantly. "I like to touch it."

His talisman.

In a box in my room were three hand-carved wooden figures. Sometimes, while Ellis was away, or sleeping, I touched the box. Sometimes I opened it and touched them.

We're not so different, Max. Holding on to our ghosts.

"I'll come by," I said. "On the day of."

He bared his teeth. Not sure if it was supposed to be a smile.

"If I have to sit on your porch in the snow, I will. I'm a stubborn bitch. You know that." I rubbed his knuckles. "You texted me for a reason. You want to talk."

"You don't come around anymore. I missed you."

"I've been busy. And you were being weird about my girl-friend."

It still gave me a little jolt, to call her that.

"I didn't mean to hurt you. Either of you. I wanted to protect you."

I looked at the hand beneath mine. "Ellis is a good person, Max. Better than I deserve. I wish you knew her the way I do."

"I wish you knew her the way *I* do."

"How is that?"

"She's hurt you. You don't understand yet, but you will."

"No more of this ominous shit, okay?" I pressed his hand. "I love her. No matter what, I will always love her. You know what it's like. You felt it for Ryan. That love will never change."

"You're young to be so wise."

"It's been a hard life. Makes you grow up fast."

"I missed this, Morgan. Your voice, your face. I missed you."

Everything. Slowed. Down.

Morgan.

I turned his hand over. Traced the smooth skin of his palm with a fingertip. Looked up. He was watching me.

"You weren't there," I whispered. "I saw everyone who walked through the door. You weren't there."

His eyes searched mine.

What had I missed? Someone in the restroom, or already seated? Dane took pics of the café; we scrutinized them later. No one looked remotely familiar.

I let go of Max and stood, dizzy.

"Don't leave me," he said.

Oh, god.

I rummaged in my coat for my phone.

Tell Ellis. Call for backup.

"You came into my life," he said. "You came in and made me feel alive again. And then you left. I need you. Please."

"How dare you, after what you did to me."

"What have I done?"

His face was dashed now in candle flame, now shadow. I couldn't read the look in his eyes.

"You catfished me. Fucked with my head, and my heart. Led me on a wild-goose chase."

"Wild-goose chase?"

"I knew it was you. You coward, watching me on cam. Bitching out in Boston. Do you know how much you fucked me up?"

"It was only a few minutes. I couldn't stand it." He glanced away. "You're like a daughter to me. It felt wrong."

"Don't fucking call me that. That's disgusting."

"I mean it. I couldn't watch. I wanted to pay you to stop."

"You did. You paid me to stop camming for anyone else." I knelt to his level, met those vivid blue eyes. "This is why you were always casting aspersions on Ellis. Trying to play me against her. Your 'archnemesis.' You fucking asshole."

Max sat up straighter. "Watch your mouth. I said it was only a few minutes. Then you left, to do a show for someone."

I was breathing hard. He faced me, unflinching.

"You were there every night, Max. For months. You and me."

"You've got me mixed up with somebody."

"What, you just stumbled across my site, despite the region ban? Accidentally used a VPN?"

He shrugged. "It's all Greek to me. I understand joints and ball bearings. Not ones and zeroes."

"How did you find me?"

"I looked up your picture on Google. It brought up other photos of you. With ties around your neck, and things like that. I was worried, so I clicked."

I laughed in his face. "Sure."

"It let me watch for free. You were right there. It broke my heart, watching you do that to yourself. Choking. You were in so much pain. I never realized how deep it went until then." His throat twisted, words straining out. "I thought it was because of Ellis. You know, the way she is. Love means being happy for someone even if it hurts, but I thought I could spare you that pain. I was wrong, Vada. You'd love her even if it destroyed you. Told you I'm bad at this father thing."

Either he had the best poker face in history, or he wasn't lying.

What the hell?

I got up, paced the bathroom. "What is this? Are you collecting dirt on us? Is this part of a lawsuit or something?"

"I haven't talked to any lawyers. I told you, I mean you no harm."

"Good, because you don't want to fuck with me. I've been collecting dirt, too." I decided to gamble. "We found Ryan's ex. And we had a nice long chat. He told us everything."

"Who?"

"His ex-boyfriend, Sergio. In Bar Harbor."

Max blinked.

"Your gay son's *partner*."

"He wasn't seeing anyone."

"Guess he didn't tell you."

"No, I'd know something like that. I spoke with his therapist." Max shook his head. "He's never been to Bar Harbor."

"We tracked this guy down, talked to him in person. He knew Ryan."

"You talked to this person, or Ellis did?"

I started to answer and then my mouth hung open, stuck.

He nodded, slowly. "You didn't actually meet anyone. You're repeating what she told you. What did this person supposedly say?"

Even though I was shaken I lobbed another dart, aiming blind. "He told us who beat Ryan up."

Max stood, grabbing the shower rod for balance. "Give me a name. Give me a name and I'll take care of it."

His hand drifted toward the gun.

He legit wanted to kill someone. Holy shit.

It couldn't be him, on the autopsy. Not his hands making those bruise patterns. He didn't hurt Ryan. He wanted to kill whoever had touched his son. The same way I'd wreck anyone who hurt Ellis.

None of this fit what I thought I'd known.

What the hell was going on?

"Who did it?" Max said.

"Answer me first. How did you watch me on cam? There's a region ban."

He exhaled, annoyed. "Ask your computer whiz friend. I don't know how that shit works."

Bugs in the code.

"You found something." Max narrowed his eyes. "You have a name. I need that name, Vada."

"I was bluffing, okay? The only name I have is Skylar. We still haven't even found her."

"What?"

"We looked everywhere. There was no Skylar at his school. Can you just tell me who—"

"You still don't see." He seemed almost about to laugh. "You looked right at her and didn't see."

For some reason I thought of Blue's last email.

you looked right at me. through me.

"See what?" I said.

"You cracked the laptop. You got the photos."

"Right."

"You saw her."

"Skylar wasn't in them."

"Yes, she was."

My thoughts skidded, losing traction.

"You're playing with me," Max said. "This is all a game to you. You and your *girlfriend*, playing detective. And you still don't realize she's playing against you, too."

He barreled toward me and I backpedaled, but he stormed past, toward the stairs. The gun was still on the tub.

"Max," I called.

"Please leave. No more of this."

"How did you see Skylar's pics?"

He turned around, leaning on the wall. In the darkness I could barely see him.

"She showed me."

"You met her?"

Now he started to laugh, dryly.

None of this made sense.

Skylar showed the photos to Max. Then Ryan died, and they disappeared.

Who deleted them?

We'd looked through every single pic. All selfies, landscapes, macro shots. No Skylar.

Unless Ellis hadn't shown me all the photos she recovered.

Like she hadn't shown me the autopsy. Like she'd lied about Ryan's ex.

"Max," I said, my body tense. "Why did you warn me about Ellis? What is she hiding from me?"

He looked at me a long time. I didn't think he would answer.

Then he said, simply, "Her."

———

Nothing moved in the woods but me. Chebeague was even more desolate than Peaks, quieter, lonelier. On a winter night there was only the soft rush of snow, the sky whispering sparkling white ellipses, words unheard. I walked carefully but my boots crunched, too loud in this deep stillness.

Our footprints had been erased on the log steps. I climbed up balancing on the railless edge, nearly falling.

Inside, small piles of snow collected in corners like pillars of salt. I went straight to the hollow rectangle traced in the paint and flicked on my phone's flashlight. Found the loose board and pressed my weight into it.

The envelope was gone.

———

"You're freezing. Did you walk here? Why didn't you call?"

Ellis was waiting in my room at the beach house. Candles lit, incense burning. Mug of tea on my desk. It all smelled like her now—my clothes, bedsheets, skin. Part of me, permeating everything. I couldn't look her in the eyes. She'd read me immediately.

How do you outwit someone who's so much smarter than you?

Think of her like a man. Prey on his weaknesses.

I flung my coat off, began to undress.

"Vada?" She followed me to the clothes rack. "What did Max say?"

"He was drunk. He didn't make a lot of sense."

"Did he want something?"

I glanced at her. "Me."

Her eyes widened. "What happened? Are you okay?"

"Nothing happened." I pulled my shirt off. Stood there in my bra, my hands lingering on my chilled skin. "I'm fine."

When I shivered Ellis moved close, circling my waist. "Are you sure? You're so cold."

I took a shaky breath.

"Did he touch you?"

"It was nothing."

Instantly she went rigid, pulling me against her. "If he did something to you, I'll—"

"It was nothing. I stopped him before anything happened, I promise." I bit my lip. "But it made me feel weird."

"In a bad way or a good way?"

"Both."

She let go and I turned around. No expression on her face, but she watched me sharply, gears turning.

"I'm sorry," I said. "I shouldn't have said anything."

"No. I'm glad you did." Her eyes danced back and forth. "How did it really make you feel, being touched by a man?"

Time to push. "Like a woman."

She stared a beat longer, not reacting, then walked toward her belongings on the other side of the room.

"Ellis, where are you going?"

"Home."

"It's late. The ferry isn't running."

"I'll call Brandt."

"It's snowing. It's not safe. Don't be like this, baby."

When I touched her shoulder she spun, seizing mine. "Is there something going on with you and Max?"

I laughed, disbelieving. "Seriously?"

"Is there?"

"Are you going to have a meltdown every time I so much as glance at a guy?" I wrenched away from her. "I knew I shouldn't have told you."

"I'm not overreacting. You still haven't let Blue go."

"I just want to know who he is. And there's a good chance he could be Max."

"Is that what you want? Do you feel something for Max?"

I sneered. "Please. I've always been faithful to you. Your paranoia is not my fault."

"You're a cam girl. You seduce men for a living. Sorry that it makes me *paranoid*."

"Well, I wasn't seducing him."

"Then why did he touch you?"

I threw my hands in the air. "Who fucking knows? He was barely lucid. He kept talking about Skylar."

If I hadn't been watching for it—if I didn't know her so well—I wouldn't have noticed the way her eyes flashed, the pique of alarm. She smothered it quickly with a frown. "What did he say, exactly?"

"Random shit. About the photos, and the autopsy. He actually met Skylar. They knew each other. I mentioned Ryan's ex, but Max had no idea who I was talking about."

"Why did you mention him?"

"Is there a reason I shouldn't have?"

"Because we should save our leverage until we need it?"

A perfectly reasonable thing to say.

Always my voice of reason, warning me back from the edge.

"You're right. I fucked up." I pretended to muse. "Now that I think about it, they never sent us that autopsy, did they?"

She looked at me for a long moment. "No. Must've gotten lost."

I headed toward the clothes rack. "I'm going to request it again. And I'm going back to Bar Harbor, to see that guy. Something doesn't add up."

"Vada." Ellis slid behind me, laid a hand on my bare back. Her fingertips glided down to the dip above my ass. Unsettling and arousing, both at once. "I think it's time we left this to Max. Let him deal with it now. It's not our business."

"Max doesn't want to deal with anything. He wants to bury it." I steadied my voice. "Sometimes it seems like you do, too."

Her hand moved to the clasp of my bra. "I want to let it go. I don't want to be haunted anymore."

"By who? Ellis, by who?"

But she didn't answer. She touched me until I stopped asking.

I let her open my bra, cup my breasts in her palms. My tension was palpable and she felt it, too. She pinched my nipples, bit my neck when she kissed it. We didn't make it to my bed. Instead she drove me up against the wall, one hand inside my jeans, the other around my throat. Her teeth shone in the candlelight, clenched. Aggressive. Masculine. Something primal in me responded. I pulled her toward the cam lights, the nightstand. Took a tie from the drawer and looped it around my neck. Put a silicone cock in her hand. "Do it like this," I said. "Fuck me like a cam girl." And she did, my legs around her waist, my spine to the wall. I looked at my fingers kinked against the wood, clawing for something to hold. There was nothing. Nothing but her.

―――――

In the morning I woke before Ellis, showered and dressed and left the house undetected. Sent her a text—running errands, nos vemos esta tarde, Christmas tree emoji—and got on the Portland ferry.

No gifts for me, she wrote back. I already have everything I want. I'll miss you.

It went in like a knife.

For a second I wanted to reply: What are you hiding? Why? But I thought of Blue, slipping away like quicksilver when I tried to catch him, hold him. I knew she'd be the same.

Not again. Not this time.

I'll miss you too, pajarito, I wrote, and turned my phone off.

All the way over on the ferry, I felt every swell and smash of the waves inside my ribs.

On the wharf the scent of raw fish and wet hemp hit me hard. I'd fallen in love with this city, too. Sometimes love for a person and a place get a little jumbled, and you can't feel one without the other. No matter what happened, Portland would always be Ellis. I'd never take that lion's head down. Brass doesn't rust. Max told me they used it on ships because it was one of the few things that could withstand the harsh salt sea. It would hang there while everything else burned slowly, disintegrating into red smoke.

I rang the doorbell.

"Vada," Brandt said, smiling. "What a nice surprise. Come in."

"Can't stay long." I kicked my boots off at the door. "Ellis sent me to pick stuff up."

Brandt was still in PJs, lounge pants and an undershirt. Bedhead and bare feet gave him a boyish air.

"Something warm to drink?" he offered.

"I'm good."

He eyed me a moment, still smiling. I couldn't tell if he read emotions as well as Ellis. "Come on."

Upstairs, we'd stacked all her boxes in the empty corner bedroom. Not our old room—*Let's be new,* I'd said. Half the boxes were open, clothes and books spilling over the floor.

"I'm helping," Brandt said.

"Uh-huh. You snoop."

"Takes one to know one."

Ellis had painstakingly labeled each box—COMICS; FIGU-RINES; STUFF VADA SHOULDN'T LOOK AT BEFORE XMAS—and something in my chest went tight at that last. She bought me gifts, after telling me a million times not to get her anything.

I waded through the mess till I found BACKUP STORAGE. Still sealed.

"Got something sharp?" I said.

Brandt snorted, as if the question were absurd. He grabbed a folding knife off the bureau and sliced through the tape.

"She sent you for hard drives?" he said.

"Yeah. You know, those bugs with the site. Guess she needs some backed-up file." Was I overexplaining? Shit. Which drive was it? These all looked the same. "On second thought, I think I will take a cup of tea."

"We're out of tea."

"Coffee?"

Brandt leaned on the bureau. He started to cross his arms and then braced on a palm instead. His right arm wouldn't bend far enough. "Let's get breakfast together."

Ellis swore her cousin had zero romantic interest in me, but he always seemed to be insinuating something. And only when she wasn't present.

"Brandt." I picked the external drive labeled R/S. Had to be this one. "You know that we're, like, serious. Me and Ellis. We're together."

"I'm inviting you to breakfast, Vada, not my bed."

Despite myself, I blushed. This guy unnerved me. I couldn't figure him out.

"Got what I need," I said, standing. "Thanks."

He stepped away from the bureau, and as I followed him out of the room, my eyes fell on the knife he'd left behind.

A large Buck knife with gold caps and a woodgrain handle.

I stopped moving. Brandt didn't notice for a few seconds. By the time he came back, I'd taken the knife and returned to the boxes.

"Forget something?" he said.

I smiled, the sultry smile I used on Ellis to get her to do what I wanted.

I cut into a random box and pretended to set the knife aside. It slid into my coat pocket.

My mouth was saying something about a favorite hoodie, mocking Ellis and her creature comforts, but my mind was playing a memory of wood shavings in the recycling bin downstairs.

I stood too fast, tried to brush past Brandt, but he caught my elbow.

I looked at the hand on me, his long, slender fingers. Thinner than Max's. Refined, elegant bones. Almost feminine, like Ellis's.

His eyes followed mine. Then our gazes rose, locked.

"Is everything okay?" he said.

where did you go?

is everything okay?

I slapped a big fake smile on my face like I did every day, as a cam girl, as a barista, as anything, because women are taught to smile, that smiling means men are less likely to hurt us.

"Everything's fine, Brandt."

I shrugged him off and walked to the stairs. As soon as I passed him my hand dipped into my pocket, gripping the knife.

He was slower than me. Bad knee. I'd pulled my boots on by the time he caught up.

someone i know used to be a star athlete.

golden boy. bright future.

"Leaving already?"

"Don't want to keep Ellis waiting."

"We're still having Christmas here, right?"

He said it in such an unassuming tone that I paused to glance at him. "Sure. Why wouldn't we?"

"No reason. I'm really looking forward to it."

He sounded utterly sincere.

Like Blue had.

"I'll see you later," I said.

I dashed down the steps and was nearly out of sight when instinct struck like lightning.

I turned around. Climbed silently back up the steps, avoiding the boards that creaked. Pressed my face to the door pane.

He stood in the hall, thumbing his phone.

My finger was pressing the bell before I realized what I was doing.

Brandt opened the door, eyebrows raised. "Forget something again?"

"I'm such an idiot. I didn't charge my phone last night." I gave him that seductive smile. "Can I borrow yours a sec?"

I was taking it from his hand before he could agree.

I flicked rapidly through the recently used apps. The last thing he'd done was send a text to Ellis.

She was here. She knows.

I opened the dialer and tapped Ellis's number, still smiling at Brandt. He watched me, not blinking.

"What did you tell her?"

The first words out of Ellis's mouth.

I pulled the phone away from my face and hit END CALL.

"Voice mail," I said.

My heart was beating so hard I could swear the air shook. I handed Brandt's phone back.

"Vada—"

"Talk soon," I said, whirling around. "See you."

As soon as I was out of sight of the house, I ran.

———

I couldn't sit still on the ferry. I paced the top deck, melting a trail of slush through the snow. My mind couldn't settle on a thought, either. Images flickered, unprocessed. The knife in his hand. His cold green eyes. His mangled arm, scarred face.

this will change things between us.

So afraid of meeting me. Of showing me his face, his body.

I called Frankie on my very well charged phone. She was waiting to pick me up at the landing.

"Want to tell me what's going on?" she said when I slid into the passenger seat of her SUV.

"Is Ellis at the house?"

"She went out." Frankie frowned. "I need to chat, but she won't answer her phone. What's wrong?"

A fleece of snow layered the windshield between wiper strokes, a constant erasure and redrawing of the world.

"Frankie, I need to ask you a favor."

She glanced at me over her sunglasses. "Yeah?"

"Can you trace some IPs from a certain client?"

"Is this about the bug?"

"No," I said, then turned to her and said, slower, "Wait, what about the bug?"

"Do you think you've been compromised?"

"Compromised how?"

"Security-wise."

"I'm not sure. What exactly does the bug do?"

She *tsk*ed, like my mother. "Didn't Ellis tell you?"

Of course not.

"It opened some loopholes in our security protocols. Some cammer safety settings were temporarily disabled."

Even though I knew, I said, "Like region bans?"

"Mm-hmm. It's fixed now. But I can pull IP logs for you. Has someone been harassing you?"

I looked out the window, into the snow.

"Morgan?"

"No. It's fine." I smiled. "Probably just being paranoid."

At the house I went straight to my room. Blood throbbed in my head as I kicked open my door, half expecting to see her. But the attic was empty.

I threw my bag onto the bed and flipped open my laptop. Plugged the external drive in.

it'll change things.

You were right, Blue.

Ellis had partitioned the drive into two volumes: RYAN and SKYLAR. I clicked the latter.

It was copied verbatim from the original. I navigated through system folders, looking for something personal.

PICTURES.

My heart hung in my throat. There was a chance these photos would be Ellis. Some weird connection, some—

Folder after folder, all filled with the same girl: blond, skinny, pretty. I clicked through them rapidly.

Skylar was just some girl. Some random girl.

Why hide her? Why did it matter?

I scanned them again, sharper. High-res photos. Professional DSLR. I recognized these places. The forest and the shore. His wood-paneled bedroom, the band posters. Peaks Island. Ryan had taken these.

Your hand sees this. But your eyes see something different.

Stop seeing with your eyes, Vada.

Skylar was pretty, though she wore heavy makeup. Extremely skinny. Skirts, combat boots, beanies. Studded chokers and bracelets. Ryan wasn't in any of the pics with her.

Something made me go back to a certain photo.

Her arms were bare. Light fell at just the right angle to reveal dozens of hash mark scars.

there's a bomb inside me, waiting to explode

"Oh my god," I said aloud.

I stood up. Walked from one end of the room to the other in a gray haze.

Took out my phone.

Ellis wouldn't answer.

I kept moving, touching things, trying to distill order from the chaos in me. I could never do it without her. She grounded me, centered me. My anchor. My everything.

I walked to the clothes rack, slowly.

On the shelf above the bar, I'd tucked the box of animals beneath a pile of old T-shirts.

But now, like the missing envelope, the box was gone, too.

————

One pair of footprints led up the snowy steps to the old oak tree house.

I followed them, stepping inside the soles. The cabin was dusky blue, the afternoon light already dying. Snow swirled in when I opened the door.

She sat hunched on the floor against the wall, knees up, head down, facing the light.

"Ellis," I whispered.

Her head lifted partway, hair tumbling into her eyes.

I shut the door. Walked to the wall across from her and leaned on it. Hands behind my back, my tailbone holding them down. Lest I do something unkind with them.

"You're angry," she said, her voice hoarse.

"Yes. About so many things."

"Do you want to hurt me?" She finally looked up. Red-eyed, her lips swollen. "I'll let you."

"I don't want to touch you."

Ellis flinched as if I'd struck her.

I took a step forward. "Give me the autopsy."

She reached into her coat, held the envelope out.

Ryan Francis Vandermeer.

I scanned through a litany of horrific injuries. Blunt force cranial trauma. Contusions, abrasions, bone fractures. I'd seen these words on my charts last year. Amazing, all the ways you could break a body and glue it back together, stronger than ever.

But not this one.

Scarring of the arms and legs, unrelated to cause of death.

Medications: spironolactone, estradiol, progesterone (for treatment of gender identity disorder).

Sex: F (transitioning from M).

The paper trembled in my hand, matching my pulse.

"Ryan was Skylar," I said. "Skylar was transgender."

Ellis didn't say anything.

It all clicked.

Rejected by the military because they didn't allow trans people to enlist. Beaten for going to winter formal in a dress. Cutting and drinking to deal with the pain. Max clinging to memories of a son. *Let me keep my memories, at least.*

How inexpressibly sad that the name on the autopsy was masculine. She didn't even get to die as herself. Skylar hadn't officially changed her name.

Like Ellis.

I knelt beside her, not quite looking at her face. Set the paper to one side and reached into my coat pocket. When Ellis saw the knife she startled, pulled away, but I seized her arm and wrenched her palm toward me.

"Give me the box," I said.

My voice was guttural, unfamiliar.

She withdrew it from her coat. I knocked the lid off. Pressed the wooden figurines into her hand, the knife into the other. I gripped her wrists, shaking so hard she trembled, too.

These were the hands that fit. The photo, the bruises in my heart. The same hands I'd drawn a thousand times yet had somehow not recognized when I thought they were a man's. Blue's hands.

We looked at each other.

"Fuck you," I said.

I rocked back on my heels, jumped to my feet. I meant to walk right out the door but when I reached it my knuckles hit a glass pane and went straight through. I pulled out and tried again, but all I did was smash another.

"Please stop," Ellis said.

My hand burned, tingling, dripping blood. I smeared it on my coat.

Red and Blue.

The same person.

In the ancient past, there was no separate word for blue. It was just an inflection of red.

I closed my eyes for a moment. Heat built there, an inferno, but of water. "Why, Ellis. Why did you do it."

"Because it's who I am."

I turned partway, feeling nastiness twist across my face. "You're some imaginary fucking guy who catfished me?"

"I think I'm like Skylar."

My entire body cringed.

"What the fuck are you saying?"

"I don't know a clearer way to say it."

"You're not this fucking man you were pretending to be."

"I wasn't pretending. I *am* him. I am Blue."

"You asshole." My hand was raw. I wrapped the fist in my sleeve. "All this time. Gaslighting me. Pretending to be jealous of yourself. What the fuck, Ellis?"

Her head lowered, half cowering. She was crying. "I don't know. I felt like two different people sometimes."

"You planted that bug in the code. That's how Max got through. You planted it to give yourself full access to me." I laughed. "Sergio never existed, did he? God, that night you walked in on my chat with 'Blue,' tricking me into thinking it couldn't be you. How'd you do it?"

"It was a macro. I knew how you'd react when I walked in."

"Where'd the money come from?"

"My mother."

"You devious little bitch." Another flinch. "You never needed the job, you just needed access to me. You are so fucked-up, Ellis. You talked about getting hard. About your fucking dick. About coming in your fist and imagining it was me." Now I couldn't look at her. I stared at the red dots spattering my boots. "I believed you. I fantasized about you as a *man*. You messed with my head. This is so fucked-up."

"It wasn't like that. It was real to me."

I laughed again, viciously. "News flash. In real life, I'm a girl. I never lied about it. But in real life, you're not a man. You don't have a fucking dick."

"That's what makes someone a man?"

"I can't believe I'm saying this. This is the most insane conversation. Anatomically, yeah, that makes you a man."

"No, that makes you male. How you feel inside is what makes you a man. Your body doesn't define you. If your hand doesn't work anymore, you're still an artist. If I'm born with two X chromosomes, I'm still not a girl."

"Stop with the fucking gender politics. The point is you catfished me. Nothing was real."

"It felt real to me. It felt real to you, too."

"Want to know what real is?" I lunged at her, dropped to my knees. Shoved my lacerated hand at her chest. "This. Flesh and blood. Not online bullshit. Not catfishing, fucking with my head. Not inventing a person who *does not fucking exist*."

"He does exist. I'm right in front of you, Vada."

I shoved her away, pushing myself back at the same time. And then sat there on the floor, crying.

God, fuck. This was happening.

"You liar," I said.

"I'm sorry."

"You broke my fucking heart, *Blue*. And you're breaking it again right now."

"Vada, I'm sorry. I didn't know how to tell you. I was scared."

I spoke to the space beside her, unable to face her full-on. "You were scared? You? The one hiding behind a keyboard, spinning out fucking fairy tales? I bared my heart to you. I built my life around you. And the whole time you've been lying to me, hiding who you really are."

"You could barely stand me as a girl. Can you blame me for hiding it?" She sniffled. "I tried to show you, in Bar Harbor. To see how you'd react to me as . . . a guy. I wasn't trying to hurt you, I was just afraid. Vada, will you look at me, please? I didn't change into some monster. It's me. Ellis."

The little wooden figures had fallen to the floor. Me, and her, and him.

I wanted to go somewhere and curl into a very small ball and cry till the world disappeared.

"I don't know who you are," I said hollowly. "And I don't think I want to anymore."

Ellis gave a miserable cry and covered her mouth, muffling it.

I had to get the fuck out of here before I lost my mind. I yanked the knife away from her, looked at the little figures.

"Don't go," she said.

don't go, Blue had said.

I could not process this.

Ellis called my name. The door banged. Cold and snow in

my face, soothing. The sting of air in open wounds. My teeth ached. I was grimacing, grinding them as hard as I could. I wished I could break my head open and let the cold inside me. Quench this feverish despair. Like Skylar.

How could Ellis have done this to me? How could she?

She? Was that even the right word?

My mind was on fire.

I stumbled down into the woods, heading toward the shore.

There was only one person who had any idea what this felt like. And I needed to tell him something.

Something I'd been trying to tell him—and myself—for a long time.

—13—

Peaks Island lay quiet and black on the horizon. Snow drifted from a charcoal sky, a billion tiny stars streaking into the ocean. The spray churning up beneath the prow flayed my skin, sharp as pins and brutally cold, and part of me wanted to drop the oars and hurl myself into the water. Let the salt eat away all the parts of me that could feel, leave my skeleton to grow coral and moss.

The shoreline was encrusted with ice and I ran the boat at it heedlessly, heard the hull screech and tear, a sound like two vehicles meeting, shredding each other. I latched the oars and leaped into the shallows, soaking my legs to the thigh.

Everything in my fucking life came down to that night a year ago. When I lost everything.

And it was all my fault.

I crashed through snow-thick woods, ran skidding over black ice on the road. Up the hill to the lonely house, only to sink to my knees in a snowbank, sucking air. I grasped soft white handfuls of oblivion.

Sharp crystals pierced the snow beneath my face. It took a second to recognize my own tears, freezing.

God, Ellis, why.

Not because of what she was. In my heart, I already knew.

Her androgyny. Her name. The way I'd never called her a girl except when I thought of our future, or when I wanted to hurt her. It wasn't so much a shock as it was stepping back from the painting, seeing all the brushstrokes coalesce into a clear image. But she lied. To the one person on earth she should have told. Manipulated me, deceived me to experiment with her identity without my knowledge or consent, made me vulnerable, took advantage of my naivete. Screwed my head up. Put my heart in danger while she stayed safe behind the keyboard.

That was it. I would have loved her no matter what, including this part of her, if only she'd told me the truth.

I got up. Snow rushed from my clothes, the shedding of some old self.

The house was dark and still, same as yesterday. I stood on the porch for a moment and then tried the door. Unlocked.

"Max," I called.

My shoes left wet prints, staining this dry, dead place. Everything looked different now. Photos of Skylar in her boy costume, standing on a pier with Max, the two of them hoisting a huge striped bass that licked up the sun. Skylar swinging a bat, smashing a baseball like a pale meteor into the aching blue beyond. Stereotypical boy stuff.

Max had always known her as a son. How do you reconcile losing someone twice—as the person you thought you knew, and the person they really were inside?

I called his name as I moved through the house. Too quiet. I peeked upstairs but there was no one. When I glanced out of Skylar's bedroom window, I noticed something.

The boat was gone.

I raced downstairs and outside into the falling snow.

The yacht floated in the water off a nearby pier. Max's Jeep sat parked on gravel. I shouted for him and a frigid gust carried my voice away.

My feet burned as I stumbled down the dock. Not good. Burning was a sign of frostbite.

The closer I got to the boat, the clearer it became:

A shadow perched on the pier, in the snow.

A man.

He sat there in nothing but jeans. Shoulders slumped, not even shivering. Snow flocked the hair on his bare chest.

I stopped a few feet away, wondering if I was hallucinating.

"Max," I said.

He tipped his head back, drained the last of a whiskey bottle, and pitched it into the ocean.

Shit.

I moved closer, careful not to startle him. "What are you doing out here? You're going to get hypothermia."

His breath formed coils of steam that laureled his head. I crouched a few feet off, ignoring the burn in my wet feet, the throb in my bleeding hand. Ice flaked off my jeans.

"I saw the photos. All of them." My breath touched his face. "Skylar was your daughter."

At last he looked at me.

"I know about denial," I said. "I've been in denial a long time, too."

"What do you want?"

"Put a shirt on, for one, before you die."

He looked back at the water. "I don't feel anything."

"That's not good, Max."

"It's what I want."

I knew that desire well.

"I get it," I said. "What you were trying to show me about Ellis. All these years I saw it without really seeing it. It was right in front of my face, in my drawings, and I just . . . couldn't name it. Neither could you. You didn't out her, even though you were worried she'd hurt me." And she did. And how could I resent her for that, if being Blue made her happy? My chest ached. "When did you know, with Skylar?"

"I always knew." Muscle twitched in his jaw. "I pushed it away. He asked for dolls and I bought him a baseball glove."

My mother, buying me dresses instead of paint.

They hadn't meant to hurt us. They thought we'd get hurt by being our true selves. And they were right, but that didn't mean we were wrong.

"What finally clicked?" I said.

"I caught him. In makeup. In . . . drag." Max exhaled through his teeth. "He took pictures, put them online. When I found out I said a lot of things I regret. But he didn't understand. None of you do. You're young and think you're invincible. You don't realize that you're branding yourself. Once you show the world you're different, you can never take it back."

"I *do* realize that. That's why I've been terrified of being my real self." Like Ellis. God, this whole time I'd been so self-righteous, thinking I was the only one struggling with my identity. "But if we're not true to ourselves, we'll never be happy."

"What's better, being happy or alive?"

"They're not mutually exclusive."

"For people like that, they are."

I reached out and brushed his bicep. His skin was rubbery with cold. "I saw the autopsy. She was on hormone replacement therapy." I thought of Ellis changing her name as soon as she turned eighteen. "When they start to transition, to become who they feel like inside, it gets better. It's like pressure letting up. A bomb being defused."

"I caused that pressure."

"How?"

Max grimaced. "When he was younger, he asked if he could

be a girl when he grew up. And I told him that was wrong. I told him not to think that way. Boys grow up to be men."

Now he knew better.

Sometimes boys grew up to be women. And girls grew up to be men.

"You still have her boy pictures all over your house," I said. "Who are those for? You think that's how she'd want to be remembered?"

"I want to remember him being happy."

"Max, being her real self made her happy."

He shook my hand off. Sloppy, uncoordinated. "You want me to put up photos of *Skylar*? To remember what a failure of a father I was? To remind me why my son committed suicide?"

This is it. This is the moment, Vada. Own it.

I touched him again, firmer. "You're not the one to blame. If you want to blame someone, it should be me."

"Why?"

Play the ace.

All the truth in me gathered in my lungs, rose, and let itself loose into the world.

"I lied to the police. I lied to Ellis. I lied to everyone. Even myself."

My voice was as soft as the snowflakes crashing against our lips and eyelashes. A hundred small impacts of crystallized sky on skin.

"I was driving, Max. And I caused the accident. On purpose."

———

The night of the crash, the sky was a clear black salted with stars. Our first winter in Maine. We spent most of it in bed watching Netflix and ravishing takeout seafood and each other. When a college friend invited me to a party down the coast, I spent hours cajoling Ellis.

"Come on, hermit. It'll be fun." I pinned her to the mattress and tickled her ribs. "I'll get drunk and table-dance. Then you can drive me home and tell your Tumblr friends how you saved a damsel from her own distress. Hashtag moral superiority."

"This is technically coercion," she gasped, laughing.

I tickled harder. "Tell me when it becomes torture."

"Vada. I can't. Breathe."

I stopped tickling and kissed her. In a second the mood shifted and she pulled me close. One hand slid under my shirt. She raked her nails across my back and arched against me, her leg between mine. It was the kind of kiss that led to coming completely undone. I had to tear my mouth away.

"We could stay in tonight," she murmured.

Tempting. Ever since we'd come to Maine, we'd been different. More intense. Like new lovers, shyer in some ways but bolder in others, pushing our boundaries farther. We didn't know anyone here. We could be ourselves, or whoever we wanted to be. Blank canvases.

I pecked her cheek and jumped off the bed. "I'm going stir-crazy. Let's go out. Just for one night."

In the car I put on K.Flay and sang along. Ellis breathed on her window, tracing words in the steam. HELP ME. ABDUCTED BY BAD SINGER. Jokingly, I threatened to wreck the car. She rubbed out the words and breathed on the glass again. I ♥ YOU.

"You big softie," I said, but my pulse skipped. "I heart you, too."

The house sprawled along the shore, bordered by a cracked stone jetty. We walked the grounds for a while, misty scarves of breath trailing after us. Ellis needed to drink in the quiet as a reservoir for social interaction. My poor introvert. Inside, I introduced her to people from my master's program. She smiled sweetly, tolerated our long obscure art convos without complaint. She even got into a discussion with some kids about re-creating famous works of art in *Minecraft,* made my friends laugh by coining the phrase "Yves Klein Blue Screen of Death." She was charming and adorable and perfect. But when I came back from the bathroom I found her out on the deck, tucked into a fold of shadow, shivering. She stared forlornly at the beating waves.

"What's wrong?" I touched her shoulder. "*Pajarito.* You look so blue."

"Nothing."

She shrugged me off and took out the vaping pen, which was Ellis-speak for *Go away.*

Prodding would only raise her hackles higher. I fiddled with the buttons on my coat. The clean air turned a spicy balsam, that forest essence that was so her.

"Please talk to me," I said finally.

She looked at me askance, struggling not to cry. "Every single person we met, you said, 'This is my friend, Ellis.' You introduced me as your *friend.*"

Fuck. This again.

"You are my friend, Elle."

"We're way more than friends."

"Yeah, but I don't have a good word for it. It's complicated. And random strangers don't need to know our personal business."

"Just admit you don't want people to see you that way."

"What way?"

"With me. As my girlfriend."

I grabbed the porch railing, glowering into the night. "Because of my internalized homophobia, right? Because I secretly hate the fact that I'm bi. Blah, blah, blah. So not having this argument again."

"You don't hate it. But you want guys to see you as available."

"What are you even talking about?"

"You were flirting with that guy. Nick."

I rolled my eyes. "God forbid I speak to a man, or I'm suddenly leaving you."

"Then why? If it's serious, why don't you take it seriously? Why don't you tell people who I really am to you?"

Ellis was too good at pushing my buttons. At getting me to spit out the nasty truth.

"Because who the fuck are you to me? I don't even know." The wood creaked under my hands. I could've shredded the house into tinder. "I'm not fucking gay, okay? It's not that simple for me. You know exactly who you are and what you want in life. I don't."

"You know why you never tell anyone we're together?" She looked madder than I'd ever seen her, which was rare enough. "Because it's temporary for you. You're just using me till you find your perfect Prince Charming. That's all I am. Your surrogate boyfriend."

It hurt. I needed to strike back.

"You're not much of a boyfriend, are you?" I said.

Ellis set the pen down on the railing. Then she turned and walked back into the house.

"Fuck," I muttered, picking the pen up. Still warm. "Fuck, fuck, fuck."

Me and my goddamn mouth.

When I found her inside a while later, she held a red cup and stood in a group, laughing uproariously at a story some girl told with finger puppets.

So it was like that, then. Fine.

I could play Ellis Carraway tonight.

I sulked in a corner, head down over a warm beer, radiating a black cloud of misanthropy. People avoided me. I stared daggers at anyone Ellis paid attention to. When she switched rooms, I followed. How does it feel? I thought. How do you like the jealous, insecure, clingy girlfriend act?

A cute girl started talking to her, and they drifted apart from the others.

My hand tightened on the beer bottle.

It feels like shit, I answered myself. No one should be made to feel this way.

I'd had one sip all night. Couldn't drink. Something dark and poisonous bubbled in my chest.

The other girl touched Ellis's arm, smiling.

I was on my feet before I realized it, slinging my arm around my best friend's shoulders. My smile was hard.

"Hi," I said loudly to the stranger. "Nice to meet you. I'm Elle's girlfriend. Life partner. Lover. We haven't really settled on a word yet, have we, baby?"

The other girl blinked. Ellis turned riot pink.

"Excuse us, please."

She crossed the house and I followed. Ellis kept moving, making me feel like a hunter giving chase. When we passed an empty bathroom I yanked her inside and slammed the door.

"What is your problem?" she said.

Tequila, heavy on her breath.

"You are my problem." I wrapped my hand around her jaw. "What do you want, huh? Want me to go out there and declare it to the whole fucking party? Tell them we sleep in the same bed? That I fuck you in it every night?"

I drove a leg between hers and held her against the door and she gasped, eyelashes fluttering.

"Do I need to fuck you right here?" I growled.

I kept her jaw in my hand. The other unbuttoned her jeans, tugged at the fly. When she fought me off I lurched back.

What the hell were we doing?

I went to the sink, flipped on the cold water. Ellis hurled herself at me.

One hand snared in my hair, twisting. I cried out in pain. Her other palm clapped over my mouth. I stared at her in the mirror, shocked.

"Like this?" she hissed. "Is this what you like? Is this what turns you on?"

Now I fought her. She clung to me, our limbs tangling. We stumbled to the wall. Her eyes were glassy, whether from alcohol or tears I couldn't tell.

"This is what you want, right, baby? A girl to share your life with, but a guy to fuck you. Wouldn't it be so much easier if I was a real boy?"

In an acid voice I said, "Sometimes I wish you were."

We stared at each other with naked resentment. Then she kissed me, meanly, gashing my lip, and slid a hand inside my jeans. A moment later mine was in hers. I'd never hatefucked someone before. I didn't think I had it in me. But there was no other word for what happened. It was crude and unlovely. Unloving. I came first, white heat knifing savagely up my belly. Then I turned tender like I always did afterward and stroked her cheek, but she grimaced and said, "Harder," and I tried to oblige. She didn't come. She pushed me away, cupped cold water to her face. Fumbled her clothes straight and staggered out.

We each had a set of car keys. I caught her before she started the engine.

"Elle, are you crazy? You're drunk."

I wrestled her into the passenger seat. When I buckled her in I knelt on the curb, grasping her hands.

"I'm sorry," I said. "I don't know how to handle this. I've never really been serious with anyone. Guy or girl. This is a first for me."

Ellis stared through the windshield, mouth drawn. Tears or water or both ran down her face, silver threads glistening in the starlight.

I kissed her knuckles. "Okay. Let's just go home."

Somewhere northwest of us, a girl with hairline fractures in her sternum left another party and got behind the wheel of her Jeep. As I double-checked the seat belt, Skylar tipped her head back, a comet tail of cinnamon whiskey trickling behind the bruises on her throat.

Ellis was eerily quiet as I drove. I glanced at her, my anxiety winding tighter. Fuck, she *was* crying, and it made me tear up, too. I could never watch her cry.

"This doesn't work," she said. "We don't work. We're broken."

"We're having an off night."

"Over and over and over."

I gripped the wheel like a vise. These were the last few minutes my right hand would be strong and whole.

"Please don't cry," I said.

Ellis took her phone out. Skylar took another slug.

I pressed the gas, felt the tires spin loosely on ice. Careful. Calm down, Vada.

But the one person who always calmed me down was the one making me unravel.

"We're not broken, Elle. We're still figuring stuff out."

"It's been four years. How long does it take?"

I never had an answer for that except *Not yet.* Everything in my life was *not yet.*

"You're wrong." She spoke in a small voice, facing her phone. "I don't know who I am, but I know what I want. And we don't want the same thing."

"What do you want?"

"You. For the rest of my life."

My palms chafed on the cold leather wheel. I didn't know how to respond.

I'm not ready, I thought. I love you but I'm not ready for something this intense, this epic. I'm not ready for my life to start. What if I choose wrong? What if I commit to something I'm not serious about? What if I grow restless and unhappy like my father? I'm only twenty-two. Still a kid, really.

Is this my fucking quarter-life crisis?

Ellis tapped her phone.

"What are you doing?" I said.

"Buying a plane ticket."

"What? Where?"

"Chicago."

Again I pumped the gas before I could stop myself. We slid over the center line, but the highway was deserted. Plenty of time to correct.

Skylar started the ignition.

"Elle, what the fuck?"

"You don't want me in your life."

"Are you nuts? You're my fucking world."

She slapped her armrest. "You moved all the way here to get rid of me. You could've gone to grad school in Chicago."

"Stop with the paranoia. They rejected me."

"Did they, or did you withdraw your app? I don't believe you. You moved here on purpose. You were hoping I'd stay behind."

My teeth ground so hard they felt like glass about to snap. No shit, I thought. Your mother promised to take care of you if I left. If I set you free. Let you find your own happiness, instead of always chasing me like a puppy. A puppy I keep kicking because I'm too scared to love it unashamedly.

I didn't hope you'd stay behind. I just wanted you to be happy. You deserve someone who puts you first.

You deserve someone better than me.

"Coming here was a mistake. And I'm going to fix it." She tapped her screen decisively. "There. Booked."

I was doing fifty in a forty zone. The road began to curve. The slightest twitch would send us flying into the other lane.

"Cancel the booking."

"No. I'm going home."

"Home is a few miles away. We'll be there soon. Then we can talk about this."

"I'm done talking. I'm just done, Vada. With everything. With you."

Her words slurred. I felt the razor edge of teeth slicing into my lip.

"You're drunk and being dramatic."

"So what if I'm drunk? Maybe I have to be drunk to stand up to you. Ever think about that?"

I winced. "What do you want, Elle? What will make you happy? Tell me, and I'll do it."

"Take me to the airport."

"I'm not doing that."

"Then you'll just keep making me miserable."

I could have screamed. "God, what do you want from me? I fucking love you. I'm sorry I don't show it exactly the way you want, but I love you. What more is there?"

"You're just using me so you don't get lonely till you find the man of your dreams."

"Give it a fucking rest. You're the only one I want. The only one who's made me feel this way."

"Liar."

"It's the truth."

"Know why it's a lie? Because you'd never marry me. Ever. But I'd do it. In a heartbeat."

Gut punch.

How can you look that far ahead? How can you imagine that, when I can barely see us getting home safe right now?

"This is so unfair, Elle. You can't judge my love based on some faraway future."

"You don't love me the way I love you. And you never will."

Fifty-five miles per hour.

"So you're just leaving? Do you know how cruel this is? I'm losing my girlfriend *and* my best friend."

"Now you call me that. Because you have nothing left to lose."

"Fuck you, Ellis."

"Fuck you, too. And slow down before you kill us. Or just kill us, actually. I don't care anymore."

A scream rose inside me. I pressed it back down.

And as I did I pressed the gas pedal, feeling the fuel burn brighter, hotter, tires devouring the road. I clung to the curve. Always in control, even when I was going too fast. Ahead of us the tree line broke and iron struts rose against the night. A bridge.

All this time, Elle had endured my misgivings in her patient, understanding way. The way that sometimes made me see her as a doormat. Not once had she pulled herself out from under my feet like this. And when Ellis Carraway had enough, that was it. She'd cut her parents off cold. She'd left her entire extended family in Chicago, for me.

Now she'd had enough of this. Enough of me controlling our relationship, framing it in my terms. Enough of it being about me and my needs and my hang-ups.

Enough of me, period.

I'd finally pushed too far. She was leaving me all alone in this cold, dark, empty place.

Who the hell was I without her?

No one. A ghost.

If I was already a ghost, then what did it matter if I sped up?

If I smashed this car into pieces.

If I broke us. Like she was breaking my heart right now.

Fifty-six miles per hour.

Fifty-seven. Fifty-eight. Fifty-nine.

The bridge came up faster than I expected. Night played tricks with distance. I braked. The car fishtailed.

Black ice.

Oh, fuck no.

Steer into a slide, I thought, steer into a slide, but it was too close and we were going too fast and we'd hit the bridge rail before I could straighten out. My first-ever accident. In this strange, lonely state where I lost everything that mattered to me. Where I lost her.

Only me, I prayed as the railing rushed up. Please, God. Let it hurt only me.

I was saying something—it wasn't until after that I'd hear the words in my memory, *I'm sorry I'm sorry I love you*—and then lights flared in the rearview mirror, and a terrible force struck deep inside my bones, and the world broke into a million glittering pieces.

———

The words hung in the air between us.

I felt so light now. The truth is a heavy thing, and you can't fight the undertow forever.

Max got to his feet. I tottered backward, slipping in the snow as I stood.

Now he'll hurt me, I thought. The way I hurt his child.

He still had his boots on, unlaced. He kicked one off and turned around.

"Max," I said.

He moved down the dock, kicking off the other. I followed.

"Max, wait."

By the time I realized what was happening and started to run, he'd reached the end of the dock. He dove headfirst into the icy water.

I slid to a halt, barely catching myself from going over, snow geysering beneath my feet. Max thrashed clumsily, more fighting than swimming. White wings of spray beat the surface at each stroke.

"Don't fucking do this," I screamed after him.

I dug my phone out, hit 911. Whirled around, peering through the snow. I needed something. Anything.

Orange caught my eye, hanging inside the yacht cabin.

I tore off my coat and pulled a life vest on, then grabbed another. The dispatcher was saying *Hello? Nine one one, where is your emergency?* in my ear.

"Peaks Island," I said, running down the boat ramp. "North side. In the water."

What is the nature of your emergency?

I stopped at the edge of the dock, staring through the snow at the splash and churn in the distance.

"Two people are drowning. Please help us." I took a deep breath. "I can't swim."

I set the phone down on the dock, pulled my boots off, and jumped.

It felt like diving into a pool of live electricity. I kicked to the surface, gasping, clinging to the other vest like a surfboard. My hair lashed across my eyes. The water was so cold it registered only as pain, not chill.

No sign of Max. I kicked in the direction I'd last seen movement.

Why the fuck had I never learned to swim?

In my dreams this past year, I drowned again and again. Always it felt less like falling to the ocean floor than falling in outer space. An abyss that kept expanding the deeper you fell. Dying would be like that, I thought. Like falling asleep without ever reaching the soft floor of your dreams. Just deeper and deeper into a blackness with no saturation point.

A hand crested, slapped the waves, disappeared.

Bastard, I thought. I'm not letting you die.

I kicked furiously, managed to propel myself little by little. Then a wave rose and flung me backward and I wanted to sob. My clothes weighed a thousand pounds. Bones made of lead.

"Max," I screamed, snowflakes filling my mouth.

My foot kicked something warm.

I kicked again, and it wrapped itself around my leg. Heavy. Pulling me under.

I kicked with the other leg and then he surfaced, spluttering, clinging to me.

"You crazy bastard," I said. "Put this on."

We fumbled at the extra vest, both inept. My fingers stuck together as if in mittens. His lips and hands were actually blue. I thought that was a thing in cartoons.

The vest finally slipped over his head but when it did, I couldn't move. My arms were too heavy. They could only clutch him, my body craving his faint heat. Max held on to me weakly, coughing.

"We're going to die," I said. "Of hypothermia."

"Swim to shore."

"I can't swim. This is all I had in me."

He started laughing, weird, shivering laughs, and wrapped me in his arms.

"Don't go to sleep," he said.

"I'm not."

But my eyelids were heavy, too.

"I'm sorry," I said. "I'm sorry for what I did."

"Don't talk. Conserve heat."

"It's not even that cold anymore," I murmured, burrowing into his shoulder.

My skin tingled, almost burning. The water lapping over us was blessedly cool. I thought of Lake Michigan in summer, driving to the Indiana Dunes with Ellis. Watching our city far away across the blue. Tracing pictures in the sand with my finger until the tide rolled in.

That's all we are, I told her. *Here for a moment, then swept away.*

It's sad, she said. *Why do we try? Nothing lasts.*

But it's beautiful for a moment. What other reason do you need?

I didn't even notice when Max's arms loosened and my head slipped beneath the surface. It was like going to sleep.

"Vada."

I stared up through the darkness, at my hair trailing above me in black vines. Cold water weighed on my chest, working steadily at my lips like a kiss, until they parted and let the ocean in. It felt strangely good. Something filling the hollow place inside me.

"Oh my god, she's alive."

Then I was rising, being hauled out of the salt and ice, dead fingers dragging below me. I felt the slow toll of my heart like a ferry bell, distantly.

Something pounded on it. Warmth against my mouth. The sear of hot air in my throat.

I vomited seawater, a brackish burn. Voices floated overhead.

"Blankets. Hurry, Brandt!"

"I'm hurrying. Fuck."

Dimly I sensed hands on my body. Something crinkling, like Christmas wrap. I opened my eyes.

A face above me, blurry. Hair plastered to her forehead, glasses knocked askew. She smoothed a foil blanket over me. Dazedly I pushed her glasses up her nose. She grabbed my hand.

"Hi," I said.

Her face did that frowning, furrowing thing that meant she was trying not to cry.

"Stay awake, okay, Vada? Please. Stay with me."

I tried, staring up into the falling snow, but after a while the sky went dark and the snow winked out like stars.

After that there was a long blankness. At times things sketched across the void: neon reflective strips on a paramedic's coat, a pouch of quicksilver saline hanging above my head. Ellis's face, mostly. Watching over me. So pretty, the pink lily petals of her mouth moving softly, saying my name. I'd inked them on Blythe's shoulder a lifetime ago. So she could remember. And I thought, If I die, that's what they'll find in me. This face, inked in the surface of every cell.

———

I woke first this time.

For a moment I thought I was still out in the snow, but the pale haze grew solid and became white walls, chrome rails. Hospital. A tube of warm fluid ran into my wrist. I was wrapped in fleecy quilts. Still shivering.

In a chair beside the bed, my best friend slept hugging a pillow.

I lay there for a while, watching.

In Life Drawing class we'd spent a whole week learning how to use our eyes all over again, like infants. How to trick our brains into actually processing what we saw instead of subbing in symbols and shorthand. Not *red-haired girl*, but Ellis. Not *Ellis* but a lopsided grin, freckles like a handful of sand blown across her face, the way she'd squint when she felt some emotion too intensely to handle, as if trying to let less of the world in.

How strange, that I could look at someone every day and every night and not really see them.

I cleared my raw throat, and she stirred.

"Hi," I whispered.

She smiled uncertainly, came to my bedside.

"How do you feel?"

"Cold."

Ellis touched my wrist and I reached over and covered her hand with mine. I heard her sigh.

"Do you remember anything?"

"I was in the water. You and Brandt pulled me out." My chest tightened. "Is Max—?"

"He's okay. He's in the ICU. They said he's fine, but they're keeping a close eye on him."

Thank fucking God.

I let go of her and looked toward the windows. Night, snow falling slowly, glittering in the hospital lights like diamond dust.

My truth was out, now.

All of our truths were.

"I'll give you some privacy," Ellis said. "I just wanted to be here when you woke up."

I caught her hand before she turned. "Don't go."

Her jaw tensed. She looked at my hand instead of my face.

"You remember that night," I said. Not a question.

She nodded.

"You know what I did."

"Yes."

"Max knows, too. I'm going to jail."

"No, you're not."

"I did it on purpose." My hand clenched. "I tried to hurt us, Ellis."

"For a second. And then you tried to stop. It was a mistake. He knows that."

"I could've killed us. I killed Skylar."

"You stopped Skylar from hurting anyone else. It was an accident. She was trying to kill herself."

"And I ended up doing it for her."

"Listen to me." Ellis worked her hand free and then laced her fingers back through mine. "We couldn't change what was going to happen that night. She had the gun in the glove box. She knew what she wanted."

How can you hold my hand right now? "Ellis, I tried to hurt *us*. You."

"I know." She gripped harder. "I've tried to hurt you, too. You make me feel things so much I can barely stand it."

I kept swallowing, but my throat stayed dry. "I couldn't have lived with myself if something happened to you. I wish I was the only one who got hurt. I'm sorry. I'm such an asshole. So selfish."

"Baby, don't cry."

Oh, that's why my throat was dry. All the water was coming out of my eyes. "I knew about it, okay? About your boy side. Not the exact details, but I've always accepted it, subconsciously. That's what came out in my art. Part of me recognized it while part of me was still in denial. I'm not as brave as you. I couldn't face it—who I am, who you are. Who we are together."

"I lied about it," she said.

"Because I made you too afraid to be honest. I'm sorry I made you afraid."

"You didn't." She bowed her head. "You're the only one who knows. The only one who really understands me."

"Look at me, Ellis."

She looked. Glassy-eyed, hair raking across her forehead. Not a boy or a girl, not any binary, rigid definition of a person. Just my everything.

"I love you. No matter who you are. Okay?" My throat felt all mucky and thick. "You're the best person I've ever known. You make me want to be better."

Ellis brushed my tears away with her hands.

"Know how much I like you, nerd? You made me fall in love with you twice."

"One of those wasn't real."

"It was all real." I brought her hand to my chest. "When I was camming, half the time I felt like somebody's therapist. But Blue was mine. He helped me work through my depression. To see myself as the person I want to be. I loved him for that."

"That's how I felt, too. You made him—you made me feel like the person I've dreamed of being."

I stared at her hands. "How did I look right at you and not realize?"

"Because you see who I am inside. Not outside."

"Sometimes I wanted so badly for you to be him. It almost feels like cheating, that you are."

"You didn't want him to be Max, or Dane?"

"No." I kissed her hand. "You're perfect. You're all I want."

"I'm sorry I broke your heart."

"*Yo también, pajarito.* Maybe we needed to break a little, so we could put ourselves back together more beautifully than before."

She was doing that squinting, this-is-too-much, I-can't-even thing.

I let her go. "It smells really good in here. What is that?"

"Oh. Almost forgot."

Ellis crossed the room and returned with a foam takeout box.

"They're not hot anymore, but I thought you'd be hungry."

Unmistakable. The scent of my childhood. Fried plantains and caramelized sugar. "Oh my god. *Maduros*? In fucking Maine?"

"I had to call a million restaurants to find them."

I flipped the box open. Golden plantain slices, still warm, topped with a dollop of cream cheese.

"My sweet prince," I said.

"My rebel princess."

I swear, my smile could've swallowed the sun.

I motioned Ellis closer and mimed for her to open. She let me feed her a slice, then took the box and fed me the rest by hand.

Things were finally starting to feel normal again.

I closed my eyes, sighing. "Why are you so sweet to me?"

"Because I love you."

"I love you, too," I said, immediately, easily.

"And you've got a great ass."

I laughed. "You sound like Brandt."

"Why was Brandt looking at your ass?"

"This may shock you, but men often find me attractive."

"I can't imagine why."

"Ask Blue about it."

She glanced away. "Brandt knew. He tried to throw you off the trail, with the knife and stuff."

She was that terrified I'd reject her. That afraid of losing me, when I'd been so scared of losing her once she knew the truth.

"It's okay. It's kind of nice, actually, that he's so loyal to you."

Ellis peered at her shoes.

"Hey," I said. "Tell me something."

"What?"

"Do you actually have Superman underwear?"

Her face went red. "I'm leaving."

"Nope." I caught her arm, yanked her back onto the bed. "This patient needs supervision. And superstrength. Super-speed."

"Will you shut up."

I couldn't stop snickering. Her expression softened.

"Still cold?" she said.

I wasn't, but I nodded.

She took off her glasses and hoodie and shoes and slid under the blanket. For a moment we looked at each other, hesitating, and then I pulled her into my arms. It felt no different from always. Holding too tightly, hearts beating in sync, her pulse matching the quick staccato in the background. I pulled the stupid metal clip off my finger so the monitor went quiet. Now we could only feel it, my rhythm against hers.

———

The headstone was blank.

We stood on a moor overlooking the ocean. Below us the drowned coast tumbled down to the water, shards of chopped rock jutting against the rush of black waves. Tide pools churned and breathed mist. At night they'd freeze solid, starfish and barnacles and other strange sea creatures trapped in ice like clear quartz. Up here, in the muddy scrub, we faced the wind and the grave without a name.

Ellis walked along the precipice. Max stood beside me, his coat flapping against his legs.

We didn't talk about what happened in the water, or on the road. Neither of us was good at expressing our emotions verbally. We spoke better with our hands. I cooked food and brought it over. Then I started inviting him to dinner at our house. He fixed the creaking floor. He hugged Ellis one night, which made me cry, for some reason. He even coaxed Brandt into helping him work on the yacht.

When the weather warmed, Max said, he'd teach me to swim. You can't live beside the ocean without knowing how to swim.

He didn't say it, but I knew he left the stone uncarved because he couldn't accept either fact: that Skylar was gone or that she was a *she*. If he left it blank, he could keep denying it. Committing to it meant the past was over, that the future had started. A future without his only child. That pretty face, those sparkling blue eyes.

"Accept her the way she was," I said. "She still needs that from you."

"Don't you see?" Ellis said, touching the headstone. Her hair streamed in the wind, a torch of color against the gray. "You're not cutting off her future by carving a name. You're *giving* her memory a future."

Blood pulsed in my head like the heartbeat of the ocean. Ellis was speaking to both of us.

She caught my eye for a second before I looked away.

Max and I understood each other in this. We hung back, hesitating.

Afraid to raise the chisel.

———

"Tell me what it's like," I said, lying on my side, gazing at her across the pillow. "What do you feel like inside?"

"Like nothing. Like everything. It's hard to explain."

Ellis turned to the ceiling, Christmas lights dappling her face. Why do we always look up when we don't understand? Maybe it's a remnant from when we're kids, tugging at a parent's sleeve. Mami, explain. *¿Por qué?*

"Do you feel like a boy inside?"

"Sometimes."

"Do you ever feel like a girl?"

"Rarely. And sometimes I don't feel like either. Like . . . a third gender. Or none at all."

"Is there a word for that?"

"Only a million. But I guess genderfluid is pretty close. It's when the gender you identify as changes."

It didn't seem strange anymore. At times I'd seen her more as a girl, a boy, both, neither. I'd never had a word for it.

Now it felt like something we could talk about. Something I could think about more clearly.

Names have power. They give contour to ideas. Lines to color inside, or to break free of.

"Does it bother you when people call you 'she' or 'her'?"

"Not really. I'm used to it. And I like it sometimes, especially when you say it. But remember those guys you scared off the first day we met?"

"Of course. I'm the cat who saved the bird."

"It bothered me when *they* saw me as a girl. To them, girls are just pieces of meat. I hate being seen that way."

"Little secret: cisgender girls hate being seen as pieces of meat, too."

"I know. And you're different. It feels equal with you. Safe. It's other people who make me feel like I have the worst of both worlds. I'm either a girl who's just a sex object, or a boy who's a weak little pussy."

Something twisted in my chest. "Is that how you feel? Like you're weak, as a boy?"

"I did until I invented Blue." Lights rippled over her skin, garlanding her in white-gold. "That was the first time it didn't make me feel ashamed. This part of myself. I felt powerful. Strong." Ellis glanced at me. "You were so different."

"How?"

"You cared more what I thought about you. You tried harder to please me."

"I was less of a selfish bitch, you mean."

"I didn't say that," she said anxiously, but I laughed and she relaxed. "I think it's more the male gaze. You felt like a man was looking at you, so you behaved differently."

"Is that really a male/female thing, or because we were strangers?"

"I don't know. But it felt good, when you treated me like a man."

A thrill shot into my belly when she said that. "Duly noted."

If we were being all confessional, it was time to own something I didn't like about myself.

"Ellis, remember when you said I'm afraid of femininity? You're right. It's why I've always been so flaky about girls. I took to you so fast because you're a tomboy. You're like, my ideal person. Smack in-between, unpindownable. But I think I've got some internalized misogyny going on, or something."

"Lots of people do without realizing it. Society wants us to see our femininity as a weakness."

"It's not a weakness in you. It's perfect. You're just right."

She smiled. "It's perfect in you, too. You're the strongest girl I know."

We looked at each other across the bed. I traced her cheekbone.

"Do you think you'll ever change yourself outside, to fit how you feel inside?"

"Not right now. Maybe not ever." She took a deep breath. "But some days I do want to be a boy. If I wanted to stay a boy, would that freak you out?"

"A little bit, yeah. Change is scary. Would it freak you out, if you wanted to stay that way?"

"A little bit, yeah."

I cupped the side of her face. "What if you're actually trans?"

"Can you be trans without wanting to transition?"

"You can be whatever feels right. I'm bi, even if I never sleep with a guy again. And I'm an artist even if I never draw."

She bit her lip. "Would you leave, if I was?"

"Nope."

"That's it? Don't you have to think about it?"

"What's there to think about? I love you no matter what you look like on the outside. It's what's inside I love. There's this—okay, I have to give you a mini art lecture. Don't roll your eyes, Ellis. *Blue* loves my art lectures."

She groaned. "I've created a monster."

"Yep. Now shut up and listen." I levered myself to a sitting position. "So, what is art? We take reality, and we filter it through our eyes and minds and hands, and remake it. What comes out is both more and less true than what went in. It illuminates some part of reality just as it obscures other parts. Art is an imperfect impression of the world. As the self is an imperfect impression of the soul."

She stared at me, her lips parting.

"Anyway, my point is that I love whatever intangible essence makes you Ellis. Your soul. The thing you don't believe exists. The rest is just very pretty art."

She fluttered her eyelashes, deliberately coquettish. "Are you objectifying me?"

"A little bit, yeah. Because I really kinda want to fuck you right now."

Ellis laughed, that pretty musical laugh, and I knelt over her and lowered my mouth to hers.

———

My gallery opened on a blue February night. Ellis's twenty-fourth birthday. I'd leased an old fishery up the coast from Portland, gutted the interior, rehabbed it with polished concrete and new drywall. Track lights glittered in the rafters like strings of diamonds. Tonight we opened with a photo exhibit. I'd angsted about what to title the show until Dane, genius of the simple, said, "Why not just *Her*?"

The gallery bustled with cammers, college kids, our friends, everyone we knew. Including the staff from my studio.

I was no longer a cam girl. I was a business owner.

My studio was basically an artist colony with a porn twist: they cammed and I comped their tuition, art supplies, gallery fees, everything. I only took people with big dreams. People who needed a leg up, pun intended. The castoffs society would have thrown away, kids with talent but no lucky break. Too many of us were drawn to camming because we'd been dealt a bad hand by life—figuratively *and* literally. They'd rather make art; I gave them a chance to make art and cash at the same time.

Technically, Katherine, I'm a patron of the arts now, too. Not bad for a twenty-three-year-old Boricua from the West Side, is it?

I found Max wandering alone, spending long minutes before each photo. We'd blown them up and printed them on giant canvases. I joined him at a close-up selfie: one intensely blue eye, half of a red lipsticked mouth. Shaggy blond hair.

Max glanced at me, expressionless.

"Let me show you something," I said.

I raised my hand, obscuring the bottom of the photo. The top half of Skylar's face looked like a pretty boy in guyliner. Then I moved my hand upward and instantly the face changed, becoming a girl's mouth, coy and alluring.

Max looked confused.

"This is very strange," he said, "but she was beautiful. She would've been a—"

He cut off, turning away, and I grabbed him in a hug. He stood still for a second and then wrapped his arms around me.

"Are you going to be okay?" I said.

"I don't know."

We leaned apart but I kept my hands on his shoulders.

"I don't know how to do this," he said. "How to feel, how to look at her. I never really had a daughter."

"I never really had a dad. Maybe we can figure this shit out together."

His eyes tightened, a smile flickering in them. He squeezed my waist and let go, and I watched him drift into the crowd.

A little thread of my heart went with him.

Naveen, one of my cam boys, caught up with me. His ears glinted with hand-tooled silver rings. My cammers all made things: Naveen worked with metal, Aurora was writing a novel, Li designed clothes.

"So, does it fit?" he said.

I smiled, the kind of smile you put on when you're actually terrified. "Don't know yet."

Naveen winked.

"Have you seen Ellis?"

"Nah, sorry, mami."

They thought that was hilarious—calling me "mami." I punched his arm.

Across the floor, Frankie and Dane stood gazing at a sad photo: a curled fist, red furrows raking across a long blue vein. Ellis and I had debated: Should we show the bad as well, or only the good? I said only the good. Why should Skylar's suffering linger on? Why not let her rest, celebrate her life? But Ellis said showing the suffering was important because somewhere in that crowd tonight, someone else suffered, too.

Someone would see those photos of her pain and feel a resonance. The point of art, of any communion between human beings, wasn't to make people feel good—it was to make them feel less alone.

She was right. Ellis was always right.

Frankie and Dane looked as elegant as the night we'd met, her in clinging pale silk and him in a smart bespoke suit. As I approached them, I froze. Dane was whispering something in her ear; Frankie's hand brushed his back. They leaned into each other, intimately.

I turned around, leaving them undisturbed.

So getting details later.

People kept detaining me to chat, and I tried to be the gracious gallery owner but a wildness brewed in me. I spied a flash of rust red in the crowd and chased, only for someone to step into my path. My body was on autopilot. I smiled, carried on entire calm conversations while my heart rampaged. It was a relief when I ran into Brandt.

He sat on a wooden bench before a photo of a washed-up sea raven, a weird fish: dark garnet scales, ragged shreds of skin trailing from its fins, as if it had been torn partially from something whole. Totally Brandt. Totally me, too.

I sat beside him. "Seen your cousin?"

"She was looking for you."

"Figures."

He gave me that trademark Zoeller squint. "Trouble in paradise?"

"You wish."

It was strange, being around him after everything. He and I were the only ones who knew the whole truth about Blue. Brandt looked up to Ellis like she was an older brother. Plus he'd driven a boat to Peaks Island in a snowstorm to rescue me, which was major Boy Scout points.

"Still sure you don't want to come home with us?" I said.

We were planning to visit Chicago soon. I hadn't seen my family in ages. And I might have news to tell, which made my insides lurch, my heart rising and teetering like a Ferris wheel car.

"Yeah. Do me a favor, by the way."

"What?"

"Don't mention my name to anyone there."

I frowned. "How come?"

"Trust me on this one." He cocked his head. "Ellis was smart to change hers. Some ghosts we deserve, and some we don't."

"You're right. I guess you and I deserve ours."

Something strange glittered in his eyes.

I still didn't know what had really happened to him, but we felt similarly about our scars: they were earned.

"You're nervous about something," he said.

"What makes you say that?"

"You keep putting your hand in your pocket. Touching something. Or maybe you're rubbing one out."

I elbowed him, and he grunted.

"That left is getting strong," he said appreciatively.

"Want to know a secret?"

"Always."

"I've been drawing with it." I flexed my hand, feeling a good, familiar soreness. Still awful drawing lefty, but every day the lines were a little less bad. "I'll probably never be as good as I was, but I won't let it stop me. This is who I am. I'm a creator. I'll keep trying till I'm dust."

Brandt gave me an odd look. " 'Out of the night that covers me, black as the Pit from pole to pole, I thank whatever gods may be for my unconquerable soul.' "

"What's that?"

"Old poem." He smirked. "A girl I knew loved poetry. You might say she beat her love for it into me."

"You are so weird."

"You have no idea. Hey, there's my cuz."

When our eyes met across the gallery, I stood, feeling weightless. Everything else went grayscale and indistinct, a faint sketch beneath the brilliant colors of the only person I really saw. I left Brandt without another word.

Ellis met me in a clear bubble of space under the bright lights. I'd seen her dressed like this a million times—hair raked boyishly above her eyes, plaid sleeves rolled up, all rustic and sylvan as if born and raised in Maine—but every detail took on deep significance. Because tonight would become a memory. One I would never forget.

"There you are," she said. "I've been looking everywhere for—"

I took her face in my hands and kissed her. Like Klimt's painting, tilting her head back, pouring all of myself into it, the world dulling, all the colors gathering inside us instead. Her lips opened against mine and she breathed into me. I kissed her like we were the only two people in the room, in the whole world, and for that kiss, we were. When I pulled back we were both hazy-eyed, smiling goofily.

"Happy birthday, baby," I said.

"Was that my present? Because that was pretty amazing."

I shook my head. Speech was hard. I took her hand, tugged. My palm was sweating. Man.

I led her through the gallery, past photos of a pretty girl we were all making new memories of, past our friends and the lights and voices to the doors that let onto the wharf. We got our coats and practically ran outside, drinking in the brisk air, the salt breeze, the stillness. When the doors shut we did run. She dashed off first and I followed, our feet thumping on the dock.

We raced to the end of the pier, screaming for no other reason than that we were alive. Screaming into the face of this cold universe. Against unkindness, against accidents and inevitabilities. Against the randomness of being born into the wrong body or the wrong family, of hurting the wrong hand. Our voices carried over the water long after we fell silent, mine throaty and brazen, hers an avian shriek. At the pier's edge I collapsed, panting. Ellis sat next to me. For a while we stared out at dark water and clear sky, wild with stars.

"Want your present now?" I said.

She nodded.

I reached into my coat. My hand shook, and she saw.

"Vada," she said, my name drifting to me in a white scroll of breath.

I withdrew a piece of paper and unfolded it in the starlight. My first sketch of her. The day we met at the train, the two of us sitting side by side. For some reason I'd drawn us with hands clasped, casually, as if we'd been best friends for years. The idea of it had seemed pretty to me. Meeting someone who felt so familiar, so much like home.

"Remember this?"

"You hid it from me. You were terrified I'd think you had a crush on me."

" 'Terrified' is a strong word. I was mildly concerned."

"You locked it in a jewelry safe, Vada."

I laughed, but my hands wouldn't stop shaking. The paper shivered.

"The truth is, I couldn't figure out what to get you. I racked my brain. But nothing was big enough, epic enough. Nothing was good enough. So this is it. I'm all you get this year."

She took the sketch, tucked it into her coat. Cupped my face. "You're good enough. And you're all I want."

My heart was too full. It couldn't hold this.

I kissed her again, pressed her down to the pier planks. I kissed her mouth, her cold cheeks, her warm throat. "I don't deserve you," I whispered. "But I want to be your everything. The way you're mine."

"You're going to make me cry."

"Not yet."

Her brow knit, but I kissed her again before she could question me. I could stay here forever. In this eternal moment, in a picture someone would draw of us, a story they would write, so it would never end.

But I wanted the next moment more than anything.

"People will wonder where we are," I said.

"Let them."

I smiled, pulled her to her feet. She hung on to my hands.

"Why are you shaking?" she said in a soft voice. "You're scared. Why?"

"I'm just cold."

Ellis squinted. I swung our arms playfully.

"Come on, birthday nerd. They're waiting."

I took off running back down the pier and she made a surprised sound and followed. I let her catch up, overtake me, fly past. Then I staggered to a halt and dropped to my knee, fiddling with my shoelaces.

Ellis spun around and walked back. "I refuse to win by default."

"Ever so noble." I beckoned. "Come here. I need you."

"Did you seriously trip over your shoelaces? What are you, five?"

"Just give me your hand."

When she reached down I clasped it firmly, lacing my fingers through hers.

"Vada, what . . ." she began, and trailed off.

I opened my other palm. Her eyes went wide and bright.

Naveen did an incredible job: he'd taken the spoon I'd given him, sterling silver with a bluebird engraved into the handle, and heated it till some melted off and the rest was soft enough to bend into a ring. Triple-coiled, the bird at the center enameled with lapis lazuli. I knew her size. Thanks for the hand pic, Blue.

Never in my life had I thought I'd go down on one knee on an ocean pier beneath the stars, but life is crazy like that.

"I meant it," I said. "I want to be your everything. Forever."

Ellis put her free hand over her mouth, starting to cry.

Told you, *pajarito*.

"Ellis Morgan Carraway," I said, "will you marry me?"

Her head bowed, a tear tracing the back of her hand. Those green eyes remained locked on mine. The tear rolled off and hung in midair for a second, a crystal thread flecked with stars, holding the whole universe. Ellis leaned close and touched my face. No fear in my heart now. We looked at each other, and she gripped my hand tighter, and her lips parted with her answer. But some part of me already knew. Like it already knew her, from the moment we first met.

(—Bergen, Vada. *She Said Yes*.
Ink and watercolor on paper.)

ACKNOWLEDGMENTS

When I was a kid, I wanted to be Robin Hood. I was obsessed with him. I watched the Kevin Costner movie a million times, begged my mom to buy me LEGO Forestmen, played the crap out of the *Robin Hood: Prince of Thieves* Nintendo game. When my little sister and I played make-believe, I was always Robin. I made swords out of sticks and capes from towels. I saved princesses. It never seemed weird, pretending to be a boy. Because I wasn't pretending.

Growing up, I never gave much thought to my gender. I didn't feel like anything specific inside—just this sort of genderless being that tended more toward masculinity than femininity, whatever those words mean. Some stuff bothered me. I felt physically sick when my parents made me wear dresses, and eventually I refused. I cut my hair short in high school and have kept it short ever since. When I was allowed to pick my own clothes as a teen, I insisted on buying from the men's section. My mom, thankfully, agreed, but if she hadn't I would've found some way to get them. Because I didn't feel right in girls' clothes. I felt like I was wearing a costume. Like I was in drag.

At the same time, I was beginning to identify as gay. Who cared about fashion? I was more worried about what being queer meant.

You can put off dealing with mild gender dysphoria for

a long time. How you choose your clothes, your hairstyle, your hobbies, the gender of your friends—all can assuage the slightly off-kilter way you feel inside, to a degree. Strangers called me "sir" and "young man." Girls gave me nasty looks when I walked into women's public restrooms. All my friends (who were mostly boys) called me a tomboy. But something about that word always bugged me. It implied that deep down, I was really just a girl acting like a boy. And I knew that wasn't quite right. Whatever I was, I *wasn't* a girl.

Say what you will about its downsides, but Tumblr is a fucking lifeline for many LGBTQIA+ people. Not until I was an adult, meeting people on social media who identified outside the gender binary, did I realize I was one of them. Everything clicked. The way I dressed, behaved, *felt* inside all finally made sense. Then the agonizing questioning phase began: So am I transgender? Am I a boy who was born into a girl's body? Do I need to change my body to match what's inside? Gender is a Pandora's box—once you understand how fluid and endlessly diverse it is, you can never go back to the simplistic binary.

From Tumblr, I learned words that fit me better than "tomboy." For starters, I was somewhere in the "nonbinary" category: someone who does not identify as a woman or a man. Like sexuality, gender is a wide, flexible spectrum with multiple subcategories. I knew I stood way farther on the masculine than the feminine side. But transgender wasn't right either, because I didn't *definitely* feel like a boy, just somewhere between boyish to neutral. So "transmasculine" fits, but "nonbinary" is where I feel more comfortable right now. To me it both encompasses a diverse sense of gender and also implies that gender itself is sort of an unnecessary concept. It's a giant middle finger to the idea that our sex should define who we are. I think in some blissful future we'll abandon the concept of gender entirely (or at least our robot masters will—what is gender to an AI?), which will be so fucking liberating.

Because really, why does it matter that my body has two X chromosomes but that I wear men's clothes and do stuff that's considered "masculine"? Why are people more respectful and attentive when they see me as "sir" and more critical and dismissive when they see me as "miss"? Why can't anyone use whichever public restroom they feel the most comfortable in? What about intersex people who destroy all our quaint ideas about sexual dimorphism determining gender? Why do stores have separate aisles for girls' and boys' toys? Why do we color-code babies by their sex, before they've had a chance to grow up and express their personality? I hated the color pink as a kid. Pink represented weakness, frivolity, stupidity, ditziness. Where do you think I got that from? Children are sponges. We readily absorb adults' fucked-up ideas about gender. We're taught to categorize, reduce, divide, judge. Break people down into stereotypes. Don't see them as *people* anymore.

In many ways the Internet is abolishing these divisions between us. We can communicate online largely free of pre-conceptions that derive from a person's sex, race, ability, etc. We can be simply and purely human with each other. And we can see examples of others like us who make us feel less alone. I didn't have Tumblr as a teen. I had no nonbinary role models to look to for comfort and guidance. Facing these issues for the first time as an adult with a fully formed sense of self is scary and depressing and confidence-shaking. But it's especially scary and depressing if you're young and uncertain and in need of support.

I was in the middle of writing *Cam Girl* when Leelah Alcorn, a transgender girl, killed herself. Leelah was assigned male at birth and came out as trans to her parents at age fourteen. Her parents refused to accept her gender identity. They tried to "fix" it with conversion therapy. Leelah had been highly active online, posting selfies and talking about trans issues. Her final post to Tumblr was her suicide note. Hundreds of thousands of people read her last words, unable to help.

Leelah had access to a supportive online community yet couldn't endure the hate and intolerance from her own family. Too many people in this world can't handle the idea that who you are is more complex and beautiful than something as arbitrary as your chromosomal sex. And Leelah's story isn't uncommon—it plays out again and again in the news. The Tragic Trans Teen. Depression. Substance abuse. Self-harm. Suicide. It keeps happening because we as a society keep clinging to obsolete, absurd ideas that our genitals have some kind of influence over our humanity.

I hope others out there who are like us, who don't fit into the cisgender binary, are someday able to live free of this bullshit. I hope books like this add one small drop to the ocean of diverse gender representation out there. And I damn well hope to see *more* books like this, where cis/straight/white isn't the stale default. I needed to see that when I was a teenager. Other nonbinary kids need it, too. Every teen needs to see that it's okay to be trans, or however they feel inside—boy, girl, both, neither, or something more nuanced and complex and mutable. Gender isn't pink or blue. It's not either/or. It's whatever the hell it means to you, personally. Maybe it means nothing, and that's okay, too.

You are okay just as you are.

———

As always, I have to begin my thank-yous with the person who shaped this book the most: my keenly sharp, smart, driven editor, Sarah Cantin. It's a pleasure to work with someone who's as Type A as I am. Sarah, thank you for insisting on nothing less than the best I'm capable of. I've learned and grown so much with you. Your guidance echoes in my work and I'm damn proud of what we've made out of these books.

Thank you also to my peerless agent, Jane Dystel, who's been a rock for me to lean on, and to everyone at both the Dystel & Goderich agency and at Atria Books. I'm honored to work with all of you.

Mad hearts to Alexander, my partner and best friend and *Minecraft* co-architect, for being the sweetest boy alive. I love you, buddy.

To my writer friends—Dahlia Adler, Bethany Frenette, Ellen Goodlett, Lindsay Smith, and many others on Twitter—thanks for inspiring and supporting the hell out of me.

To all the bloggers and reviewers who make these books possible at all, thank you. Special shout-out to the *Cuddlebuggery* girls for being rad af. #sorrynotsorry that I used your names in this book.

And of course, crazy love to my Facebook fan group, the Raeder Readers. You guys are my everything. Thank you for sharing your stories and passion and humor and art with me, for being there when I need an escape from reality, for sticking with me through these increasingly challenging books. I promise to keep writing the best I can and to give you stories that provoke intense feelings, push you out of your comfort zone, and generally make you go OMGWTF. No compromise, no surrender.

I hate to end on a sad note, but there's a deep sorrow in this book that's haunted me even after the happy ending. Because too often in real life, trans people don't get HEAs. I was nearly one of those tragic statistics, too. It's sheer luck that I'm here instead, writing books about it. I feel indebted to light a candle and try to guide others out of the darkness.

Leelah, this book is for you. You're one of the girls I've lost. We've all lost you.

All my love,
Leah Raeder
Chicago, August 2015